D.L. Klason is an award-winning Australian author and amateur historian specialising in premodern Japanese history. With master's degrees in both Research and International Relations, he has combined his love of research and detail to provide his readership with an exciting insight into the events and characters of this important but turbulent era.

To Lyn

David Klason

An Age of War and Tea

The Rise and Fall of Ishida Mitsunari

AUSTIN MACAULEY PUBLISHERS™

LONDON • CAMBRIDGE • NEW YORK • SHARJAH

A CIP catalogue record for this title is available from the British Library.

ISBN 9781398477322 (Paperback)
ISBN 9781398477339 (ePub e-book)

www.austinmacauley.com

First Published 2023
Austin Macauley Publishers Ltd®
1 Canada Square
Canary Wharf
London
E14 5AA

I am indebted to the late Japanese historical novelist, Eiji Yoshikawa, whose retelling of Japanese historical classics in his own style, provided the inspiration to write this book.

My gratitude also to Martin Bridgewater, whose invaluable advice and feedback guided my hand in polishing the manuscript. A special thanks to the Simpson family for their support and finally, my gratitude to the Publishers Austin Macauley for allowing me to bring this story to life.

Table of Contents

Map

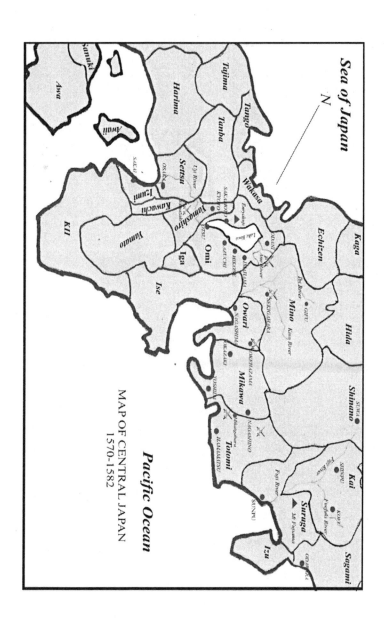

Sea of Japan

Pacific Ocean

MAP OF CENTRAL JAPAN
1570-1582

List of Characters

*Fictional Character

AKECHI HIDEMITSU: Samurai retainer to Akechi Mitsuhide.

AKECHI MITSUHIDE: Daimyo & vassal of Oda Nobunaga.

AKECHI SAMA: Samurai retainer to Akechi Mitsuhide.

ANAYAMA NOBUTADA: Samurai retainer of Tokugawa Ieyasu.

ARAKI MURASHIGE: Samurai retainer of Oda Nobunaga.

AZAI HISAMASA: Father of Azai Lord Nagamasa.

AZAI NAGAMASA: Daimyo of Omi province and brother-in-law to Nobunaga. Husband of Oichi.

FUJITA DENGO: Samurai retainer to Akechi Mitsuhide.

HAJIKANO MASATSUGU: General of Takeda Shingen, Sakichi's alleged father.

HATANO HIDEHARU: Head of the Hatano clan and retainer of Lord Miyoshi.

HATTORI HANZO: Retainer to Tokugawa Ieyasu.

HAYASHI HIDESADA: Samurai retainer of Oda Nobunaga.

HIDEYOSHI: Retainer to Nobunaga. Originally known as Kinoshita Tokichiro, then took the name Hashiba Hideyoshi.

HIROKOHIME: Principal wife of Akechi Mitsuhide.

HOJO MASAKO: Wife to Takeda Katsuyori, son of Takeda Shingen.

HOJO UJIYASU: Daimyo of Sagami province.

HONDA TADAKATSU: Samurai retainer of Tokugawa Ieyasu.

HOSOKAWA FUJITAKA: Advisor to Shogun Yoshiaki.

IMAI SOKYU: Noted tea Master and Sakai merchant.

ISHIDA MASATSUGU: Sakichi's adoptive father.

ISHIDA MASAZUMI: Eldest son of Ishida Masatsugu, Sakichi's stepbrother.

KENSHO-IN: A daughter of Takeda Shingen.

KUNITOMO ZENBEE: A Kunitomo Sword smith.

MASTER IGARASHI: Lacquer ware artisan in Kyoto.

MIKO*: Childhood friend of Sakichi.

MOCHIZUKI CHIYO: Female Kunoichi (Shinobi/Ninja) leader. Agent for the Takeda clan.

MORI TERUMOTO: Daimyo and Mori clan leader, an enemy of Nobunaga.

NAO*: Courtesan.

NENE: Hideyoshi's wife.

OBAI-IN: A daughter of Takeda Shingen.

ODA NOBUKATSU: Second son of Nobunaga.

ODA NOBUNAGA: Daimyo, Warlord & the first 'Great Unifier' of Japan.

ODA NOBUTADA: Eldest son of Nobunaga.

OICHI: Wife to Azai Nagamasa and sister to Nobunaga.

OKO*: Childhood friend of Sakichi.

OKUBO TADAYO: Samurai retainer of Tokugawa Ieyasu.

ONA*: Courtesan in training.

SADAKO: Wife of Ishida Masatsugu and adoptive mother of Sakichi.

SAITO KURA: Samurai retainer to Akechi Mitsuhide.

SAITO TANEOMI: A Sakamoto pottery merchant.

SAKAI TADATSUGU: Samurai retainer of Tokugawa Ieyasu.

SAKICHI: Boyhood name of Ishida Mitsunari.

SANADA YUKITAKA: One of Takeda Shingen's twenty-four generals.

SHIBATA KATSUIE: Samurai retainer of Oda Nobunaga.

SHIZEN: Akechi Mitsuhide's daughter from his concubine.

TAKEDA KATSUYORI: Son of Takeda Shingen by concubine Suwa Goryonin.

TAKEDA SHINGEN: Pre-eminent Daimyo of Kai province. Also known as Harunobu.

TAMA: Akechi Mitsuhide's daughter from Hirokohime.

TANAKA YOSHIMASA: Samurai. Also known as Atsuji Sadahide in a past life.

TOKUGAWA IEYASU: Daimyo of Mikawa province and ally of Nobunaga.

TOKYUSAEMON: A Kunitomo blacksmith.

TOMO SUKESADA: A *jonin* (master ninja) of the Koga Ninja clan.

Part One

Prologue

Anegawa: Summer, Northeast of Lake Biwako, Omi Province
First Year of Genki (1570)

It is said, 'A man who cheats death regrets life.' These were the thoughts that the young Azai warrior, Atsuji Sadahide, dwelt upon as he stood on the battlefield for the fight that was to come. Though he had lived his life as if he were already dead, Sadahide stood before the first rays of a rising Sun and prayed for death. The sweet smell of the sandalwood incense he had burnt inside his helmet lingered in the morning air and he smiled. Should he lose his head this day, he would take comfort in knowing that a fragrant aroma would greet his enemy.

Sadahide touched the musket ball dent in his breastplate armour and reflected on that near miss. He was pursuing the retreating army of the great lord Oda Nobunaga as he abandoned the Asakura Castle of Kanegasaki that he had recently taken. The Azai lord, Nagamasa, who was also Nobunaga's son-in-law, had betrayed Nobunaga and attacked Kanegasaki with overwhelming force, forcing Nobunaga to flee the castle.

Along with his mounted Azai warriors, Sadahide chased Nobunaga into the nearby woodlands, scattering many of the enemy in confusion. And then it happened, a trap. He heard the sharp crack of musket fire and felt the impact of the ball striking him in the chest, nearly unseating him. Dropping his sword, he kept control of his horse, and under the heavy volley of musket fire, he retreated out of the woodlands with the rest of his band.

Sadahide finished his prayers and wiped away the beads of morning dew that had accumulated on the leggings of his crimson red amour. He looked across the Anegawa River but could see nothing past the dense mist rising above its slow-moving surface. The river separated his outnumbered army from the twenty-eight thousand Oda and Tokugawa forces he knew to be on the other side.

Nobunaga had returned to deal with the Asakura and to punish Nagamasa for his treachery. Still focused on the mist, Sadahide knew it would delay the battle until it clears.

Across the river, the Oda sentry, Yoshi Kenosuke, also watched the mist and listened intently to the mixture of sounds he could hear within. Yoshi was an *Ashigaru* foot soldier in his late fifties who had reluctantly found himself conscripted into Nobunaga's army.

Why am I here? At my time of life, I should be home tending to the farm, thought Yoshi.

"As there won't be any fight till this mist clears, I may as well have some breakfast," he muttered to himself as he retraced his steps back towards the large piece of driftwood he had earlier tripped over. Yoshi sat down to unwrap his meal of rice balls and hungrily devoured his meal, as the familiar sounds of men and horses within the mist distracted him. He looked across the river and thought he could see the faint outlines of moving shapes; dancing like ghosts over the surface of the slow-moving river. A startled, Yoshi resolved to head back to camp and make his report when one of his ghosts suddenly materialised before him, taking the form of a mounted warrior. The *Nobori* (banner) he carried showed he was Azai, his enemy. Enemies. Upon seeing Yoshi, the Azai warrior called out to proclaim his pedigree and issue the customary challenge for single combat.

"Ho!" the warrior exclaimed, "I am Atsuji Sadahide, retainer of Lord Azai Nagamasa and descendent of Ashikaga Takauji. Who do I have the honour of facing today?" It was an act of foolishness or careless bravado, but Yoshi taunted the warrior before him with his own exaggerated pedigree and provocatively dismissed his challenge as being unworthy of his attention. An infuriated Sadahide charged at Yoshi with sword held high, and Yoshi, who felt the warmth of an ever-widening damp patch in his loins, turned and ran. He managed only six paces before his head left his body.

As more Azai warriors emerged from the mist, the echo of war horns reverberated along the river, and it was not long before both sides waded into the shallows of the Ane to battle. Sadahide discarded his *Nobori* and galloped directly towards the Oda lines with Yoshi's head still tied to his saddle. It had crossed his mind to deceive the Oda into believing he had taken the Azai lord's head and to present it to Nobunaga, hoping to kill him. He knew such an undertaking was a suicide mission, but he was already dead. With his path blocked by a group of Oda Ashigaru bearing muskets aimed directly at him, Sadahide halted and called out.

"I am Hachisuka Masakatsu, retainer of Lord Nobunaga. Make way, for I have the head of the Azai enemy lord to present to Lord Nobunaga." A distant voice called out a command and the line of Ashigaru before him parted. Confident the gods were still on his side, Sadahide trotted on, only for two Ashigaru to grab the horse's bridle, and bring him to a halt.

"What is the meaning of this?" demanded Sadahide. The reply came swiftly as a well-placed blow. He felt the heavy impact of steel across his face armour toppling him from his saddle and a jarring pain in his back as his body landed heavily on the ground. As he tried to get up, he felt the pressure of a foot on his back and the piercing pain of a blade. Unable to move, he gasped for air as blood flooded his mouth. Ahead, in the undergrowth, he watched as two intense yellow eyes stared at him. The white fox blinked and disappeared.

That was the last thing Sadahide saw before a wave of darkness washed over him. His lifeless body lay on the dew-laden grass, and his pooling blood glistened in the bright sunlight. He never heard the horns of war sound out and the clash of the battle that raged about him. If he had crossed the 'Floating Bridge of Heaven' that dead warriors used to access the home of the god's, he would have seen the battle went badly for the Oda that day until the tide of war changed.

Having disposed of the Asakura forces, Nobunaga's allies, the famed Tokugawa fighting men of Mikawa, attacked the Azai right flank to seal victory, forcing Azai Nagamasa to retreat to his nearby castle at Odani. At nightfall, with the battle over, he would have also seen the Tokugawa Samurai relieving the corpses of their heads before the scavenging women descended onto the field to pick the corpses clean of valuables. That day, they presented over three thousand heads to Nobunaga and Tokugawa Ieyasu for their viewing pleasure.

Chapter One

Kyoto

Summer: Mount Hiei-Zan

Tanaka Yoshimasa was a young Samurai in his late twenties, but the noticeable flecks of grey in his otherwise black hair made him look much older than his years. He had just left the Tendai Buddhist Temple of Enryaku-ji atop Mount Hiei and strolled along the steep walking trail leading down the mountain towards the nation's capital, Kyoto. The temple of Enryaku-ji, besides providing rest and shelter for weary travellers in return for suitable donations, was also home to the fearsome *Sohei* (warrior monks) who were continually agitating for power and influence in the capital.

Even at this high altitude, Yoshimasa found the summer heat oppressive, and he struggled to keep the beads of sweat dripping from his forehead away from his eyes. He also knew the humidity would become worse as he descended. Only two access routes led from the Enryaku-ji to the base town of Sakamoto; the narrow, well-worn path he now travelled on, used by merchants and travellers, and another jealously-guarded shorter route known only to the temple.

Yoshimasa had not travelled far before he cautiously halted. Ahead of him, a large menacing group of snow monkeys had gathered on the nearby rocks, seeking the shade of the tall canopies of cedar and fir trees that filtered the bright mid-day sun. As he neared the monkeys, the forest echoed with their alarm calls, and they defiantly stood their ground. With his hand resting on the hilt of his sword, Yoshimasa continued along the path, keeping as far away as possible and being careful not to look them in the eyes. Several of the larger monkeys jumped in front of Yoshimasa and attempted to intimidate him by baring their teeth, but they quickly moved aside as Yoshimasa continued walking, deliberately ignoring them, but ready to strike.

He soon reached a clearing in the trail, affording expansive views of the distant capital, and assessed that a further day's walk lay ahead just to reach the city outskirts. Given the heat of the day, Yoshimasa resolved to rest and continue at dusk in the cooler part of the day. He rested at the base of a nearby cedar tree and drank the last of his water, wiping away the last few drops from his mouth to dampen and cool his disfigured face, the left side of which had a long scar running from the temple to the chin that intersected with a missing eye. He laid down in the soft undergrowth at the base of the tree and closed his eyes. The peaceful silence of his surroundings inspired him to compose an impromptu poem.

An ancient silent path
A deer crashes through the trees
Snap. Silence again.

He had come to the Enryaku-ji to deliver a message to the abbot from his employer, Mochizuki Chiyo, after which he was to continue to the capital and find the *Kunoichi* (female ninja) operative in Kyoto to deliver another message. Chiyo came from an extensive line of Koka ninja in Shinano province and at the warlord Takeda Shingen's behest, she built an extensive network of trained female operatives who would function as spies and agents for the Takeda clan.

The nearby scratching of a badger digging in the fading light of dusk awoke Yoshimasa, and he was soon on his way down the mountain. Several hours later, and just before midnight, Yoshimasa reached the eastern outskirts of the capital. A bright full moon bathed the city in an eerie, colourless light, prompting Yoshimasa to rest in a nearby copse and gather his thoughts.

How do I find this Kunoichi? I am told she is using the cover of a high-ranking geisha. How am I going to find her pleasure house in this city? There is sure to be more than just one.

As the distant sound of nine bells rang out, announcing the midnight arrival of the hour of the rat, Yoshimasa set out towards the city. The extent of the destruction these troubled times had inflicted on the capital surprised him. Many of the wealthier homes now resembled minor fortresses, surrounded by walls of bamboo and extensive earthworks. The neighbouring streets of these homes had become deep trenches to function as protective moats.

Yoshimasa approached the checkpoint ahead that controlled the eastern entrance to the city. He found it manned by four Oda guards, and given the time and quietness of the night, they appeared to be in a relaxed mood and content to drink the night away.

"Forgive my intrusion on your time, Sir's, but can you direct me to the best pleasure house this city offers?" Yoshimasa asked. One guard, assuming Yoshimasa to be just another *Ronin* (masterless Samurai) and an unwelcome distraction, rose from his makeshift table of baskets and strode menacingly towards Yoshimasa with his hand tightly gripping the hilt of his sword.

"And who might you be, sneaking around at this time of night?" the guard demanded. Sensing trouble, Yoshimasa replied,

"I am merely a traveller seeking comfort in the city. Sorry to have bothered you." In an unfortunate moment, as he turned to walk away, the tip of Yoshimasa's sword accidentally brushed against the guard's sheathed sword. Knowing this to be a dangerous breach of etiquette, Yoshimasa quickly apologised, but the belligerent guard would have none of it. Intent on making an issue of this perceived insult, the guard challenged Yoshimasa to defend himself. He shouted out that he would remove this *Ronin's* head for his rudeness, and custom dictated that Yoshimasa had no choice but to accept the challenge.

Noticing what was about to happen, another guard stood up and called out whilst pointing towards a nearby street, "If you continue in that direction, you will come to the Rokujo-Misujimachi, where the pleasure quarters are. You can't miss it. Just look for a painted vermillion lattice frontage." Yoshimasa bowed in gratitude to the guard for his help. If the guard intended to diffuse the situation, it had the opposite effect on his colleague. Yoshimasa heard the soft click of his opponent's sword, being released from its *Saya* (scabbard), and stepped back as the guard raised his sword over his head in an offensive, striking position. Fully expecting the guard's next move, Yoshimasa drew his sword, its tip pointing towards the guard's raised wrist.

As expected, the guard made a lunge for Yoshimasa's left side, who easily stepped backwards and avoided the strike, and then aimed at the guard's sword hand, instantly slicing off his thumbs. Yoshimasa quickly followed with a reverse strike, cleaving the guard's head in two. The guard's comrades not wanting to involve themselves in this duel, continued their drinking while one of them ran off, no doubt to alert their superiors. Using the leggings of the fallen guard, Yoshimasa wiped the blood off his sword before sheathing it and addressed the dead guard's companions.

"My apologies for again disturbing your leisure, but if you would be so kind as to direct me to the local magistrate's office, I will report this occurrence as required by law." It later turned out that the local magistrate, Murai Sadahiko, was very accommodating, considering Yoshimasa had killed one of his men. Sadahiko informed Yoshimasa he was free to go, but not to leave the city while he made enquiries, a proposition Yoshimasa readily accepted, and he resumed his search for the Kunoichi.

As Yoshimasa wandered the dark alleyways of the Rokujo-Misujimachi in search of the pleasure house as described by the guard, the quiet stillness of the night, broken only by the constant pitch of cicadas in song, unnerved him. It was an eerie silence that would have continued had not a certain house in a quiet nearby off-street erupted into flames. Like much of Kyoto, the Rokujo-Misujimachi district was a dense concentration of wooden townhouses, and the impact of any fire would be devastating. Noticing the distant glow of a fire, Yoshimasa headed towards its source in time to see hundreds of concerned Kyoto residents lining up to pass water buckets to wet down adjacent buildings, while others used long-handled hooks to pull as much of the burning townhouse down as they could, to limit the spread of the fire.

It was amid all this confusion, that Yoshimasa noticed the solitary figure of a woman conspicuously dressed in an elaborate red kimono shuffling effortlessly on her black high wooden *Geta* shoes enter one of the long dark narrow lanes leading away from the fire, towards the *Kamo* River.

She dresses like a courtesan. She can help me find the Geisha I seek.

Yoshimasa followed the solitary figure, who he noticed was clumsily carrying a black lacquered box that was swinging by its hemp rope ties. He kept a respectful distance away to not scare her off, but he was close enough to notice that she wore an obi of gold silk brocade tied in the front with an enormous knot, a feature many courtesans used to symbolise their availability.

So, she is a courtesan, Yoshimasa thought, and he continued to follow her for some distance, only to arrive back at the source of the fire.

Does she suspect someone is following her? She is going to great lengths to conceal her true destination.

Yoshimasa watched from the shadows. The courtesan paused and looked furtively up and down the street before continuing her journey. This time, she entered another nearby lane way where rows of lit lanterns hanging on the eaves of tightly packed townhouses swayed in the warm evening breeze, resembling dancing fireflies. The courtesan approached the doorway of one house and knocked on its solid wooden door; two quick knocks followed by three long knocks, finishing with one quick knock. Under the light of the house lantern, the courtesan's features were now visible to Yoshimasa. Her chalky white face and blood red lips stood in stark relief to the shiny black loops and coils of her hair, held in place by ornamental *Kanzashi* (hairpins). A headdress of dangling mother-of-pearl ornaments with strings of coral weighted with gold leaf blossoms sat atop.

She dresses as a high ranking Tayu, which fits the description Chiyo provided. Could it be her? The courtesan was about to knock again when the door suddenly opened, and a balding old man in a cheap linen kimono beckoned her inside.

They clearly know each other, Yoshimasa observed. Noticing an interior light in a small open window to the left of the door, Yoshimasa looked inside to see a low table set out for tea and a steaming kettle on a nearby hearth. The courtesan was kneeling opposite the balding man, who attended to the kettle and poured boiling water into a bowl, carefully whisking its contents before passing the bowl to the courtesan. The courtesan ignored the tea and placed the box she has carried onto the table, along with several coins. It is only then she picked up the tea bowl and carefully sipped its contents.

Disturbed by two noisy drunken Samurai who had rounded the corner, Yoshimasa moved into the shadows to hide until they have passed. Again, at the window, he watched the old man untie the hemp cords securing the courtesans lacquered box and lifted out the severed head of some unfortunate Samurai by its topknot, allowing fresh beads of blood to drip onto the tabletop.

"Ah-ha!" the old man exclaimed. "He is, or should I say was, known to me. If I am not mistaken, what we have here is the very recent head of Katsurayama Ujimoto, a high-ranking official in the Shoguns service. I do hope you have considered the repercussions of this?" He asked the courtesan.

"Yes, I have, but it is such a handsome face, is it not?" she replied, dipping her finger into the glistening beads of blood that lay on the table. "I think our 'Abbot' Shogun will soil himself when he finally discovers what Ujimoto was doing behind his back."

"Treachery is a double-edged sword, as the Shogun will also find out," the old man replied, "I find it odd that the Shogun continues to scheme against his benefactor, Nobunaga."

It was two years earlier in the tenth year of Eiroku (1568) that Yoshiaki, as the abbot of the Ichijoin temple in Nara sought the help of the warlord Nobunaga to displace the two-year-old child Yoshihide, who succeeded his assassinated brother Yoshiteru as Shogun. Even then, Nobunaga had formed a view of Yoshiaki as a person of weak character and of little significance, but to realise his ambitions, he needed two things: the favour of the imperial court and legitimacy. The latter required a pliant Shogun he could control. So, it was that on the seventeenth day of the ninth month of Eiroku, Nobunaga set out from Gifu ahead of the massive armies of four provinces Owari, Mino, Ise and Mikawa to escort Yoshiaki into Kyoto. With Emperor Ogimachi's blessings on the twenty-second day of the tenth month of Eiroku, the emperor feted Nobunaga and Yoshiaki at the imperial palace and invested Yoshiaki as Seii Taishogun, the fifteenth Ashikaga Shogun of his line.

Still unsure if the courtesan within was the one he is looking for, Yoshimasa knocked on the door, using the same sequence of knocks he watched the courtesan use.

"Are you expecting someone?" the courtesan cautiously asked the old man.

"No, that signal was our secret arrangement. Who else have you told?" the old man replied with concern.

"No one, I can assure you." the courtesan snapped back. "There is only one way to find out though," she said as she signalled the old man to open the door. With the head quickly returned to its box, the old man moved hesitantly towards the door, first sliding back the small inspection hatch in the door to see outside.

"Hmm. Strange, there is no one there," he mumbled before unbolting the door to step outside and check. No sooner had he unbolted the door than he found himself pushed with such a force that it sent him flying across the room. It was then that Yoshimasa entered and shut the door behind him as quickly as he had pushed it open. He stood in the doorway surveying the room and its occupants, his hand resting on the hilt of his sword, poised ready to strike. His next words would settle the question of the courtesan's identity finally.

"Yumiko, I presume?" Yoshimasa said, addressing the courtesan.

"You have me at a disadvantage, Sir," she replied, "you seem to know me, but I know nothing of you." Satisfied he had the right Tayu, Yoshimasa moved to face her.

"My name is of no consequence; what matters is that our mutual employer has instructions for you. You are to establish yourself in *Gifu* before the next full moon and await further instructions." The Tayu who had remained kneeling now rose and bowed to Yoshimasa.

"Sir, I find it hard to believe Chiyo would employ someone with such bad manners. Here, I am known as Yoshino. The Yumiko you speak of was of a past life." Ignoring her barb, Yoshimasa continued to study the Tayu.

Chiyo had warned me that with Yumiko, nothing is what it seems. The story that Chiyo told was of a young girl found lying naked in a ditch, left to die. She had, of course, been raped and the child she later carried was fostered out as soon as it was born. Chiyo, seeing potential in her, had her raised as a *Kunoichi* and once her training was over, sold her to the 'Pillow World' as a courtesan and spy.

"Forgive this intrusion, master Igarashi," Yoshino said, addressing the old man and ignoring Yoshimasa. "Our business here is not finished."

"Yes, my lady, I have it ready," Igarashi replied, and he beckoned her to follow him. The backroom they had entered was devoid of any furniture save a low workbench surrounded by scattered tools and remnants of broken lacquerware. Igarashi removed the red silk cloth covering an object on the bench to reveal a skull with its top section missing.

"The bowl, Master Igarashi, the bowl. Where is it?" Yoshino shrieked. Igarashi removed another cloth covering an object next to the skull, revealing a saucer-shaped cup lacquered in black and inlaid with gold and mother-of-pearl.

"Yes, master Igarashi, this is indeed a fine piece of work," Yoshino said, approving of her acquisition, and handed Igarashi a pouch of coins. "I think this concludes our business for today," she said as he picked up the saucer. Yoshimasa, who had followed them into the backroom had watched the macabre transaction and now interjected.

"And mine too," Yoshimasa added, "I will take my leave of you and report back to our employer."

26

"Sir," Yoshino replied, "I still do not know your name, but if you would escort me back to my lodgings and take refreshments with me, I can provide you with news of the latest developments here which I am sure will interest Chiyo." Tapping the lacquered box, she had brought with her, Yoshino spoke to Igarashi as she rose to leave.

"I will send word of where to deliver this when I am settled."

For such a high-class courtesan, the Tayu's lodgings in Kyoto's Gion district were modest by Kyoto standards. The house featured shoji-screened outer walls and a formal entry alcove lay to the right as you entered. Aside from the main residential room, the house had two other smaller rooms and a separate kitchen. The principal room with fire pit opened onto a landscaped garden complete with its own teahouse and save for a large wooden chest decorated with carved herons, there was no other furniture.

Suspecting her guest would prefer sake instead of tea, Yoshino opened the chest, and withdrew two shallow lacquered sake cups and filled a pouring flask with sake. She raked the dull, glowing firepit coals she had used earlier and brought the fire back to life, and set about heating a pot of water to warm the flask. Once satisfied with the temperature of the sake, she poured a cup and placed it before her guest. As he sipped the warm sake, Yoshimasa noticed its unusual symmetry, and its similarity to the cup Igarashi had presented Yoshino with earlier. The revelation unsettled him, and he immediately dropped the cup in disgust, only for Yoshino to catch the cup at the precise moment it was about to hit the floor with ease.

"Careful now, such fine work is to be treated with respect," rebuked Yoshino.

I have no desire to anger this unfortunate's spirit any further. Yoshimasa thought before replying.

"My task here is ended, and I have delivered our employer's message. My instructions are to report back straight away, so if you have nothing further to add, I will be on my way." Without waiting for Yoshino's reply, he picked up his swords and rose to leave.

"There remains the matter of my contract here with the pleasure house," Yoshino suddenly called out.

"I had forgotten about that," Yoshimasa said. Reaching into his robe, he withdrew a pouch of coins and threw it at Yoshinos' feet.

"Our employer has foreseen your indebtedness. There is more than sufficient for there to buy out your contract." Yoshimasa then slid open the screen door to leave when he remembered a further instruction from Chiyo.

"I am reminded to tell you to leave no loose ends. Chiyo says you will understand."

"Then, till we meet again, unknown warrior," the Tayu replied, smiling but inwardly seething at the slight.

At the distant sound of the six bells announcing the approaching hour of the hare and dawn, a weary Yoshino slid back the painted *Fusuma* screen door of her quarters and laid down to rest. She rested her head on her *takamakura,* a cradle-like pillow, and closed her heavy eyes. Yoshimasa's words returned to taunt her, '… leave no loose ends.' *Have I been careful enough*? She thought.

A few hours earlier, she had been naked and taking part in a sexual liaison with Nao, one of the house's lower-ranked courtesans who was astride the late Ujimoto and riding him hard until they were both spent. She recalled it was Nao who had first approached her for help as she was fearful of complaining to the *Okasan* (housemother) in case she might take offence and withdraw her sponsorship as a courtesan in training. The severe bruising on Nao's face betrayed the abuse she had suffered, but that was the nature of her profession.

Ujimoto was a frequent client of hers, who not only enjoyed the voyeurism of watching Nao and Yoshino having sex, but he preferred his sex to be rough and would delight in brutally sodomising his choice for the night. Although still a novice by house standards, Nao had become accustomed to the deviant desires of her clients, but she found Ujimoto different. He relished not only the sex but the cruelty he inflicted, while he boasted about his privileged position with the Shogun.

Nao's troubles began when Ujimoto, in one of his drunken states, bragged about having powerful connections that even the Shogun knew nothing about. Once he had sobered up, he came to realise his indiscretion and began threatening Nao should she dare speak of it to anyone. Despite Nao's pleadings, Ujimoto insisted on a guarantee to secure her silence and set out to incriminate her by recruiting her to spy on her clients and report back to him.

Yoshino cared little for Nao's dilemma and ignored her pleas for help until Nao mentioned Ujimoto's latest boast. He had bragged about his cleverness in arranging a secret alliance between Lord Nobunaga and Uesugi Kenshin, and the promises of lands and titles he would receive. Yoshino also knew that an alliance between two of the most powerful Daimyos in the land, Oda Nobunaga, and Uesugi Kenshin, would place her own lord, Takeda Shingen, in grave peril. Kenshin and Shingen's had long been bitter rivals, and an alliance with Nobunaga would end any hope of expelling Kenshin from his recent encroachment into neighbouring Shinano province, leaving Kenshin free to threaten Kai.

What to do? Yoshino thought. She knew there was no time to get a message to Chiyo for instructions and resolved to eliminate the threat herself.

Expecting Ujimoto's return to the pleasure quarters later that evening, Yoshino suggested Nao include her again as an added sex partner, which should easily be enough to ensure Ujimoto's enthusiastic participation. That night, Yoshino, dressed in her finest silk Kimono of crimson red with white Sakura flowers, stealthily entered Naos' bed-chamber. Lit by two small lanterns on the wall, the interior remained hidden within the shadows they cast; Yoshino easily made out the two naked bodies entwined before her.

Ujimoto was middle-aged and was taller than most men his age, but his years of inactive service first at the court, then under the Shogun had taken their toll. Fat replaced muscle in most areas, and he no longer kept the athleticism of a warrior's body. His bright piercing eyes flickered as he sighted Yoshino and he eagerly disengaged himself from Nao's embrace in anticipation of pleasures to come. He sat up, naked, and stroked the small beard he wore beneath his cruel mouth as he watched Yoshino seductively disrobe in front of him. She stood before him naked, her breasts heaving, her nipples erect, and her eyes now focused on Ujimoto's arousal. Before Yoshino could move any closer, Ujimoto grabbed her and mounted her from behind. Having penetrated her, his thrusting became violent, and Yoshino tried hard to contain the anger she felt. As suddenly as it began, it was over. Ujimoto collapsed onto the futon alongside Nao, bringing Yoshino down with him, and he lay there grinning.

After a while, Yoshino sat up and set about tidying her dishevelled hair. She withdrew one of her long ornamental hairpins and with effortless speed drove the hairpin into the sleeping Ujimoto's left ear. She remembered the look of bewilderment on his face before his eyes rolled upwards, his body arched, and at the puddle of piss gathering around him. Realising what was happening, a horrified Nao sat up and tried to scream, but the second hairpin Yoshino had thrust into her right eye, piercing the brain, silenced her. She regretted having to kill Nao but leaving her alive would just complicate matters. *No loose ends*, she thought.

Yoshino searched through her discarded clothes and retrieved her *Kaiken*, a single-edged dagger she had hidden in the sleeve of her kimono. Grasping Ujimoto's well-oiled top knot, she bent the head backwards and slashed at his windpipe, continuing the cut to sever the spinal cord. Cutting through the remaining sinew, Yoshino removed Ujimoto's head from his body and placed it inside Nao's wig box. At the washstand, she wiped away the blood sprays, mottling her naked milky white skin and then dressed in her discarded clothes. Yoshino removed the two lanterns on the wall and extinguished the flame before emptying its oil onto the naked corpses. She rummaged through Ujimoto's clothes for anything that might immediately identify him and pocketed the few silver coins she found. As she left the room, Yoshino hurled the other lamp at the room's paper screen walls, setting the room ablaze.

Momentarily awake, Yoshino opened her eyes. Her throat felt dry, and her cheeks flushed. *The fire, yes, I remember the fire;* she thought as she recalled the details of her crime and resumed her sleep. She saw herself dressed in her red Kimono escaping the raging fire at the pleasure house she had started, shuffling effortlessly through the long, dark narrow lanes away from the fire towards the *Kamo* River carrying a plain black lacquered box.

Chapter Two

Sakichi

Mount Hiei-Zan: Autumn

Second-year of Genki (1571)

The aesthetics of the *Chanoyu,* or 'Way of Tea' as the tea ceremony became known, had long captivated the interest of the thirteen-year-old Samurai boy known by his boyhood name of Sakichi. His father, Ishida Masatsugu, a vassal of the Azai clan, was head of an important Samurai family from Omi province and was now castellan of Ishida castle. Masatsugu had tried to introduce Sakichi to the customary martial arts expected of young Samurai boys, but without success. Sakichi's lack of enthusiasm showed that his interest lay elsewhere.

To the annoyance of his father, Sakichi would spend most of his time spying on his mother, watching her prepare the tea and taking notice of her skills as she performed the *chanoyu.* One day, his mother caught him spying and thought it prudent to teach him the purpose of these rituals. She lectured him on how the rituals of classical refinement symbolise the Buddhist teachings of man and nature being bound in an endless cycle of harmonious coexistence. It was a lecture completely wasted on Sakichi, whose inattentiveness to her teachings matched the attention he gave to his martial lessons. In frustration, Masatsugu entrusted Sakichi into the care of the local Tendai warrior monks at the Kyoto Enryaku-ji temple at Mount Hieizan. He had hoped that they would be better able to instil into him an education befitting a Samurai warrior and prepare him for his *genpuku* (coming-of-age ceremony) that would mark his formal transition to adulthood.

At first, Sakichi found his duties at the temple confined to performing menial tasks and household chores and would often be at the receiving end of an occasional beating for no reason other than to instil a sense of humility into him. When the time came to begin his studies, he proved to be a conscientious student who took his learning seriously. He would often pour over various translations of ancient classical Chinese texts well until the early morning hours, and his tutors reported daily to the abbot to outline his progress or lack of it. Masatsugu had earlier briefed the abbot about Sakichi's obsession with spying on his mother performing her various rituals, which intrigued the abbot. Like Sakichi's mother, the abbot would lecture Sakichi on the spiritual aesthetics and Tendai Buddhist precepts that were associated with these rituals, especially the *chanoyu*. However, this time the abbot rewarded Sakichi's inattentiveness with more beatings and made him write everything he had understood. If his responses were unsatisfactory, he kept Sakichi writing until they were.

The abbot also had a keen interest in the tea ceremony, besides being a keen collector of fine tea ware. It was Dengyo Daishi, the founder of the Enryaku-ji Temple, who introduced tea to Japan from China. The abbot took immense pride in his collection and would often invite Sakichi to view his latest acquisitions. On one occasion, he showed Sakichi several elaborate tea caddies and bowls recently imported from China, only for Sakichi to exhibit disinterest. He was more impressed by the simpler, locally-made rustic pieces in the abbot's collection, for it reminded him of the sober coloured pottery used by his mother.

The abbot also liked the refined simplicity of the local pieces and lectured Sakichi that as imperfect as these utensils were, they were more in keeping with true Zen principles, and that is why the noted tea master, Murata Shuko set about transforming the traditional Chinese styled tea ceremony into a uniquely Japanese one. He continued to lecture Sakichi that such was the power of the *chanoyu,* that all the great lords and noted Samurai of the realm aspired to host one. He also told of a story concerning three famous, large, and expensive tea caddies known in the realm as the *Hatsuhana,* the *Nitta* and the *Narashiba*. It was said that if you owned all three, you would own all of Japan, and the *Narashiba* was the only one his enemy that lord Nobunaga had yet to obtain.

#

As the months progressed, the abbot became increasingly worried about the news coming out of Kyoto concerning Nobunaga's intentions to punish the monks of the Enryaku-ji. He had earlier rebuffed Nobunaga's entreaties to cease providing sanctuary for his enemies and to ally with him. Instead, Nobunaga had countered the abbot's refusal with the demand that he at least remain neutral, which the abbot again refused. With a powerful army of warrior monks at his command and an overblown confidence in the impregnability of the Enryaku-ji, the abbot convinced himself Nobunaga would not dare attack. That was until news reached him of a great army now massing at the foot of the mountain. The abbot had decided to write to the Shogun and appeal directly for his help. He would remind him of the temple's sacred status as the spiritual guardian of the capital and have him order Nobunaga to withdraw his forces. He would add that such an assault on the Enryaku-ji would offend the emperor and the Shogun as guardian of the peace would be blamed for allowing it to happen. Having finished writing his appeal to the Shogun, the abbot summoned Sakichi to the main hall.

"Ah. Sakichi, I need you to do an errand for me," the abbot said, instructing the boy to sit down.

"Of course, Father. How can I be of help?"

"You remember Saito Taneomi, the local pottery merchant in Sakamoto?"

"Yes, Father. He visits here often to show you his latest teaware acquisitions."

"Yes, I need you to deliver this letter to him," said the abbot handing Sakichi a folded and sealed parchment, "and while you are there, have a look at his recent imports and see if there is anything worthy there."

"Of course, Father. When do I leave? And am I to wait for a reply?"

"No, that is unnecessary, but I need you to leave immediately. One more thing: make sure this letter does not fall into anyone else's hands other than Taneomi's. One of my Sohei warriors will escort you down the mountain."

"Excuse me, Father, why not just let the Sohei deliver the message?"

"Do you think my Sohei has the skills to appraise the value of Taneomi's teaware?" Sakichi accepted the abbot's point and returned to his quarters to prepare for the journey down the mountain.

The abbot had meanwhile summoned the Sohei Gozo to discuss Sakichi's mission.

"Gozo, the message the boy carries is important, and it cannot fall into the wrong hands. Guide him to Sakamoto and find out what you can about Nobunaga's troop deployments there and hurry back."

"What about the boy?" Gozo asked.

"Once you are sure he has delivered the message, leave him to make his way back. The information you gather will be too important to delay," said the abbot.

With the mid-morning sun at their backs, Sakichi, and his Sohei escort began their descent down the eastern side of the mountain and followed the secret route towards the merchant town of Sakamoto at its base. It was well past mid-day and into the hour of the sheep before Sakichi and Gozo finally arrived at Sakamoto. The town was a busy complex of temple shrines, retirement houses for the Enryaku-ji monks, and trading stores for merchants and craftsmen. Like most of the buildings, Saito Taneomi's pottery store was an unassuming structure of unhewn stone and whitewashed walls with very few windows. Were it not for the sign outside, no one would have known that it was a merchant's pottery shop housing some of the finest imports of *karamono* (Chinese porcelain).

As Sakichi and Gozo entered the store, Gozo hit his head on the doorway sill and exploded with obscenities. Unlike most of the Enryaku-ji warrior monks, Gozo was unusually tall with gleaming dark eyes and wore a white head cowl that was wrapped around his head, contrasting with the saffron colour of his robes. The only weapon he carried was his 'Bo' staff, a six-foot-long wooden pole made of oak. Hearing Gozo's expletive-laden rant, a voice from across the room called out.

"May I be of help, sirs?"

"We seek the merchant Saito Taneomi," Sakichi called out in reply. It was then that a small man with a shiny shaven head glistening in sweat appeared from behind a table of stacked earthenware jugs.

"Oh. Forgive me. I had thought you were one of the Oda soldiers returning. How can I be of help?"

"We are looking for Saito Taneomi," Sakichi answered.

"Why, I am he. What business do you have with me?" the man asked. A confused Sakichi inquired, "Forgive me, but you look very different from the times I saw you at the Enryaku-ji." The merchant laughed.

"That was my brother," he said. A worried Sakichi glanced at Gozo, and he remembered the abbot's instructions *Make sure this letter does not fall into anyone else's hands other than Taneomi's.*

"I have a letter from the abbot of the Enryaku-ji for Saito Taneomi," said Sakichi.

"I can take it, if you like. He will be back a little later on."

"I am sorry I am under strict instructions to deliver this only to Saito Taneomi. Is it all right if we wait for him?"

"Of course, make yourselves comfortable over there." The merchant pointed to a corner of the room with a low table and cushions.

"I will prepare us some tea," he said and encouraged Sakichi to browse around the shop while he arranged the refreshments. Sakichi noticed a particular bowl laying on a nearby shelf. The unusual nature of its blue glaze led Sakichi to believe it was from China's Jiang province, but on closer inspection, he remained unconvinced. Sakichi was about to seek the merchant and inquire further when they heard sounds of panicking people and agitated horses whinnying outside. A curious Sakichi and Gozo stepped outside to see what the fuss was about and caught the attention of a panicking peasant running past them.

"What is going on?" Sakichi called out.

"Soldiers are coming," he replied, "if you want to live, flee to the temple." It was then that Sakichi and Gozo caught sight of a large group of Ashigaru foot-soldiers led by a group of mounted Samurai appearing in the narrow street. Gozo recognised the *Nobori* banners they carried emblazoned with the bell flower emblem.

"They are Akechi," he muttered to Sakichi. By now, panic had well and truly set in and people scattered in all directions, leaving Gozo and Sakichi conspicuously alone in the street, and now the focus of attention. A mounted Samurai broke formation and rode ahead towards them. Sakichi noticed the Samurai wore a distinctive *maedate* (helmet crest) that signified someone of importance, and he wondered who it might be. Gozo, now realising the gravity of their situation, implored Sakichi to make a run for it.

"Go now, boy. This day will not end well," Gozo urged.

"Gozo!" Sakichi pleaded in protest, but he knew he was right and reluctantly took off. The mounted Samurai had halted just a few feet away from Gozo, who prepared himself to make a stand. Turning his face to the heavens, Gozo appealed to the compassionate Bodhisattva for help, believing that all are saved who call upon his name. He positioned his Bo on his right shoulder and assumed a defensive stance. His right leg was out in front and bent at the knee, his back leg straight. Recognising that the monk was preparing for a fight, another of the mounted Samurai charged with his sword held high above his head slashing downwards at Gozo, who just pivoted to avoid the blow but quickly followed through with a return strike striking the Samurai on the left shoulder and dismounting him.

Seeing their fallen companion, two more mounted Samurai now charged at Gozo, this time with Yari spears. Gozo parried the spear of one rider, the force of which disarmed him, but the second threw his spear, striking Gozo in his left thigh. Both Samurai dismounted and approached the wounded Gozo with swords drawn. Armed with only his staff and with a spear protruding from his thigh, Gozo faced his attackers. His eyes bulged as arrows thumped into his back and he briefly saw the ground rushing up to meet the falling top half of his body.

Gozo's distraction had enabled Sakichi to escape the confrontation, and he ran as fast as he could down an alleyway behind Saito's shop towards the mountain, and hopefully safety. Sakichi found the end of the alleyway blocked by a loose stone wall a little over waist high, which was easy enough to leap over, and he ran towards the cover of a nearby thicket that lay mere metres away from the forested slopes of the mountain.

Sakichi crouched low within the thicket and rested to catch his breath, while he vainly fought off the wave of tiredness and despair that swept over him. He had briefly fallen asleep and woke to sounds of soldiers taking up positions on both sides of his hiding place.

How am I going to get out of this? Sakichi thought. *Has the great Bodhisattva Hachiman seen fit to end my days now?* He watched as the Ashigaru formed a single line at the foot of the mountain with mounted Samurai lined up behind them.

There must be thousands of them. I had better wait till nightfall before making a run for it. Sakichi looked skywards and sighed. *It will be hours yet before sunset.*

Just as Sakichi resigned himself to more hours of cramped waiting, he suddenly felt the grip of powerful hands pinning him down.

"What have we got here? A spy?" exclaimed the Akechi Ashigaru who stood over Sakichi whilst his two companions held his feet and arms.

"Talk boy or you will see your ancestors in the afterlife," the Ashigaru demanded as he rested the tip of his naginata on Sakichi's throat. A fearful Sakichi in a panicked voice explained to the Ashigaru in a panicked voice how he got scared and ran away when he saw soldiers heading into town. The Ashigaru studied the fretting boy at the end of his naginata.

"It would not go well for us to kill a spy without first getting any useful information. It would be more sensible just to hand him over and have done with it," the Ashigaru said to his companions. Having bound Sakichi's hands, the three Ashigaru delivered him to the command tent set up at the eastern foot of the mountain where he was dragged before the Oda general, Akechi Mitsuhide.

For a young warrior in his early forties, Lord Mitsuhide had already served three masters before swearing allegiance to Nobunaga: Saito Dosan of Mino, Asakura Yoshikage of Echizen, and most recently, the Shogun Ashikaga Yoshiaki. It was a habit that saw him often change loyalties, depending on which master star was in the ascent. To Sakichi, he was a fearsome figure who sat before him on a camp stool in full battle armour, and he nervously recognised the distinctive helmet crest he had seen earlier in the street with Gozo.

"And you are?" demanded Mitsuhide. Sakichi gave the same story he told the Ashigaru who captured him when Mitsuhide cut him off.

"What were you doing in the town?" said Mitsuhide.

"Looking at teaware, sir," Sakichi replied. Then he remembered he still had the letter the abbot had given him and became anxious.

"Teaware?" Mitsuhide exclaimed with interest.

"Why, of all things, were you looking at teaware?" Sakichi again told the truth, leaving out the primary reason for his mission. He explained how the abbot, being a keen collector of teaware, had sent him to view the merchant Saito Taneomi's latest imports and to advise him if there was anything of value.

"You are asking me to believe the abbot would send a boy of your years to judge the value and quality of imported tea are?" Mitsuhide said in a condescending tone.

"Yes, sir," Sakichi replied nonchalantly.

"And your observations, master expert," Mitsuhide snapped back sarcastically.

"I found an interesting piece in the store. It was a *Chawan* style tea bowl with the characteristic bluish glaze of Chinese Jiang ware but on closer inspection, I was thinking it might be of local origin when your soldiers appeared."

"Why would you think it is locally made?" an intrigued Mitsuhide asked.

"I thought the style simplistic, somewhat like the pieces the abbot obtained from the tea master, Murata Juko. I am told there are many local potters following the Murata Juko style, which, as you know, aims to blend both the aesthetics of Japanese and Chinese tastes in a simple and rustic style."

"And what else did you learn at the temple?" Mitsuhide probed. Sakichi related his study of *Hanzi,* the Chinese writing system, to study the texts of the holy books of Buddha. He told how he spent each day from sunrise to sunset

37

with his tutor reciting sutras and pouring over Chinese classics, and when the sun finally set, he would continue at his books until his lamp went out.

"What to do, what to do with you?" Mitsuhide mumbled aloud, and without thinking, Sakichi asked.

"May I ask what became of the monk who was with me earlier?"

"You mean the Sohei?" Mitsuhide snapped back.

"Yes, sir," replied Sakichi.

"His head now watches over the sacred mountain, if you get my meaning?" Forgetting himself, Sakichi screamed, "Why did you have to kill him?"

"Quite simple, boy. He fought, and he died. Had he surrendered, his fate would have been a lot worse." Mitsuhide studied the confused expression on Sakichi's face and spoke.

"This venerated mountain has been sacred since Heian times, giving spiritual protection to the capital and protected by successive emperors. So, what did the monks here do? Aside from colluding with our enemies to protect their extensive land interests, they have set themselves up as a power unto themselves using religious justifications for private wars. All the great clans of history: the Fujiwara, Taira, Minamoto, Ashikaga, Takeda and Mori, have had to fight and deal with these warrior priests. Do you realise that the number of temples and monasteries on this one mountain alone exceeds three thousand? The enemy is not this mountain, nor is it Buddhism, but if we don't address this issue now, no one will ever do so."

Mitsuhide frowned and mulled over what he had just said. A few hours earlier, lord Nobunaga had given him orders to attack the Enryaku-ji and burn it to the ground. As a devout Buddhist himself, Mitsuhide protested Nobunaga's order and tried to think of another way to bring the recalcitrant monks to heel, but, in the end, Nobunaga would have none of it. The order to 'spare no one' reverberated in his head. "Hunt them all down and burn their lair. Then maybe the fire will purify their religion anew," Nobunaga had said.

Mitsuhide's steely eyes again rested on Sakichi, whose dark eyes were now glistening with the welling of tears.

"I have yet to decide what to do with you, boy, but I feel you may yet be of some use. I hear our general, Kinoshita Hideyoshi, is currently looking for a sandal bearer and has sought my advice on this matter, and I am due to meet with Hideyoshi and Lord Nobunaga soon, so you shall accompany us."

It was several days later when Mitsuhide, following Nobunaga's orders, torched the town of Sakamoto at the foot of Mount Hiezan in a deliberate act to drive the townsfolk and the retired priests to seek refuge up the mountain into the monasteries and temples above. As Sakamoto burnt, the war horns sounded and Mitsuhide's army of 30,000 that had completely encircled the mountain began moving upwards, burning every building they came across and killing all before them, sparing no one, be it man, woman, or child. By nightfall, only the smouldering ashes of the Enryaku-ji temple and the two thousand other buildings remained. Twenty thousand monks, men, women and children were slaughtered in the initial attack and their corpses lay strewn about the mountainside like forest litter, and those that were captured alive had their heads chopped off one by one. Nobunaga had intended the devastation of Enryaku-ji to serve as a warning to all temples throughout his domains that he would not tolerate religious militancy, and he took comfort in knowing the political influence of the Enryaku-ji was finally at an end. Throughout the onslaught, Mitsuhide sat emotionless on his camp-stool in his tent at the foot of the sacred mountain, receiving regular reports of the slaughter's progress.

The 'lord fool' lives up to his nickname, he thought, referring to Nobunaga.

Only a blind fool ignores the fact that the nation will be in an uproar over this.

It was whilst he dealt with the Enryaku-ji that Mitsuhide had Sakichi consigned to the care of his first wife Hirokohime at his new residence at Usayama castle, which lay atop Usayama Mountain just across the valley from Mount Hiezan. The sight of Hirokohime in the castle kitchen brought a relaxed smile to Sakichi's face, for she reminded him of his mother, and it made him realise how much he missed her. He stood at the doorway, watching Hirokohime gently tend the embers of the fire pit and coaxing them into life. Sensing someone was watching her, Hirokohime turned and saw Sakichi in the doorway.

"Your poor boy," she exclaimed, "I can see living with those greedy monks has put no meat on those bones of yours. Come and sit next to me and tell me about yourself while I prepare your meal." Sakichi nervously moved towards the fire pit and sat alongside her, staring. She was a woman of youthful years, as the skin of her face appeared smooth and lacked the wrinkles that age brings. Yet on closer inspection, Sakichi noticed her left cheek seemed marred by the pitted scarring typical of smallpox infections. The plain grey kimono she wore was of expensive silk and fastened with a half-width *Obi* sash tied in a butterfly knot. Her radiant black hair held in place by a silver clasp, also in the shape of a butterfly.

"There. I will not bite you. I am the wife of Lord Mitsuhide and daughter of Tsumaki Norihiro of Mino," Hirokohime said by introduction, but Sakichi had other things on his mind.

"What will happen to me?" he asked.

"My husband informs me you are coming with us when we journey to Kyoto and he further directs that I am to shall we say, 'look after you.' So please tell me about yourself." Sakichi, feeling a bit more at ease, opened up.

"My name is Sakichi, and I have an elder brother called Masazumi, and my father is Ishida Masatsugu, a retainer of Azai Nagamasa."

"Oh dear, my husband did not mention this," Hirokohime said. "who else knows about your family?"

"Only the abbot," said Sakichi.

"You must understand, Nagamasa betrayed our Lord Nobunaga, and he is furious with this lord, so it would be wise not to discuss your family connections with anyone at this stage, not even with my husband."

"Why? He knows my father sent me to the temple for an education?"

"Did he ask who your father was?" replied Hirokohime. Sakichi carefully thought before answering,

"Come to think of it, no."

Lowering her voice, Hirokohime said, "I will wager, he is as yet not aware that your father is a retainer of Nagamasa. Understand this, we are at war with the Azai, and should your father fall into Nobunaga's hands, he and all his family, including you, are at risk of beheading." The gravity of Hirokohime's words sunk in and Sakichi returned to feeling fearful once more.

"I think I understand," Sakichi replied. "Lord Mitsuhide said we are going to Imahama to visit Lord Hideyoshi after visiting Kyoto. As my home is only just a little north of there at Ishida, do you think he might permit me to visit my family?" Sakichi thought to ask.

"Silly boy," an exasperated Hirokohime said. "Have you not learned anything from what I just said? You are my husband's hostage, and that, dear boy, is why you are still alive." Hirokohime moved to attend to the fire pit and sympathetically added,

"We shall have to just wait and see what develops."

"My husband also tells me that for one so young, you have a keen interest in the *chanoyu,* especially it would seem, the teaware. I should like to know why you are so interested, but first, have some food and then you can tell me." Sakichi did not realise how hungry he was and quickly wolfed down the freshly made rice cakes with bean paste Hirokohime offered. Feeling fuller and more relaxed, Sakichi spoke of the times spent watching his mother prepare the *chanoyu* and his interest in teaware that he developed from studying the abbot's collection.

"Let me tell you something, Sakichi," Hirokohime said. "The tea ceremony is not just about enlightenment and striving for perfection. It is also a valuable tool of state. Wars have been averted by simply having rival Daimyo engage with each other using the ritual of the tea ceremony and even trade expensive teaware for territory? You must understand that teaware is now a measure of status and power and is useful in the motivation of vassals."

"How so?" Sakichi asked, looking confused.

"Our Lord Nobunaga realised rather astutely there is a limit to how many domains and castles you can keep awarding subordinates for valuable service. He considered it was far better to create a new means of reward that is equally prized." Sakichi was so intent on listening to Hirokohime that he declined her offer of more rice cakes.

"If you have finished eating, then let me tell you a story," said Hirokohime. "Lord Nobunaga rewarded one of his retainers for meritorious service with a fife in Ise province. The retainer, Takigawa Kazumasu, made it known the reward disappointed him, as he had been hoping for a tea set as a reward. Nobunaga immediately corrected the situation and presented Kazumasu with pieces from his collection. The humble tea utensil, if used strategically, can unite this land. Now, let me show you to your quarters, for we leave at first light."

With the first rays of the rising sun breaking over the horizon, the assembled Akechi retinue began their advance towards Kyoto. Fifty mounted Samurai of Lord Mitsuhide's personal guards led the procession, followed by Lord Mitsuhide with his coterie of retainers. A little way back were two palanquins carried by six bearers each, and behind them walked Sakichi amongst the two-hundred-armed Ashigaru foot-soldiers. A day's march later, the procession arrived at Nijo Castle, the Shogunal residence that Nobunaga had rebuilt for Yoshiaki's pleasure. There, they waited for some time for the Shogun to approve their letters of credentials and gain entry to the castle.

Whilst preparations were underway for their evening meal, Sakichi explored the gardens adjoining their assigned residence. He headed for the large pond ahead with its three islands. The garden featured a spring, a narrow stream, and even a miniature hill overlooking the pond upon which he climbed. Where he stood, he noticed how each of the islands featured neatly manicured trees, together with a careful placement of assorted stones and large rocks. His eyes settled on the huge rock that rested on the largest of the three islands.

That must be the Fujitoishi, he thought. He remembered hearing how Nobunaga had one thousand workers bring the abandoned old rock from Lord Hosokawa's mansion on the faraway island of Kyushu, all the way here to the Nijo Castle.

Sakichi sat down on the soft grass of the hill and watched the large Koi carp break the surface of the pond as they fed on the insects and larvae gathering on the water's surface. A pair of nesting bush warblers who had made their home in the nearby tall box hedge that ringed the garden sang out at the approach of dusk. Not wanting to disturb them, Sakichi approached the nest cautiously to see if it contained eggs and he heard voices coming from the other side of the hedge. He recognised one voice as Lord Mitsuhide's, which made him nervous, but he continued to listen in.

"You need to be careful, Lord Mitsuhide, and be thankful the peasant Hideyoshi is not around to hear you."

"Seii Taishogun, I merely commented that my lord, Nobunaga, plays favourites with General Hideyoshi."

Seii Taishogun? It must be the Shogun Yoshiaki himself. Sakichi thought to himself, and he became more worried than ever. He thought about sneaking away, but curiosity got the better of him, and he continued to listen in.

"Mitsuhide, have you not heard? Nobunaga intends to appoint Hideyoshi as his liaison officer to oversee my dealings with him. Does he take me for a fool? More likely, it is another excuse to spy on me. He already vets every piece of communication that passes through my hands. Who does he think he is?"

He is the power behind you. Mitsuhide thought. *I can imagine you would never be grateful to Nobunaga for being his puppet.*

"Your part in this crime against the sacred mountain Mitsuhide has not gone unnoticed."

"Seii Taishogun, my Lord commanded me, and you know I must obey."

"That may be Lord Mitsuhide, but it has appalled his excellency, the emperor."

"In every calamity, an opportunity lurks," Mitsuhide replied.

"What are you talking about?"

"You may yet have your opportunity to be rid of him."

"Explain yourself, Lord Mitsuhide."

"The attack on the Enryaku-ji has made many of the Daimyo uneasy in their support for him. Already it has provoked the Ikko-Ikki monks of Nagoya who have now openly revolted and challenged Nobunaga's authority. Reports are also coming in that other sects are rising in response to the desecration of the Enryaku-ji and have fortified their temples."

"Yes, yes," Yoshiaki said impatiently, interrupting Mitsuhide. "The point is?"

"I have also heard that the monks of the Ishiyama Honganji in Nobunaga's own Osaka fife have revolted," Mitsuhide said. "If you can get Nobunaga's nemesis, Takeda Shingen, to support our cause, he is close enough to threaten Nobunaga's base at Gifu."

"Yes, Mitsuhide. I recall you once saying, 'control Gifu, and you control the country?' Nobunaga has stretched himself to the limit. The Azai and Asakura are pinning down his armies while his Tokugawa allies are busy suppressing the Ikko-Ikki revolts in Mikawa. To deal with the Osaka Honganji revolt, Nobunaga will have to split his forces to face the Miyoshi and Mori clans, who will move to support the Honganji monks." Excited by his analysis of the situation, Yoshiaki pressed Mitsuhide. "Get word to Shingen's that he has the support of the Shogun and plead with him to make his move against Nobunaga, now."

In the long interval of silence that followed, Sakichi strained to hear anything and moved his ear closer to the hedge, only to feel a vice-like grip on his shoulder and a hand smothering his mouth. He tried to cry out, but all he could manage was a muffled groan before finding himself wrenched to the ground.

"Be quiet if you value your life," a hushed voice whispered into Sakichi's ear. With an arm locked around his neck and his mouth smothered, Sakichi's assailant dragged him away towards the seclusion of the nearby Koi Pond.

"If I take my hand away, do you promise to be quiet?" the assailant whispered to which Sakichi nodded and gasped for air as he removed his hand.

"My name is Tanaka Yoshimasa. I am a retainer of Lord Nobunaga, who is here to meet with the Shogun. What are you doing here spying on the Shogun?"

"I wasn't spying, I just overheard," Sakichi pleaded.

"Who are you, anyway? And what are you doing here?" Sakichi explained his capture by the Akechi soldiers, and how he came to be Lord Mitsuhide's hostage.

"Now, what do you think would happen if I dragged you over there and informed Lord Mitsuhide and the Shogun that I caught you eavesdropping?" What Yoshimasa had just said now made him realise the danger he is in. He looked up and studied his captor's face. It was youthful but badly disfigured by a menacing scar running down the left side of his face, which only added to the gravity of the situation, making Sakichi break down in tears. Yoshimasa looked on sympathetically.

"Look, my purpose here is to protect my lord and secure the grounds against potential assassins. How do you think it looks seeing you crouched here spying on a meeting with Lord Mitsuhide and the Shogun?"

"I heard nothing," Sakichi sobbed. "Whatever you heard is of no interest to me, and I would not persist with your denials as no one would believe you, anyway. A bit of torture is all it takes to loosen tongues. I am inclined to let you go, but I suspect others have seen us; in which case the Shogun's spies will watch to see what happens to you. Your best bet is to take your chances with Lord Nobunaga, and you can tell him about what you heard."

Sakichi, now resigned to his fate, quietly followed Yoshimasa away from the gardens and through the big imposing Karamon gate that led to the outer palace buildings of the Shoguns residence. Yoshimasa led Sakichi down an avenue lined with cherry and plum trees towards the palace guard house where he would detain Sakichi until summoned by Nobunaga. At the guardhouse, Yoshimasa grabbed Sakichi by the shoulders and turned him around to look into his eyes. Unable to explain it, he felt a bond with the boy. He cared for him, and deep in his eyes, he saw the boy before him in another time and place. He saw Sakichi dressed in one of the brightest and elaborate kimonos he had ever seen, playing with a group of boys all flying their kites in clear blue skies. The kites, emblazoned with the emblems of the old Taira and Minamoto clans, rose and fell as the boys did battle, re-enacting the legendary battles of the Genpei wars. Returning to reality, Yoshimasa handed Sakichi into the charge of the palace guard and returned to the palace, along the way reflecting on his missing childhood.

I have no memories of that part of my life, and I cannot recall any part of my life before waking up and seeing Izuma's face. Having nursed my wounds and restored me to health, she later told me how she found my partly submerged body in the shallows of the river Ane, and with the help of local river workers, they carried me to safety. As I recall, she claimed to have come from the Mochizuki clan of Omi Province, one of the original fifty-three ninja clans of the Koka-Ryu, and my survival is a testament to her ninja healing skills.

Yoshimasa touched the hilt of the *Tanto* knife nestled in his Obi alongside his long sword-*Katana* as if seeking reassurance that the one remaining possession of his past life was still there. Izuma had salvaged the *Tanto* from the mud under his near-naked body. Picked clean by scavengers, his clothes, armour, swords and anything else of value had been taken. Izuma had said of the *Tanto*, "this is not the common sword of a country Samurai; I suspect it has a pedigree and believe it to be one of Sengo Muramasa's forgings. Like all his swords, they are said to possess a life of their own. Beware, young warrior, it has a history. Guard it well." Izuma had grown tired of calling him 'young warrior', and named him Tanaka Yoshimasa after her late son. How he died is unknown as she steadfastly refused to discuss it, and when the time came for Yoshimasa to resume his place with the living, she arranged for him to meet the family benefactor, Lady Mochizuki Chiyo.

In the hour of the rooster just after dusk, Sakichi arrived under escort at Nobunaga's quarters in the palace complex. He had imagined Nobunaga as some fearsome devil-like persona and grew afraid at the prospect of meeting him. Yet, before him sat a composed, slender, middle-aged man wearing a gold brocade coat over a pair of simple black *Hakama* pants. His face exuded serenity, broken only by malevolent eyes.

So, this is the great fool of Owari, Sakichi thought. He had long heard tales of the 'Lord Fool', as the local populace referred to him. What started as a childhood nickname came to reflect his reputation for being brash, foolish, and reckless, but what struck Sakichi most about Nobunaga was his prominent nose; that and his goatee beard reminded him of the demon *Tengu*.

"Well, little songbird, I am told we caught you and your nesting warblers spying on the Shogun and my Lord Akechi?" Nobunaga said. Sakichi looked towards Yoshimasa, seated off to the side of Lord Nobunaga as if to appeal for help, but he remained emotionless and still. Sakichi prostrated himself before Nobunaga and nervously replied.

"Forgive me, Lord, I was not spying. I was watching some nesting birds in a hedge behind which I heard the lord's conversing."

"So, what did you hear?" Nobunaga asked. Sakichi made a point of saying that he only paid attention to a few of the words spoken and did not understand what they meant and relayed to Nobunaga what he remembered.

"They talked about there being an opportunity and to get word to Shingen's, that's all I understood." Nobunaga was about to respond when Yoshimasa bowed and approached Nobunaga, intent on asking to speak privately. In response, the two Samurai sitting behind Nobunaga immediately drew their swords and rushed at Yoshimasa with swords held high. Recognising the danger to Yoshimasa, Nobunaga called out for everyone to stop.

"You should know better than to try such an approach, Yoshimasa," Nobunaga said.

"Forgive me, Lord. I mistakenly thought I had your permission to approach. May I again approach and speak in private, Lord?" Nobunaga grinned and dismissed the Samurai guards and had Sakichi wait outside.

"We are alone, Yoshimasa. What is it you wish to say?"

"My Lord, Lord Akechi intends to place this boy in the employ of Hideyoshi and considering the conversation between the Shogun and Lord Akechi some of which I also overheard, I suspect they intend to use him as a spy to advance whatever it is, they are planning." Nobunaga sat in meditative silence for quite some time before addressing Yoshimasa's concerns.

"I think we should let this 'songbird' of yours return to its nest and let the game play out. The Shogun's spies will have noticed the boy's presence here, so you must return him to Lord Akechi with my command to punish him for wandering around the palace without permission. Now, have the songbird brought back." Again, a nervous Sakichi prostrated himself before Lord Nobunaga, anticipating his execution at any moment.

"Understand this, songbird. Should Lord Akechi or the Shogun learn of your eavesdropping activities, they will not allow you to live," Nobunaga said. "No amount of pleading innocence will save you this time, for the very simple fact you are a loose end and ending your life will solve their problem." Nobunaga studied the boy for a reaction but found none. Sakichi just continued to stare at something behind him.

"What are you staring at, boy?" Nobunaga demanded.

"Forgive me, Lord, but is that the famous *Hatsuhana Katatsuki* over there?" A startled Nobunaga stammered a reply.

"How do you know of this?" said Nobunaga, acting surprised.

"My lord, such a distinctive tea container with a unique iron brown glaze can be none other than the famous *Hatsuhana Katatsuki*."

"Yes, you are correct," Nobunaga nodded proudly. "One day, if you live long enough, I may let you touch it, but for now, you must accept whatever punishment Lord Akechi inflicts on you and do his bidding. You are walking on a fence between two pits: mine and Lord Akechi's. To fall in either is to invite certain death, do you understand?" Sakichi nodded. "Now wait outside." With Sakichi again gone, Nobunaga spoke with Yoshimasa.

"I share your concerns about the Shogun, and I will instruct Hideyoshi to accept Akechi's proposal to employ your songbird. I am also sending you to Hideyoshi's household as his tutor. He will soon be of an age to have his *Genpuku* and will need a good tutor and someone to steer him away from trouble, but your real purpose will be to monitor events and see what Akechi and the Shogun are up to."

Later, Yoshimasa drank alone in his quarters and again thought about his saviour, Izuma. He recalled helping her with the household chores and finding the work rewarding, despite the lingering pain from his injuries. He still chopped the firewood, and it was on such an occasion he recalled seeing the approach of a lone rider galloping towards the house. The small chestnut Kiso mare halted in front of him, its rider, who wore a conical straw hat covering the face, dismounted and handed Yoshimasa the reins of the horse. He ran his hand along her lean flanks admiringly, for he knew the Kiso was a highly priced and expensive breed of a horse, valued for its temperament as a warhorse and surmised its rider must be somebody of rank. He looked closely at the stranger's demeanour and judging by the riding clothes worn, a short-sleeved robe of silk kept closed with a thin Obi sash he knew this was a woman, not just any woman but a strangely unescorted woman of importance.

Yoshimasa called out to Izuma to alert her to the stranger's arrival, and she hurried outside and bowed as she recognised her visitor. Izuma introduced the visitor as the family benefactor, Lady Mochizuki Chiyo, prompting Yoshimasa to acknowledge her with a deep bow. Chiyo removed her straw hat to respond and allowed her loosely tied black hair to unravel gently and cascade down to drape over her shoulders. Yoshimasa found her alluring, and his eyes locked onto her youthful face which was absent of the white makeup, usually worn by such ladies of status.

Chiyo approached Yoshimasa and extended her hand to caress his long facial scar. She delicately traced its outline, beginning from his temple on the left side of his face to the corner of his mouth. She lingered at his mouth for a while before cupping his chin with her hand and looking deep into his eyes. As suddenly as she began, she withdrew her hand and returned to her horse and climbed into the saddle. After a lingering look at Yoshimasa, she goaded the mare forward and trotted off, leaving her straw hat lying in the dust where she discarded it. Yoshimasa looked at Izuma, his eyes searching for an explanation, but there was no response. Much later, when he questioned Izuma about the visitor's strange behaviour, all she would offer was that the lady seemed pleased and never spoke of it again.

#

"From what I have just heard, you have become a nuisance," Mitsuhide berated Sakichi. Yoshimasa had just finished explaining to Lord Mitsuhide the contrived circumstances of Sakichi's arrest at the Shogun's palace and Lord Nobunaga's instructions to mete out an appropriate punishment.

"I should have you beaten, if not beheaded, straight away," Mitsuhide added. Sakichi swallowed hard. His facial expression betrayed his anxiety and fear, but he remained silent. Yoshimasa, considering his task complete, glanced at the downcast Sakichi, and excused himself, leaving Sakichi to his fate.

"So, what do you have to say now?" Mitsuhide demanded. Sakichi struggled to fight back the tears welling up in his eyes and quietly prostrated himself before Mitsuhide, half expecting a sword to separate his head from his body any minute. He snatched a glance at Mitsuhide, who showed no outward signs of being annoyed. On the contrary, he noticed the lord's little smirk betraying his amusement.

"No matter," said Mitsuhide, resorting to a more friendly tone. "I have today received news from Lord Hideyoshi advising he has accepted your placement in his household as a servant. I will, of course, have to inform him of your latest troublesome adventure and assure him I have taken steps to ensure your best

48

behaviour in his service." Sakichi's downcast eyes came to life as he now focused on what Lord Mitsuhide had said.

What did he mean by that? He wondered, and as if reading Sakichi's mind, Mitsuhide elaborated.

"I found it necessary to locate and inform your father that you are now under my protection and should have no concerns for your wellbeing. However, I have also discovered your family are vassals of Azai Nagamasa, an enemy of my liege lord. By rights, I should have you and your family put to death, but as no one knows about this and I am both benevolent and merciful, your ongoing loyalty to me will stay my hand." Sakichi understood. Lord Mitsuhide's intention was clear enough. The life of Sakichi and his family would now depend on his continuing cooperation as an Akechi informant.

With Sakichi and the attendants dismissed, Lord Mitsuhide turned and slid back the painted screen behind him, revealing a grinning Shogun, fanning himself.

"Lord Mitsuhide, what I heard was amusing, but of what use is the boy to us?"

"Seii Taishogun, Hideyoshi is the key to Nobunaga's success. He has forces stationed here as your bodyguard and will report to Nobunaga any move you make. Where Hideyoshi is and what Hideyoshi does is what we must know, and this is what I expect the boy to tell me."

"Yes, I see some advantage here, but my spies tell me Nobunaga is sending his retainer Yoshimasa as his tutor and to monitor his activities."

"Yes, Seii Taishogun. May I suggest you take a keen interest in the boy's wellbeing and offer to sponsor his education while taking steps to remove this tutor?"

"Now, how would I achieve that?" Yoshiaki smiled.

Chapter Three

Nene

Spring: Third Year of Genki (1572)

Sakichi stood on the bow of the Maruko-Bune, a single-masted sailing vessel just out of Otsu, heading for the port of Imahama on the north-eastern shore of Lake Biwako. In warm sunshine, the south-westerly winds from Osaka Bay filled its sail and propelled it forward to meet the strong westerly gusts descending from the local Hira Mountains that created huge swells, forcing the Maruko-Bune to zigzag across the bay.

From his position on the bow, Sakichi watched the boat plough through the dark foaming water, and he looked to the distant shoreline of Hikone and the mountains that lay beyond. He knew the area well and took comfort in that they were less than half a day away from their destination, and the sheltered approach to Imahama would mean calmer waters.

It was only yesterday when Sakichi had departed Kyoto with Hirokohime. An overnight stay in the lake town of Otsu was necessary while the Maruko-Bune finished unloading its cargo of rice and salt from the northern provinces and prepared for an early morning departure. Their destination was Hideyoshi's home at Imahama and Sakichi's family home in Ishida lay tantalisingly close, less than a day's ride away, but Sakichi was mindful of Mitsuhide's threats and resigned himself to wait for another opportunity to see his family.

With the approach of sunset at the beginning of the hour of the rooster, the Maruko-Bune finally docked at the small port of Imahama. A palanquin for Hirokohime and six porters were waiting with lanterns to ferry the landing party to Hideyoshi's new residence in the hills. The procession left the docks with Sakichi walking behind Hirokohime's palanquin, flanked by an escort of four Akechi Samurai. The pace was quick, but luckily the terrain was mostly flat as they headed towards the village of Kunitomo on the southern banks of the Ane River. Beyond the hill that overlooked the village lay their destination.

Although this was familiar territory to Sakichi, Hirokohime had earlier explained Nobunaga's keen interest in the area. It was less than thirty years ago, the then Shogun Ashikaga Yoshiharu commissioned the famous swordsmith Kunitomo Zenbee to reproduce the barbarian matchlock guns the Portuguese introduced to the Daimyo of Tanegashima Island. From that time on, the town of Kunitomo, which was an Azai fife, grew in importance and quickly developed into one of the major gun-production centres in Japan. With the routing of the Azai and Asakura at Anegawa, Nobunaga took control of the Kunitomo region together with its foundries and workshops. Hirokohime added there was a purpose to Hideyoshi establishing his residence close by Kunitomo. His orders were to not only secure the fife but also to improve the output at the Kunitomo foundry.

By the time the procession finally arrived at Lord Hideyoshi's villa, it was well past dusk and late in the hour of the dog. A solitary servant had waited outside the gate, holding a lantern to guide them in. As they approached the main house, the light of more lanterns appeared along the eaves of the house, allowing Sakichi to see that the residence was an incomplete single-storey mansion, as evidenced by the signs of ongoing construction. Assorted materials and tools lay scattered everywhere. Inside, he noticed the sleeping area was finished, and the elaborate paintings on the screen doors decorating his assigned quarters impressed him.

"Sakichi, I trust these lodgings are comfortable enough for you?" Hirokohime said, laughing. "I am told Lord Hideyoshi is away, and unsure when he will return, but your tutor will arrive tomorrow."

"My tutor? What tutor?" Sakichi exclaimed.

"Lord Nobunaga was mindful of your purpose at the Enryaku-ji and has ordered that your education is to be continued. My Lord Mitsuhide has also reminded me to make it clear to you that he has gone to significant effort and expense to secure this position here for you with Lord Hideyoshi and he expects your complete dedication."

"And what is my position here to be?" Sakichi meekly replied.

"Why, I thought my husband would have explained all that to you."

"You are to be schooled in martial arts to be of practical service to your lord as a page. Remember, you are not far off from your *Genpuku,* coming-of-age ceremony."

If only I had applied myself with my father's teaching, then he would not have sent me away, and I would not be here. Sakichi thought.

"May I ask who is schooling me?"

"All I know is that my husband has told me that Lord Nobunaga has sent one of his retainers to tutor you. He is travelling overland and is expected to arrive sometime tomorrow. Meanwhile, you are to meet with Lady Nene, Lord Hideyoshi's wife, who is eager to hear everything about you, so clean yourself up."

#

Yoshimasa crossed the Inukami River to reach the outskirts of Takamiya-juku, a post town at the foot of the Suzuka Mountains, which was part of the Tosando eastern mountain route connecting the north-west provinces with the capital. Coaxing his struggling Kiso mare onwards, Yoshimasa rued the oppressive heat and humidity that hung in the mid-morning air. Even the rice fields straddling the town looked like steaming cauldrons.

With the town in sight, the heavens cracked with the sound of thunder and the grey skies released a downpour of rain so intense it quickly filled every available fissure and threatened to flood the road. His clothes now sodden, Yoshimasa hurriedly dismounted and sought shelter among a group of cryptomeria trees. The rain was relentless and seemed to go on forever when it stopped as abruptly as it began. The briefly cooled earth quickly warmed up again, creating more mists, and the oppressive heat returned.

A soaked Yoshimasa continued towards the town on foot, holding the reins of his horse, desperate for food and a change of clothing at one of the town's inns. A peasant farmer pulling a cart of melons had caught up with him and Yoshimasa sought directions to an inn. The farmer pointed towards a nearby street lined with shops and outside-produce stalls, explaining that the town's only inn lay at its end, but as it was market day, he doubted there would be any rooms available. Undeterred, Yoshimasa continued in the direction the farmer had shown, only to find his path blocked by a gathering crowd of townsfolk.

Ahead, he could see a group of Oda Samurai menacingly brandishing their swords, threatening the crowd to move aside. Wet and hungry, Yoshimasa pushed his way through the crowd to see the body of a Samurai lying face down in the mud. He continued and skirted the crowd to reach the inn at the end of the street, and for his offer of two silver coins, which was double the going rate, they made a vacancy available where none had existed before.

Refreshed and dry, Yoshimasa was enjoying his meal in the inn's common room when he overheard a conversation between two Oda guards sitting at a nearby table.

"I don't like it. This is the second body that's turned up today."

"Yes," said the second guard. "And it's strange that both bodies show no signs of how they died," provoking a chuckle from his companion before downing his bowl of sake.

"What's so funny?" the second guard snarled.

"Don't you remember? You saw his face when we turned it over. He was smiling, and no trace of blood anywhere."

"Maybe, they met up with some witch or demon," said the second guard.

"Well, I've sent a message alerting the local magistrate, so it's not my problem."

Completing his meal, Yoshimasa left the inn to pause on the veranda and mull over the conversation he had just overheard. Night had descended and a gusty cool breeze blew through the town. He watched the *Kakeandon* lanterns hanging under the eaves of the inn flicker and rock in the wind and decided to stay the night in town. Imahama was still a day's ride away, and he would leave at first light. He turned back to go inside when he felt something pass close to his left ear and the sound of a dull thud. Turning in the sound's direction, he noticed a *Fukibari* dart embedded in dried earth used to seal the gaps of the inn's walls and pulled the dart out, scrutinising every detail.

This is a Ninja dart... whoever fired this did not want me dead, for any competent ninja would not have missed. Was it a warning? A message, perhaps?

Yoshimasa woke up much later than intended, and it was mid-morning before he finally set off for Imahama. He had slept in after being kept awake for most of the night, agonising over the meaning of the dart attack. By now, the sun was fast approaching its zenith in a clear blue sky, and he felt the return of the oppressive heat. He was not long out of town before he became conscious of someone or something following him.

#

The hour was late, and the evening was still warm. A mild breeze rocked the room's solitary lantern, casting moving shadows against the white expanse of Sakura blossoms that decorated the *Fusuma* screen doors in Lady Nene's drawing-room. Sakichi gazed in awe at the lady who knelt alone before him. Flanked by Hirokohime, he felt her discrete nudging, reminding him respectfully to bow. Hirokohime had earlier coached Sakichi for this audience, informing him he would meet a lady of extensive pedigree, and held in high esteem by Lord Nobunaga himself. The daughter of Sugihara Sadatoshi, a favourite retainer of Lord Nobunaga, Nene became Nobunaga's closest aide and confidant. Many have remarked that her marriage to Lord Hideyoshi was initiated by Nobunaga, as he felt his aspiring general needed a consummate politician and advisor.

Nene's loosely-flowing black hair, her delicate application of white face powder and rouge-coloured lips, contrasted elegantly with her elaborately heavily brocaded red silk kimono with white cranes. Given the warmth of the evening, it surprised Hirokohime to see her choice of outfit as it was usually the prevail of ladies from the imperial court who would dress with such extravagance. Acknowledging Hirokohime's surprise, Nene addressed her.

"My dear, Hirokohime, given the lateness of the hour and having just entertained the emperor envoys at Lord Nobunaga's request, I should like to meet with our new servant and retire."

"Of course, my Lady. I present your servant Sakichi. He is yet to come of age and has much to learn, but my Lord Mitsuhide is confident he will prove to be worthy of your employ," said Hirokohime.

"Thank you, dear Hirokohime. There is no need to keep you up. If you would care to leave us, I shall attempt to get to know our young charge here." Relieved to be excused, Hirokohime left to retire to her quarters, and when Nene was sure Hirokohime was out of earshot, she quietly addressed Sakichi.

"Tell me, young Sakichi, why do you wish to work for my husband, or is it perhaps you have no choice?" Sakichi shuffled nervously, unsure how to reply.

"Before you answer, let me tell you something: my husband is a simple man, but a brilliant strategist, and he is currently away campaigning for Lord

Nobunaga. It was near here at Anegawa that the defeated Azai and Asakura clans both battled Lord Nobunaga, and the traitor Azai Nagamasa retreated to his base at nearby Odani Castle. To this day, Nagamasa remains secure and defiant in his castle and continues to receive aid from the Asakura. Why am I telling you this, you may ask?"

"I am informed your family are Azai vassals. You realise, of course, the leader of your clan Azai Nagamasa is also married to Nobunaga's younger sister Oichi and has now betrayed his brother-in-law by openly siding with his enemy, the Asakura. You are also my lord's enemy, and your loyalty could be questionable."

Sakichi's mood changed, and his heart raced as he swallowed hard. He wanted desperately to tell her about Mitsuhide's threats but thought it better just to keep quiet and see how things play out. Nene noted his downcast expression and silence and smiled as a mother would with a wayward child.

"It is getting late." Nene sighed. "I need to retire. You have a big day ahead of you tomorrow, and we will have many more opportunities to get to know each other." Nene rose, gathering in her long kimono as she summoned her chamberlain to show Sakichi to his quarters and promptly left, leaving Sakichi alone to mull over her words.

#

Yoshimasa was conscious of someone following him and had varied his route into Imahama by circling back and forth, frequently stopping to hide, hoping to catch sight of his follower. All he saw for his efforts was an entourage of four Samurai leading a palanquin carried by porters. He promptly recognised the Bellflower crest they wore as those of the Akechi clan. With the sun at its highest, and the heat taking its toll, Yoshimasa headed directly for the Hideyoshi residence.

At the Hideyoshi villa, he came across scores of working people scurrying back and forth; the sound of hammers and sawing rang loud, and the scent of freshly-sawn lumber permeated the air. In the chaos of all this construction, it was some time before he attracted the attention of what he assumed to be the household guards to announce his arrival. In the end, they escorted him to a drawing-room still under construction and devoid of any matting to wait. As he was about to sit down on the bare timber floor, the painted Fusuma panel doors at the end of the room slid open and the Lady Nene entered. She knelt before Yoshimasa, resting back on her heels, and bowed low to the ground, as is customary for a woman receiving guests even though she was the host. Yoshimasa responded with a low bow, then at her instructions, took a cross-legged sitting position in front of her.

"I trust your journey here was uneventful?"

Yoshimasa hesitated but replied, "Yes, my Lady, it was. May I present a letter of introduction from our lord?"

"I feel it would be unnecessary. Lord Nobunaga has already confided in me your true purpose here, but we have another problem." Noticing Yoshimasa's confused expression, Nene realised she would need to explain further.

"Lord Shogun has this day sent one of his retainers as a tutor. Here, read his letter."

My dear Lady O-Nene, please accord the bearer of this letter the hospitality for which you are renowned. Regretfully, it has been a while since I last beheld your radiant beauty. My Lord Akechi Mitsuhide has exemplified the true nature of Bushido and spared the life of one of his young enemies, and your husband has graciously found a position in your household for this young viper. As any mother would know, this is a headstrong age requiring love and, above all, discipline to forge his character into a vassal loyal to the realm. Indeed, your husband himself has risen from lowly beginnings to become a lord, no less. It is my direction that we shall recompense you for any costs incurred in the upbringing of your young charge. My gift to you is the bearer of this letter who I deem to be most qualified to act as a tutor; an expert in martial arts and indeed the refined classics.

Seii Taishogun Yoshiaki

Yoshimasa handed back the letter to Nene.

"The cheek of him," she remarked. "He knows I have been desperate to be a mother, and the raising of my husband's modest beginnings is insulting. But I dare not refuse his offer. He is the Shogun, and I am required to obey. Why is this boy so important?"

"My guess is that our Shogun intends to keep a close eye on our 'songbird', and I would suspect this tutor has additional instructions to eliminate him, should it be necessary. Has the boy arrived yet?"

56

"Yes. The boy arrived late yesterday accompanied by Lord Akechi's wife, the Lady Hirokohime, who has since departed this morning. Perhaps, you met her on your way here?" Nene said.

"Yes, I believe I saw her escort this morning, but where is the boy now?"

"Why, in the garden, training with the Shoguns tutor? I have yet to reconcile the conflict of having two tutors here and would ask that you receive instructions from our Lord Nobunaga in this matter. In the meantime, I deem it prudent to play along with our Shoguns offer."

"A wise move, my lady. It cannot harm to play along. You should also know that Shingen's has left Kofu and marched into Totomi province. His general, Yamagata Masakage, is also marching against the Tokugawa in Mikawa province. When I left, Shingen's had already captured the Tokugawa castles of Yoshida and Futamata. It would seem Nobunaga's ally Ieyasu has retreated to his Hikuma Castle and has appealed for reinforcements."

"So, war is coming?" inquired Nene.

"Yes, my Lady, the reason I am telling you this is that your husband will be instrumental in that war, and knowledge of his movements will be vital information for Yoshiaki's plans to break free of Nobunaga. So, you see the connection?"

Nene frowned. "So, the boy is a spy, then?"

"Yes, but an unwilling one that will allow us to keep one step ahead of Yoshiaki," said Yoshimasa. "Now if you will excuse me, my Lady, I should like to meet the Shoguns tutor and our pupil." Nene pointed towards the other Fusama screen decorated with nightingales, and Yoshimasa exited onto a veranda overlooking a garden of dust and weeds, beyond which lay the courtyard.

Covering the glare of the sun from his eyes with a cupped hand, he saw Sakichi in a white cotton *Yukata*, a short Kimono more akin to a bathrobe, grappling to control a Bo staff as he duelled against an opponent who was continually striking him without making contact. His opponent in his black jacket and pants appeared to be not much taller than Sakichi and of slender build, with long black hair tied up in a warrior's ponytail.

Yoshimasa watched the duelling pair, observing Sakichi's frustration as he struck out blindly against his opponent. Predictably, it was not long before a well-placed blow struck Sakichi's left shoulder, and he went careering to the ground screaming in pain.

"That hurt," Sakichi cried out to his opponent. Getting no response, Sakichi rose and lunged out, swinging his staff wildly at his opponent's head, only to feel a sharp pain land on the back of his knees and the jolt of a hard landing as he struck the dusty earth on his back.

"Enough," his opponent barked. "If you do not wish to be carried from here in pieces, stay down." Sakichi's opponent, sensing another's presence, turned to face Yoshimasa and smiled. Yoshimasa instantly recognised this was no man, but the woman he had sought in Kyoto, Yoshino.

"So, it appears we meet again," Yoshimasa said coolly as he politely bowed.

"Indeed, Sir Yoshimasa. It has been a long time," said Yoshino.

How does she fit in this? Yoshimasa now wondered.

"Will you not walk with me? We have much to discuss," Yoshino said as she dismissed Sakichi from his lessons. She walked on ahead, beckoning Yoshimasa to follow, and several minutes later found a shaded spot under a cryptomeria tree where they could sit and talk. Yoshimasa sat and produced from his Kimono the *Fukibari* dart he had retrieved from the inn wall at Takamiya-juku.

"Yours, I suspect?" Yoshimasa inquired. "Was this an attempt on my life or merely a message?"

"Neither," Yoshino replied, changing the subject.

"May I ask how you now serve Nobunaga?" Yoshino asked.

"May I ask how you now serve the Shogun?" Yoshimasa snapped back.

Yoshino paused for several moments before answering and glanced up at the overhanging branches filtering the sun's rays while she thought of a reply.

"I recall there was a time we both served the same master. Lord Shingen's grows stronger by the day. Already he has taken Futamata Castle from the Tokugawa and threatens Kyoto. Tokugawa Ieyasu is not strong enough to resist Shingen on his own and depends on the support of his ally Nobunaga. The winds of change are blowing."

"You have not answered my question," said Yoshimasa. "You know as well as I do your master Yoshiaki seeks to ally with Shingen, but he is a fool if he thinks Shingen will let him remain as Shogun, for he covets that title himself. He also has a better pedigree to qualify him than Nobunaga. His wife, Lady Sanjo, is the daughter of Sanjo Kinyori, the emperor's most favoured noble, and once he controls Kyoto, the emperor would not hesitate to make him Sei-i Taishogun."

Yoshino nodded in agreement but remained silent.

"One thing bothers me," Yoshimasa added. "Why is Shingen moving now? He cannot risk marching on Kyoto while his nemesis Uesugi Kenshin still threatens him in the north."

Yoshino smiled. "The Uesugi-Hojo alliance hemming Shingen in is now at an end. The Odawara Lord, Hojo Ujiyasu, has died and his son Ujimasa now seeks a rapprochement with Shingen, who has now given his daughter, Obai, in to be Ujimasa's wife. This will secure his eastern flank and the Hojo in adjoining Sagami and Musashi provinces will now become allies. He already controls most of neighbouring Shinano with his new allies, the Suwa, and Sanada clans."

Yoshimasa's mind raced, "But Kenshin still threatens him in the north."

"Yes, it is true, but thanks to Shingen's meddling brother-in-law, the priest Kennyo Kosa, Uesugi Kenshin is now forced to deal with a revolt of militant monks in his home province of Echigo," said Yoshino. Yoshimasa reflected on this and in his mind reviewed Shingen's moves as one would place pieces on a *Go* board.

Yes, it is all about opportunity and timing. This explains why Shingen has moved on Ieyasu. He cannot march on Kyoto with Ieyasu flanking him to the east, and he also knows with Nobunaga stretched thin, he cannot afford to support Ieyasu with many troops.

Frustrated, Yoshimasa returned to his original question, "Again, I ask, how is it you serve Yoshiaki?"

"Our previous employer, Chiyo, directed I serve Shingen's daughter Matsuhime, who has now married Nobunaga's oldest son, Nobutada, as part of a peace agreement. Sometime later, Matsuhime received an envoy from our Lord Shogun, requesting my services."

"And you expected me to believe that? More like Shingen informed Yoshiaki he now had a plant in the Nobutada household."

An annoyed Yoshino snapped back, "And are you also a plant in the Nobunaga household?"

"If I was, we would be on the same side. No, I have sworn fealty to Nobunaga."

"Do you intend to betray me, then?" Asked Yoshino.

"No, but I suspect your presence here is not merely to teach." Yoshimasa suddenly became distracted by a rustling sound coming from the nearby bushes.

And looked beyond the cryptomeria tree to see the head of a red fox poking through the leafy branches. It's bright yellow eyes locked onto his.

Kitsune. He thought.

With Yoshimasa distracted by the fox, Yoshino quietly rose and walked a few paces away. As Yoshimasa turned to face Yoshino, she unleashed the *Bo Shuriken* blade concealed in her hand. The blade found its mark, striking Yoshimasa in the neck. Stunned, and with eyes wide open, he tried to rise only to stumble, falling face down into the dry earth under the cryptomeria tree. The last thing he heard was Yoshino's warm breath whispering in his ear, "We can't have loose ends, can we?"

Chapter Four

The Tiger of Kai
Winter: Third year of Genki to First Year of Tensho
(1572–1573)

With the onset of winter, a light dusting of snow fell on the thirty thousand Takeda army as it marched out of Kofu, Takeda Shingen's capital of Kai province. This was Shingen's opening gambit in his risky move westward towards the capital Kyoto and eventually all of Japan. But first, he would have to pass through Totomi and Mikawa, territories held by Nobunaga's ally Ieyasu, who would threaten his rear.

As he approached Totomi province, Shingen split his army. Generals Yamagata Masakage and Akiyama Nobutomo each led a division of five thousand. Yamagata headed for Ieyasu's Yoshida Castle in Mikawa, and Akiyama marched on the Oda Mountain stronghold of Iwamura Castle in eastern Mino. With luck, Yamagata, and Akiyama would then trap Nobunaga in a pincer movement. So, it was under a cold grey winter's sky, Shingen led his huge army comprising the men of Kai, Suruga and Shinano provinces into Tokugawa territory.

News of Shingen's march out of Kai soon reached the ears of Nobunaga and Ieyasu. They both expected him to take the most direct route to Kyoto, a westward approach through neighbouring Mino province, which would have brought him into a decisive confrontation with Nobunaga's army. However, in a completely unexpected move, Shingen's army turned northward out of Kai and followed the Kamanshi River Valley towards Suwa, the opposite direction from Kyoto. A confused, Nobunaga and Ieyasu deduced he had returned to campaigning against his rival Uesugi Kenshin, 'The Dragon of Echigo'. The symbolism of Shingen's as the 'Tiger of Kai' and Kenshin as 'The Dragon of

Echigo' had not escaped Nobunaga, for legend has it the dragon and tiger will always try to defeat one another, but the result always ends in a draw.

It was at Lake Suwa that Shingen turned his army south towards Totomi, using the Tenryugawa River Valley as cover. In three days, the vanguard of the Takeda army crossed into Totomi and besieged the Tokugawa Fortress of Futamata. Ieyasu's spies had already alerted him to Shingen's encroachment into his territory, and despite being outnumbered almost three to one, General Honda Tadakatsu and three thousand Tokugawa warriors valiantly attempted a surprise attack on the Takeda vanguard. Unfortunately for Tadakatsu, the discovery of his rouse meant the Takeda cavalry easily routed his Tokugawa foot-soldiers, and they forced him to retreat to Hikuma Castle, Ieyasu's seat of power.

The Futamata Fortress enjoyed a natural hilltop defensive position, protected on three sides. The meandering Tenryugawa River protected its western and southern approaches, whilst the nearby Futamatagawa River protected its eastern approach. Futamata's castellan was a man by the name of Okubo Tadayo who also had been part of Honda Tadakatsu's failed attack on Shingen's vanguard. Standing on the 'stone-throwing shelf' of the castle's wooden palisade, Tadayo nursed his injured arm and surveyed the amassed Takeda army before him.

"How many would you say are there?" asked Tadayo, to the archer standing next to him.

"At least four or five hundred, Sir."

"That's about what I would say. The rest of the Takeda army is yet to assemble. Let us test the mettle of these Takeda dogs before they dig in," Tadayo said. Shouting to one of his captains, Tadayo ordered his troops to sally forth and watched as three hundred of his mounted warriors charged out of the northern castle gate towards the Takeda lines. As the castle defenders held the high ground, the Takeda were at a disadvantage, as Tadayo well knew. The Futamata warriors charged and crashed down the slopes towards the Takeda positions, but the Takeda did not break and run. Their commanders rallied their Yari-Spear, carrying foot-soldiers to close ranks in front of the advancing wave, and just as the Futamata warriors were about to clash, the Takeda parted their lines like gates, allowing the Tokugawa to charge through unhindered before they quickly closed ranks again cutting off any hope of retreat. Tadayo, watching from his vantage point, already knew the fight was lost.

"Look, over there," another archer on the palisade began shouting frantically to catch Tadayo's attention, who now looked towards the grey northern skyline and saw a horizon full of fluttering Takeda banners. The main army had arrived.

Within the central keep of the castle's two-storey Tenshu tower, Okubo Tadayo and five of his remaining commanders sat in readiness to receive the inevitable messenger from the enemy, demanding their surrender. The sun had just set when the expected Takeda messenger arrived and handed Tadayo a letter from Shingen. The messenger also informed Tadayo of his instructions to wait for a reply. Clearly irritated, Tadayo glanced through the letter, dismissively rejecting its contents, for the tone of the letter and the terms dictated were what he had expected. Surrender or die.

"Tell Lord Shingen, my orders are to hold this castle, and until my lord directs otherwise, my duty demands that I and all my men must defend it to death." The Takeda messenger returned to his lines and entered Shingen's large multi-striped *Akunoya* command tent hidden in a copse of trees, where Lord Shingen sat on his campstool together with his son Katsuyori and his generals. At the age of fifty, Shingen's dark bushy moustache contrasted with his hair heavily streaked with grey and his eyes glowered at the messenger prostrate before him.

"So, the castellan's response to my demands was both predictable and understandable," Shingen boomed. "What is unacceptable is that we can ill-afford to dally here. We must move on. While Ieyasu is confined in Hikuma, we must take Kakegawa Castle. With Futamata and Takegawa in our hands, Ieyasu's supply lines will be in peril, and he will be too weak to attack our rear. We already vastly outnumber him." Shingen's General Baba Nobuharu was the first to reply.

"What about Nobunaga? Surely he will race to aid his ally?"

"My spies tell me Nobunaga has at yet made no moves to mobilise. I suspect his forces are stretched to their limits, and he has no desire to confront us just yet. Yet as a Tokugawa ally, he will have no choice but to send some token reinforcements. I have no desire to waste men here fighting Ieyasu when the major prize lies west. Gentlemen, speed is of the essence. Our general, Yamagata Masakage, already marches on Mikawa with five thousand to prepare the way and take the Tokugawa stronghold of Yoshida Castle. It is imperative our army quickly takes nearby Kakegawa Castle and links up with Masakage to permit his western advance on Okazaki castle held by Ieyasu's son, Nobuyasu. With

63

Nobuyasu in our hands and our rear protected from Ieyasu, we can safely march west into Owari and meet Nobunaga with confidence. Now, gentleman, tell me about your plans for Futamata?"

Shingen's brother Takeda Nobukado spoke first, outlining his appraisal of the castle's defences, suggesting the fortress can easily withstand a long siege. Its only weak point was its water supply. As the castle abutted the Tenryu River, they draw water from the river by lowering buckets using an impregnable purpose-built tower.

"We can use the river to our advantage," interrupted Sanada Yukitaka. "The swollen Tenryu flows fast with the winter rains. As the castle abuts the river on a bend where the current is strongest, we only need to build rafts and launch upstream using the river's flow to collide with the tower at its base and undermine its supports." Shingen nodded his approval at Sanada's plan but worried at the time this would take.

"How many captured Tokugawa soldiers do we have?" Shingen asked his general, Kosaka Masanobu.

"About two hundred, my Lord."

"Then have all of them beheaded at once and have their heads displayed in front of the castle walls. Let us see if such a sight speeds up the surrender process." Turning to his son Katsuyori, Shingen said.

"If this does not work, then proceed with Sanada's plan. Meanwhile, the main army will strike camp and leave immediately and take Takegawa before Ieyasu reacts. I am counting on you."

On the eleventh day of the tenth month, after two further months of siege, the garrison of Futamata Castle finally surrendered. The sight of mutilated corpses and the assembly of heads on stakes had failed to coerce the castle defenders into submission. Sanada's strategy of undermining the water tower worked as planned. Deprived of a water source, Okubo Tadayo decided not to punish the villagers anymore and surrendered unconditionally. Unexpectedly, Katsuyori spared Tadayo and his depleted garrison of soldiers. Stripped of their weapons, they were permitted to march to Hikuma to serve as both a warning and appeasement to Ieyasu. Katsuyori knew that whilst the Tokugawa were heavily outnumbered, Ieyasu was also a man of pride, and he would never let us pass through his lands unopposed. The needless slaughter of his Futamata garrison would only provoke him and further hinder the Takeda advance.

Meanwhile, Sakai Tadatsugu, 'The boar of Mino' and castellan of Yoshida Castle, was faring much better against the Takeda, having repelled Yamagata's assaults. Shingen now believed Yoshida would take at least three months to subdue and ordered Yamagata to break off the siege and head instead for Okazaki Castle. While at the Yamashino, mountain fortress of Iwamura, General Akiyama Nobutomo must have somehow found favour with the gods. Toyama Kageto, the ageing castellan of Iwamura, had fallen ill and had now departed this mortal life, leaving his widowed wife, Lady Otsuya alone to defend the Oda Fortress. Nobutomo knew Lady Otsuya was Nobunaga's aunt and offered to marry the widower in return for a peaceful surrender. Otsuya accepted and Iwamura had a new lord.

#

Spring: Second Year of Genki (1571)
Tsutsujigasaki Yakata Palace: Kofu, Kai Province.

The sun shone brightly, and the Sakura cherry blossom was now in full bloom, and today the blossom provided the perfect backdrop to showcase the splendour of Tsutsujigasaki Yakata Palace, the Kofu residence of Takeda Shingen. The Lord of Kai had long recognised the palace was not suitable for defence, for it was small and sited on a moderate slope much too difficult to defend, so he had nearby Yougaiyama Castle built as a supporting castle for shelter in case of dire need.

Long before Shingen entertained the idea of seizing Kyoto and claiming the title of Shogun, his pre-occupation lay with consolidating his conquests in Shinano, Kozuke and Suruga provinces. It was memories of the Suruga campaign with his former ally Tokugawa Ieyasu that now consumed most of his anger. Having summoned Mochizuki Chiyo, Shingen sat and waited alone in the palace common room. The screen doors within the common room were open to the garden, and Shingen looked out, admiring the elegant but rustic simplicity of his tea garden. The opening framed a view of maple and cypress trees planted to filter the harsh rays of the mid-day sun. A steppingstone path with stone lanterns on either side and bordered by moss snaked across the ground to the covered gate of a teahouse lay directly opposite.

His sense of serenity now disturbed, Shingen grumbled at Lady Mochizuki Chiyo, who arrived dressed in a lightweight blue-cotton summer kimono with a white peony flower, bowed and greeted her lord.

"Congratulations on your Suruga campaign, my Lord. The screen I use as a map of your conquests is already falling over under the weight of all the flag pins I am placing, yet I sense something displeases you."

"Chiyo, enough of the formalities. I have summoned you because I need your services." Chiyo again bowed as Lord Shingen continued.

"Yes, I am displeased. Matsudaira Ieyasu has betrayed me, and he must be punished."

Chiyo didn't have to know why or even understand the nature of Ieyasu's betrayal. It was enough that her lord had commanded, and she must obey. She looked into his dark eyes and saw a coldness in him such as an executioner might have in dispatching his victim. She, of course, knew the real reason. Shingens and Ieyasu were allies, and they struck a grand bargain to split the spoils in taking Suruga and Totomi provinces from Ujizane of the Imagawa. Whilst Shingen was nursing his wounds in defeat from his attack on Suruga, Ieyasu struck a deal with Ujizane. Ieyasu would get Totomi in exchange for helping Ujizane against Shingen.

"I want you to send an operative and rid me of him," said Shingen.

"My understanding is that Ieyasu has recently left Okazaki and now lives at his Hikuma Castle. Is that not so, my Lord?" Chiyo replied.

"Yes, you are as knowledgeable as ever, Chiyo. That is why I have someone like you around. Except, he is expanding the castle fortifications and renamed it Hamamatsu."

Shingen closed his eyes and smugly wondered if Chiyo did not know that, or as is her way, limits what she reveals.

"Why Ieyasu would leave Okazaki for an unfinished castle?" Shingen inquired of Chiyo.

"My Lord, it would seem he craves respite from his wife, Lady Tsukiyama, who remains at Okazaki with his eldest son, Nobuyasu. She is, I am told, prone to bouts of temper and makes her lord's life, shall we say, somewhat uncomfortable?"

"There are other ways of reminding a wife of her place rather than running away, do you not think?" Shingen said.

"Perhaps, the more likely reason is his affair with the Lady Saigo," said Chiyo. His interest aroused, Shingen pressed Chiyo to elaborate.

"Lord Ieyasu has recently conferred on Lady Saigo the title, Saigo-no-Tsubone, thus elevating her status to a concubine of the highest ranking. We know she was adopted into the Saigo clan by her father, Tozuka Tadahara, and she is also a devout Buddhist with considerable influence on Ieyasu. If cultivated correctly, she could be an asset. Unfortunately, Lady Tsukiyama remains jealous and has frequent tempestuous moods."

"Hmm, I can almost sympathise with him for that," Shingen muttered under his breath.

"My Lord?" Chiyo queried.

"It is nothing. Attend to my request, Chiyo, and remember, leave no trails back to me."

"May I suggest, my Lord, that Ieyasu has more value to you alive than dead?"

"You may be right, Chiyo, but that game takes time. I have only a brief window to move west and removing the dagger at my back takes precedent."

Chiyo rose and with a touch of fanfare opened and closed the loose flap of her over kimono and bowed to her lord before excusing herself. Shingen remained seated and watched her glide away before returning to the uninterrupted view and tranquillity of his tea garden. He entertained more thoughts about Ieyasu's marital woes and chuckled before he relived the painful memories of how unkind he was to his late wife, Lady Sanjo. Although he had never physically mistreated her, his aloofness and coldness towards her were just as cruel. He bedded her occasionally, as custom demanded to produce the much-needed heirs to the Takeda clan, but otherwise made no effort with any further intimacy. He was certainly capable of love, for as a youth he had once fallen in love with a priest's daughter and begged his father Nobutora for permission to marry to no avail. It was common knowledge Nobutora considered Harunobu as Shingen was then called a weakling. Marriages were to be treated as a commodity. Their purpose was to buy alliances, political power and wealth. Love was for fools and weaklings.

Any thought of Harunobu marrying a priest's daughter was out of the question, but the young Shingen would not take no for an answer, and they continued their liaison. Shortly after this latest confrontation with his father, the priest's daughter disappeared, her broken body was eventually discovered in the nearby woods. Word had it bandits had attacked and killed her, but Shingen never believed this story and always suspected his father's part in this.

For the good of the clan, he agreed to the arrangement to marry Lady Sanjo, the wealthy daughter of a powerful court noble and then took his revenge by hastening a coup against his father, replacing him as head of the clan and promptly exiling him. Sanjo finally bore Shingen, his son, and heir, Taro, who became known as Yoshinobu. While he doted on Taro, he remained aloof from Sanjo. He was grateful for a son, but he could not warm to her and continued his cold behaviour towards her; an aspect not lost on Taro as he grew up to resent his father, just as Shingen had done with his father.

Shingen threw his energy into expanding Kai's borders and completed his conquest of neighbouring Shinano province and the Suwa clan. With the defeat of Suwa Yorishige, Shingen took his daughter Sanjo Goryonin as his concubine who later gave him a son, Katsuyori, before she died. Considering his mother's treatment and estrangement, Yoshinobu's resentment of Shingen festered. Both Sanjo and Yoshinobu came to fear Shingen would make the younger Katsuyori heir instead of himself, and like father like son, Yoshinobu rebelled and plotted to assassinate his father. Under pressure from his general, Shingen had no choice but to denounce his son and order Yoshinobu to commit the ritual of seppuku.

Having Yoshinobu confined to his quarters, Shingen pleaded with him to make the lifesaving gesture of an apology to no avail. On his last visit, Shingen handed Yoshinobu his tanto and left with tears in his eyes. With no *Kaishakunin* or assistant to relieve him of the agony of disembowelment and cut off his head, they found Yoshinobu dead the next morning. He had completed the *jumonji,* a second and more painful vertical cut to the belly once the first crosscut of the abdomen was complete. It was the sign of a true warrior and a most impressive seppuku.

Yoshinobu's suicide had a devastating effect on Sanjo, only worsened by Shingen's decision to proclaim Katsuyori as the new Takeda heir. She naturally blamed Shingen and withdrew from life, harbouring a festering hatred towards her lord until her death from consumption. In her last moments, Shingen attended and tried to comfort her. He regretted the pain he had caused her and what he had done to Yoshinobu. Sanjo had her revenge, for Shingen would also later suffer from the consumption.

Shingen was of the view that all the women in his life had caused him nothing but pain, joy and sorrow, so it was with sympathy he considered that Lady Tsukiyama contributed to Ieyasu's desire to move to Hikuma. He felt the need to escape the pull of Sanjo's incessant pleadings to return to the court life of Kyoto, but he felt his destiny was to enter Kyoto as the new ruler of all Japan, with Sanjo as the principal wife.

Chapter Five

Kunoichi

Hikuma Castle: Totomi Province. Autumn
Second-year of Genki (1571)

Yoshino crouched under a large and old white pine tree that commanded good views of the South *Koguchi* gate of the castle. The flattened canopy of the ageing tree not only provided her with shade from the harsh mid-day sun, but it was a convenient place to watch the castle unseen. Like most hilltop fortresses of this warring period, they built Hikuma Castle in the classic *Hirayama* style, highlighting its distinctive terraced fortifications. Originally built by the Imagawa clan to control the trade routes between the capital Kyoto and the coastal towns of Edo, the layout of Hikuma Castle centred around three 'U' shaped compounds, each separated by high stone walls and moats.

For two days and nights, Yoshino watched the castle traffic and guard movements. On the third day, she allowed herself to drift into sleep, to wake at sunset when a sprinkling of light falling rain on her face induced her eyes to open and focus on the murky dark sky above. Springing to her feet, she felt her mind was clear and focused. She had decided how to proceed.

In the early morning, the local traders, and merchants made their way towards the castle to make their deliveries. The misty light rain that fell overnight had given way to rolling thunderstorms, and the heavy downpour that followed offered a brief respite to the oppressive humidity of the last few days. Yoshino along with three others struggled to keep the cart laden with bales of tea they were pulling from being bogged in the deepening mud.

It was during the night that Yoshino had sought the help of Tomo Sukesada, the local *Jojin,* or head ninja, who ran the area. Chiyo had suggested Yoshino enlist Sukesada's help, and even though he was in the pay of Ieyasu, he had fulfilled several contracts on her behalf, and she felt he could be trusted. Yoshino knew many of the Koka ninja clans prided themselves on being neutral players and would often find themselves pitted against their other clan members in the service of rival lords. Yoshino learnt from Chiyo that Sukesada earned his reputation as a shrewd tactician by leading a group of his *Shinobi* (Ninja) to infiltrate and raid this very castle on behalf of Ieyasu and setting it on fire whilst slaughtering two hundred of its garrison. For the right amount of Shingen's gold, Sukesada obligingly provided Yoshino with three of his Shinobi for infiltrating Hikuma in secrecy.

Disguised as merchants and at the tail end of a long queue of other anxious merchants, Yoshino and the three Shinobi wearing straw raincoats and hats pushed the tea cart towards the castle gates, often relying on her Bo staff to help steady her footing in the ever-deepening mud. It was late in the afternoon when they finally reached the South Koguchi gate. The rain had eased off a bit, and the air was full of the shouts and noises of wealthier merchants berating their cart pullers for being too slow. They all wanted to be out of the castle before nightfall.

Yoshino knew from her observations that being late at the gate was an advantage, as the first arrivals seem to receive the most scrutiny. It was much later that the guards would become bored and lax in their searches. As expected, when their turn came, the two guards, who were not keen to be out in the wet, performed only a cursory inspection of the tea cargo and waved them through. They followed a convoy of traders, first into the outer compound which housed the main castle garrison, then through another gate into an inner compound. According to Sukesada, it was here that the castle's administrative offices and her target, Ieyasu's residence, lay.

The convoy continued and headed for the stores at the castle's keep, well beyond the inner compound. Yoshino knew she needed to break away now and, leaving her *Shinobi* associates to continue, she quietly slipped into the gap between two of the nearby office buildings they were passing. Satisfied the buildings were unoccupied, she discarded her cumbersome raincoat and crept under the veranda decks and waited for nightfall.

At the castle stores, the Shinobi agreed to stage an accident, sufficient for their cargo of tea to be unsalvageable. Yoshino knew once they arrived at the castle stores, if they tried to deliver the tea, the quartermaster would certainly notice there was no requisition for this cargo, and it would raise awkward questions. The feint of an accident should be enough to cover their withdrawal from the castle without attracting undue attention.

Bright rays of moonlight filtered through the wooden decking of the veranda, and Yoshino realised the sky must have cleared. She would need to be careful and eased herself out from beneath the deck and sprinted for the darkened crevices along the stone wall that separated the compounds. Dusting the dry earth from the dark cotton jacket and pants she wore; she untied the pouch she carried on her back and withdrew two dark reddish pieces of cloth. With one, she formed a hood and with the other; she wrapped around her face to form a *fukumen* (mask) to hide her face. Lastly, she withdrew a thin pair of black *Tabi* boots and discarded her straw sandals. The *Tabi* would be vital in providing the tactile contact between her feet and the ground as she navigated the *Uguisubari* (Nightingale) floors waiting for her. She twisted the lower section of the Bo staff she carried and separated the two halves, revealing a hollowed-out section hiding her *Fukiya* blowgun. Strapping the *Fukiya* to her back with a loose hemp cord, she cautiously moved among the shadows and headed towards the dancing lights marking the entrance to the compound housing Ieyasu's residence.

As part of the deal, she had struck with Sukesada, Yoshino received detailed information on Hikuma Castle's layout and how best to gain access to Ieyasu's palace quarters. What the deal did not include was the assassination of the Tokugawa Lord. Sukesada knew perfectly well the blame would fall on his clan and feared Ieyasu's retribution should any attempt fail. Yoshino had lied about the reasons for enlisting Sukesada's help, indicating her mission was to deliver Ieyasu a message from her employer, an act that would leave him in no doubt of his vulnerability despite his castle.

With the gate to Ieyasu's residence in sight, Yoshino halted in the shadows and studied the layout. She noticed a gate set in a palisade of thick, rough-hewn *hinoki* logs. To access it meant crossing a long narrow wooden bridge, some twenty feet across a deep dry moat, designed to choke a mass assault by limiting the number of the enemy that could attack at once. And should they breach the gate, an inner compound would trap them, while archers and muskets finished them. Safe in the belief that no frontal assault was possible, no sentries were posted at the gate, Yoshino looked up at the lights within the covered watchtower above the gate and thought, *the guards must be in there.*

Yoshino climbed under the bridge and used its support structure to swing from beam to beam, quickly crossing the moat. As the watchtower overhung and spanned the width of the gate, it afforded blind spots for hiding at its base. Moving from shadow to shadow, Yoshino exercised the skills she had learnt in her training under Chiyo. Helped by the rolling cloud cover that masked the moon's brilliance and using the Shinobi art of *Ninpo* (hiding), Yoshino stepped in and out of her own shadow unseen.

It was around midnight and well into the hour of the rat by the time Yoshino had scaled the watchtower and reached the first of the palace buildings; a feat she had found easier than expected. According to Sukesada, Ieyasu's quarters were in the second building, and, like the other buildings, they were interconnected by corridors featuring Uguisubari 'nightingale floors' laid at strategic points. Whilst ordinary floorboards often make a creaking sound when walked on, these floors used special flooring nails in certain sections that rubbed against a special type of iron clamp. When trod, these boards created a sound resembling the singing of a Bush Warbler and this was an effective security measure against intruders.

Yoshino placed her ear to the building's outer shoji screen doors, and listened, remaining motionless for some time. Satisfied that no one was inside, she carefully slid the screen door open and stepped into a room. No lanterns had been lit, but enough of the weak moonlight could shine through for Yoshino to make out her surroundings. She found the room was devoid of furnishings. All she could see was a large empty room of mat flooring and panelled walls, decorated with scenes of pine trees contrasting against a golden background. A plain *Fusama* screen door lay on the other side of the room, and this, according to Sukesada, opened onto a corridor leading to Ieyasu sleeping quarters.

Yoshino slid open the *Fusama* door, just enough to survey the dimly lit corridor in both directions. All seemed quiet. Several floor lanterns lined the corridor and not far along the corridor, she made out a lone guard sitting motionless outside a room.

That must be Ieyasu's quarters, she thought. *I trained to walk stealthily, but I have never attempted a nightingale floor. One song from the Uguisu and the game is lost. Is there another way?*

She counted the number of sliding doors leading to the sitting guard and estimated her target was two rooms away. Promptly closing the *Fusama* door, Yoshino withdrew her *tanto* knife and cut a small hole in the paper wall panel to the adjoining room and looked inside. Once she was confident the room was empty, Yoshino enlarged the hole enough to crawl through, but first, she retreated outside the building and took one of the *Kakeandon* lanterns, hanging under the eaves. Using the lantern's oil, Yoshino doused the outside screens and ignited the screens. The fire took hold quickly, and Yoshino returned to the 'room of pines' and crept through the hole she had made into the adjoining room. The fire spread rapidly, and she heard the panicked voices raising the alarm. Once in the adjoining room, she cautiously slid open the *Fusama* door that opened onto the corridor and saw the corridor rapidly filling up with smoke. Ahead of her, towards Ieyasu's sleeping quarters, she noticed the guard was no longer there.

The distraction worked. She thought. Her face covering would serve another purpose this day, protecting her from the smoke. Unslinging her *Fukiya* blowgun, Yoshino loaded it with a poison dart she kept in her hair and sprinted out from the room, using the cover of smoke towards the door where the guard had been. Wasting no time, she slid the door open and aimed.

Where is he? She thought. *The rooms were deserted. No futon, no pillow rest, no sign anyone has even slept here.* She sensed a movement behind her, but the sudden breakthrough of men through the room's walls distracted her. It was the last thing Yoshino remembered of that night.

She found herself floating in a world long past and looked down at the bloodied body of a young girl lying naked in the ditch below her. The girl's eyes opened and screamed, and she took possession of the body. She felt the touch of groping hands on her naked flesh and smelt the oppressive odour of the heavy body lying on top of her. She now grimaced as the body rhythmically thrust deep inside her, and she offered no resistance, for fate had given the cruel gift of *Fudoshin,* an immovable heart, a mental dimension that suspended any pain or emotion under stress and allowed the mind to process events freed from its reality. She left the girl's body and adjusted to the glare of a blistering sun heating the raked earth of the courtyard she now found herself in.

Aware of her nakedness, Yoshino tried to stand and immediately fell over, not realising that they had bound both her feet and hands. She sat up and focussed on a group of armed Samurai sitting in front of an empty dais ahead of her. Sensing activity behind her, she turned and saw several men glistening in sweat and naked save for their *Fundoshi* loincloths, attending to an enormous cauldron atop a burning fire.

"I see you have noticed the preparations for our morning's entertainment," said a calm, commanding voice.

Yoshino's head turned in the voice's direction. A man of some status wearing expensive blue silk robes sat flanked by two Samurai on the dais that was empty only moments before. He was a thin-set man with a shaved pate, thin moustache and had a small queue of oiled hair folded onto the top of his head. By introduction, the man remarked, "In case you are wondering, I am the one you had set your sights on killing." Yoshino remained silent. She concluded with her fate now sealed, death will surely follow.

"I know Sukesada is greedy, that's why he is in my employ," Lord Ieyasu barked. "But seriously, did you believe he would bite the hand that feeds him? If it is of any consolation to you, my spies alerted me of your mission much earlier on, and I am sorry to say, we monitored your every move in true Shinobi fashion."

Yoshino sat expressionlessly and just stared at Ieyasu.

"However, I am disappointed Sukesada took your lord's gold before informing me of your intention to infiltrate my castle to leave me some memorable message." Ieyasu summoned one of his retainers and quietly issued instructions before continuing his interrogation.

"Now, did you know your master, Lord Shingen reserves a special punishment for his enemies, which I find distasteful? Boiling people alive." Ieyasu looked to Yoshino for a reaction.

"Did you also know how the Mongol barbarians fed their captive slaves? Every week they would round up the old and infirm and chop an assortment of arms and legs off to cook in their giant cauldrons." Yoshino feared where this conversation was heading but remained steadfastly silent. Distracted by a commotion behind her, she turned to see a lengthy line of bedraggled, semi-naked prisoners roped together being led into the courtyard. Before them, kneeling in the dust, were the three men she recognised as the Shinobi accomplices she had entered Hikuma with.

Ieyasu stood up and descended the dais with his bodyguards and approached Yoshino. He looked into her eyes and stood, surveying her nakedness. Then he smiled.

"I see you are not afraid. Could it be you are a true Kunoichi?" Ieyasu said before making a cutting gesture with his fan and walked back to the dais. As quickly as it began, it ended. Several Samurai walked down the line of prisoners hacking off a hand here, a limb there, leaving a line of pooling blood congealing in the raked earth. The *Fundoshi* clad workers followed behind, gathering the severed limbs, and tossed them into the now smoking cauldron.

"You will never make me eat that," Yoshino screamed at Ieyasu, breaking her silence.

"I have no intention of doing any such thing," Ieyasu snapped back in annoyance.

"I reserved the feast for those accomplices of yours. Sukesada needs an object lesson in the pitfalls of biting the hand that feeds him." A confused, Yoshino called out, "What do you intend to do with me, then? Have you devised something worse?"

"For you, yes. I have devised a much worse torture; I am going to set you free."

Chapter Six

Saru

Autumn-Winter: The First Year of Tensho (1573)

From the Veranda, Yoshino took pleasure in watching the dying moments of a setting sun. As the red and orange hues of the sun's rays gradually sank beneath the darkening horizon, she heard shouts and turned to see the small figure of an old man running towards her.

"Oh, there you are," the old man loudly shouted. His shout was not enough to interrupt the chorus of cicadas that permeated the evening air, and Yoshino watched as he stopped to adjust his loose black cotton kimono, stroking his long grey wiry beard before continuing. The old man knew Yoshino as the Shoguns emissary and greeted her with a bow befitting her status, whilst Yoshino in token acknowledgement merely nodded her head.

"My lady is frantic with worry. We cannot find Sir Yoshimasa, Lord Nobunaga's messenger." The old man blurted out. "May I ask if you have any knowledge of his whereabouts?"

"And who is your lady?" Yoshino asked.

"My apologies, my Lady. I am Chamberlain for the lady of the house, Lady Nene." Remaining silent for a moment, Yoshino studied the old man. His nervous twitches and the beads of perspiration gathering on his forehead betrayed his anxiety.

"I may have news that will ease her ladyships' distress," Yoshino calmly replied, adding, "take me to her."

#

"Hey, hold up," shouted Oko, the older of the two servant boys running after Sakichi. Sakichi turned and instantly recognised the boys as the ones who were harassing him earlier when they chased him away from the stables. He was about to make a run for it when the oldest boy shouted, "Don't run away, we just want to talk." Sakichi hesitated, allowing Oko to catch up to him. Oko gasped as he tried to catch his breath and stammered,

"Are you Samurai?"

Sakichi eyed the bedraggled and mud-stained pair now before him and judged they posed no threat. Cursing himself for showing fear, he relaxed.

"My family is Samurai," Sakichi replied, "but I have yet to have my *Genpuku*."

"Look, we are sorry we chased you away from the stables just before," Oko pleaded. "The truth of the matter is, one of the house servants saw us chasing you earlier and told us who you were and gave us a good beating for what we did. My name is Oko, and this here is Miko. I hope we can be friends."

Sakichi eyed his prospective friends with caution and smiled. Oko grinned in return and dusted down his badly stained, rough grey cotton robes he wore while Miko edged behind him as if to hide.

"Don't mind him. He's my little brother, and fears Samurai."

"What do you do here?" enquired Sakichi.

"We both work in the household, doing chores and occasionally helping in the stables. One day, I hope to be a page for the lord like you."

"How long have you been here?" Sakichi asked.

"As long as I can remember. I'm about twelve years old now and Miko here is seven." Frowning, Oko continued, "I am a *Sutego*, one of the many abandoned children in these parts. I never knew my actual parents. My foster parents told me how they could not have children and would regularly visit the crossroads outside the town where children were abandoned, hoping to find a child to adopt. One day, they found me at the town crossroads and took me in, while Miko here was found abandoned at the local temple and given to my foster parents by the temple priest."

"Where are your foster parents now?" enquired Sakichi.

"They are both dead, cut down by passing *Ronin* a few years ago. I do not know how old I was then, but I remember seeing my father arguing with one of them, and the next thing I knew, his head landed at my feet. I escaped with Miko in my arms, and we lived in the woods for a while. One day, we got lucky when one of Lady Nene's house servants discovered us whilst out foraging for kindling wood. She pleaded with the lady to take us in to help with the chores. So here

78

we are." Before Sakichi could ask any more questions, they heard loud shouts coming from the house.

"We are being summoned," exclaimed Oko, as he saw the newly lit household lanterns appearing in the distance. "We have to go," he said.

Sakichi watched the boys head off towards the lights and thought of his own house and parents. He so wanted to be home again, but his rumbling stomach got the better of him and he raced off towards the lights. Just as he had the villa gates in sight, he found himself face down in the dirt. He felt the pressure of a foot on his back keeping him down and heard the voice of a man.

"Be quiet and don't look up," demanded the voice. "You passed a large maple tree with red-purple leaves back there; do you remember it?"

"What do you want with me," cried Sakichi and in response, he felt the pressure of the man's foot become more intense and painful.

"I asked you a question," the voice again demanded. With tears welling up in his eyes, Sakichi cried out, "Yes."

"Good, then every second day you will meet me here and give me a report on Hideyoshi's movements."

"But I haven't even met him yet," stammered Sakichi.

"You will. He is returning tomorrow."

Sakichi felt the pressure release and for a while, he heard no more from the voice. Unsure, he continued to lie face down in the dirt for some time, and then cautiously raised his head. The expected blow never came, and a wave of relief flooded over him.

Whoever he is, he appears to have left. It must surely be one of Akechi's men.

He thought about running away, but he remembered Akechi's threats and what it would mean for his parents. Picking himself up from the ground, he wiped the dirt from his face, dusted his clothing, and then ran through the gate to safety.

#

The *Chakai,* or tea gathering ritual, can be an endlessly simple, or an elaborate and sophisticated affair. It required the meticulous following of every detail and movement as prescribed by tradition. The *Chakai* Nene, now hosted in her drawing-room, was a simple ceremony. Sitting around a brazier, Nene served her guest, Yoshino, an assortment of sweets accompanied by thin tea. Protocol demanded her guest comment on the ritual and the aesthetics of the utensils and tea bowls used, but Nene had other priorities and set about questioning her guest about Yoshimasa's disappearance.

"My chamberlain tells me you have information concerning the whereabouts of my guest," Nene enquired. Without making eye contact, Yoshino paused before answering. First, taking three sips of the tea presented to her before wiping the rim and handing the bowl back to Nene.

"I was in the garden instructing your new servant when your guest approached and introduced himself. It was not long after that, a messenger interrupted us urgently requesting to speak with Yoshimasa in private, and that was the last I saw of him."

"This is most awkward," Lady Nene exclaimed, not wanting to appear overly anxious, but thought.

Yoshimasa's disappearance would appear to leave you free to control events concerning Sakichi's presence here.

Nene summoned her chamberlain to enquire why no one had alerted her to the messenger Yoshino had just mentioned.

"My Lady, we know nothing of this messenger," the old man nervously replied. Yoshino, who had moved to study the calligraphed scrolls hanging on the wall, turned to address the chamberlain.

"Sir, I suggest you take the issue with your household staff for neglecting to inform you of a stranger's arrival. You would do well to consider the grave risk you may have placed your lady in." Casting a glance at Nene, the old man bowed low in deference. The implications of Yoshino's rebuke had sunk in.

"Given the lateness of the hour, I excuse you, chamberlain. We will discuss this further," Nene replied. "But first, inform Sakichi that Lord Hideyoshi will arrive tomorrow, and he is to report to the stables at first light to help. Oko will show him the ropes." As the evening wore on, Nene and Yoshino continued in their battle of wits, each trying to pry some insight into the other's thoughts. Eventually, the lateness of the hour decided the outcome, with both retiring for the night.

The first rays of the rising sun broke over the horizon, revealing clear skies for the day ahead, and Sakichi was hard at work oiling the horse's tack, while

Oko and Miko cleaned out the stables to prepare for their lord's return. The hour of the hare had just passed, giving way to the hour of the dragon and Sakichi yearned for breakfast, but the sudden arrival of two of Hideyoshi's mounted Samurai put paid to that. At the news of their lord's imminent arrival, the household staff went into a state of excitement and panic. At the sound of the approaching conches, the villa gates opened, and household staff, workmen, and retainers assembled in the courtyard to welcome home their lord. Sakichi watched from the stables, the two thousand grim and tired looking Oda troops pass through the gate into the compound with the Lord Hideyoshi at the head. Once the entire Oda contingent had assembled in the courtyard, Hideyoshi dismounted and, still holding the reins of his bay Kiso mare, he readied to address his troops.

Nene, who had been closely watching the gathering assembly from the doorway, left the veranda and made her way through the assembly of *Ashigaru* towards her husband. She noticed the wind suddenly pick up and heard a loud fluttering noise that caught her attention. Each of the *Ashigaru* had a bamboo pole strapped to their backs, holding an unfurled white *Sashimono* banner bearing the Oda *Kamon* of flowering quinces, which fluttered noisily in the strengthening breeze, and the Lady Nene smiled at the sea of white.

A good omen. She thought. *Not bad for the son of a farmer and part-time Ashigaru from the provinces, eh! I knew him then as Tokichiro Kinoshita, a lowly suitor, who my parents did their best to dissuade me from seeing. Let me see. It must be some twelve years now since we married. Not much of a catch I remember: Just another lowly Ashigaru with big ears and a reputation for drinking and womanising. But I love him all the same. Now, look at him, an Oda general, and a Daimyo in his own right.*

Hashiba Hideyoshi kept the address to his troops brief. The two-day forced march from Odani warranted sake and refreshments for all.

"Men, you have deserved your rest," Hideyoshi boomed. "Eat well and drink well, for tomorrow the army prepares its campaign, and all leave is cancelled."

A mixed chorus of grumbling and cheers rose from the ranks, and Hideyoshi instructed his commanders to dismiss the men as he left to stable his horse and greet Nene. He insisted on leading his mare towards the stables alone and dwelt upon Nobunaga's latest directive, ordering him to regroup and prepare for the inevitable Takeda assault on Owari.

I fear that with our allies the Tokugawa now defeated at Mikatagahara, there is now nothing to prevent Shingen's conquest of Totomi province and threaten us.

All for what? Pride? Ieyasu ignored Nobunaga's advice. He should have just let the Takeda army pass through Hikuma and let Nobunaga deal with him further South, while he attacked Shingen on his rear. Instead, he committed his eight thousand Tokugawa troops and three thousand of our Oda troops against Shingen's 35,000. Utter madness.

By now, the sun was directly overhead and Hideyoshi felt its heat. He stopped to remove his *Kabuto* helmet just as Sakichi came running out of the stables, chased by Oko. Sakichi halted in front of Hideyoshi and could not help staring at the odd-looking short and thinly proportioned Samurai with a shaved head, big ears, and sunken features standing before him holding the reins of a horse.

"And you are?" enquired Hideyoshi.

"My name is Sakichi, I am page to Lord Hideyoshi."

"So, you're the one I was told about." A confused, Sakichi looked around for Oko and saw both him and Miko prostrate in the dirt before this odd-looking Samurai.

"What are you doing? Get up." He shouted to Oko, who remained prostrated but raised his head slightly to utter.

"This is Lord Hideyoshi." Sakichi suddenly realised he was in deep trouble and a wave of fear swept over him as turned to look at Hideyoshi.

"Your friend is correct," said Hideyoshi. Sakichi fell to the floor and prostrated himself, convinced his life would be soon forfeit.

"Will someone take care of this horse?" shouted Hideyoshi angrily. Oko got to his feet and took the reins from Hideyoshi and led the mare into the stables.

"Oh, get up, will you," Hideyoshi ordered Sakichi. "If you're my page, then you can help me unsaddle my horse." In the stable, Sakichi clumsily untied the large hemp bag hanging from Hideyoshi's saddle while Oko moved to unbuckle the mare's saddle girth.

"Hey. Careful with that," Hideyoshi shouted. "It's a gift for Lord Nobunaga. A valuable Chinese tea jar I bought from a Sakai merchant." His curiosity piqued, Sakichi felt brave enough to ask if he could look at it, and Hideyoshi, being so proud of his acquisition, readily obliged. Hideyoshi peeled away the bag covering and reverently held out the tea jar in both hands to show Sakichi.

"Well, what do you think? Magnificent, isn't it?" Sakichi drew closer and manoeuvred to study the jar from every conceivable angle without touching it, paying particular attention to its glaze.

"My Lord, you said this was Chinese *Karamono?*"

"Yes, what of it? I am told it is a valuable and fine example of Southern Song dynasty porcelain, and so it should be for the price I paid." Hesitantly, Sakichi murmured,

"It's just that the glaze of this tea caddy is flawless."

"What's wrong with that?" exclaimed Hideyoshi. "That is a good thing, isn't it?"

"No, my Lord, quite the opposite. If this were indeed from the Song Dynasty, one would expect to see minor imperfections."

"What are you talking about, boy?"

"Because of their pottery processes, minor imperfections such as rust spots from the iron in the clay and little depressions from flecks of contaminated material are most common in *Karamono* of the Song Dynasty." Sakichi shifted nervously, wondering if he should continue, but decided the truth should be, told.

"My Lord, the absence of any imperfections shows the item has a more recent history. I have seen comparable items traded by the merchants in Sakamoto that are also flawless but are widely made in Busan."

"Are you trying to tell me this is fake? What would someone like you know?" demanded an astonished, Hideyoshi.

"Forgive me, Lord, I have long held a keen interest in tea utensils, and during my time at the Hiezan Temple, I also learnt pottery trade from the Sakamoto merchants who traded fine *Karamono* with the abbot, who is a keen collector."

Hideyoshi mumbled, and his demeanour showed he was becoming angrier by the minute and quickly re-wrapped his gift.

"I am no expert, I admit," said Sakichi, "but if it was later discovered to be a fake, then passing this gift off as genuine to Lord Nobunaga could be viewed as an insult." A stunned Hideyoshi also noticed Oko, who had just finished unsaddling his horse, stood looking at him with his mouth agape. Hideyoshi immediately seized Sakichi by the collar of his Kimono and dragged him kicking and screaming out of the stables to a spot just out of sight of Oko, by an old black pine tree, and released him.

"Now, stop crying. Nobody can hear us. If what you say is true, you have saved my life," Hideyoshi whispered. "Lord Nobunaga has also instructed me to search the land for valuable tea utensils for his collection, so I will need someone like you around. Come, let us find Lady Nene, and discuss your future."

Chapter Seven

Yoshiaki

January-Winter: The First Year of Tensho (1573)

Yoshiaki, the fifteenth Ashikaga Shogun of his line, sat with his retainer Hosokawa Fujitaka in the resplendent hall of cranes within the Nijo Palace. Landscape paintings of soaring cranes in the Kano style decorated every one of the vast halls' *Fusama* screen doors. Yoshiaki listened intently to Fujitaka's latest reports concerning the rapidly changing political situation in the East.

He felt uncomfortable in his heavy gold brocaded kimono and fidgeted so much that the black lacquered *eboshi* hat he wore was in danger of sliding off. Yoshiaki listened intently to Fujitaka's reports of Takeda Shingen's victory over Ieyasu at Mikatagahara, which did much to lift his spirits.

"At last Yoshiaki shouted, Shingen had finally made his move. You see, Fujitaka, a chance, at last, to be rid of the meddling lord fool." Fujitaka bowed to his lord in agreement.

"It would seem Nobunaga has his hands full of problems right now," Yoshiaki said before continuing. "He will now have to face Shingen's vast army which already approaches his own fifes borders, and deal with the Azai and the Asakura of Echizen who are even now amassing against him in northern Omi."

"Quite so, my Lord," Fujitaka said. "Even the great Nobunaga cannot overcome all these threats at once."

"Listen Fujitaka, we must send word to the Azai, Asakura, Miyoshi, and the Takeda that their Shogun is counting on them to march on Nobunaga immediately and restore the peace under heaven that he has defiled."

"My Lord," Fujitaka said alarmingly, "to do so would openly expose your intentions to Nobunaga and risk retaliation." Yoshiaki ignored Fujitaka's concerns and, with smug satisfaction, stroked his pencil-thin moustache as he continued to savour Nobunaga's plight.

"My Lord," Fujitaka again said, trying desperately to get his attention, "did we not receive Nobunaga's envoy in this very hall only yesterday? He relayed to you Lord Nobunaga will provide hostages as a measure of his sincerity and undertake written oaths to you as a demonstration of his loyalty and atonement for the current discord that exists between you and him."

"Bah! I am not interested in any reconciliation," said Yoshiaki. "You are not in league with him, are you? No matter, I will be at peace when I see his head in the viewing pile."

"My Lord, my loyalty has never been in question. As you know, I have served the Ashikaga court all my life. I came into your service from your late brothers' assassination at the hands of the very Miyoshi you now seek to enlist in support. Did I not get Nobunaga to be your patron when no other Daimyo would? And was it not he that restored you to your rightful place as Shogun? In these uncertain times, can you not just sit back and see where the righteous flow takes us?"

"As long as Nobunaga has the power, I will forever be his puppet. No, Fujitaka, I cannot sit back and do nothing." Fujitaka sighed and bowed in acceptance. He knew further protest was useless.

"Send the letters Fujitaka," Yoshiaki demanded, "but for Nobunaga's benefit when he intercepts them, carefully couch the letters to say that their Shogun seeks to get as many horses as can be spared for a new breeding project. They will understand the true meaning."

"What of our reply to Nobunaga's entreaties for reconciliation?" Fujitaka asked.

"There is no need for a reply, Fujitaka. If all goes as I have planned, then future events will serve as my response. One more thing Fujitaka, this appointed bodyguard of mine, Hideyoshi. He has Oda troops garrisoned here. Remember, we must know what he is up to." Fujitaka's eyes narrowed with concentration.

"I recall you had what you term as a 'songbird' planted to provide this intelligence?" Fujitaka replied.

"Precisely. It bothers me we have heard nothing yet. Come to think about it, I have yet to hear from Mitsuhide either, which also concerns me."

"I will make enquiries, my Lord," Fujitaka replied and bowed, seeking leave to depart.

"By the way, Fujitaka, that Akechi daughter-in-law of yours, what's her name, Tama, isn't it?"

"Yes, Lord,"

"Find out if she has been in contact with her father of late."

Alone in the palace garden, Fujitaka felt the icy chill of the morning air and clutched his kimono, drawing it tighter around him. A light sprinkling of early season snow fell from the penetrating winds sweeping Kyoto. In better times, he would often spend time in this corner of the garden by the Koi Pond, inviting the cool summer breezes to circulate and refresh his perspiring skin while he meditated. This time, his thoughts turned to his eldest son, Tadaoki, who recently married Akechi Mitsuhide's strongly principled daughter, Lady Tama.

I will serve the Shogun as I have always done, but his strategy is false and ungracious. I only hope that the Hosokawa clan will survive, though either through Tadaoki or my other sons. But I fear Tadaoki will become my enemy and the Ashikaga line will cease to exist.

#

Nene sat alone with Hideyoshi in one of the villa's few furnished rooms, tenderly replenishing her husband's bowl of warm sake. As Hideyoshi reached for the bowl, the screen door slid open and household servants entered, carrying an assortment of dishes, each selected earlier by Nene herself for the evening's meal.

"You may go," Nene instructed the servants as they placed the last dish. "And inform the guards and the household we are not to be disturbed."

"Oh, it is good to be back," said Hideyoshi as he wiped his mouth with the back of his hand, having finished his stake in one gulp.

"It seems I continue to be in great favour with Lord Nobunaga. You watch, Nene. I will soon have a castle of my own. Oh, life is good." Impatiently, Hideyoshi offered his bowl to Nene for a refill when she snatched the bowl from his hand and broke it upon his head.

"What was that for?" a dumfounded Hideyoshi exclaimed.

"That, my dear husband, is to knock some sense into you."

Nene had finally snapped and had enough. For the months he was away, she constantly sought news of her husband only to hear continual reports of his drinking and womanising. It would seem being an important general in the Oda army was not the only reputation he had amassed.

"What are you talking about, Nene? Have I upset you?"

"Without a doubt, Lord Nobunaga considers you a valued loyal vassal and has heaped many rewards upon you, but you are also rapidly gaining another reputation, one that is a disservice to our lord." The comment touched a nerve, and Hideyoshi felt the stirrings of anger within him.

"Have I not provided you with fine things and a pleasant house? Where are the thanks I get?" The tears that had been building in Nene's eyes gave way and cascaded down her cheeks. She knelt before her husband and with muffled sobbing withdrew a letter and gave it to Hideyoshi, who immediately recognised the characters of Nobunaga's seal, respectfully opened the letter, and read.

... it has been quite some time since I last saw you, but your beauty grows day by day. Tokichiro complains about you constantly, and it is outrageous. While the Bald Rat flusters to find another wonderful woman, you remain lofty and elegant. Do not be envious. Show Hideyoshi this letter.

Nobunaga.

Had it been anyone else but Nobunaga, Hideyoshi could have dismissed the letter out of hand. But it was not just anyone. Lord Nobunaga had now delivered judgement on his moral standing. He knew he had done nothing wrong, for, after all, this was the way of things, but he also knew that even though this behaviour would not hinder his advancement, it certainly would not help either. Whether it was through a sense of guilt, genuine remorse or just making the best of an unpleasant situation, Hideyoshi approached Nene gently, putting his arms around her.

Still sobbing, Nene said, "My Lord, I may mind, but I cannot complain. I will just have to learn to control my feelings. As your wife, I have failed to provide you with children and heirs. The Gods have seen fit not to bless me in this, so I have no right to complain that you seek solace in other women. Notwithstanding, I am your wife and will continue to devote my life to your wellbeing and pray to the Gods. They keep you safe. You will achieve remarkable things, this after all, is your destiny."

So moved by Nene's response, Hideyoshi drew her closer to him in a tight embrace. His hands slipped between the folds of her kimono, cupping her breasts, and moulding them in response to the rapid building of excitement now stirred within his loins. Despite the tightness of his embrace, Nene loosened and freed the restrictions of her husband's kimono and guided him down onto the floor to mount him. Several thrusts later, a sated Hideyoshi rolled over and closed his eyes, allowing his laboured breathing to subside, while Nene readjusted her kimono and dutifully poured her husband a bowl of sake.

By mid-morning, the sun's rays had broken through the grey expanse of sky and quickly melted the light dusting of snow covering the ground. Sakichi was hard at work in the stables with Oko grooming *Giri*, Hideyoshi's Bay mare, while Oko cleaned out the soiled straw. Sakichi stood cautiously at the mare's side, just out of striking range of her legs, combing out the dung matted hairs of the mare's tail.

"A strange name to call a horse," said Oko.

Sakichi did not answer and recalled the abbot's teaching on *Giri*. It is the essential quality of devotion, loyalty, and obligation a young Samurai must learn in service to his lord, the abbot had said, and he at once understood why Hideyoshi would name his horse Giri.

A horse and its rider have a relationship. One is master and one is subordinate. And each has an obligation to the other. Such is the duty of care. Giri!

Miko, who had rushed into the stable in a highly agitated state yelling, "Sakichi!" interrupted Sakichi's thoughts.

"What's the matter," said Sakichi, dropping the comb. Miko stopped and stooped over to catch his breath. "I've got something to give you" He held out a baton size object wrapped in a faded blue silk cloth bag.

"What's this?" asked Sakichi.

"Don't know," said Miko. "You remember the old maple tree just down the road from here? Well, I was just passing it on the way back from the river when a well-to-do looking Samurai sitting at the foot of the tree called me over to ask if I knew you. He said he had come a long way to deliver a message to you and was in a hurry to leave. He said you would know what this meant."

Sakichi opened the bag and withdrew a half metre long bamboo shaku-hachi (flute). Turning it over in his hands, he sensed something familiar about it. He noticed it must be old, as the lacquer had flaked, and when he saw the unusual Kamon inscribed at the end of the fifth finger hole, he recognised its owner. The

Kamon was the family crest of the Azai clan. Three turtle shells in a diamond shape with a *hanabishi* flower in the centre of each shell. This was his fathers', a treasured family heirloom.

My father would never part with this voluntarily. This is surely a warning from Mitsuhide. He has already threatened to harm my father if I failed to cooperate.

"Hey, are you all, right?" Miko asked. "You look pale." A dark mood descended over Sakichi, and he stormed out of the stables, clutching the *shakuhachi* close to his chest. In a quiet spot behind the stables, under a persimmon tree, he fell to the ground and sobbed uncontrollably.

What am I doing? If I spy for Mitsuhide, it will not be long before I am discovered and killed, and if I run away, my father's life will be forfeited. As he searched for an answer, he felt the grasp of a hand on his shoulder, levering him over onto his back to face Hideyoshi.

"What have we here?" Hideyoshi asked. "I went looking for you in the stables and the boys said you hurried off, upset." Sakichi felt he had no choice now. He was desperate to tell someone, and he trusted Hideyoshi, even at the risk of Hideyoshi executing him on the spot. Sakichi quickly reasoned that if he was dead, they might leave his father alone as he would be of no further use to them, and so he explained to Hideyoshi how he became ensnared in Mitsuhide's scheme and about the run-in with the *Ronin* at the maple tree the other day. Hideyoshi listened without expression, but gradually his face transformed into a beaming smile.

"Did you take me for a fool?" Hideyoshi asked. "I found it odd that Mitsuhide would offer me your services so unexpectedly? And I questioned why the Shogun would involve himself in this and provide a tutor for you? And then I hear the tutor assigned by Lord Nobunaga has now vanished without a trace?"

"Are you going to kill me?" asked Sakichi.

"Not yet," Hideyoshi said with a wide grin that seemed to make his big ears stand out, making Sakichi stifle a laugh.

"We are but stones on Yoshiaki's *Go* board as he games with Nobunaga. Sometimes, Sakichi, it pays to be just an ignorant country bumpkin like me."

"What am I to do?" a relieved Sakichi asked.

"As my whereabouts are of such importance to the Shogun, I feel you should not disappoint him."

Following two more days of light snow, patches of blue sky finally appeared, and Sakichi took advantage of the brief sunshine to sit under the maple tree, savouring a breakfast of rice cakes and bean paste. This was the third time he had come at dawn's first light, waiting patiently for contact by Mitsuhide's agents. He sensed someone was watching him and thought it was only a matter of time before he was approached. Sakichi had just finished the last of his breakfast when the passing rider he had just seen doubled back and inquired of directions to Hideyoshi's villa.

"Why do you want to know?" Sakichi asked.

"Your answer tells me you know, and I would also like to know," the stranger replied.

"Why should I tell you?"

"Because, young sir, your father's life depends on it."

Sakichi felt stunned, and any pretence of confidence quickly dissipated as he looked up at the man seated on his horse before him. He seemed of middle age and wore fine robes of black silk which blended in with the black colouring of his mount. He wore the two swords of the Samurai class and spoke with a tone of authority.

"Now, I will ask again. Which way to Lord Hideyoshi's villa?" Sakichi rose and pointed in the direction he had just come.

"Good. Perhaps you can also tell me if the lord is in?"

"No, he has left for Totomi to confront Shingen's army."

"Is that so? Why should I believe you?"

"Because I value my father's life." The traveller tightly gripped his horse's reins and stared at Sakichi.

"So, when did he leave and how many troops accompanied him?" The traveller demanded.

"I do not know," replied Sakichi. "He wasn't around yesterday, and I overheard the day before he was withdrawing the army from Nijo, leaving only a skeleton force behind to guard the Shogun."

The traveller slowly turned his horse around away from the direction of Hideyoshi's villa and lent over to give Sakichi a small package wrapped in white cloth.

"Only one left, young Sakichi, the rest is up to you." The traveller picked up the reins and galloped back the way he had come. With the traveller out of view, Sakichi carefully unwrapped the cloth package and stood transfixed at the ear nestled in its folds. The traveller's last words continued to echo in Sakichi's mind.

'Only one left, young Sakichi, the rest is up to you.'

#

Yoshiaki was in a good mood. Fujitaka Hosokawa's interruption to his evening meal would normally have prompted outrage, but on this occasion, the Shogun calmly gulped down the last of the sour plums on offer and gracefully accepted his retainer's intrusion.

"You must try one of these plums, Fujitaka. They are delicious," Yoshiaki muttered as he cleaned up the plum drips on his chin with a napkin.

"So, what good news do you have for me today, Fujitaka?"

"We have received news from our agent in Imahama. He has contacted the songbird." The Shogun's eyes gleamed in anticipation of the good news to come.

"It would appear Hideyoshi and his army have departed for Totomi province to meet up with Ieyasu and confront Shingen," Fujitaka calmly relayed before adding.

"I have also checked the veracity of this report and confirm that only two hundred of Hideyoshi's men remain garrisoned here."

"This is good news indeed, Fujitaka. It should not be too hard to neutralise that number. I am told Shingen is fielding an army of thirty thousand. How many are with Hideyoshi?"

"My Lord, our intelligence suggests that of the five thousand Hideyoshi fielded at the recent siege of Odani, he would be lucky to have three thousand left if one takes into consideration those wounded and killed and the troops he has garrisoned here."

"Excellent. Did you despatch those letters to our allies, Fujitaka?"

"Yes, my Lord."

"Another thing, Fujitaka. Asakura Yoshikage is still holed up in Otake Castle with his twenty thousand men, is he not?"

"Yes, Yoshikage has sent word that he must return home to Echizen before the winter worsens. He fears once the snow closes the mountain passes, he will be trapped."

"Just as trapped as Nobunaga will be," said Yoshiaki.

"Inform Yoshikage of this latest news of Hideyoshi's movements and tell him we must coordinate plans. Nobunaga and Hideyoshi will now have to face Shingen's army, in the north and the east, with the Asakura and the Azai threatening Nobunaga's western flank. I suspect as soon as the southern Daimyo scent blood, they will join in so as not to miss the spoils. Even the Nobunaga cannot withstand an attack on simultaneous fronts."

Yoshiaki had grown confident the outcome was without doubt but grappled with a nagging doubt that something was missing. He had Fujitaka bring in his *Go* board table and laid out the black stones representing the forces arrayed against the white stones of Nobunaga and played Nobunaga's hand to study his predicament.

What would I do if I were him? Yoshiaki thought as he encircled one of Nobunaga's stones for capture when the sudden arrival of a messenger with a letter from Akechi Mitsuhide broke his concentration. With Yoshiaki's permission, Fujitaka took the letter and read it.

"Well?" Yoshiaki barked at Fujitaka while he still studied the board.

"My Lord, the letter is brief and to the point. Lord Mitsuhide wishes to warn you that Nobunaga is aware of your plans to garrison Imakatata and construct fortifications at Ishiyama and has instructed him to attack them both at the earliest opportunity. He further adds as he is under orders to comply, he trusts this advance-news will provide the Shogun time to extricate himself from the bind he now finds himself in." Yoshiaki was about to explode with anger when Fujitaka pleaded for calm and interpreted Mitsuhide's true meaning.

"My Lord, Mitsuhide is a vassal of Nobunaga, and he has no choice but to obey his command. His warning clearly shows he is still in alliance with us and will continue to serve your interests by remaining inside Nobunaga's circle. At least you get the benefit of being forewarned and prepared."

"How did that fool get wind of Ishiyama?" Yoshiaki demanded, "Tell me that Fujitaka, tell me that."

"My Lord, it is obvious Nobunaga's spies have reported our moves to garrison the Imakatata Fortress, and the extensive defensive preparations that have begun at Ishiyama would have hardly gone unnoticed." Yoshiaki looked at the solitary sour plum on the table, beckoning to be devoured.

"My Lord," Fujitaka continued, "as we have not replied to his entreaties for a reconciliation, it is not surprising he suspects your intentions."

"How dare you, Fujitaka, what are you implying?"

"Nothing, my Lord, but if we were to send a message to Nobunaga that you are still exploring ways for a reconciliation, it will buy us time till he is forced to deal with Shingen?"

Yoshiaki's rage grew, and he curled his lip and began snarling at Fujitaka.

"I will not reconcile with that, fool. Let him attack. If he purports to support the office of Shogun, he will heed my warning. I will not betray Mitsuhide, but once Mitsuhide makes a move against Imakatata or Ishiyama, you are to send word to Nobunaga in the emperor's name that these actions constitute a rebellion against the lawful governing authority of this land. We have enough influence at court to persuade the emperor to order him to stand down. Nobunaga will have no choice but to comply or risk being declared a rebel."

Part Two

Chapter Eight

A Coming of Age
Spring: The First Year of Tensho (1573)

Nene's hand servant, Koro, escorted Sakichi along the long dark corridors towards Lady Nene's quarters. Still half asleep, Sakichi looked anxiously at the shadows cast by the lantern Koro carried. It was well past midnight and into the later part of the hour of the rat. Nene was particular about the time chosen for seeing Sakichi, for she knew her household would all be asleep, and with less chance of prying eyes and ears about. At Nene's bedchamber, Koro slid open the screen and ushered Sakichi in and then left.

"Come in, Sakichi, and sit with me. We have much to discuss," Nene said. The room was dark and what small light there was emanated from a solitary lantern, giving Nene's face a ghostly appearance. Sakichi also noticed she was still wearing her formal Kimono and wondered if she ever slept.

"As you know, my husband has left here, but not to Owari."

"Oh!" said Sakichi. It was the only response Sakichi could muster as he gradually woke up. Sakichi knew of Hideyoshi's plan to resolve his dilemma with Mitsuhide and had followed his instructions. He had let it be known to Mitsuhide's agent that Hideyoshi had left for Owari to join Ieyasu and hold off Shingen's till Nobunaga could reinforce him.

"My husband has told me all about your recruitment as a spy," said Nene, prompting Sakichi to speak and explain, but Nene held up her hand to stifle any attempt at replying.

"There is no need for further explanation, but we need to deal with some pressing issues at hand. First, we have concerns about Nobunaga's retainer, Yoshimasa's sudden disappearance. Lord Nobunaga is aware of these events and directs us to continue to follow my husband's plan. Therefore, I cncourage you to embrace the tutelage of the Shogun's tutor and to prepare for your *Genpuku* ceremony within the month." A downcast Sakichi bowed in acceptance.

"Sakichi," Nene quietly said. "Do you trust Hideyoshi?" Sakichi knew he was in too deep not to trust Hideyoshi, but there was something about Hideyoshi that made him want to trust him.

"Yes, my Lady, I do trust Lord Hideyoshi."

"Then do not complain and consider yourself fortunate that your lord has a plan to extricate you from your dilemma."

At least he is not thinking of executing me, Sakichi thought to himself.

"May I ask what the Lord Hideyoshi has in mind for me?" Sakichi asked.

"My husband has not seen fit to confide in me all his plans, as I know it involves many people. You must understand that all this has the full knowledge and approval of Lord Nobunaga, as the stakes here are higher than just the life of one worried pageboy. Besides, we have your *Genpuku* to arrange at the earliest opportunity and you have much to learn and master before then. Now go." Nene gestured to Sakichi before adding.

"After your stable duties, you are to report to your tutor in the courtyard."

The next morning, with his stable chores finished, Sakichi sat with Miko and Oko under the persimmon tree near the stables and ate a breakfast of rice cakes and dried fish under its shade.

"You are going to need a good bath before you head back inside the house," Sakichi said to Miko, twitching his nose in disgust.

"You knew *Giri* was going to do that, didn't you?" Miko shouted at Oko, venting his anger.

"What fool would sweep under a horse with a raised tail, anyway?" Oko sniggered before breaking out into laughter. Miko reached for the horse comb he still carried and tried to comb away the traces of dung clinging to his hair. Sakichi watched and joined in Oko's laughter.

"Admit it was funny, Miko," said Sakichi. "The look on your face, and you wiping the steaming dung away from your eyes, it was enough to make even the gods laugh." Determined to appear aggrieved, Miko shouted, "Laugh all you want." Then he got up and walked away.

By mid-morning, the sun was at its highest, and beads of sweat ran from Sakichi's forehead as he made his way towards the courtyard to report to his tutor. Despite the hour, it surprised him to find the courtyard deserted, and the freshly raked gravel unspoilt.

Where is she? Sakichi queried, fully expecting his tutor to be here and ready. He sat on one of the smaller low setting stones, flanked by a tall vertical rock in the centre of the courtyard, and passed the time thinking of a way to get Hideyoshi's permission to visit his parents in nearby Ishida.

The hour of the dragon had passed into the Snake when the thud of some rock landing in the gravel at Sakichi's feet restored him to reality. Shading his eyes with his hands from the glare of the sun, Sakichi re-focussed and saw a *Katana* in the grip of an extended hand in front of him. It looked odd and then he realised the sword's hilt was much longer than usual.

Looking up, he saw his tutor dressed in black pants and jacket. She held in her other hand a wooden bokken (training sword).

"Sakichi, I presume. Take the sword and let us see what you know." Sakichi grabbed the *Katana* and withdrew the blade from its *Saya* and held it in his right hand. It felt uncomfortable. Yoshino moved closer, raising her wooden sword high over her head, gripping the hilt with both hands.

"Watch and learn, Sakichi," Yoshino shouted. "You will learn the sword style of the Tamiya Ryu as practised by Tamiya Hebei Narimasa. You will notice your hilt is longer than normal to allow greater control." But before Sakichi had time to think about this, Yoshino made her move and in three quick successive moves, delivered a forceful slap to his abdomen, and Sakichi fell to the ground in agony.

"In a proper fight you would have been split in two, like a pig on the butcher's block," Yoshino said.

"Now, pay attention. The purpose of the *Jodan No Kamae* move I just did was simple. You, like most novices, are more focussed on the blade above your head, and oblivious to your opponents' foot movements."

"Now watch again and pay attention to my feet." Yoshino crouched on the ground, assuming a sitting position while resting on her heels. Her *bokken* rested in the gravel on her left alongside her. With lightning speed, she gripped the sword and in one movement she advanced upright with her right foot forward, then bringing her left foot up. Simultaneously, she raised the *bokken* above her head, then with blinding speed followed through, performing a vertical to horizontal sweeping cut whilst keeping her feet parallel to the front. In a commanding tone, she called out to Sakichi, who was still nursing his soreness.

"Now you try," she said. Sakichi picked up his sword and positioned himself with sword upraised as he had seen Yoshino do.

"Good," shouted Yoshino.

"You at least know enough to assume the stance correctly but keep the left foot parallel to your leading right foot."

Sakichi stood motionless, waiting for Yoshino to call out her instructions. Finally, he broke concentration and lowered his sword to see Yoshino appear transfixed with her sword still in her hand.

"Is something wrong?" Sakichi asked.

"That mark under your arm. Where did you get it?" Yoshino coldly responded.

"Do you mean this?" Sakichi raised his right arm over his head and pointed to the small, elongated patch of dark, pigmented skin under his arm.

"Yes, that,"

"I don't know. I was born with it. Must be a birthmark, I suppose."

"The lesson is concluded. We shall resume again tomorrow," Yoshino said in a tense voice and then left, leaving a bewildered Sakichi to search for the swords *Saya* he discarded earlier.

What was that all about? Now, where is this Saya?

As Sakichi crossed the courtyard towards the villa, Nene's chamberlain nervously approached, notably wary of the naked *Katana* Sakichi held in his hand.

"Oh, sorry," he exclaimed to the visibly shaken chamberlain. "I've just had a lesson and cannot find its *Saya*," Sakichi said apologetically.

"Lady Nene has instructed me to bring you to the audience room at once," the chamberlain uttered, feeling a little more relaxed at Sakichi's explanation.

"You cannot bring weapons inside. I will have to take this and return it to your tutor." Sakichi offered the chamberlain the sword's hilt, and he smiled with amusement at the nervous way the old man took charge of it.

I do not think he has ever held a sword before.

A dishevelled and sweaty Sakichi sat cross-legged in front of Lady Nene. Koro was to one side, preparing tea. Another servant attended to a steaming kettle of water.

"You will, of course, join me in tea," Nene said. "We have much to discuss." Koro placed a low table between them, and Nene produced two black, glazed *Chawan* tea bowls.

"What do you think of these bowls, Sakichi? For someone so young, it surprised me to learn from my husband that he considers you something of an expert in such things," said Nene.

Sakichi reached over and picked up the bowl, running his finger over its tapered mouth, and caressing its brown and black glaze before turning it over and replacing it on the table.

"My Lady, it is a delightful piece. It is a *Tenmoku Chawan.* I suspect you are already aware of its origins. It is not Chinese Karamono, as the whiteness of its unglazed foot betrays it as being a copy made here in Seto."

"You are correct, young Sakichi. Karamono is popular but is too expensive to get hold of. These are a little more affordable."

"Was this some kind of test, my Lady?"

"Indeed, it was Sakichi, indeed it was."

Nene gestured Koro to pour the tea, and they both drank in silence. Sakichi had just finished his second bowl when a smiling Nene was first to break the silence.

"I watched your lesson and there is a story Lord Nobunaga once told me, that I should like to tell."

"As a reward, a meek tea master was made Samurai by his lord, but a jealous retainer challenged him to a duel. Knowing he was going to die, and determined not to dishonour his Lord, he sought the help of a *Kensei* (swordmaster) to teach him how to die with honour. In return, the *Kensei* asked the tea master to perform the tea ceremony for one last time. As the tea master performed the ceremony, all traces of fear disappeared. He became entirely focused on the ritual, leaving no room in his mind for anxiety. When the ceremony was complete, the *Kensei* declared there was no need for the tea master to learn anything of the way of death. When you see your challenger tomorrow, imagine you are about to serve tea for him. The next day, the challenger beheld a different man altogether. The tea master was calm and fearless; thus, the challenger's eyes were opened, and he apologised for his rude behaviour." Sakichi's eyes narrowed as he tried to discern her meaning.

"I sense you still do not understand. The tale of the tea master shows that with mastery over your mind and spirit, you can overcome anything. The impossible now becomes possible." Sakichi nodded as if to say he understood, as it was pointless to argue.

"We have decided to hold your *Genpuku* at the next full moon. This will hopefully allow enough time for you to show some progress in your lessons," said Nene in a sarcastic tone.

"My Lady," Sakichi pleaded, "I will never be a warrior, so why is all this necessary?" At this, Nene became visibly annoyed.

"You need to understand. This is not all about you. My husband is of the opinion that Azai Nagamasa will eventually suffer defeat and be forced to commit Seppuku. As is the custom, if Nagamasa ends his life as an enemy, then as the head of the Azai, all the rest of his clan, including you and your family are likely to be put to the sword, or at the very least have all their lands and titles confiscated. Should your parents be spared this fate, then as Azai vassals they will be become masterless *Ronin* with no inheritance they can give to their children? You, however, can protect your father and mother by becoming one of my husband's retainers. As an Oda vassal, you and your family will now share Nobunaga's fate, but to become one of Nobunaga's vassals, you must be Samurai. Perhaps you might now understand now how important it is for you to have your *Genpuku* and achieve Samurai status."

While Nene attempted to instil upon Sakichi the importance of his education, Yoshino sat meditating within her quarters, her screen doors open to receive the cooling relief of the light breeze that had sprung up. She stared out at the dry barren earth of a garden that yet did not exist and thought.

Is it possible? She lifted her right arm before bending it at the elbow and raised it above her head to better study the birthmark etched on her skin. *The similarities are uncanny. Is it possible?*

Several long weeks had passed under Yoshino's tutelage, and Sakichi noticed a transformation taking place. The muscles in his arm and legs had grown stronger, and like the 'tea master', he felt his mind was clearer and the more he focussed, he felt less afraid and confident. His proficiency in the sword style of the Tamiya Ryu had increased, and on one rare occasion, he even beat Yoshino in a practice session. Yoshino used the time to probe into Sakichi's background, asking questions of his birth and his parent's lineage, but Sakichi could only tell what he knew, so Yoshino discovered nothing of significance.

102

At his lessons, Sakichi practised all his sword moves with the Muramasa blade that Hideyoshi had recently given him, which he named *Jiko,* which attracted repeated criticism from Yoshino.

"You performed better with the other blade," Yoshino observed. Hideyoshi had obtained the sword from Ieyasu as a gift, who let slip he was eager to be rid of it. The Tokugawa Lord was not one given to superstitious beliefs, but whether it was by coincidence or design, he could not overlook the fact the deaths of his grandfather, Matsudaira Kiyoyasu and his father Matsudaira Hirotada had one thing in common, death by a Muramasa blade, and he was taking no chances.

"Yes, I agree. The other blade seemed more balanced and comfortable to grip," he replied.

"Let me look at it," Yoshino demanded as she grasped Sakichi's sword by its hilt and frowned as if disappointed. She performed a series of sword moves to assess the sword's characteristics.

"I see what is wrong here. It is a fine blade, but the hilt is too short," said Yoshino. "I will speak to the swordsmith and see if we can put a longer hilt on." Without waiting for Sakichi's permission, Yoshino walked away, taking Sakichi's sword with her, leaving him to assume the lesson for today was once again over.

At the next two sessions, Sakichi drilled with the blade Yoshino had originally given him, and as much as he wanted to, he resisted the temptation to ask her how the work on his sword was going. Yoshino would occasionally compliment him on his progress, and he took his instruction from her without question and with complete focus, until one day.

The day had been warmer than usual. Even the slight breeze that blew was insufferably warm and Sakichi felt the beads of sweat trickling down his back. The intense sunshine that reflected off the clean white gravel of the courtyard made him squint and added to his discomfort. He had assembled in the courtyard for his daily instruction when he noticed three large stakes driven into the ground, and only two of them had straw dummies attached. Yoshino came into view, approaching from behind the dummies, still dressed in her usual black clothes and carrying *Jiko.*

"Try this. Go through the moves I have taught you," said Yoshino as she handed Sakichi his sword.

Sakichi tucked *Jiko* in his Obi on his left side, with his left thumb resting against the sword guard, and immediately withdrew *Jiko* from its *Saya.* Gripping the new hilt with both hands, he performed the *Kata* (movements) instilled into him by Yoshino and nodded approvingly at the modification. The weight and balance of the new, longer hilt were perfect.

"That is much better," said Yoshino with an approving nod.

"Now let us test if you and the blade are fit for purpose. Demonstrate the *O-kesa* move and let me see you cut one dummy on the diagonal, then the other on the horizontal in one fluid movement." By now, the sweat was running down in rivulets from Sakichi's forehead and he tasted its saltiness. Taking a cloth headband from his Obi, Sakichi tied it around his head to absorb the sweat. He was hot but composed, focussing intently on the first dummy. Sakichi willed the blade to guide him and struck downwards at the diagonal entering the base of the dummy's right neck, proceeding through the body, and exiting through the left armpit. Instantly. he reversed direction, cutting horizontally across the second dummy's midsection. He had executed the move perfectly, despite his concerns that he might lack the strength. Yoshino nodded her approval.

He shows promise. He has come a long way in such short a time, but is he ready?

"Not bad, Sakichi," Yoshino shouted across the courtyard as she walked towards Sakichi and looked him in the face. "But can you kill?" she said. The question unsettled Sakichi, for it was one he could not answer. He thought momentarily about not answering, hoping the conversation would pass, but Yoshino grabbed him by the lapel of his Hitatare and pulled him close towards her. She wondered if she could smell fear.

Even at such an early age, Sakichi accepted death would always be a close companion. To protect his family, he undertook to learn the 'Way of the Warrior' and master the very set of skills that would equip him to kill. He also knew the sole purpose in the path fate had chosen for him as a Samurai was to fight, kill, and die for his lord. In truth, he had never expected to face that reality.

"Tell me Sakichi, as Samurai if your lord tells you to kill a peasant, can you do it without question?" Yoshino demanded as she continued to hold him close to her face.

"Don't bother answering," she said, before releasing her grip. and signalling with a nod of her head towards a group of household guards who were loitering at the edge of the courtyard. As Sakichi dwelt on Yoshino's question, two of the household guards entered the courtyard, dragging a poor wretch, clad only in a loincloth and tied him to the third stake. Pointing to the man, Yoshino spoke to Sakichi, but loud enough for all to hear.

"This man has killed. He raped a young child and then brutally murdered her. The *Shugu* (magistrate) has sentenced him for immediate execution, but the manner of his death was left to the girl's family to decide." The hapless wretch raised his head and defiantly spat a ball of spittle through his toothless mouth towards Yoshino.

"Sakichi," she called out. "Would you say this creature is deserving of his sentence?" Sakichi remained motionless with *Jiko* still in his hand at his side and nodded. He had seen executions before. The necessity of ridding the world of such foul creatures was a reality that would not affect him until now.

"What did the girls' family decide?" a genuinely concerned Sakichi asked.

"At first, they produced many imaginative ways for the cruellest of deaths, some of which were quite ingenious, but in the end, the prospect of compensation was far more motivating than revenge. So, in exchange for a purse of copper coins, they allowed me to determine the manner of this criminal's death." It was at that moment Sakichi had an uneasy feeling where this was leading to.

"Sakichi, just as you demonstrated the *O-kesa* on those dummies, you will execute the move on this criminal." Sakichi remained motionless. The pit of his stomach was in turmoil. He is being told to kill.

He is a dead man already. If not me, it will be someone else. If I refuse, I will not only be humiliated, but I will have failed at securing my parents' lives. I cannot do it. I cannot kill. Not like this. Yoshino understood the dilemma Sakichi was agonising over and whispered.

"Your mission is not simply to kill. As Samurai, you have a duty not only to your lord but also to those beneath you. What of your duty to the girl's family? I can end this now and kill him myself, but you will have avoided dispensing the justice that is asked of you, out of fear." Sakichi's mind raced.

Yes, I am scared, but you only want me to kill to test me and not because of any obligation of duty.

Sakichi thought of the 'tea master'. *What would he have done? To refuse will mean dishonour and the wretch still dies. What will I have achieved, other than acknowledging my shame and losing my parents' lives?*

Sakichi stared at the ground for a few moments, as if deep in thought. He looked at the wretch before him, his eyes still defiant as if goading him to end his torture. The wretch smiled and spat again, this time at Sakichi, and *Jiko* descended on the diagonal, slicing cleanly through his neck. The wretch's eyes remained open as if stunned, and the thin red line stretching from his neck to his armpit gradually became larger and darker. Just before his upper body completely detached, Sakichi reversed his strike, and cut horizontally through the wretch's midsection. *Jiko* fell from Sakichi's hand onto the ground and Sakichi doubled over and retched, his vomit mingling with the blood on *Jiko's* blade.

Chapter Nine

Genpuku

Spring, May: The First Year of Tensho (1573)

Nobunaga had opened the screen doors to his sparse sitting room that also served as his command post atop Mount Toragoze, to bask in the warmth of the early morning sunshine. The night had been exceptionally cold and as he breathed, wisps of cloud rose from his mouth. Toragoze and nearby Yokoyama Castle were both bases built to support the campaign he waged against his brother-in-law, Azai Nagamasa.

Despite his victory at Anegawa, Nobunaga still seethed that Nagamasa escaped and continued to taunt him from his impregnable mountaintop fortress of Odani, a mere two kilometres away. He looked out northward towards Odani Castle atop nearby Mount Ozuku and thought of his sister, Oichi. He regretted forcing her to divorce her rebellious husband Shibata Katsuie and using her to cement an alliance as the wife of the lord of Omi province, Azai Nagamasa.

Nobunaga looked out towards Odani Castle and even at this distance, he could see the enemy movements as one would watch a nest of ants. His concentration disturbed by the entry of three of his generals: Hayashi Hidesada, Maeda Toshie and Kinoshita Hideyoshi, Nobunaga waved for them to take their positions in front of him. He remained sitting opposite the open screen door, keeping one eye on Odani. Maeda Toshie was the first to speak.

"I notice Shibata Katsuie and Akechi Mitsuhide are absent, Lord."

"Yes, they are busy elsewhere," said Nobunaga, glancing towards Odani.

Why am I always betrayed? He thought of his then brother-in-law Katsuie, who conspired with his younger brothers, Nobuyuki and Hayashi, to usurp his leadership of the clan.

I killed my brother Nobuyuki, yet I pardoned both Shibata and Hayashi. I am what they call me, 'lord fool'.

"Gentlemen," Nobunaga said, snapping back into reality.

"You are no doubt aware of the Shogun's latest manoeuvres at Imakatata and Ishiyama. If he establishes a foothold there, he will set back our campaign against those troublesome Ishiyama Ikko-Ikki monks. We cannot afford to allow him to link up with the monks. I have ordered Shibata and Akechi to prepare for an immediate attack on the Shogun's forces in Imakatata." Maeda Toshiie gave out a low whistle of surprise.

"Does the dog have something to say?" inquired Nobunaga, using the pet name he had for Toshiie. Despite the differences in their upbringing, Hideyoshi, the son of a peasant and Toshiie, head of the Maeda clan, both Toshiie, and Hideyoshi became good friends but still career rivals. Nobunaga would tease Hideyoshi and Maeda and remind them that 'dogs and monkeys' are never friendly to each other.

"Is this wise, my Lord?" Hayashi asked. "Attacking the Shogun when we are facing more important threats?"

"Hmm, do not forget, we are in this position because of the Shogun, Hayashi. His meddling and conspiring with our enemies have emboldened Shingen, and the Shogun feels the time now is ripe."

"Then let us deal with the Shogun after we have dealt with Shingen," Hayashi pleaded. "To do so now will surely weaken us more." Nobunaga did not reply to Hayashi, instead, he turned to Hideyoshi.

"Monkey, explain our current thinking to Lord Hayashi here," said Nobunaga before resuming his watch over Odani and recalling the events of a few hours earlier. He had received a messenger from Shingen. An arrogant Takeda Samurai with an insolent manner, who treated him as if he were some inconsequential provincial lords.

I should have your head for your insolence, Nobunaga remembered thinking. And he did.

The only message Shingen had sent him was the head of Hiraide Norihide, the commander of the reinforcements he had recently sent to help Ieyasu. It was a warning, not lost on Nobunaga. It was clear Shingen had coached the messenger what to say and lay the bait. Should the messenger survive, Shingen would know Nobunaga could be coerced into compromise. The head of Hiraide

108

Norihide served as an admonishment for breaking off the friendly relations that had existed between the two of them, and for supporting his enemy, the Tokugawa. In response, an enraged Nobunaga beheaded the messenger and kicked his severed head to the far corners of the room.

While Lord Nobunaga watched over Odani, Hideyoshi explained to Hayashi his master's reasoning.

"Lord Hayashi, we have reports that Shingen has moved on from his victory at Mikatagahara to siege Ieyasu's under-manned castle at Noda. We find it strange that his army of thirty thousand appears stalled in their siege against a garrison of only five hundred. There are also reports indicating that Shingen's army is on the move and returning to Kai."

"Why on earth would Shingen, on the cusp of victory, want to give up and return to Kai?" Hayashi uttered incredulously. "Surely, the reports are false?"

"Or perhaps Shingen is ill, or even wounded," Hideyoshi replied. "We have cross-referenced all the reports and believe that for whatever reason, the Takeda march is at present halted."

"Yes, yes, yes," Nobunaga muttered, returning to the conversation, and cutting short Hideyoshi's assessment.

"We have a small window of opportunity available to us. Our enemies are relaxed in the belief that Shingen's move on the capital will precipitate our downfall. If we strike quickly, we can not only neutralise a meddling Shogun but finally deal with the Azai and Asakura." Nobunaga was about to outline his plan when a guard interrupted to announce a messenger from Mikawa.

"Show him in at once," said Nobunaga.

"Reporting," shouted a dishevelled-looking Samurai in a grubby kimono.

"Lord, we have confirmed reports the Takeda army has abandoned Noda Castle and moved on towards Nagashino."

"What!" exclaimed Hayashi. He clearly understood the implication. *Shingen is moving in the opposite direction.*

"Who are you? You are not Tokugawa," Nobunaga inquired of the Samurai.

"My name is Gorozaemon, I am one of Lord Hideyoshi's men, sent to Mikawa to observe Shingen's movements."

"Aha, one of monkey's spies," shouted Nobunaga.

"Hideyoshi, can you vouch for him?"

"Yes, sire. He is one of my men. His instructions are to report to you directly of any developments."

"We will need to you question you further Gorozaemon," said Nobunaga. "But first, rest and have refreshments." Hideyoshi looked towards Nobunaga, who remained still and expressionless, as if deep in thought. Hayashi and Toshiie meanwhile began arguing with each other, each trying the decipher the true meaning of the news they had just heard when Nobunaga suddenly dismissed everyone. The last to leave was Hideyoshi, who Nobunaga discretely made it known he was to stay behind.

"Monkey, send spies and report back. I must know if Noda Castle has fallen, Ieyasu's whereabouts, and if the Takeda army has moved on to Nagashino. None of this adds up."

"Yes, my Lord," said Hideyoshi.

"Oh, another thing. This issue with the 'songbird' you spoke to me about. It would seem Yoshiaki's obsession with your whereabouts could be just the advantage we need. I believe you have allowed him to think that you are moving to help Ieyasu in Totomi."

"Yes, my Lord," replied Hideyoshi.

"So, where have you parked your army, then?"

"We have set up camp at Shimizudani."

"Good. If Yoshiaki believes you are on your way to Totomi, he also knows I will have to reinforce Nagoya Castle to defend Owari against Shingen. He will, therefore, entice Yoshikage and Nagamasa to strike now. Spread the rumour that preparations are underway for the army to march to Nagoya and keep your little army out of sight and ready at Shimizudani. Be sure to send messages of your progress to Nene, who will inform the 'songbird'. Meanwhile, I will have Shibata and Akechi clip the Shogun's wings."

#

For several days, a lack of wind and cloudless skies over Imahama had left vast expanses of Lake Biwako as calm as a 'millpond', which had led to an unusual build-up of hot weather. Such was the extraordinary nature of the heat that the village headman suspended all work for the day, and children and workers alike played in the warm waters of the lake. It was on the fifteenth day of the new month, the date of Sakichi's Genpuku ceremony, that the rumbling in the heavens grew louder and the skies darker. North-westerly winds now blew in from the lake, pushing a storm front towards Imahama where it unleashed torrential rains which exacerbated the already oppressive humidity.

The sudden storm scattered the small procession, leaving the Hachimangu Shrine dedicated to *Hachiman*, the patron deity of warriors and the venue for Sakichi's *Genpuku*. Nene had stopped to gather up the bottom of her now sodden kimono and kicked off her *Geta* sandals to run for the cover of her waiting palanquin, leaving Yoshino and the rest of the entourage to make their way through the downpour back towards the villa.

A brief time earlier, Sakichi had undergone the rites of his *Genpuku*, marking his passage to adulthood. He felt alone and sorely missed his parents on what should have been a proud day for them. He also missed his lord, Hideyoshi, who was away somewhere in Owari. Nene had stood in for Hideyoshi as Sakichi's patron at the ceremony and formally presented him with new adult clothes. Of note was the new black silk kimono emblazoned with a gold Quince flower Kamon of the Oda clan. The Kimono was a gift from Lord Nobunaga and symbolised Sakichi's new vassalage to Nobunaga.

A few weeks before Sakichi's Genpuku ceremony, Hideyoshi had arranged with Nene to present Sakichi with the first of his two swords he would carry as a Samurai. A Muramasa Katana. Forged by the great swordmaker Muramasa Sengo, which Sakichi named *Jiko*, but today Nene would present Hideyoshi's gift of a *wakizashi* short sword, also by the famed swordmaker, to complete Sakichi's *Daisho* of two swords. Her gift to Sakichi was a simple *Kabuto* war helmet that once belonged to her father, Sugihara Sadatoshi. He had gained it on his own *Genpuku*, and Sugihara had bequeathed it to Nene to pass on to the eventual grandson she sadly could not bear.

Sakichi's *Genpuku* concluded with the shaving of his pate at the top of his head and tying his remaining hair in the characteristic topknot of the Samurai, and the bestowing of his adult name. Lord Nobunaga had chosen for him the name 'Mitsunari', the characters for which are 'He who sings of life', ironically mimicking his nickname, the 'songbird'. For his family name, Sakichi chose the village of his birth, Ishida and Nene announced to all that henceforth, Sakichi was to be known as Ishida Mitsunari.

Oblivious to the storm raging outside, Mitsunari had stayed behind after the ceremony to offer prayers for the protection of his parents when he felt the gentle pressure of a hand squeezing his right shoulder. He turned to see a man with a shaved head and weathered face dressed in the white *Kariginu* robes of a Shinto priest grinning at him. Mitsunari instantly recognised the prominent scar running across the priest's face intersecting where his right eye should have been. His eyes lit up as he recognised Yoshimasa.

#

Just after daybreak at the hour of the dragon, Shibata Katsuie, and Akechi Mitsuhide attacked the Shogun's forces at Imakatata, a small hilltop fortress overlooking the Seta River. The fortress controlled the approaches and the supply lines to the Ikko-Ikki stronghold at Ishiyama, at the mouth of the nearby Yoda River. For three years, Nobunaga had laid siege to Ishiyama, tying up many thousands of his forces in a war of attrition against fanatical warrior monks and commoners. The Ikko-Ikki was a populist religious movement determined to overthrow the ruling Samurai class and had unlikely Samurai allies in the Mori Clan, the Takeda and Uesugi Kenshin of Echizen. These allies also feared the threat posed by the Ikko-Ikki, but now they were more useful in keeping their enemy, Nobunaga distracted.

With Ishiyama well protected by the Seto Sea and the Mori navy, Imakatata remained vulnerable to seaborne attack, a feature Akechi exploited. Using warships brought down from Otsu on Lake Biwako, Akechi attacked offshore from the east, while Shibata attacked by land from the south. By mid-day around the hour of the horse, it was all over. Mitsuhide had been the first to break through the Imakatata defences, slaughtering many of its defenders and those that survived were given the option to either swear fealty to Nobunaga or die. Mitsuhide had two of the defenders sent back to Yoshiaki with important news he needed to alert him to.

At the Nijo Palace, Yoshiaki sat with Hosokawa Fujitaka going through the latest news from the field, when Fujitaka announced he had just received a report which, unknown to Yoshiaki, he had deliberately suppressed for several hours.

"My Lord, Nobunaga has attacked Imakatata, and your castellan Akai Nagato has surrendered with a significant loss of life." Yoshiaki did not react. He remained emotionless but calm, his attention fixed on the six-panel painting of birds in flight by the famous artist Sesshu he had recently obtained to hang in the Hall of Cranes.

"My Lord," Fujitaka once again called out to gain Yoshiaki's attention. He again attempted to persuade the Shogun to come to immediate accommodation with Nobunaga. At the mention of Nobunaga's name, Yoshiaki instantly sprang to life.

"I would rather walk alone in *Yomi,* the land of the dead than reconcile with that fool," he declared in a tone laced with venom. Fujitaka's heart sank, but he steeled himself to reply.

"My Lord, we also have reports Nobunaga has assembled a large force and has left Gifu and is marching on Kyoto. Again, I plead for the sake of the Shogunate and your ancestors. Please, reconcile with Nobunaga."

Something here is not right. Yoshiaki thought.

"Fujitaka, were we not led to believe he was heading for Nagoya?" Yoshiaki snapped. "No matter, send word to the imperial court at once. Inform the court that Nobunaga has rebelled against the emperor's authority and his Shogun requests His Highness declares Nobunaga a rebel and rescinds all titles and honours afforded to him."

"My Lord," Fujitaka pleaded, "despite Nobunaga's ambitions, he can only succeed if the people see him acting under the legitimacy of the Shogun and the emperor. Remember, his gains are your gains, and his failures are something you can disown. Would it not be to your advantage to indulge him and reap the rewards? After all, he had the Nijo rebuilt just for you."

Yoshiaki quietly rose without replying and moved to open a large painted screen door opening out onto the palace gardens. He looked out upon a landscaped vista of manicured hedges, Koi ponds and fruit trees. He paid particular attention to the placement of various sized large stones designed to represent the eight Islands of Japan that Nobunaga himself had designed. For a moment, Yoshiaki seemed lost in thought, then he calmly turned to Fujitaka.

"Fujitaka, see that you despatch my letter to the court at once without delay," further adding, "have the gardener sent for, at once."

The gardener, now worried his labours had somehow caused offence, prostrated himself in front of the Shogun and pleaded forgiveness. The old man had laboured in this garden for the past five years in all weathers, giving his tanned skin a weathered texture akin to leather. In restoring the Nijo, Nobunaga had taken upon himself to oversee much of the landscaping and instructed the gardener to achieve the designs he envisioned. He need not have worried, for Yoshiaki was full of praise for his diligent work and even discussed with him those aspects of the garden he enjoyed the most and those he felt were out of place. In noticing the gardener's nervousness, Yoshiaki again reassured him he was not in trouble and had merely summoned him for a special task. Feeling relieved and important, the old man raised his head and smiled with an air of self-importance.

"You have a family I believe that lives with you in the house which I have provided?" Yoshiaki inquired about the gardener. The old man's eyes suddenly narrowed in concern, and he immediately again prostrated himself.

"Yes, my Lord," the old man nervously mumbled.

"Good," Yoshiaki exclaimed and turned his attention back towards the garden.

"Then if you wish to see them again, you will perform the task I am about to give you with the same enthusiasm you applied in creating this masterpiece of tranquil beauty." Looking back at the gardener, Yoshiaki summoned his guards.

"Escort the gardener here to the Ninomaru Palace that Lord Nobunaga so generously restored. He is to gather his tools and to enlist as much labour as he requires and tear down its very structure. Let me be clear. I do not want it dismantled, I want it destroyed, and the task completed by sunset today." The gardener, together with hundreds of workers, armed with axes and saws, began their systematic destruction of the palace, and the Kyoto citizenry with Yoshiaki's connivance helped themselves to the lumber and anything of value.

It was mid-morning and approaching the hour of the snake by the time Nobunaga and his army reached the outskirts of Kyoto. Word had already reached him of the destruction taking place at the Ninomaru Palace, and he vented his fury on the Kyoto citizenry. Every temple in Kyoto's Kamigyo area was reduced to ashes and by the next morning, a further fifty villages around Kyoto had also suffered the same punishment. Realising his weakened position and hoping to stave off Nobunaga's vengeance upon him, Yoshiaki despatched a messenger to sue for peace.

Nobunaga had demanded Yoshiaki meet him at Shoryuji Castle on the southern approach to Kyoto to discuss terms, knowing the venue would annoy him. He had taken the castle five years earlier from the Miyoshi clan and had it governed by his retainer, Hosokawa Tadaoki, who was Fujitaka's son. It was Yoshiaki's intention for a grand entry into the castle as a statement of Shogunal power even if it was only illusionary, so it came as a bitter disappointment that he and his retinue in full battle dress entered Shoryuji Castle unseen hidden by the dense early morning fog.

114

The meeting between Nobunaga and Yoshiaki had gone well for Yoshiaki. He took great satisfaction from the fact that Nobunaga was visibly annoyed, and the terms for reconciliation were not much different from those that currently existed. Nobunaga even accepted counter proposals put forward by Yoshiaki, making Yoshiaki suspicious of Nobunaga's eagerness to accept them. It was not long before the reason for this became apparent, when Nobunaga showed Yoshiaki the royal edict from the emperor, compelling him to reconcile and end hostilities with the Shogun. So, it was that Yoshiaki left Shoryuji under a new understanding with Nobunaga that he had no intention of honouring, and Nobunaga returned with his army to Gifu to wait out the Shogun's next betrayal.

At the Nijo Palace, Yoshiaki sat with Hosokawa Fujitaka, deliberating the terms of his reconciliation with Nobunaga to progress his plans to rid himself of Nobunaga. Shingen's stalled army was worrying, but not fatal to his cause, for Azai Nagamasa and Asakura Yoshikage remained as allies and a continuing threat to Nobunaga. He noted an intelligence report showing Nobunaga had committed only five thousand of his army to attack Kyoto, which reinforced his belief that the rest of Nobunaga's army were still on their way to Nagoya to meet Shingen's threat, as were Hideyoshi's troops. Feeling more confident, Yoshiaki stroked his pencil moustache with satisfaction and addressed Fujitaka.

"Losing Imakatata is a minor setback. The game has not much changed and remains in play." It had crossed Fujitaka's mind to make another attempt to plead with the Shogun to abandon his schemes, but he realised the futility and grovelingly replied.

"Yes, my Lord, indeed it does."

"Another thing, Fujitaka, why have we not heard from our spies confirming Nobunaga's and Hideyoshi's movements?" Before Fujitaka could answer, a palace guard announced the arrival of the two Imakatata defenders sent by Akechi Mitsuhide, noting one of them has an important message for the Shogun.

"Show them in at once," demanded Yoshiaki.

The two Ashigaru soldiers from Imakatata bearing the grime and wounds of battle prostrated themselves in front of Yoshiaki.

"Which one of you has a message for me from Akechi?" shouted Yoshiaki.

An Ashigaru raised his head and squinted at the Shogun, his other eye remained closed with congealed blood.

"So, you have a message for me, I believe?"

"Yes, my Lord," rasped the Ashigaru.

115

"And your friend here? Does he have a message for me as well?"

"We both have the same message, my Lord, to ensure it reaches your ears."

"And what is the message?"

"The Akechi Lord said to tell you Nobunaga's spies have confirmed that Shingen has died from his wounds. His son, Katsuyori, now leads the Takeda, and his army is returning to Kai." Yoshiaki stared at the Ashigaru and remained motionless. Nobody in the room dared to make a move or utter a sound. Eyes darted everywhere, waiting for a sound, a movement, anything that would relieve the tension. Fujitaka was the first to break the silence and instructed the guard to remove the Ashigaru's. He had an urgent need to discuss with the Shogun the situation in private. Just as the guard moved to comply, Yoshiaki came to life, shouting.

"Stop! What are you doing?"

"Clearing the room, my Lord," said Fujitaka. "We must talk urgently."

"Is that so?" Yoshiaki replied coldly.

"Have everyone remain in the room and summon the captain of the guard at once," Yoshiaki snapped. Fujitaka issued instructions, and moments later the captain of the palace guards arrived, and Yoshiaki took him aside to whisper instructions.

"You are to take these deserters away from here quietly, without fuss, and behead them. The guard who brought them in is also to be beheaded, as he has heard too much. Be thankful you were not present as well." With the room cleared, Yoshiaki raised his voice and addressed Fujitaka.

"The game is not yet over. Make immediate arrangements for us to leave for Makishima Castle."

"But that lies in Yamashiro province," a surprised Fujitaka responded.

"Yes, and we will soon be out of Nobunaga's reach."

Chapter Ten

Past Ghosts

Summer: The First Year of Tensho (1573)

At the Hachimangu Shrine of Imahama, a surprised Mitsunari returned Yoshimasa's beaming smile and attempted to resist the urge to embrace him. The ceremony of his *Genpuku* had just finished, and Mitsunari now wondered if being an adult had somehow changed him.

"Where have you been all this time?" Mitsunari said. Ignoring his question, Yoshimasa studied the young man standing before him. He noticed how much the boy had changed, the musculature of his body, and the fine clothes he wore. Yoshimasa's eyes lingered on the two swords nestled in the young man's obi, noting his status as Samurai. He felt his fondness for Mitsunari intensify and he moved his hand to caress lovingly the young man's cheek.

"I see you shave now," Yoshimasa said with an admiring smile. "I watched your Genpuku ceremony earlier. It seems we are now both sworn to serve the same master, but to more important matters. Your parents' lives are in danger." Mitsunari immediately gripped the hilt of *Jiko,* resting alongside its new companion, the *Wakizashi* short sword he called *Jiro.*

"What do you mean?" Mitsunari asked.

"I am aware of the arrangement you have with Lord Hideyoshi to deceive Lord Mitsuhide and the Shogun. Yoshiaki is not stupid; he is an experienced *Go* player who always plans his moves well ahead. Mitsuhide will have already informed him by now of Nobunaga's plans against him, and the Shogun will query the value of your intelligence and that of your tutor."

"Yoshino? What has she got to do with this?" Asked Mitsunari.

"Like me, she was sent to keep an eye on you, but by different masters, and she, too, will shortly disappear."

"What do you mean? What's going on?"

Yoshimasa paused and thought carefully about his reply.

How much should I tell him? He recalled his last encounter with Yoshino, and how he later woke up unable to move any part of his body. He wondered if he still had his fingers and toes, for he lacked any feeling, but he knew he could see, even though he could not move his eyelids. Also, he could hear and remember the kind, soothing words coming from a wrinkled grey-haired woman's face as it hovered above him. On his back, he could see the roof made of straw, supported by rough poles, and knew he must be in a peasant's house. He tried to cry out, but his mouth remained still, and his throat felt numb. With the woman's face above him, he felt some sort of obstruction in his throat, followed by the warmth of liquid as the old woman administered soup through a bamboo tube.

By the time he eventually sat up, he had regained most of the feeling in his fingers and toes but could only just move his arms and legs. His throat remained sore from the bamboo tube the old woman used to feed him. The old woman said her name was Akira and continued to hand feed him for several more days but remained silent for most of the time. He noticed one time the woman wore a smart sky-blue cotton kimono with an orange sash, which he thought odd, as it was not what one would expect a peasant to wear. He also recalled the only visit Yoshino had made to see him and how she explained how he came to be here, but not why she did it. She had arranged with a local *Ninja* tribe to hide his body here and later came to administer an antidote to the frog poison; she had coated her Shuriken blade with.

"One day, I will tell you the entire story," said Yoshimasa, "but the sudden death of Shingen will require Yoshino to return to her true employer."

"I thought she worked for the Shogun?" Mitsunari asked quizzically. Yoshimasa ignored Sakichi's question and looked outside. The rain was heavy and the visibility poor, but a large red fox sheltering under a nearby bush caught his attention, its eyes locked onto his. Yoshimasa blinked, and the fox disappeared. In its place sat a beautiful young woman dressed in white, impervious to the heavy rain falling around her. He again blinked and suddenly noticed all that remained of the woman in white was a pile of broken twigs.

"Are things truly what they appear to be?" Yoshimasa quietly said to Mitsunari.

#

It was near dusk and well into the hour of the monkey by the time Yoshino reached the forested foothills of mount Ibuki-Yama. The incessant rain had eased, and the first rays of late afternoon sunshine pierced the pillowy, dark clouds shrouding the mountain. Looking back towards Imahama, she noticed the rain shadow blanketing the town was also breaking up.

Good, she thought. *At least the night will be clear. It will be well after sundown before I can reach the hut.*

Yoshino followed a trail known only to the woodcutters and slowly climbed up the slopes of Ibuki-Yama. A dense canopy of pine trees blocked much of the remaining daylight, making sticking to the trail difficult, but at least the ground was dry. Gradually, the denseness of the forest thinned as she climbed, and overhead, she watched the orange orb of the sun beginning its disappearance into the darkening horizon. The trail she followed now led downhill to a clearing in the woods bathed in the moon's eerie light, and within the clearing, a rustic looking thatched wooden hut local woodcutters once used stood dark and deserted. It was the same place she had hidden Yoshimasa, and she casually entered, knowing no one would or should be here. Discarding the sodden straw cape and hat she wore, Yoshino laid down on a rough mattress of straw and momentarily rested her eyes. She dwelt on Shingen's death and knew she must return to Chiyo. Even though Chiyo had founded the *Shinobi* network, it was Shingen who pulled the strings, and without Shingen, the network was rudderless.

Soon, the land will once again be in turmoil as the news of Shingen's death spreads. Nobunaga will be free to purge and conquer. I owe my life to Chiyo, and she will need my help. But first I must find Mitsunari's parents. I must find out what they know.

At first light, Yoshino left the hut and set out through the rising mists, resolved to find Mitsunari's parents. With the eastern ranges impenetrable because of dense forests, she followed the downhill trail south to the plains of Sekigahara. This was Oda territory, and she would need to avoid the many checkpoints along the way to avoid unnecessary delays. All being well, she would turn north again and follow the Ibi-gawa River to the Azai castle town of Ishida, home of the Ishida clan and Mitsunari parents. With luck, she should make it by mid-day during the hour of the horse.

119

It was well past mid-day and into the hour of the sheep by the time Yoshino reached the outskirts of Ishida. She paused and pulled down the brim of her straw cone-shaped hat to better shield against the intense sunshine. Beads of sweat trickled down her face, irritating her eyes, and even with wiping the sweat from her eyes, the sun's haze distorted her view of the town ahead of her. She followed a well-trodden path that led into the town's major thoroughfare, a long and very narrow street flanked by tightly packed two-storey townhouses. Despite the heat of the day, the street was busy and crowded. Townspeople brandished colourful paper umbrellas for sun protection, and workers clad only in their *Fundoshi* (underwear) toiled, pushing their carts.

Yoshino followed closely behind a heavily laden cart of sake casks, as it ploughed a path through the busy crowds. Like most castle towns, the various artisans, and craftsmen lived and traded in their assigned areas and Yoshino recognised the distinctive latticework fronting most of the townhouses she passed, confirming her assessment that this must be the guild area reserved for sake brewers. The cart she had followed suddenly lurched on its side with a broken axle, and several loose barrels rolled away, one of them colliding with a passer-by and pinning him to the ground. As a crowd gathered around to enjoy the mayhem taking place, Yoshino hurried into one of the many narrow sidelanes that fed off the main street, and at its end, she stopped and looked up at the four-tiered sloping stone walls surrounding Ishida Castle.

At the castle entrance, a solitary guard was busy fanning himself to keep cool, oblivious to the trickle of artisans and merchants coming and going.

Yoshiaki had demanded Yoshino deal with Mitsunari's parents as retribution for the false information he provided, and at Yoshiaki's direction, she met with the *Ronin* he had first sent to Ishida Castle, who updated her on their findings. Yoshino had two objectives in mind, and it occurred to her she could achieve both at the same time; Yoshiaki would have his revenge, and she might finally put an end to the suspicions that plagued her that Mitsunari could be her child. Yoshino approached the guard and politely inquired if the lord was at home?

"What's it to you?" the guard replied gruffly.

"I have come a long way with news concerning the lord's family and must speak with him," said Yoshino.

"Have a look up there," the guard said, pointing to a blackened head impaled on a pole high above the gate and still picked at by the birds. "That is the fate that befell the last guard who let someone in to see the lord. We did not catch the assassin, but poor Yasuke here paid the price. You're not an assassin, are you?" he asked sneeringly.

"No, but what if what I say is true? And the lord cannot hear the important news concerning his family I bring I will wager that your head will soon be alongside that of your friend." Quickly realising he was out of his depth, the guard nervously called out to one of his companions. His companion wisely suggested that they let their captain decide and save both their necks, and Yoshino shortly found herself flanked by two Azai guards kneeling before Ishida Masatsugu, castellan of Ishida Castle.

Masatsugu sat with his wife Sadako and eldest son Masazumi in his living room, a gloomy, sparsely decorated room lacking any decoration to brighten it up, but it had excellent views of the dry, overgrown castle moat. Yoshino studied Masatsugu and noticed the hostility in his eyes as he returned her stare. She thought it odd that a lord, even a provincial one, would present himself to guests wearing soiled brown outer garments over a cheap cotton kimono. She noticed the chiselled features of his sunken but clean-shaved face, and the deep scar on the side of his head where his right ear should have been.

"You state you have news of my son?" Masatsugu asked.

"Yes. Your son has recently had his *genpuku* and has been given his adult name, Ishida Mitsunari. As is the custom, he has sworn fealty to his patron Lord Nobunaga."

"So, he still lives and serves our enemy, then?" Masatsugu replied. Yoshino thought to lessen the blow and explain Mitsunari's entrapment, as an unwilling spy was through no fault of his, whilst embellishing her role as his tutor and protector. She was aware of movement in the corner of her eye and looked at Masatsugu's eldest son, Masazumi, a gangly looking creature, constantly fidgeting as if uncomfortable. Next to him was his mother Sadako, who remained impassive and silent at her husband's side and, like her husband, also dressed plainly. But at least, they were clean.

Masatsugu looked at Yoshino and began stroking the scar of his missing ear.

"Do you want to know how this happened?" Masatsugu asked and without waiting for Yoshino's reply, he told his tale. He then spoke of a recent visit by two *Ronin,* also claiming to have news of his son and how, if he wanted to see him again, he was to comply with their anonymous masters' bidding. He gave serious thought to having them beheaded, but they warned him that should they fail to return, their master would immediately execute Sakichi. Masatsugu demanded to know what they wanted from him, but all they said was that they needed something of his that Sakichi would recognise to secure his son's cooperation. He gave the *Ronin* a *shaku-hachi* that had been in the family for generations and Sakichi would instantly recognise it, for he had practised on it for months. He also spoke of how the *Ronin* continued to quarrel and argue that the flute was not enough and how his rage grew. Finally, he reached for his *Tanto* knife and without hesitation sliced his right ear off, presenting it to the shocked *Ronin* in a clean white cloth, as an atonement for his *Haji* (shame).

Masatsugu angrily said to Yoshino that he should have let them kill his son. He knew his son would never become a warrior and contemptuously spoke of Sakichi's obsession with the womanly rituals of classical refinement.

"He was not like the other boys," said Masatsugu. "He was always teased for his womanly ways, and now you tell me he is a dishonourable spy." Yoshino tried to argue that his son's involvement in this intrigue was not of his choice.

"One always has a choice," Masatsugu snapped back. "A true warrior would have preferred to die than live such a dishonourable life." He described with pride his clan's direct lineage from the Miura clan, a cadet branch of the Azai, but they could also claim descent from the imperial Taira clan just as Nobunaga's clan does.

"And now you tell me he has also sworn allegiance to our enemy." Yoshino again attempted to defend Mitsunari, but with his patience wearing thin, Masatsugu cut Yoshino off in mid-sentence and rose to leave. Looking down at his wife Sadako, whose cheeks were now wet with tears, he said,

"I am sorry, Sadako, that we ever took him in. He is a disappointment." To Yoshino, he said, "I cannot say I am grateful for your news, but you are free to go," and left the room followed by Masazumi, who scurried after him. Sadako continued to sniffle and compose herself, and once the room was clear, she dismissed the guards and addressed Yoshino.

"I thank you for your news, but as you can see, my husband's mind is made up." With her mind preoccupied with something Masatsugu had said, Yoshino seemed to ignore what Sadako was saying.

'I am sorry, Sadako, we ever took him in.' What did he mean by that?

"Sadako, did you adopt Sakichi?" Yoshino bluntly asked.

"Yes. That is correct. My husband longed for a son to carry on the Ishida name."

"But you have your eldest son, Masazumi?"

"Masazumi is not a leader and is of ill health, and Masatsugu has no other family to carry on the name."

"May I ask how you came to adopt Sakichi?" Yoshino asked, deliberately referring to his childhood name.

"It was a strange event. Emissaries from the Takeda, Lord Shingen, approached us to consider adoption. They said one of his noted generals had just died in battle, leaving a son. The mother who had desired to follow her husband into the next world and could not bear to kill her son left him in the care of the local priest. Such was the spread of Shingen's tentacles he was aware of Masatsugu's dilemma for a suitable heir and proposed adoption would also cement our ties with the powerful Takeda clan." Memories of Chiyo telling her child had gone to a loving home now flooded back in Yoshino's mind, and she rued never asking if it was a boy or a girl.

"But Masazumi is still the rightful heir?" Yoshino asked.

"Yes, he still is. Although Masatsugu views him as a disappointment. Masazumi is no warrior, even though he pretends to be. He once confided that he was keen to abdicate the responsibility of being an heir in favour of his younger brother. The prospect of risking his life as clan leader was too much for him. Now, it is getting late, and I am sure you must be exhausted. You are welcome to stay the night here. As our guest, of course."

Yoshino knew the journey to Kai would be both long and arduous. Crossing the Kiso Mountains would take at least three days and a further two days to reach Kofu. She reconciled it would be better to rest up here and leave at first light. Thanking Sadako, Yoshino accepted her hospitality, and Sadako rose and bid Yoshino farewell, summoning a maidservant to prepare for suitable sleeping quarters. For such a small castle, most of the few rooms it had were large, but again sparsely furnished. Ishida Castle's function was neither strategic nor defensive. It was an outpost for Masatsugu to collect taxation revenues on behalf of his Lord Nagamasa from the trade route connecting the provinces of Omi and Mino via the local Ibi-gawa River crossing.

The only furnishing in Yoshino's sleeping quarters was a cotton quilted futon mattress stowed away in the room's corner and a solitary Andon lantern. Despite her exhaustion, she found it impossible to get to sleep. Her mind continued to dwell on her conversation with Sadako.

Chiyo must tell me. Yoshino thought. *She must. I need to know. But first I must kill Masatsugu and Sadako.*

Chapter Eleven

Last of the Ashikaga's
Autumn: The First Year of Tensho (1573)

The polished nightingale floors of the Nijo Palace sang out under the weight of Yoshiaki as he quickly made his way down the corridor towards one of several audience rooms. "Fujitaka where are you?" he shouted in a loud, frustrated voice. As he slid open the screen door to the audience room, the Shogun snapped at the retinue behind him.

"Find him," Yoshiaki ordered and took his seat in front of a four-panel paper screen with painted scenes of cypress trees against a backdrop of gold-leafed clouds. The painting by the famed painter Kano Eitoku was one of Yoshiaki's favourites and just one of the many that adorned the walls of the Nijo, courtesy of Nobunaga.

Despite the coolness of the morning, an agitated Yoshiaki sat fanning himself with a plain cedar fan, as if to cool his mounting frustration and anger. The black lacquered hat he wore, further annoyed him as its ties rubbed against his chin, and the stiffness of his heavy gold brocaded kimono further added to his discomfort and irritability. It was sometime later that his advisor, Hosokawa Fujitaka, finally entered. Anticipating an angry reception, Fujitaka prostrated himself at the Shogun's feet and made his excuses.

"So, you are finally here, Fujitaka," Yoshiaki said in a conciliatory tone.

"I have heard no further news from you since my return from the reconciliation meeting at Shoryuji castle, which I believe Nobunaga has now given to your son," said Yoshiaki sarcastically.

"My Lord, as you seem to have reached an accord with Lord Nobunaga, no developments require your urgent attention."

"Fool," Yoshiaki said, his anger now rising.

"I have no intention of coming to an accord with that fool. I want to know when Asakura Yoshikage will move against Nobunaga. Shingen's demise is an unfortunate setback, but not enough to change the play of the game. I still have support in Kyoto and as agreed, Nobunaga has returned his army to Gifu. Should he decide to attack us again, he must now endure a long march overland and try to cross the Ujigawa, which is now in flood and impassable."

A worried Fujitaka looked pensively at Yoshiaki. For generations, the Hosokawa clan has faithfully served the Ashikaga line, and Fujitaka was now concerned that Yoshiaki would end up destroying the very Shogunate he helped re-establish. Again, he attempted to counsel Yoshiaki against reigniting a confrontation with Nobunaga, but the Shogun would have none of it and insisted on finishing the game.

"Fujitaka, how are the arrangements progressing for our move to Makishima? There will never be a better time than now. At Makishima, I will be free to guide events." Fujitaka tried to protest, but Yoshiaki abruptly silenced him.

"Oh, be quiet, Fujitaka. You know as well as I do that the fortress at Makishima is impregnable. Should Nobunaga move against me, all I need to do is delay him long enough for Yoshikage and his coalition to move, then the trap is sprung."

"My Lord, what about the Nijo? Are you abandoning the palace?"

"Our generals Terasuke and Nagasuke will remain and hold the Nijo. If Nobunaga attacks, he will have to split his forces, which will also buy us more time. Now, listen carefully, send word to Yoshikage and Nagamasa that I will move before the end of the month, and you will, of course, not mention any of this to your son, will you?" It was the tone of that comment that made Fujitaka suspicious.

What if this is an elaborate trap? Set up for me. Fujitaka now thought.

"Another thing," Yoshiaki said, "it has not escaped my notice that our 'songbird' appears to have deliberately misinformed us." Fujitaka shuffled nervously.

"I also find it odd that the tutor I sent to monitor this brat has also provided no information. Am I to believe they are in league together? No matter. I have sent word to her to proceed with haste and eliminate the brat's parents at once."

Fujitaka later sat in his quarters preparing the inkstone to compose the coded messages he would send to Yoshikage and Nagamasa. He picked up the brush and hesitated, instead he stared at the blank mulberry paper laid out before him.

Is this part of the Shogun's plan to trap me? But how?

Fujitaka was aware Nobunaga used Yoshiaki to further his ambitions, but in this, he did not differ from any other Daimyo. Yoshiaki had made his dispute with Nobunaga personal and was now in grave danger of not only losing the Shogunate but his head. After which, Yoshiaki's sons and family would also be killed, putting an end to both the Ashikaga and Hosokawa clans.

If only he would listen to reason. Fujitaka again thought, but he knew better and wrote the required letter to Yoshikage and Nagamasa. When he had finished, he picked up another blank sheet of mulberry paper and penned another message, this time to Nobunaga. He would not betray Yoshiaki, but he would offer his allegiance to Nobunaga, and his service to the Ashikaga's would be over.

#

At the beginning of the midnight hour of the rat, Yoshino was still awake. The restlessness that had kept her awake had subsided, and she felt a wave of weariness threatening to overtake her. The implication, however slim that Mitsunari could be the child she gave up long ago, preyed on her mind. She needed more proof, but Yoshiaki's command for her to eliminate Mitsunari's parents threatened to throw her plans into chaos.

Masatsugu and Sadako mean nothing to me, but if he is my son, I would be killing the very people who have raised and nurtured him. If he is not my son, then I will have completed my duty and have no regrets. But if he is my son... I need to be sure; I need Chiyo to set the record straight.

Yoshino slept well into the hour of the tiger, just before dawn, and awoke at the sounds of nearby thunder and the heavy rain that shortly followed. She quickly gathered her belongings and slipped away unnoticed. Under the cover of darkness and driving rain, Yoshino left Ishida Castle to begin her journey to Kai.

Yoshiaki watched the sunrise from the uppermost balcony of Makishima Castle. He vigorously shook the lapel of his summer kimono to circulate the warm night air to cool his skin. The lack of even a slight breeze had meant an uncomfortable night. Below him, the murky and swollen Ujigawa river that ran alongside the castle had broken its banks. The recent heavy rains had raised the river's level and Yoshiaki watched the strong currents carry off the remains of trees felled by the floods. On the other side of the river, the lifeless white banners bearing the Kamon of flowering quinces of Nobunaga's army stood silent. Yoshiaki smiled in smug satisfaction. It was as he had expected; the river had stalled Nobunaga's advance, and he felt more confident in both his security and his plan.

Makishima was a formidable fortress, built by the powerful Makishima clan, and its castellan was one of Yoshiaki's magistrates who enthusiastically contributed its sizable garrison to Yoshiaki's war plan. A frontal assault on the castle was useless as the Ujigawa River blocked the castle's only approach, and the swampy waters of the surrounding Ogura-ike Lake protected the castle's other three sides. Yoshiaki saw the amassing Oda army on the other side of the river and revisited his plan.

It seems I was right about you, Fujitaka. How dare that fool Nobunaga try to insult my intelligence by saying he intercepted communication between me and Yoshikage? He even waved the letter you penned in my face, accusing me of going back on my word. Well, I wonder how he came by that letter, Fujitaka? No matter. I had the foresight to despatch a messenger directly to Yoshikage myself, and by now Yoshikage will have distributed my edict to the Takeda heir Katsuyori, as well as the Azai, Miyoshi and Mori. Not to mention the bonzes of the Ikko-Ikki. Together, we will put an end to the excesses of this fool Nobunaga.

Preoccupied in his thoughts, Yoshiaki had only just noticed the turn of events now developing on the Oda side of the Ujigawa, and his facial expression reflected his mood. A look of worry appeared over Yoshiaki's face as he watched a solitary mounted Oda Samurai wade into the roaring current of the river. With his eyes riveted to the lone rider, Yoshiaki watched the Samurai cross the raging waters to reach his side of the river. It was not long before the entire Oda army moved to emulate the lone rider's feat and began its crossing of the Ujigawa.

On the second day of the Makishima assault, at first light, at the start of the hour of the hare, a messenger arrived at Nobunaga's new campsite on the Makishima side of the Ujigawa. He delivered news of the Shogun's offer for a reconciliation, and as a measure of his good faith, the Shogun offered to send his eldest son Isshi Yoshitaka as a hostage. Nobunaga immediately summoned Hashiba Hideyoshi, Akechi Mitsuhide, and Niwa Nagahide for council to discuss the situation, only to fly into a rage when told Lord Mitsuhide had already left the camp earlier.

It was not until mid-morning around the hour of the dragon that Akechi Mitsuhide returned to Nobunaga's camp with a young boy under escort. The Shogun's son, Yoshitaka, who would have been only seven years of age, accompanied Mitsuhide into Nobunaga's command tent. *Sashimono* battle flags in their stands lined the walls of the tent, and Nobunaga, Hideyoshi and Nagahide in full armour squatted on their camp stools around a low table. A visibly distressed Yoshitaka rubbed his eyes to wipe away his tears and prostrated himself on the trampled grass and dirt floor before Nobunaga.

"So, young Yoshitaka, it would seem your father now proposes to use you as one of his '*Go*' pieces," said Nobunaga. Yoshitaka raised his head and looked up at Nobunaga through red inflamed eyes but remained silent. Pointing to a corner of the enclosure, Nobunaga told Yoshitaka to wait over there, but Mitsuhide, acting as if his prize might escape, dragged him over to the corner himself whilst calling out for one of the Ashigaru's outside to stand guard over him.

"Akechi, how is it that the Shogun has confidence in you to entrust his son to the camp of his enemy?" asked Nobunaga.

"My Lord, I have always strived to cultivate a good relationship with the Shogun that might one day prove useful. The Shogun advises me he has learnt the error of his ways and seeks reconciliation."

"Indeed," said Nobunaga, "how many more times must I trust the word of this snake? I think this time I will see his head on a stick. What he has done is entirely his fault."

"Forgive me, Lord, what you say is true," said Hideyoshi, interrupting. "But Makishima is about to fall, and should the Shogun be killed, whether, by assassination, suicide or execution, you will be held to blame. Is your legacy to be known as the Murderer of a Shogun?" Nobunaga growled and pointed his war fan accusingly at Hideyoshi but said nothing. Undeterred, Hideyoshi continued.

"Sire, you will recall the legacy of the Lord Miyoshi Nagayoshi, guardian of the respected Shogun Yoshiteru, who also is the elder brother of Yoshiaki. Nagayoshi also fought against and defeated Yoshiteru, but had the Shogun killed at the Nijo and found himself reviled all over the land as a traitor. As you know, not long after that, the power and influence of the Miyoshi crumbled."

Nobunaga, still growling, stood up and walked around the enclosure, deep in thought, continually slapping his war fan against his thigh. Finally, he stopped and addressed Hideyoshi.

"What you say makes sense, monkey, but unless I stop this now, Yoshiaki will always be a dagger at my back." Turning to Mitsuhide, Nobunaga said, "Seeing as you and the Shogun are on such good terms, tell him I will accept his unconditional surrender. He is to leave the castle before sunset and suggest to him he head for Wakae Castle. I am sure his brother-in-law, Miyoshi Yoshitsugu will welcome him with open arms, and the two of them can plot and scheme to their heart's content in far away in Kawachi until I deal with them. If there is to be no surrender, then we will attack at nightfall and I promise you this, every man, woman, and child, including the Shogun in Makishima, will be put to the sword." Mitsuhide bowed and excused himself, glancing sideways at Yoshitaka as he left the tent.

"I see you are surprised, monkey. If you want to find out what a rat is up to, send in another rat." Mitsuhide stopped outside the command tent and deliberated if he should despatch a messenger to Yoshiaki with Nobunaga's ultimatum or go himself. It crossed his mind there was a risk if he sent a messenger that Yoshiaki might be inclined to divulge to Nobunaga more than he should about their relationship, especially if he thought he could gain some advantage from it.

I would not put it past that fox to sacrifice me for better terms. No, I will go by myself.

Once again, Mitsuhide climbed the steep road leading to Makishima Castle alone. He wore his dark-green laced body armour and a white *Hachimaki* headband and stopped halfway up the road to tie a prepared flag to the scabbard of his Katana. As he approached the two large wooden castle gates before him, he waved the flag. Yoshiaki had given Mitsuhide a piece of cloth with two horizontal white bars on a black circle, the Mon of the Ashikaga Shoguns, to identify and signify safe passage to the bearer. He shouted to the guards on the castle ramparts, identifying himself, and demanded access to the Shogun to deliver a message. On his earlier visit, he collected the boy Yoshitaka outside the gates. This time, he would enter alone.

Mitsuhide cautiously entered through the gate into the courtyard and noticed Ashigaru milling around without weapons. Arquebuses and Naginata lay stacked in neat piles on the dirt floor of the castle compound.

They are completely unprepared. Most of them are not even wearing armour.

Escorted to the Shogun's quarters, Mitsuhide found Yoshiaki pacing the room in an agitated state. He wore a black and white patterned kimono, which had seen better days. Gone were the flamboyant and expensive robes that were his trademark. Mitsuhide was the first to speak.

"My Lord, I bring…" whereupon Yoshiaki interrupted, cutting him off mid-sentence.

"How is my son? Was he delivered safely?" Yoshiaki asked.

"I bring news from Nobunaga," and again, Yoshiaki interrupted.

"Yes, but what news of Yoshitaka?"

"Yoshitaka is safe, albeit for now," said Mitsuhide.

"What do you mean for now?" An exasperated Mitsuhide tried to continue.

"You had sent him as a hostage, therefore his safety depends on your conduct. Nobunaga is insisting you formally surrender by sunset today and exile yourself to the care of your brother-in-law, Miyoshi Yoshitsugu, at Wakae Castle, which he believes should be acceptable to you."

"I will do no such thing," a stunned Yoshiaki replied.

"You can tell him I am prepared to reconcile our differences and return to the Nijo. He has my son as a guarantee does, he not?"

"That might well be the case, my Lord, but Nobunaga is insistent on your exile to Kawachi. Do not underestimate his anger. Should you refuse, he will repeat what he did at the Enryaku-ji, and have every living thing within these walls put to the sword. You and your son's heads will look down from the prison gates of Kyoto for all to see."

131

"As for your Nijo Palace," Mitsuhide continued, "do you know it fell to Nobunaga's army without a single loss of life? Your brave generals, upon hearing of Nobunaga's approach, opened the gates and cravenly apologised for any misunderstanding." Yoshiaki appeared floored, but his mind was still razor-sharp.

"How could he possibly have got to Kyoto in such a brief time? And why wasn't I forewarned of this, Akechi?" Mitsuhide recognised the implicit accusation that he failed to warn the Shogun.

"My Lord, I was not privy to Nobunaga's' plans, but I later learned that as he had no faith in you keeping to the terms of your last reconciliation, he built a fleet of warships at Hikone on Lake Biwa in case he needed to move a large army quickly to Kyoto again. To divert attention, he had it rumoured he was planning to launch a coastal strike against the Asakura in North Omi next spring. None of his generals, including Hideyoshi or myself, knew the true reason." Yoshiaki stood silently, gazing down at the floor, and Mitsuhide continued to press home his reply.

"My Lord, you are in no position to win this battle. Your messages to Yoshikage were intercepted by Nobunaga's spies and no help is on the way. Should you resist, you and your son will die and the Ashikaga line with you, and you will have handed Nobunaga a glorious victory. Retire gracefully to Kawachi and watch developments. I will let you know when the moment is right, and you can emerge to resume your rightful position as Shogun."

The following day at mid-day at the beginning of the hour of the horse, Nobunaga and an honour guard of fifty mounted Oda Samurai in full battledress, including Mitsuhide, Hideyoshi and Nagahide assembled in two lines outside the gates of Makishima. The sun was now at its highest and the heat was making its presence felt when an Ashikaga Samurai walked through the open gate to announce the passage of the Shogun. Shortly after the Shogun, Yoshiaki walked through and stopped at the head of the Oda guard before him. Beads of sweat ran down his face, threatening to ruin the chalk makeup he wore. He kept up the pretence of his position to the very last by wearing his heavy gold brocaded overclothes, which were hardly appropriate for travelling in this heat.

As the Shogun passed between the lines of the Oda Samurai, each of them bowed one by one like an undulating wave. Yoshiaki looked up, his hand shielding his eyes from the glare of the sun as he looked for Nobunaga. Recognising the waterfowl plume atop a helmet, Yoshiaki walked over.

"Well, it has finally come to this," Yoshiaki said, summoning all the composure he could muster. "I see my son has not come to see me off."

Nobunaga remained silent astride his black Kiso stallion, which snorted loudly and stomped the dirt with its feet as if agitated. Nobunaga had forbidden the Shogun, the use of a horse and had insisted that all depart Makishima for Wakae on foot. Gathering his pride, Yoshiaki turned away from Nobunaga and began the long walk to Wakae. The rest of his retinue of wives, concubines and handmaids quickly followed. Deprived of their palanquins, the ladies wailed at the discomfort of walking on foot and once through the great Hinoki gates of Makishima fortress, several had already succumbed to the heat and remained where they fell. Yoshiaki turned and briefly paused just in time to see the Oda guard and Nobunaga enter the fort.

We are still in the middle game, fool. Yoshiaki thought.

Chapter Twelve

The Fall of two clans
Autumn: The First Year of Tensho (1573)

Nobunaga had gathered his five most important generals, Akechi Mitsuhide, Hashiba Hideyoshi, Niwa Nagahide, Shibata Katsuie and Maeda Toshiie, in the autumn room at Gifu's Inabayama Castle for a rare viewing of his acquisitions from the recent *Meibutsugari* (tea utensil hunt). On his orders, Hideyoshi had scoured the land to buy with force valuable tea utensils for Nobunaga's collection.

Nobunaga had all the screen doors in the autumn room opened to receive the morning sunshine and to experience the traditional viewing of the autumn foliage. Inabayama Castle, which sat atop Mount Inaba, afforded breathtaking views of the Nobi Plain and the Nagara River, which also served as the castle's moat. The view from the autumn room took in a colourful palette of vibrant red, orange and yellow leaves from the forests lining the mountain slopes, and it was, according to Nobunaga, the perfect backdrop for the occasion.

His generals were encouraged to get on their hands and knees and examine the Meibutsu from every conceivable angle, but not to touch. Hushed tones of amazement filled the room as individual items were identified. Mitsuhide was first to identify the famous *Tsukumo Nasu*, a rare imported Chinese ceramic tea container in the Nasu or eggplant shape, and for his efforts, he received a thunderous applause from Nobunaga. Hideyoshi, having learnt a little more about ceramics from Mitsunari, identified the three famous tea caddies, the *Hatsuhana*, *Nitta* and *Narashiba*, only to receive nodding approvals from his lord and encouragement for his interest. With the sun about to set, Nobunaga announced the meibutsu viewing at an end, and dismissed his generals, but called for Mitsuhide and Hideyoshi to stay behind.

"Hashiba, you may bring your new sandal bearer in," said Nobunaga. Hideyoshi left and returned with Mitsunari, whose eyes locked with Mitsuhide's. He noticed Mitsunari had changed since he last saw him. Gone was the lanky emotional boy that had fallen into his hands. The evidence of Mitsunari's training was there on show, for he carried himself with confidence, clutching the hilt of his Katana as it rested in his obi, his arms revealing the musculature of a seasoned warrior. The Akechi Lord now suspected what was coming next.

"You appear to have come a long way since our paths last crossed," said Mitsuhide, addressing Mitsunari. Hideyoshi's restraining hand on Mitsunari's shoulder halted his impulse to answer back.

"Mitsuhide, it would appear you and Mitsunari know each other?" Nobunaga boomed from across the room. The ability to think quickly on one's feet was a trait Mitsuhide excelled in.

Mitsunari's presence here can only mean Nobunaga knows about my involvement with Yoshiaki. No matter, I had prepared for this eventuality.

"Yes, my Lord, we have met. I enlisted the songbird here to spy on Hideyoshi for information I might pass on to the Shogun to cement my usefulness to him." Mitsuhide's stark admission took not only Nobunaga by surprise but also Hideyoshi and Mitsunari, who looked at each other to communicate their confusion.

Has the idiot just sentenced himself to death? thought Hideyoshi. A perfectly composed Mitsuhide continued.

"As I have said to you before, my Lord, it was always my intent to cultivate a useful relationship with the Shogun to facilitate your command, requiring me to find out what I could about his communications with Asakura Yoshikage. In short, a spy for you, my Lord."

Nobunaga rose and ambled over to the open screen doors and stood still, hands clasped behind his back, admiring nature's autumn vista. He breathed deeply and cleared his mind.

Hmm. I do recall getting Akechi to find out more about Yoshiaki's involvement with my brother-in-law, Nagamasa. As he was once a senior retainer of Asakura Yoshikage and then Yoshiaki before swearing allegiance to me. I remember thinking he could be useful.

"Why did you need to spy on Hideyoshi?" Nobunaga asked.

"Simply, my Lord, I don't trust him. Your pet monkey here makes a habit of drunkenness and womanising. He is privy to all our operational plans, and I held concerns that, in his carelessness, he would let slip things that are best-kept secret."

Hideyoshi's arm tensed, and his hand crept to the hilt of his Katana, a reaction that had got gone unnoticed by Nobunaga.

I believe the monkey's version, but his drinking and womanising ways must stop. Mitsuhide is not the first to have betrayed me. Matsunaga Hisahide and Katsuie have both betrayed me, yet I have pardoned them because they are useful, and I can control them as I will control Mitsuhide.

"Mitsuhide, how can I be sure your involvement with the meddling Yoshiaki is at an end? The nation has surely seen through this Shogun. I have absolved the citizens of Kyoto and Sakai of tax imposts, so they might rebuild with vigour. I have also removed the merchant checkpoint taxes levied by the Shogun to cover his expenses at the Nijo. Overall, I do not think the Shogun will be sorely missed." An angry Hideyoshi interjected.

"My Lord, should the Shogun feel betrayed by Lord Mitsuhide then he cannot present a risk to us."

"What had you in mind, Monkey?" Nobunaga asked, his curiosity piqued. Mitsuhide, sensing Hideyoshi, was up to something, interrupted.

"My lord, you have the Shogun's son as a hostage against any betrayal." Hideyoshi looked directly at Mitsuhide and argued.

"Yes, we have the Shogun's son as a hostage against betrayal by the Shogun, but not you," Hideyoshi said, looking towards Nobunaga before continuing.

"My Lord, If Lord Mitsuhide were to put an end to the boy's life, then Yoshiaki will no longer feel tempted to trust him," a shocked Mitsunari looked at him, horrified that his master could even contemplate such a thing. Nobunaga also looked at Hideyoshi, and his eyes narrowed as he thought.

I am seeing the monkey in a new light.

"Mitsuhide," Nobunaga shouted. "Take up the monkey's suggestion. I need to be sure I have your loyalty."

Yoshitaka's quarters were close to those of Nobunaga, and those responsible for protecting Nobunaga also guarded Yoshitaka against escape. It was well after dusk and into the hour of the dog when Mitsuhide approached Yoshitaka's rooms. Nobunaga had not yet retired for the night, so only one of Nobunaga's guards was on duty and readily accommodated Mitsuhide's orders to enter Yoshitaka's room. Sliding open the screen door, Mitsuhide silently stepped into Yoshitaka's room to find the boy awake and bent over his writing-table, composing a letter. Sensing someone else in the room, Yoshitaka turned to see Mitsuhide at the doorway and then resumed his attention to his writing. He heard the soft click of Mitsuhide's Katana as it was freed from its scabbard and turned his head towards the sound. At that moment, Yoshitaka's cleanly severed head fell onto the tatami mat floor and rolled away, leaving a bloody trail. His headless torso sprayed a fountain of blood onto the writing table and the letter he had composed disappeared beneath a pool of slowly congealing blood. Emotionless, Mitsuhide stooped to pick up a clean blank sheet of mulberry paper off the table and carefully wiped the blade of his Katana clean before finally returning to its scabbard. Sliding open the screen door, Mitsuhide stepped outside and called for the guard.

"I have eliminated the hostage. Inform Lord Nobunaga and see to it they clean the room up. Have the head made presentable and delivered to my quarters without delay." It was near midnight at the beginning of the hour of the rat that the same guard Mitsuhide had charged with taking care of Yoshitaka's corpse announced his arrival at Mitsuhide's quarters. Mitsuhide admitted the guard and resumed his seat at a low table whilst the guard placed a plain cedar box in front of him. Mitsuhide opened the lid to inspect the contents, and without the slightest remorse, he stared at the head of Yoshitaka. He reached into the sash of his kimono and withdrew the folded cloth Yoshiaki had given to him, the same one he used to gain access to Makishima, and covered Yoshitaka's taunting eyes. Closing the lid, he ordered the box delivered to Wakae Castle without delay.

#

It was the eighth month in the first year of Tensho, and the fortunes of the Oda clan since the death of Takeda Shingen's were in the ascendant. Hideyoshi, who now garrisoned at Fort Toragoze, prepared his army for another assault on

Odani Castle, the seat of Nobunaga's estranged brother-in-law, Azai Nagamasa, whilst Nobunaga was away campaigning against the Asakura in the north.

Late into the hour of the rooster just after sunset, Hideyoshi, and Mitsunari sat in Nobunaga's living room silently, drinking sake. They listened to the sound of heavy rain falling on the tiled roofs and the whistling of the wind as it blew through the castle eaves. Despite the weather, the screen doors to the living room were open to the elements, providing a refreshing and welcome relief from the warm night air. A troubled Mitsunari broke the silence by clearing his throat several times.

"You wish to say something, Mitsunari?" Hideyoshi said, detecting Mitsunari's agitation.

"Yes, I wanted to ask why you suggested to Nobunaga that they should execute the Shogun's son just to secure Lord Mitsuhide's loyalty."

"Songbird, Lord Mitsuhide's explanation did not ring true, and Lord Nobunaga knows it. Anyway, Lord Nobunaga had no intention of getting rid of him. With Yoshiaki out of the way, we need Mitsuhide's attention and his army to fight the wars ahead of us. Besides, by betraying Yoshiaki, we will not have to worry about Mitsuhide's involvement when the Shogun rebels again."

"But we had the Shogun's son as a hostage?" Mitsunari queried.

"Yes, we do. But Yoshiaki would not be the first lord to sacrifice his family for ambition. So, when Yoshiaki rebels again, Nobunaga will put him to death, anyway. Yoshitaka would die anyway, so his death may as well be of benefit to our cause."

Mitsunari frowned and thought to argue this logic when Hideyoshi pushed his bowl over to Mitsunari, reminding him of his status and his obligation to keep his master's bowl full. Mitsunari had just finished pouring the sake when the guard interrupted, announcing a visitor, Shibata Katsuie.

Still wet and looking bedraggled, Katsuie greeted Hideyoshi and invited himself to the table opposite Hideyoshi whilst Mitsunari poured drinks for both.

"Welcome back, Katsuie, how is our lord's campaign going?" Katsuie downed the sake down in one gulp before replying and then wiped his mouth with his sleeve.

"Lord Nobunaga launched an attack on the Asakura Fortress at Mount Yamada, north of Ozuku, with such overwhelming force that he took the fortress in a matter of hours. He then moved on in heavy rain to attack Asami Tsushima at nearby Yakeo Castle. Guess what? Tsushima lets Nobunaga in and surrenders with no loss of life. With the road back to Echizen now cut off, Nobunaga goaded Yoshikage to attack before he finds out Yamada and Yakeo had surrendered. And it worked. Yoshikage broke through with huge losses and retreated into Echizen with Nobunaga snapping at his heels. The lord now has his head, and the Asakura is finished."

Hideyoshi's eyes lit up and indicated for Mitsunari to keep refilling the bowls. The more he drank, the sadder he felt at not being there to take part in the victory, while Katsuie would burst into laughter and song as he told of his exploits in Echizen. In the end, Hideyoshi and Mitsunari both helped drag Katsuie to his sleeping quarters to sleep off the sake, leaving Mitsunari surprised that Hideyoshi was still standing, albeit a little unsteadily after matching Katsuie bowl for bowl.

Afterwards, Mitsunari assisted a now unsteady Hideyoshi to his quarters and left him to retire for the night when Hideyoshi's voice called him back. He turned to see Hideyoshi's smiling head poking out through the partially open door.

"Songbird, have you ever killed before?" Hideyoshi asked.

Without waiting for Mitsunari's reply, Hideyoshi continued.

"It's time for your first battle. You will be in the vanguard with me when we take Odani," and Hideyoshi shut his door. Mitsunari returned to quarters with Hideyoshi's words echoing in his mind.

Have you ever killed before? Memories of *Jiko* descending and decapitating the poor wretch of a criminal once again haunted him. He shuddered, and with each step he took, he relived being the instrument of the wretch's death.

Nobunaga had returned to Toragoze, and Hideyoshi was keen to boast about his success in peeling off one of Nagamasa's principal Samurai retainers to defect.

"How do you do it, Monkey?" Nobunaga said, chuckling before adding, "it certainly wasn't because of your good looks, eh?"

"My Lord, I have outside a senior retainer of Nagamasa's father, Azai Hisamasa."

"I know who Hisamasa is, Monkey?" Nobunaga snapped back.

"My apologies, Lord, the retainer's name is Hineo Takayoshi and has valuable knowledge of the layout of Odani Castle."

"Bring him in then," said Nobunaga. A smiling Takayoshi entered the room and knelt before lord Nobunaga, who promptly turned away and looked at Hideyoshi.

"Monkey, ask your new friend here to tell me why I should not execute such a disloyal retainer such as himself?" Hideyoshi, now clearly worried, explained Takayoshi's inside knowledge would be invaluable for the upcoming assault on Odani.

"Monkey, if information was all I needed, I would have this traitor tortured and get it out of him, anyway," Nobunaga said. Although Takayoshi was in his fifties with a shrivelled weathered face and white hair, he had the physique and athleticism of men half his age. He had dedicated his life to the service of his lord and feared a wasted life more than he did death. Nobunaga's accusation shamed him, and the tone of his voice showed it.

"My Lord," Takayoshi spoke out, "is it wrong for a Samurai to want to leave his master's service because his master is vain, lacking in honour, and thinks only of himself? I have served Lord Hisamasa since my coming-of-age, and he shamed me by refusing to grant my request to leave. Age, it seems, has taken his reason, for it was he who convinced his son Nagamasa to side with the Asakura over his allegiance to you. He and Nagamasa are leading our clan to destruction, and if I am so wrong lord, then order me to commit seppuku and I will die knowing I have upheld the values of Bushido." Takayoshi's outburst surprised Nobunaga and made him pause his thoughts.

"Yes, Takayoshi, Hisamasa, and my brother-in-law are all those things, but a vassal's loyalty is sacred and if need be, you must follow your master into the void," said Nobunaga.

"My Lord," said Hideyoshi, raising his voice. "What you say is true, but Takayoshi did not betray his master. He asked to be dismissed, but Hisamasa refused. If a Samurai swears allegiance to a new Lord, does it also make him a traitor?"

"If his lord dies, then he is free to seek another master," Nobunaga snapped back.

"Did not the Lords Mitsuhide and Katsuie serve other masters, and they did not die?" Hideyoshi replied carelessly.

"Careful, Monkey, you are in dangerous territory daring to lecture your lord, but I will concede there is perhaps something in what you say." Nobunaga turned to face Takayoshi and again locked his eyes with his.

"Tell me, Takayoshi, that you will swear fealty to me, and I will accept you as one of my retainers." Overjoyed, Hineo Takayoshi at once prostrated himself before Nobunaga and swore an oath of fealty. He then requested paper and ink to explain the Odani Castle layout and the best ways to conduct an assault. Takayoshi crudely drew a diagram explaining the construction of Odani was based on a series of terraced fortified compounds occupying the entire Odaniyama mountain ridge, and a huge dry moat separates the castle complex into two principal parts, the Komaru, and the Kyogokumaru. Lord Nagamasa occupied the Komaru compound, and his father Hisamasa occupied the Kyogokumaru, which was also the weakest point as it was the least defended.

It was late into the hour of the rat and well after midnight, when Hideyoshi led his vanguard of five thousand, in heavy rain, up the steep hill of Odaniyama Mountain to attack the Kyogokumaru. Mitsunari, unaccustomed to wearing armour, wore a style known as *Tameshi gusoku,* which used thick iron and steel plates instead of the usual thin iron strips to make them more resilient to the bullets of the enemy matchlocks. Like Hideyoshi, he found the armour cumbersome and restrictive, but he also knew the damage a musket ball could cause.

Nagamasa was not yet aware of Yoshikage's defeat or the fact his nearby forts had recently surrendered, nor was he expecting a direct assault on Odani. Hideyoshi's assault on the Kyogokumaru had taken him by surprise. Hideyoshi easily penetrated the under-manned garrison of the Kyogokumaru and quickly overwhelmed it. Mitsunari followed close behind Hideyoshi, nervously wielding *Jiko,* slashing and parrying, not knowing or caring who he killed or maimed.

Hideyoshi and Mitsunari had reached the external stairs leading to the Kyogokumaru citadel with little opposition, where Hideyoshi instructed Mitsunari to search the rooms on the lower floors whilst he would ascend and search the upper floors. Mitsunari, accompanied by several Oda Samurai, broke their way through several screen doors as they searched the rooms adjoining the corridor on the bottom floor. He halted when he came across the retired lord of the Azai clan, Hisamasa, alone in his room, preparing himself for suicide. The old man looked solemnly at Mitsunari and murmured.

"Young man, my time on this earth is over. Would you begrudge an old man the dignity of his death? Would you serve as my Kaishaku?" The seppuku ritual was not new to Mitsunari, for it had been part of his martial training, but now it was real, and he had to face it. His concern was, could he, do it? Dutifully, Mitsunari nodded, for he had no choice. To refuse would bring eternal dishonour and shame.

Hisamasa resumed his position at a low table and dropped the shoulder of his kimono, exposing his bare torso. He reached for the Tanto that he had prepared by wrapping it in clean white paper to prevent the blade from slipping during the cut. Without hesitation or any warning, Hisamasa thrust the tanto into his abdomen and performed the single line cut of the *ichimonji-bara* across his abdomen, followed by a second vertical cut from the pit of the stomach to below the navel. His eyes bulged in agony, and he looked at Mitsunari, pleading for relief, but Mitsunari, sword in hand, remained frozen. It was at that moment Hideyoshi had entered the room and within three paces took aim, struck at Hisamasa's neck, severing the head. Hideyoshi once again calmingly gripped Mitsunari's shoulder and ordered him to pick up the head and follow him.

When news reached Nagamasa that they had overrun the Kyogokumaru; he ordered the burning of the Komaru and upon seeing the fires, Nobunaga's forces halted their advance as the quickly spreading flames reached the outer buildings. Hideyoshi too watched the fires from the front lines. He had Hisamasa's head put on an Ashigaru's halberd and had it waved at the Komaru defenders to intimidate them. Finally, accepting imminent defeat, Nagamasa despatched a messenger to Nobunaga requesting safe passage for his wife, Lady Oichi, and their three daughters. He and his retainers would commit seppuku. Nagamasa expected Nobunaga's favourable response, for he doubted he would allow his sister and nieces to be killed. As expected, Oichi and her children walked out of the burning Komaru into the waiting Oda army. Rumours later abounded among the townsfolk that, amid the smoke and flames of the Komaru, a group of beautiful *Tennin* (angels) were seen to fly out of the gates of Odani.

Nobunaga wasted no time in securing the safety of his sister and nieces. Katsuie was ordered to escort them to safety at Gifu while Hideyoshi launched the final assault on the Komaru before the flames consumed the citadel. Mitsunari was instructed to remain behind to guard Hideyoshi's rear. In truth, Hideyoshi was worried Mitsunari might shame himself before others in battle.

Accompanied by fifty seasoned fighters, Hideyoshi broke into the citadel and quickly located the Azai Lords' quarters. It was a ferocious fight, and less than half of Hideyoshi's men made it to Nagamasa's quarters. The Azai Lord was already dead, having disembowelled himself along with his three other retainers. Three heads lay to the sides of their bodies, the fourth body, being Lord Kaishaku's, was not decapitated. Hideyoshi examined Kaishaku and, noticing he had completed the *ichimonji-bara* unassisted, stood to attention and reverently bowed. A valiant adversary who had completed his last act of service to his lord and died in terrible agony. Hideyoshi had the heads of Nagamasa, and his father sent them to Nobunaga for viewing.

Back at Toragoze, Hideyoshi took a late evening meal in his quarters with Mitsunari, who attended to the pouring of sake. Wiping his mouth, Hideyoshi looked directly at Mitsunari and said, "I once asked if you had killed before and recall not getting an answer."

"Yes, I have killed," Mitsunari said. "I was once tricked into killing a common criminal who, under sentence of death, was going to die anyway, possibly, in a more horrible manner than anything I would inflict upon him. I convinced myself it was a question of duty, and I was dispensing justice no more, no less, but it still bothers me." Hideyoshi reached and took another sip from his bowl before replying.

"But I saw you kill and maim many in our attack on the Kyogokumaru. How did you feel about that? You were not afraid of death." Mitsunari paused and thought for a moment before refilling Hideyoshi's bowl.

"I felt nothing, I reacted. I did what they trained me to do, but when I saw the old lord, his eyes pleading for me to end his suffering, I just couldn't bring myself to do it."

"You know Mitsunari," said Hideyoshi, slurping up another bowl of sake.

"A true warrior serves his lord's cause, and only kills to protect, and end suffering. Let me tell you something. Before I entered and ended Hisamasa's suffering, I had searched the floors above and discovered Hisamasa's wife, the lady Ono-dono, silently kneeling on the floor with her back to me. I spoke to her and, receiving no reply, moved closer and noticed she was sitting in a large pool of congealing blood. In front of her was a low table upon which lay the bloodied remains of her fingers she had cut off. She was barely still alive, her face devoid of makeup was ashen white and her eyes, oh, those eyes, blazed hatred and defiance. She had tried to bleed herself to death and could have been saved, but she too would die one way or another, as it was her duty. So, I took to relieving her of any further suffering and decapitated her. Now, pour me another drink, then I shall retire. I am summoned to Gifu, and we leave at first light."

#

143

The autumn rains had persisted for much of the day, but by the time Hideyoshi arrived at Inabayama Castle, the dark grey clouds were gradually breaking up, revealing patches of blue sky. Hideyoshi entered Nobunaga's living room and took his position along with Akechi Mitsuhide, Niwa Nagahide, Shibata Katsuie and Maeda Toshiie in front of Nobunaga. Mitsunari, along with the other servants and retainers, waited outside.

With a beaming smile, Nobunaga announced the next stage of his campaign to crush the Miyoshi before taking on Shingen's successor, his son Takeda Katsuyori. Nobunaga's words aroused Mitsuhide's curiosity, and he chose his words carefully.

"Is not the former Shogun under Miyoshi protection?" asked Mitsuhide.

"You know damn well he is Mitsuhide," Nobunaga replied, "I must deal first with Miyoshi Yoshitsugu. If Katsuyori is anything like his father, I do not want this Miyoshi thorn in my foot distracting me." Nobunaga clapped his hands to break off the conversation and summoned the scribes to come in. Today, he was to announce the customary distribution of rewards and had the two scribes unravel a long roll of blank mulberry paper. The scribes took their places alongside their ink tables, ready to write Nobunaga's dictates.

Nobunaga looked around the room. He liked to study the faces and body language of the candidates before announcing his decisions. "Let it be recorded that Lord Akechi Mitsuhide is awarded the province of Tamba together with a stipend of 100,000 koku. Let it also be recorded that Shibata Katsuie is awarded the province of Echizen. He will take up residence at Kitanosho Castle along with my sister Oichi and her three daughters." Instructing the scribes not to write for a moment, he continued, "you can have her back again, Katsuie, and get her off my hands." On Nobunaga's clap, the scribes resumed their writing. "Let it be recorded that Hashiba Hideyoshi is given all the Azai lands held by Nagamasa and a stipend of 180,000 koku."

So, a peasant is worth more than I am, Mitsuhide thought as he glared at Hideyoshi.

With the distribution ceremony finished and everyone dismissed, Nobunaga had Hideyoshi secretly recalled.

"Monkey, with the Azai clan finished, I expect you to take up residence at Odani and protect my flank."

"My Lord, you say the Azai clan is now finished, but I believe Nagamasa had a son and heir, although I am told he is only ten years old. Will you now adopt him and raise him as one of your own?"

"Yes, Monkey, you are astute. I have indeed promised Lady Oichi that the young Manpukumaru will be adopted and raised as one of my sons. She had him sent away to Edo just before the assault on Odani, to be cared for by the priests at the Yogo temple." Nobunaga got up and walked over to the screen door, pulling it back slightly to check on the weather. He felt an icy wind on his cheeks and shut the door. Turning to Hideyoshi, he said, "I want you to leave for Yogo immediately. Take as many men as you need."

Hideyoshi, anticipating his lord's meaning, asked, "Do you want me to return him to you here at Inabayama?"

"No, Monkey, I want you to find him and behead him." Startled, Hideyoshi thought Nobunaga was making a jest and again repeated his question.

"I see you are confused, Monkey. Let me make it clear, I want Manpukumaru executed, and not one word of this is to reach his mother, Lady Oichi. See that any witnesses to this event are also killed. Do you understand now?" Hideyoshi silently nodded and bowed.

"Monkey, I have sent the heads of Nagamasa and Hisamasa to Kyoto for display. When the citizenry has finished with them, have them lacquered and gilded, and returned to me. Now, I must be off to visit Oichi and tell her the good news she is to be reunited with her former husband, Shibata Katsuie."

145

Chapter Thirteen

Masako

Autumn/Winter: First year of Tensho (1573)

It was late autumn when Yoshino secretly set out for Kofu, Takeda Shingen's capital in Kai province. Despite having left under cover of darkness and relentless rain, it was a journey that should have taken only three days, but it took closer to five. Early snow had fallen across the Kiso Mountain ranges, and the heavily forested slopes soon became snowbound and impassable.

Yoshino made progress by keeping to the long-established woodcutter trails that crossed the ranges, but wind squalls and driving snow forced her to shelter under a canopy of low-lying pine branches to await an improvement in the weather. It was several hours later that the wind finally abated, and Yoshino moved from her position. She eventually broke free of the dense forest and deep snowdrifts to reach the snow carpeted clearing that abutted one of the many meanders of the Kiso River. At this bend in the river, the Kiso ran fast but also shallow, and Yoshino attempted to cross its icy waters. She gathered up her damp winter kimono and held her straw sandals as she slowly waded across her numb feet, seeking a firm footing among the loose stones of the river floor. Once across, she strained to see signs of her path ahead amongst the deep carpet of snow covering the land but noticed in the distance the smoke of a checkpoint manned by soldiers.

Why is there a checkpoint here? This trail is no trade route. Are they looking for someone or something? She crept closer. *Three guards standing around a brazier. No shelter was erected. Who are they looking for? The mon of four diamonds on the soldier tells me they are Takeda. That must mean I have crossed into Shinano.*

Yoshino thought about bypassing the checkpoint, but that meant more treks through the forest and in this weather, a greater risk of getting lost. Tightening the chin straps of her *Amigasa* straw hat, she brazened it out and passed through the checkpoint.

As Yoshino approached, one of the Takeda Samurai, warming his hands over a brazier, called out, "Halt, take off your hat, and let's have a good look at you." Yoshino obeyed and removed her *Amigasa*, shaking her head to allow her hair to cascade down. The Samurai, who had been expecting a man, and clearly startled, called his two companions over for a look, and despite the strong wind and heavy snow, they stood transfixed, ogling at Yoshino. Against the noise of the wind, Yoshino shouted out her intentions to pass through and reach Kofu.

"Now, why would a woman be out travelling in this weather and dressed as a man?" the Samurai responded whilst pointing to the Wakizashi resting in her Obi. Yoshino, who was quickly becoming annoyed, snapped back that she too was Samurai, and not some peasant, to be intimidated.

"Oh, it's respect you want, is it?" one of the other guards sneered before breaking out laughing and making a lunge towards her with his arms outstretched, intent on grabbing her. Yoshino easily sidestepped his lunge and with blinding speed slashed at the gropers neck with her Wakizashi. A spray of blood caught her in the face, and his head fell to her feet. The other two stunned Samurai were slow to react and clumsily slashed at Yoshino with their swords. She easily parried both strikes and stepped to one side, reversing her sword, and struck one Samurai across the thigh, feeling the cut stop at his bone. He dropped to the ground, grimacing in pain. Blood spurted from the severed artery, which rapidly pooled at his feet. The remaining Samurai lunged at Yoshino with his sword, but his strike went wild, allowing her to follow through with a strike to the neck, nearly decapitating him.

Yoshino returned her attention to the wounded Samurai, still clutching his leg and yelling curses. She grabbed him by his topknot and pulled his head back. Her sword cut through his throat, severing his head, and then threw it into the snow. The Samurai she had wounded earlier writhed on the ground before her, clutching the wound in his neck. Yoshino calmly looked into his terror-stricken eyes and with the tip of her Wakizashi, she lifted one of the lamellar armour plates of his cuirass body armour and smiled as she plunged the tip of her sword into his heart.

147

Yoshino shook the blood off her sword, and, with handfuls of snow, she wiped the blade clean before returning to its scabbard. She used more snow to wipe the blood from her face and extinguish the brazier. The heavy snow and wind gusts made it difficult to see ahead, but she could just make out the edge of the forest beyond the checkpoint and the road she was to follow. Yoshino replaced her *Amigasa* hat and securely tied the cords tightly against her chin, then made her way towards the woods. She paused and glanced back, satisfied the settling snow would soon cover the evidence of what happened.

It will not be long before the guards are missed, and once the snow lifts, they will send out a search party. I must stay in the woods away from the road, but I need shelter.

She knew the area well enough and how to find one of the many woodcutter huts in the hills around these parts. She would find shelter first and wait until the weather lifted. Then, if she could cross the Kita Mountains ahead of her, she would reach Kai province and her destination, Kofu.

A day and a night had passed before the foul weather eased enough to continue travel, and at first light, Yoshino left the shelter of the woodcutter's hut. The wind had died down and some patchy light snow continued to fall, but the biggest concern was the deep snow hindering her progress towards the Kita Mountains. Yoshino eventually cleared the densely forested slopes of the Kita Ranges and emerged to find the snow had stopped and looked up to see patches of blue sky appearing. She descended into the valley of the Kofu Basin and basked in the welcome warmth of the emerging sunshine.

It was mid-morning and well into the hour of the snake when Yoshino again approached a group of Takeda Samurai who were manning the checkpoint guarding the approaches to the castle town of Kofu. Keeping her hat on, she walked up to one of the Samurai manning the barrier and withdrew from her Obi a small silver token to show the guard. The Samurai looked at the token and noticed its inscription. The characters read *Shin-Gen,* and he immediately bowed.

"Let him pass," he shouted to the other guards. "He has the lord's seal. Escort him to the palace."

#

At Tsutsujigasaki Yakata Palace, Yoshino received fresh clothes to change into and waited in one of the palace's living rooms for Lady Mochizuki Chiyo. She inspected some of the many ink monochrome paintings of waterfalls and rocks that decorated the room and, out of curiosity, slid open an elaborate screen door of painted white peony flowers. Before her lay an expansive view over the Kofu Valley and the snow-capped mountains that surrounded Kofu. Directly ahead, beyond the mountain ranges, lay the towering snow-capped peaks of Mount Fujiyama.

The sudden arrival of Lady Mochizuki Chiyo interrupted Yoshino's admiration of the view. Chiyo shuffled into the room wearing a vivid blue heavyweight silk kimono that was unusually long and trailed behind her. She knelt at Yoshino's side and adjusted her loosely pinned long black hair.

"What do we call you these days? Yumiko, Yoshino, or something else, perhaps?" Chiyo said in a soft tone.

"Yoshino will do," Yoshino replied. Chiyo pointed to the screen door Yoshino had opened and commented,

"Seeing as the weather and view are perfect today, let us fully open the doors and enjoy the view, for we have much to discuss." As they moved towards the doorway, Chiyo called out for refreshments and Yoshino began a debriefing of her latest contract with the Shogun to eliminate the castellan of Ishida Castle.

"You should know, I failed to complete the assigned contract," Yoshino said.

"Was your failure deliberate or unintentional?" asked Chiyo.

"Deliberate," Yoshino casually replied.

"Then, you must accept the consequences of your actions. However, I doubt any repercussions will ensue considering the Shogun is in exile and has limited ability to act."

Yoshino looked at Chiyo and said, "I should say I paused my contract depending on the information you will supply me." Yoshino savoured one of the sweet-bean paste dumplings on the table in front of her and continued.

"My Lady, I know I owe you, my life. You rescued me from the gutter, took me in and gave purpose to my life. I am what you moulded me to be, but I have a past, and I cannot recall it. I need to know about my parents and the name of the man who raped me."

"And if I tell you his name, what will you do?" Chiyo said. Still gazing out at Mount Fujiyama, Yoshino softly replied,

"Kill him, of course." Chiyo looked carefully at Yoshino. She sat erect and tense like a coiled spring waiting for release, and through her watery eyes, Chiyo saw the inner pain of her suffering.

"My dear, it seems only yesterday when your broken body, soon with child was, brought here. I looked into your eyes, into your very soul, and saw a desire to live. I knew then you would not only survive but thrive, for I needed someone like you. You must forgo any ideas of revenge. A lot has happened since you have been away, and with Lord Shingen's death, I fear I will have to disband this Shinobi network that Shingen and I painstakingly set up."

"What about his son, Katsuyori? Will he not want to continue his father's work?" Yoshino asked. Chiyo glanced up and looked out as if drawn to Fujiyama's magnetism before replying.

"Katsuyori is now head of the Takeda clan, and their future rides on his shoulders. He is a skilled and brave fighter, but is brash and headstrong. He lacks the cunning and the strategic skills that made his father both feared and respected throughout the land. Shingen sought knowledge and used it for his people's benefit. He astutely adopted many of the ancient treatises of war and was a master tactician and just ruler. He was undoubtedly cruel, but he was always fair. Katsuyori has no time for the old ways, and, like Nobunaga, he believes power comes from the end of a sword. With Katsuyori at the helm, the Takeda are doomed. He has no use for me and I for him." Chiyo picked up one of the sweet-bean paste dumplings and stared at it for a while, allowing her mind to drift to another place before replacing it on the plate untouched.

"The man who raped you is Hajikano Masatsugu. He was one of Shingen's favoured generals, and the lord was distraught when he found out what Masatsugu had done. Not out of any empathy for you, you understand, but because it required him to punish Masatsugu for a capital crime and lose a valuable general. Shingen's laws proscribed death as the punishment for rape, and as clan leader, he must dispense justice equally to Samurai and peasant alike. The lord found himself torn between ordering Masatsugu to commit seppuku or having him executed. In the end, he merely admonished Masatsugu for his drunkenness and debauchery. He accepted his defence that too much sake caused the crime and had him exiled to the nearby Daizenji Temple, where he shaved his head and took the priesthood for an undetermined period as penance. My understanding is, he is still there."

"Why are you telling me this now?" Yoshino replied.

"You wanted vengeance, did you not?"

"That is not an answer," Yoshino remonstrated before adding, "what about my parents? What became of them?"

"As far as I can gather, they were wealthy merchants from Sakai who fell on tough times after fleeing Sakai from Nobunaga's onslaught. Masatsugu would frequently visit them here in Kofu after his regular drinking sessions and pay them."

"What do you mean, pay them?" Chiyo frowned.

"For you, of course. Masatsugu would visit frequently. One night, your mother had enough, it seemed, and attacked him with a knife, prompting Masatsugu to draw his sword and cut your mother in two. Your father was spared, but the next day he killed himself by drowning in the river."

"Why is it I have no memory of this?" a confused Yoshino asked.

"My dear, do you not remember your Kunoichi training? You were taught how to administer a certain potion that would induce amnesia, but it is not without risk. Throughout your confinement, your rage grew, and you became more hysterical. The physicians who attended you warned that your body and mind were fighting at the expense of the unborn child in your womb. We had even considered killing you to save your child, but as a last measure, you were given the amnesia potion and you slept for four days before waking. It is Buddha's mercy that you were saved from the pain of recall."

"Will I ever remember?" Yoshino pleaded.

"To my knowledge, no one who has had the potion has ever recovered their memories."

"All this makes little sense. Why then was Masatsugu not held accountable for the slaying of my mother?"

"Child, think. Why would Shingen execute a loyal retainer for paying for the services of a prostitute and for killing one of the merchant classes for attacking him?" Chiyo's logic was obvious, but it did not help. Yoshino broke down distraught and sobbed and leaned forward, low enough to just touch the floor in front of her. Her tears fell onto the polished floor, beading like pearls on its surface. She heard a door slide open and the soft, comforting voice of someone calling out to her. And looked up to see the smiling features of a young woman. She had a kind face, she thought, and her long raven black hair hung loosely around her shoulders.

"My name is Hojo Masako. I am sorry to see you are so distressed." Yoshino sniffled and tried to regain her composure. She looked around with red puffy eyes, expecting to see Chiyo, but there was no sign of her. Masako asked if she needed anything, but Yoshino only asked where Chiyo had gone.

"Who was it you were talking about, Masako again asked inquisitively?"

"The Lady Mochizuki Chiyo, who was here just a few moments ago," replied Yoshino.

"I am sorry, but I do not know of any other guest here, save you." Yoshino had regained enough of her composure to suspect something was amiss and knew there had to be a purpose to this charade. For the moment, she would keep quiet and play along.

"My apologies, Masako. It is just I had arrived here earlier to speak to the Lady Mochizuki Chiyo, and a servant escorted me to this room to meet with her. It was the same servant who had just brought in these refreshments," Yoshino said, pointing to the low table of plated sweet bean paste dumplings.

"The palace guards informed me earlier that a visitor had arrived bearing the *Shin-Gen* token. It is a token given only to those considered important, so I gave instructions to give you a warm change of clothes and escorted here to be supplied with refreshments. Forgive me, but I feel I must repeat I do not know of this Lady Mochizuki Chiyo," said Masako. Yoshino knew pursuing this would get no further.

Why does she deny Chiyo's existence? I must find out.

"Forgive me, Masako, I have been unwell. I think my mind must be playing tricks on me."

"May I now ask who my guest is?" said Masako. Yoshino paused to consider. She certainly would not tell the complete story about being a Kunoichi in Chiyo's network.

"Yes, of course, I am sorry. My name is Kusumoto Yoshino. I am, or rather I was, physician to the Lord of Kai, Takeda Shingen."

"But you seem to be so young to be a physician."

"My father was also a physician to the lord, and I learnt his craft from an early age."

"Yes, it is sad about the lord's death. My husband tells me news of his death was kept secret for some time. One of his generals donned Lord Shingen's armour and pretended to be Shingen as he led the army home to Kai."

"Forgive me. You said your husband knew about this deception?" Yoshino asked.

"Yes, my husband is Lord Katsuyori, Lord Shingen's son and now the ruler of the Takeda clan." Yoshino's mind raced.

What am I to do? Katsuyori will not remember me as one of his father's physicians.

It was as if Masako pre-empted Yoshinos' dilemma for her explanation of Katsuyori's life restored her cover story. Masako added that Katsuyori, as the fourth son of Shingen, had spent most of his life in far off Shinano province, away from his father and isolated from the Takeda court. He succeeded his mother, one of Shingen's favourite concubines and a princess of Suwa province, as the new lord of Suwa. It was not until his stepbrother and Shingen's heir, Yoshinobu, committed suicide for plotting against his father that Katsuyori returned to Kai to become Shingens' heir.

"Yoshino, we must get to know each other better," said Masako. "It would honour me if you would consent to stay awhile. I already have your quarters prepared and look forward to continuing our discussion when you are feeling more refreshed."

Yoshino later retired to her assigned quarters to find her meagre belongings and her short sword neatly laid out on the rolled-out futon, along with several changes of clothes. On the headrest lay a neatly folded sheet of mulberry paper and unfolding it she read a letter from Mochizuki Chiyo.

By the time you read this, I will have been long gone. With Shingen's death, my time here is finished. I do not regret taking you in and moulding you. Out of all my pupils, you alone held the most potential. What is done is done, and we cannot undo the past? You need to decide to embrace a future or live in the past. Take care of Lady Masako, for both you and she are the same.

Mochizuki Chiyo

Yoshino stared at the letter. *So, she was here. I did not imagine it. Why did Masako lie? Why the charade?* She felt cheated, crumpled the letter, and discarded it.

To hell with you. I came here for answers, I still do not know what became of my child. I will stay and seek this Daizenji Temple and Masatsugu.

Yoshino's time at Tsutsujigasaki Yakata palace went quickly. The passing weeks soon led into months, and Yoshino and Masako grew closer by the day. Yoshino was a woman in her early thirties and Masako, a much younger woman of only nineteen, but the two became as close as sisters until one day.

When the long winter passed into spring and the blossoming of the Sakura had ended, summer enticed Yoshino and Masako to visit Lake Kawaguchiko, near Mt Fuji, and immerse themselves in the sacred waters of the goddess Asamano-Okami. Kawaguchiko was a day's ride out of Kofu, and soon after daybreak at the start of the hour of the dragon, Masako led a contingent of fifty Takeda Samurai towards Kawaguchi Asama Shrine near the lake. Yoshino and several maids rode at the rear.

It was early summer, and the cooling westerly winds blowing in from Biwako, together with the warm sunshine, made the excursion even more pleasant. It was well after noon into the hour of the sheep when Masako and Yoshino arrived at the home of the Asama shrine's priest. Eager to receive guests and their donations the Kannushi-priest instructed the shrine maidens in their distinctive red and white livery to accommodate the Samurai and the horses in the stables and prepare quarters for the Takeda Lord's wife and servants at the nearby Asamano-Okami shrine.

The priest escorted Yoshino and Masako along a pathway lined with ancient cedars and through a large red Torii gate to the shrine of Asamano-Okami, the goddess of volcanoes. For eons, the shrine had harnessed the power of Asamano-Okami to quell the once violent eruptions of Fujiyama and bring calm to the land. The hot springs at Kawaguchiko, whilst renowned for their curative effects, to bathe in its waters, were seen as an act of devotion to the goddess. Legend has it an injured white heron found the springs at Kawaguchiko and flew here to the springs every day until it completely cured its injured leg.

As the sun dipped below the horizon, an eerie silence descended on the calm waters of Kawaguchiko, broken only by a chorus of cicada calls. Even in the moonlight, the bubbles of the hot springs were visible, quietly breaking the water's surface amid the mists of warm air that rose from its waters.

Yoshino had disrobed and sat luxuriating in the spring's warm waters when Masako appeared. Her heart fluttered as Masako shed her clothes and entered the warm waters alongside her. She never gave it much thought before, but now she admired Masako's slender youthful body and wondered to herself was this admiration or desire. She focussed on Masako's beautiful bosom with erect nipples, her oval face and deep brown eyes. The more she looked, the more desire she felt. There were other bathers in the waters immersing themselves in spiritual submission to Asamano-Okami, but they were oblivious to the developing passion engulfing Yoshino. She felt Masako's eyes on her and immediately pulled Masako's naked, lean body against hers. Masako's small breasts flattened against hers and her lips pressed against Yoshino's, who felt Masako's tongue darting between her lips, and her soft moans became screams as her breath became faster. They pawed each other, exploring every orifice, until in unison they climaxed and sank back, partly submerged in the warm waters feeling reborn. Relaxed, Yoshino's mind wandered, and she recalled an aspect of Chiyo's message that was still nagging her.

Look after the lady Masako, for both you and she are the same. What did she mean by that?

Back at Tsutsujigasaki Yakata Palace, Yoshino rose the following morning at dawn in the early hours of the hare and stepped outside into the garden to watch the sun begin its ascent. The sky was a brilliant hue of orange and red, indicating another warm day ahead. She heard voices in the courtyard just beyond the gardens and walked over to see soldiers taking advantage of the early cool air to practice their martial skills. It surprised her to see Masako, who in the centre of the courtyard was wielding a practice Naginata against several soldiers. Yoshino watched as Masako skilfully swung her bamboo bladed Naginata at six opponents armed with bamboo Shinai swords. Masako struck the body of five of her opponents and disarmed them, but on the sixth one, her strike broke the Naginata shaft. Upon seeing Yoshino, Masako bowed to her opponents, signalling the end of practice, and walked over to Yoshino.

"You are very skilled, Masako," Yoshino complimented.

155

"Thank you. I have trained in this for as long as I can remember. It is a woman's weapon; one that can counter the advantage of a man's strength in close-quarter combat."

I wonder if you possess other martial skills, thought Yoshino.

"Maybe, one day you would teach me," Yoshino asked. Angling for a way to test her out.

"It would honour me, Yoshino. Now come, let us have refreshments." Yoshino and Masako breakfasted on fried bean curd with abalone and rice in another one of the palace's living rooms. Today, Masako seemed agitated and explained to Yoshino that her husband Katsuyori is soon expected.

"Why does this upset you? Or is its lustful anticipation?" Yoshino asked, grinning.

"No, it's just that I am reminded I have failed in my duty as a wife to produce an heir. His first wife, Toyoma Fujin, died while giving birth to their only son, Nobukatsu. Did you know she was the adopted daughter of our enemy, Nobunaga?"

"You are young Masako and have plenty of time," Yoshino tried to reassure her.

"I fear losing Katsuyori. He has taken unnecessary risks lately to prove himself as a worthy successor to Shingen. He has already achieved what his father failed to do by capturing Ieyasu's impenetrable castle, Take Tenjin in Totomi." Yoshino knew while the Takeda held the eastern mountain provinces of Kai and Shinano, the road to controlling Japan lay through Kyoto, with the Tokugawa standing in the way. Shingen's victory over Ieyasu at Mikatagahara had reignited Katsuyori's ambition to complete his father's task and rule Japan.

#

Spring: Third Year of Tensho (1575)

Yoshino once again wintered with Masako at Tsutsujigasaki Yakata Palace. When Katsuyori was away, as he frequently was, they would often revisit the hot springs of Lake Kawaguchiko and rekindle their passion for each other. Japan was changing. They talked about how Nobunaga had grown more powerful since crushing the Azai, Asakura, and now the Miyoshi clans. The latest news was that

156

Yoshiaki fled his Miyoshi patrons in fear of Nobunaga's wrath and fled to the island of Shikoku, where he took the tonsure of a monk.

The brief blooming period of the Sakura had just ended, and Katsuyori was away once more, this time campaigning in Ieyasu's heartland of Mikawa. Yoshino sat in the living room alone with Masako, who officiated over a *Chakai* or simplified tea gathering for them both, serving various sweets and thin tea. Between sips, they both looked out through the screen doors that opened out onto the garden and talked of the recent times in this very room when they both watched over three days the intoxicating, but tragically short-lived blooming of the pure white Sakura blossom. Green fruit awaiting ripening now hung heavily from the many Sakura trees on the palace grounds.

Yoshino picked up one of the exquisite *Chawan* tea bowls they had just drunk out of and thinking them to valuable pieces of Karamono inspected its pale blue glaze and carelessly allowed it to fall to the floor. With astonishing speed, Masako lunged and caught the bowl before it crashed into the floor.

"Forgive me, Masako, I am so careless," Yoshino pleaded.

"No harm done, it is safe," Masako said. The incident made Yoshino recall Chiyo's message... *Both you and she are the same. I wonder?*

A brief time later, the sliding door to the living room slid open and Katsuyori, with two retainers, stepped inside. Masako and Yoshino rose and bowed. The Takeda Lord wore a red laced chest armour, which had seen better days, and Yoshino eagerly eyed his handsome features and fine musculature. He wore no helmet, and his untidy long black hair, tied loosely in a ponytail with coarse rope, gave him a dishevelled appearance. Katsuyori returned Masako and Yoshino's bow and took his seat at the low tea table. His retainers knelt on either side of the door.

"I have missed you, husband," Masako said.

"I too Masako," said Katsuyori, reaching for Masako's hand to pull her gently closer.

"How did the campaign go?" Masako asked.

"Well enough, but we leave again for Mikawa in five days."

"Why must you depart so soon? You have only just returned."

"We received word that one of Ieyasu's officials at Okazaki Castle has offered to open the gates to us."

"Why would your enemy want to do such a thing?"

"Why for land and a sizeable stipend, of course? Don't you see? Taking Okazaki would isolate Ieyasu from Nobunaga and allow us to destroy the Tokugawa with ease." Having only just noticed Yoshino's presence, Katsuyori asked.

"Forgive me, who is your guest?"

"Husband, this is Kusumoto Yoshino, one of your late father's physicians." Katsuyori raised his thick, bushy eyebrows in surprise. "Physician, you say," adding in a concerned voice, "are you unwell, my dear?"

"Not at all, husband," Masako said, almost blushing. "Yoshino has returned after a long absence and keeps me company while you are away. Which, as you know, is most of the time." Katsuyori sheepishly nodded and invited Yoshino to sit alongside him while Masako left briefly to have the servants bring in sake and refreshments.

"The Tokugawa are finished," Katsuyori bragged as the sake flowed. "All that stands between me and Kyoto now is Nobunaga and that monkey of his, Hideyoshi. I hear he is now lord of Odani and has a new pet."

"A pet?" Yoshino queried.

"Yes. The monkey's sandal bearer; never leaves his side and is making a name for himself. He is called Mitsunari, Ishida Mitsunari." Yoshino's heart fluttered. It was a name she thought she had let go of. Her relationship with Masako these last two years had provided a convenient escape, but she knew there could be no future for themselves, she a lord's wife and her, a masterless Shinobi. Her situation reminded her of the transient life of the Sakura blossom, and she quietly murmured to herself, "Life and passion are but fleeting moments in the cycle of life."

"Did you say something?" asked Masako.

"No, I was just saying a prayer," Yoshino replied, still looking outside.

Chapter Fourteen

Shitagahara
Summer: Third year of Tensho (1575)

The evening was warm and sultry and in the grounds of the Tsutsujigasaki Yakata Palace, the shrill scream of a female fox briefly shattered the calm, but the stillness returned, broken only by the sharp clap of the *Shishi-Odishi*-deer scarer striking a rock in the nearby garden. It was well after dusk at around the hour of the dog when Yoshino secretly crept out of her quarters at the palace and headed for the stables.

The journey to Kashioyama Daizenji Temple was only a half-day walk from the palace, but Yoshino had arranged for a saddled horse to be ready. She led the horse out of the stables and headed for the palace gates, where after showing the *Shin-Gen* token to the guards, they allowed her to pass through. Yoshino mounted her horse and galloped towards the nearby Fuefuki River and crossed at its narrowest point where it split into the Hi and Omo rivers, to arrive at the Daizenji Temple around midnight in the hour of the rat.

The temple was still in darkness with no visible signs of life, and none of the lanterns rocking violently in the strengthening breeze was alight. Yoshino climbed onto the roof of the main shrine and crept across the roof towards the temple compound, looking out for signs of life. In one corner of the compound, she noticed a faint light in one outbuilding and dropped to the ground. At the source of the light, she noticed a covered window with gaps just wide enough for Yoshino to peer inside and see the figure of a priest tending to a brazier.

Within minutes Yoshino was inside and from the shadows, she watched the priest who wore the white *Kariginu* robes of a Shinto priest ladle broth from a pot hanging above the brazier into a bowl. He seated himself at a low table to eat, just as Yoshino, disguised with a *fukumen* covering her face, stepped out into the shadows, and surprised him. Believing his unwelcome guest was here to rob

159

him, the priest begged for the intruder to spare his life and quickly offered a small pouch of coins. Yoshino calmly reassured him she was not here to rob him but to talk to a priest called Masatsugu.

"That is a name I have not heard for many years," answered the priest, feeling a little more relaxed.

"Do you of know of him then? Where can I find this Masatsugu?" demanded Yoshino. The priest looked nervously at Yoshino with his sunken, dark eyes. His pale, lean, and wrinkled face was evidence he spent little time outside. Using the sleeve of his robe, the priest wiped away, beading sweat collecting on his shaven head.

"What is it you want with Masatsugu?" the priest asked cautiously.

"So, you do know him. Tell me where I can find him," Yoshino demanded. By now, it had become clear to the priest that the slim frame and voice of his intruder indicated it was a woman, and he felt his confidence returning.

"The one you seek sits before you, but tell me, how did you know my name?" The moment had arrived. Yoshino's hand went to the hilt of the Wakizashi she carried in her Obi and stood silently staring at the man before her. She found it difficult to believe this could be the same man who had violated her all those years ago. Yet he paid good money and had permission from her parents, who should have protected her. She also knew in law Masatsugu had nothing to atone for, but he had violated a child against her will for his pleasure, and for that, she must dispense justice.

"So, it is you, after all these years," said Yoshino.

"Have we met before?" Masatsugu asked inquisitively.

"I do not expect you to remember me, but cast your mind back to the time of your service with the Lord Shingen. After your many visits to the local sake shops, you would seek a certain merchant's house and buy a girl for the night. Were you not banished here by Lord Shingen to reflect on your crime?" Yoshino questioned.

"Let me see, your crime was drunkenness and debauchery, and bringing disrepute to the Takeda clan, was it not?" Masatsugu remained silent. His downcast eyes fixed on the floor in front of him. After a moment, he looked up at Yoshino and spoke.

"I take it then, you were that girl," Masatsugu said as he moved to a corner of the room to sit at another table. Looking at Yoshino, Masatsugu opened the front of his robes and freed his right shoulder.

"Give me a knife. I am ready to die. I am prepared to atone for my crimes," said Masatsugu. Yoshino stared at Masatsugu. She had come here to kill him and satisfy her thirst for revenge. So why, she thought, *am I hesitating*? On her way over to the temple, she fed her desire for revenge by imagining the type of death she would inflict upon him. A quick death was out of the question, as she wanted him to suffer. She thought of taking his head and having it turned into a lacquered drinking cup to add to her collection. It excited her to think of the pleasure she would have, savouring her revenge each time she drank from it. But first, she needed answers.

"You knew you made me with child?" Yoshino said, and Masatsugu nodded.

"Yes, I knew. Lord Shingen had your child, a boy, delivered here for me to care for as penance. For a couple of years, I tended the child until news came from Lord Shingen that an Azai family was looking for a boy child to adopt. Shingen sent word that I was to leave immediately and hand over the boy. When I tracked down the family and I found out they already had an older son, I thought it strange they did not ask questions about the child's pedigree, as one might expect."

"Who was this family?" demanded Yoshino.

"A minor retainer of Azai Nagamasa and castellan of Ishida Castle, Ishida Masatsugu."

So, Mitsunari may be my child? But why would Shingen involve himself personally in this? Chiyo still had some more explaining to do, but where to find her? And what to do about Masatsugu?

"Why did you think it strange they did not inquire about the child's pedigree?" Yoshino asked.

"Maybe, they did not care, or maybe they knew," said Masatsugu. She had got some answers, but some things still made little sense. But first, she had to get back to Tsutsujigasaki Yakata before she was discovered missing. She looked down at Masatsugu, his torso exposed, calm and ready to die. She placed her tanto knife on the low table before Masatsugu. The priest raised his head and looked deep into Yoshino's eyes and smiled. Her meaning clear, he bowed and picked up the Tanto and prepared himself for the ritual suicide. When he next looked up, Yoshino had disappeared and was nowhere to be seen.

It was mid-morning late into the hour of the snake back at the Tsutsujigasaki Yakata Palace when Masako tapped loudly tap several times on Yoshinos' screen door, attempting to rouse her.

"Is anything wrong?" shouted Yoshino, waking to the noise and feeling sluggish. Upon hearing Yoshino's voice, Masako slid open the door and stepped inside. Yoshino was sitting up, her arms wrapped around her knees, basking in the diffused light shining through the *washi* paper screens.

"I am sorry to disturb you, but I became worried. I felt it unusual for you to sleep in this late, especially as we had arranged to meet earlier in the courtyard."

"Forgive me, Masako; I was up all night, only a mild illness. I did not get to sleep until late," Yoshino said, lying. The look of concern on Masako's face made her want to hold her tightly and tell her the truth.

"Should I send for a physician?" Masako asked before correcting herself. "Silly me, you are a physician."

"Masako, you know how fond I am of you, but there is something I need to tell you. I am not who you think I am, but first I must dress." Yoshino quickly changed into the plain crimson kimono laid out for her at the foot of her futon and then took Masako's hand. They both knelt alongside each other in front of the paper screen, and Yoshino explained her identity as one of Chiyo's Kunoichi and the events that led her to be here. Worried her deceit would destroy the relationship they had fostered, Yoshino bowed and begged forgiveness, only to find Masako giggling and with her hand over her mouth, stifling her growing laughter.

"Yoshino. I am sorry. There is no need to torture yourself any further. I knew full well who you were when I first laid eyes on you," said Masako.

"How was that possible? Unless…"

"Yes, Chiyo told me all about you. I too am Kunoichi, and I knew you suspected me when you purposely dropped the tea bowl."

"Masako. Why did you lie to me about Chiyo not being here and making me think I had imagined it all?"

"That was Chiyo's idea. She forbade me to reveal myself to anyone, especially you. She was fond of you, but always had doubts about the strength of your mind and had said that If you came to doubt what your own eyes saw and told you, then you were of no use to her."

"So, this was a test? But she said she was disbanding the network, anyway."

"Yoshino. Chiyo was talking about this network, the one that serves the Takeda. Do you not think other networks with other masters exist? Shinobi are no different from Samurai. They exist to serve, and without a master, our tradecraft is useless and would wither." Masako stood up and gently took Yoshino's hand.

"Let us walk together in the garden. I too have much to explain." Masako and Yoshino walked past the weeping pagoda trees onto a long path lined on both sides with four hundred Sakura trees. They both recalled the times they walked this path together when the trees in bloom formed a tunnel of falling blossom. Masako explained she was the daughter of Matsuda-dono, one of Hojo Ujiyasu concubines. Her mother came from the Fuma Ninja clan led by Fuma Kotaro, which developed independently from the Iga and Koka Ninja. The Fuma served the Hojo clan at Odawara, and as there was no place for women within the Fuma Ninja, Matsuda-dono made secret arrangements with her friend, the Lady Mochizuki Chiyo, from the rival Koka Ninja to raise Masako in the Koka arts. It was an age of shifting alliances, and the Hojo later dispensed with their alliance with the Imagawa clan to seek closer ties with the Takeda. When Katsuyori's principal wife, Toyama Fujin, died in childbirth, Masako's name was put forward as a potential bride for Katsuyori.

"Masako," Yoshino asked. "Do you know where Chiyo is?"

"I am not privy to where she is, but I know that wherever my husband is, Chiyo is sure to be close by."

"Why is she so tied to Katsuyori?" said Yoshino.

"Ever since Shingen told Katsuyori on his deathbed, his great secret?"

"Perhaps, a useless question, but what secret?"

"I do not know, except that it was important enough for Chiyo to ensure Katsuyori does not reveal it."

"So, your husband does not confide in you then. Where is Katsuyori now?"

"He is currently relieving his frustration at Nagashino Castle in Mikawa."

"Is this personal?" queried Yoshino.

"My husband has made it so. The castellan of Nagashino is Okudaira Sadamasa, once a vassal of Ieyasu who defected to Lord Shingen and served him for many years. Katsuyori grew up with him, they even flew kites together. When Lord Shingen died, Sadamasa refused to submit to Katsuyori as clan leader, for he was unfit to lead the Takeda. With Ieyasu's forgiveness and blessing,

Sadamasa re-joined the Tokugawa, and when Katsuyori heard about Sadamasa's betrayal, he had his wife and brother who were hostages, crucified."

"Masako, I have to find Chiyo and sort this out."

"Yes, I understand. It would seem you have missed knowing about your child. If I were you, I too would want to know for sure and watch him grow?"

Yoshino embraced Masako, first kissing her neck, then her lips. Her hands caressed her firm bottom, inching towards her front. Masako put her finger on Yoshino's lip and spoke.

"Not now. Find Chiyo and return to me." Yoshino quickly disengaged and walked away.

Katsuyori had since departed his home territories around the end of the fifth month, taking half of the Takeda army of approximately 15,000, and marched on the Tokugawa stronghold of Okazaki. The other half, led by Kosaka Masanobu, went north into Shinano to keep Uesugi Kenshin in check. It was while he was on his way to Okazaki that Katsuyori received news that the plot to open the gates of Okazaki castle had unravelled. The head of the traitor they were relying on now sat on a tall pole overlooking the castle.

Katsuyori accepted that a frontal assault on the heavily-fortified Okazaki Castle was not workable, so he bypassed the castle to attack the nearby Tokugawa Fortress of Yoshida to the south as it guarded the coastal road into Mikawa from Totomi. Unfortunately for Katsuyori, Ieyasu had anticipated this move and had Yoshida heavily reinforced, leaving a disappointed Katsuyori to retreat up the Toyokawa River and take his vengeance out on the castellan of Nagashino Castle. If he could take Nagashino with its paltry garrison of five hundred defenders, it would decisively end Tokugawa power in Mikawa. Katsuyori knew that with most of the Tokugawa army tied up defending Okazaki and Yoshida, Ieyasu would be no match for his army.

#

Unlike the autumn room of Inabayama Castle, with its extensive views over the Nobi Plain, the summer room where Nobunaga's war council had now gathered looked onto a small garden, but it was one that Nobunaga himself had spent much time and energy designing. The screen doors of the summer room were open not just to allow in the cool mountain breezes, but to provide a scenic backdrop where the Oda Lord could sit and meditate.

Hideyoshi had answered Nobunaga's summons to attend, and at Nobunaga's insistence, brought Mitsunari along. Mitsunari had guided Hideyoshi's purchases of tea utensils, even if some of them were bought at the point of a sword. Nobunaga, suspecting Hideyoshi had guidance in his purchases of teaware, confronted him, and Hideyoshi confessed to relying on Mitsunari's extraordinary talent for identifying Meibutsu. Mitsunari was subsequently invited to Inabayama Castle for a private viewing of his own Meibutsu collection.

At Nobunaga's insistence and contrary to protocol, Mitsunari sat alongside Hideyoshi at Nobunaga's war council, along with other commanders. Shibata Katsuie and Maeda Toshiie sat alongside each other, and seated opposite were Niwa Nagahide, Akechi Mitsuhide, and Takikawa Sakon. Lord Nobunaga sat alongside his eldest son and heir, Oda Nobutada, on a raised dais in front of them.

Akechi Mitsuhide appeared resentful as ever. He considered Mitsunari's presence in the room as an affront to the status of those in attendance and was about to speak up and complain when Niwa Nagahide sensing his friend's mood calmly put a restraining hand on his shoulder and suggested to Lord Nobunaga that the council acknowledge Lord Mitsuhide's latest success in routing the Mori. Nobunaga wholeheartedly agreed and offered some carefully worded praise but stopped short of offering any reward.

Attending to the matter in hand, Nobunaga announced to the council that Katsuyori's army of 15000 had bypassed Okazaki and Yoshida castles and entrenched themselves at Nagashino Castle. Maeda Toshiie was the first to speak, curious why Katsuyori had bypassed the castles.

"Lord Ieyasu informs me Katsuyori did not intend to waste needless lives there and moved on to Nagashino, knowing Ieyasu would have to split his army and draw forces away from Okazaki and Yoshida." A worried Hideyoshi who rapidly analysed the consequences of Nagashino falling spoke up.

"Lord, if Katsuyori takes Nagashino, the Tokugawa are finished."

"I think Ieyasu realises that and has petitioned me for reinforcements at the earliest opportunity," Nobunaga said.

"How many Tokugawa can the Lord Ieyasu field?" Hideyoshi asked.

"He says around 8000," said Nobunaga. Turning to Katsuie Nobunaga asked, "Given our other commitments, how many we can afford to field to help Ieyasu?"

"Without withdrawing completely from the Honganji Ishiyama siege, about 26000," said Katsuie.

"What about the Teppo units?" asked Hideyoshi.

"We have 3000 Teppo matchlocks deployed at Ishiyama which are not having much of an impact, so we may as well release them," Katsuie argued. Mitsuhide now spoke up, questioning the viability of using matchlock weapons.

"Lord, the use of matchlocks is questionable, as we found in Ishiyama. They are vulnerable to the weather, which made our last assault useless, and with a range of only eighty yards, we cannot get close enough to the fortress walls before being cut down. Even our archers have a greater range and can release sixteen arrows in the time to reload one musket."

"I take it you are not a fan of the barbarian weapons," Nobunaga said, smiling.

"Lord, I heard that at Mikatagahara, the swiftness of the Takeda Cavalry easily overran our 300 teppo rifles," Mitsuhide argued.

"We are here to decide how to help our Tokugawa allies, not to debate strategy at Ishiyama or cavalry tactics," shouted Nobunaga, becoming visibly annoyed. Mitsuhide's arguments had hit a nerve. Mitsunari waited till everyone had finished before asking the permission of Nobunaga to speak.

"If your appraisals of Meibutsu are as accurate as your opinions, then we would do well to listen," said Nobunaga. As Mitsunari prepared to speak, he felt all the eyes in the room were upon him.

"Several months ago, Lord Hideyoshi and I visited the siege of Ishiyama. It was noticeable that the defenders using their numerical advantage in matchlocks easily repulsed your repeated assaults on the fortress. The barbarian weapons have advantages, for had it not been for the guns the Honganji used, the fortress would have fallen much earlier. Lord Mitsuhide has correctly pointed out the fundamental weakness of matchlocks, the weather and the time taken to reload. Protecting the powder from dampness is harder, but I believe we can turn the firepower of three thousand muskets into 15000 easily." Mitsuhide, keen to show Mitsunari in a poor light, spoke up to remind everyone of Mitsunari's youth and that matters of tactics and warfare are better left to generals of experience. Undeterred, Mitsunari asked Lord Nobunaga for ink and paper to illustrate his theory.

Unfurling a long roll of blank mulberry paper, the scribes had brought in, Mitsunari illustrated an arrangement of three hundred Teppo Ashigaru covering an area of four hundred yards and split into four ranks. He explained that the first line would fire, then kneel to reload while the second line fired. This would continue until the third and fourth rank had fired, by which time, the first line would have reloaded and been ready to fire again. In short, the arrangement would provide continuous firepower, decimating any enemy advance. Mitsuhide was quick to respond.

"May I ask how the young strategist here proposes to protect these Teppo units from the successive waves of Takeda cavalry, known for their speed?" Mitsunari had no answer to Mitsuhide's question, and the room fell silent. Nobunaga suddenly rose and walked over to Mitsunari and sat alongside him. Using Mitsunari's sketch, Nobunaga added a series of fences arranged in a zigzag fashion in front of each of the Teppo ranks illustrated by Mitsunari.

"If these fences were to be movable palisades, the Teppo Ashigaru will have protection from a direct cavalry assault, and if arranged in such a fashion, it would create chokepoints for any cavalry that survived where our spearmen could finish them," said Nobunaga, adding, "with this, we have them," as he slapped his hand down on the paper, hard.

"It would seem, Monkey, your songbird has a skill for detail," Nobunaga said, addressing Hideyoshi. "He will accompany us to Nagashino." Nobunaga then directed Mitsuhide to have the Ashigaru Teppo units at Ishiyama and their commander, despatched to Nagashino.

"Well, songbird, we will soon see how good your skills are," Nobunaga said in a hushed voice to Mitsunari before he rose and addressed his council to outline his plans.

"The army will leave in two days and meet Ieyasu in the village of Shitara. Nobutada, Hideyoshi, Katsuie, Takikawa Sakon, and Niwa Nagahide will accompany." Turning to Mitsuhide, Nobunaga said, "Continue the siege at Ishiyama and keep the pressure on, and hopefully, when I return, you will have better news for me."

As the afternoon ended, Hideyoshi and Mitsunari walked together on the wide veranda that connected the summer room to the autumn room and watched the sun begin its slow descent. The early evening air was still warm but lacked the oppressive humidity of the lower plains, and Mitsunari sat on the steps leading to the garden with Lord Hideyoshi.

"Why does the Lord Nobunaga want me to accompany him to Nagashino?" Mitsunari said. "You know I have a problem with killing. I do my best to avoid it."

"Forget all that. What I want to know is how you came to know so much about these barbarian weapons?"

"I spent a lot of time in the company of pottery merchants and came to know a few barbarian traders. Portuguese, they said they were. The barbarians were here to trade their matchlock firearms for silver and silk, and I took an interest in their craft. They told me of the way their nations fought with these weapons and from this, I could see the way we currently use them is not effective as it could be."

"You never cease to surprise me, songbird. In your presentation back there, you laid your life on the line, which is why Nobunaga wants you with him."

"My life?" questioned Mitsunari.

"Yes, Nobunaga has staked a lot on your opinion. He is an excellent judge of character and makes use of those with talents. But make no mistake, if your theory falls, so will your head." Hideyoshi continued. "Nobunaga sees many advantages in using the barbarian weapons and believes these firearms will help him realise his ambitions. Nobunaga also realises, as you have pointed out, that our failure to overrun the Ishiyama Hongan-Ji is because they have put firearms to better use than we have." Hideyoshi rose and gently patted a worried Mitsunari on the shoulder, and the two continued towards their quarters.

On the fourteenth day of the month, exactly two days since Nobunaga convened his war council, he led his army of 26000 out of Inabayama. The oddity of this procession was that Nobunaga had each Ashigaru carry a long, thin wooden log. The army pressed on in the relentless heat and humidity, finally arriving at the village of Shitara on the eighteenth day after mid-day around the hour of the sheep. Nobunaga had pitched camp on nearby Mount Gokurakuji while his son Nobutada encamped on Mount Niimido. Both elevations looked down onto the plains of Shitagahara, and Nagashino Castle lay only three kilometres to the east. Tokugawa Ieyasu brought his army of eight thousand to Shitara and set up camp on the slopes of Mount Takamatsuyama at a place called Koromitsu. Takikawa Sakon, Hideyoshi and Niwa Nagahide meanwhile set up camp on Mount Takamatsuyama overlooking the Arumihara Valley.

Mitsunari dismounted and marvelled at the view of Mount Horaiji directly in front of him. The sky was clear, and he could see in the distance a vast range of mountain peaks stretching from east to west. Towards the east, Mitsunari saw the Onagawa River snaking its way south along the contours of the great peaks, and at the confluence of the Onagawa and Takigawa rivers, he made out the outline of Nagashino Castle. Before long, Hideyoshi rode up beside him and told of the summons to attend Nobunaga's war council on Mount Gokurakuji. Less than three kilometres separated the camps, but climbing the slopes of Gokurakuji proved tiresome. Arriving at Gokurakuji, Hideyoshi and Mitsunari set off for Nobunaga's command tent, a hastily erected three-sided windbreak enclosure. Inside, the Oda Lords and Lord Ieyasu sat on camp stools while Hideyoshi and Mitsunari took their position and sat on the soft dirt alongside Takikawa Sakon, Niwa Nagahide, and a Tokugawa Samurai not known to them. The famous Oda captains Sakuma Nobumori and Okubo Tadayo had the honour of sitting on Nobunaga's right side.

Nobunaga snapped open his war fan and demanded of his generals the latest information on the Takeda deployments. Katsuie announced that the Takeda army of 15000 had deployed west of the Rengogawa River on the Shitagahara Plain below. A scout sent to assess the siege at Nagashino had suddenly returned and interrupted Nobunaga's council.

"Reporting," the messenger shouted, announcing his presence.

"What news of Nagashino?" Nobunaga asked.

"Lord, Nagashino remains under siege. The Takeda now control the fort overlooking Nagashino Castle at Mt Tobigasu and hold it with a garrison of some three thousand men." Nobunaga frowned as he digested the information.

"Who is in charge at Tobigasu?" thundered Nobunaga.

"Lord, we believe it to be Kawakubo Nobu Zane, the younger half-brother of Takeda Shingen," the messenger replied. Lord Tokugawa Ieyasu now opened his war fan and pointed to his vassal Tadatsugu, directing him to speak up.

"I am Sakai Tadatsugu, vassal of Lord Ieyasu. The key to relieving the siege is the fortress on Mt Tobigasu. Just below Tobigasu is the village of Ariake Mura, which controls the only passable route the Takeda can take to return safely to Kai. Take Tobigasu, and you not only end the siege but cut off any Takeda retreat." Hideyoshi listened intently and requested permission to speak.

"Lord, even though we outnumber the Takeda, it would take at least 5000 men to assault Tobigasu, and with many lives lost." Niwa Nagahide also requested permission to speak.

"Lord, the Takeda spies surely know where we are and that they are outnumbered. The fort Tadatsugu spoke of is only one of the Takeda forts on Mt. Tobigasu. Securing all these forts will take time and delay the relief of Nagashino, as Katsuyori will surely divert resources to protect them."

Nobunaga conferred with Ieyasu, and then thanked Tadatsugu for his assessment and opinion, but reiterated that the army will proceed with preparations for an expected frontal Takeda attack at daybreak. He instructed Hideyoshi to have the logs the army had carried erected as palisades. They were to be wide enough to conceal thirty to fifty Teppo Ashigaru at intervals of fifty yards. Nobunaga estimated this would provide a two kilometre defensive front against the Takeda.

With specks of rain falling on his face, a worried Nobunaga looked up at the sky. It was mid-afternoon, late into the hour of the sheep, and although several hours of daylight remained for preparations, the prospect of rain now worried him. Nobunaga dismissed all those in attendance except Tadatsugu, who remained behind at Ieyasu's insistence. When everyone had left, Nobunaga took Tadatsugu aside and whispered.

"Tadatsugu, what you say makes sense, and Ieyasu here agrees, but there are too many Takeda spies afoot. My commander Nagachika Kanamori has three thousand troops and five hundred Teppo ready at your disposal. Leave at nightfall and take Tobigasu, but tell no one."

Once alone, Nobunaga reflected.

Katsuyori is brash, impulsive, and overconfident. Even if his spies inform him of the Tobigasu assault, he will not resist the temptation to repeat Mikatagahara. He knows this weather will favour him as it did at Mikatagahara. Without a doubt, he will meet me on the plains of Shitagahara.

A light drizzle fell upon the plains of Shitagahara, and Yoshimasa and Mitsunari continued with their preparations for the next day's battle. Yoshimasa supervised a group of Ashigaru spearmen on how to lash the logs together in such a way that the gap would allow the Teppo to fire at the oncoming enemy. Meanwhile, Mitsunari gathered a Teppo unit of about thirty men and, with their rifle commander, drilled them in volley fire according to his plan. By making the riflemen carefully imitate the same motions they would normally use used to load a matchlock, he would calculate the reloading time required and space his men accordingly. He eventually settled on positioning one gunner every five feet to suit the width of the palisade but four ranks deep and drilled each rank to perform the firing, the withdrawal, the reload and firing again in sequence. Once satisfied, Mitsunari gathered another group of thirty riflemen and despatched the trained rifle commander with his men to teach the others. Mitsunari also arranged and drilled the support crews stationed behind the Teppo units to provide a steady supply of ammunition and gunpowder.

Tadatsugu and Kanamori's small army crossed the Toyogawa River downstream in secret, and the drizzling rain continued well into the night. They travelled through the low hills, passing behind the Takeda army, sieging Nagashino Castle, and reached the fort on Mt Tobigasu just before daybreak. From their vantage point, they could see the Takeda and Oda alliance armies below, positioning themselves for the coming battle on the Shitagahara Plains.

The Rengogawa River divided the two armies and irrigated the rice fields straddling both sides of the river. On the east bank, the main Takeda army had taken up positions less than three hundred yards away from the Oda lines, and only eighty yards west of the river stood Nobunaga's defensive perimeter of palisades. Nobunaga, his son Nobutada, and Ieyasu had set up at the rear also some three hundred yards away from the river, while Shibata Katsuie and Hashiba Hideyoshi protected Oda's northern flank. Okubo Tadayo and five hundred Teppo Ashigaru took up their positions on the southern flank, well outside the limits of Nobunaga's palisade. It was left for Sakuma Nobumori to set up in the centre, deliberately outside the palisade to act as bait and draw the Takeda cavalry in.

Daybreak on the morning of the battle revealed another day of grey skies and continuing light rain that showed no signs of easing. Overnight on Tobigasu, Tadatsugu, and Nagachika Kanamori launched a successful surprise attack on the forts and the Tokugawa and Oda flags were raised. Tadatsugu then moved his forces down towards the Ariake-mura Village, just below Nagashino Castle, and quickly overran the Takeda troops stationed there. Upon seeing the Takeda in disarray outside his walls, the Nagashino castellan Okudaira Sadamasa rode out to reinforce Tadatsugu's men, ending the siege. Word of the fall of Tobigasu and Ariake-mura quickly reached the main Takeda army, and Katsuyori, afraid of his retreat being cut off, moved to begin the battle.

Mitsunari, along with his Teppo unit, waited behind a palisade for the battle to start as a thick mist descended, obscuring his view of the enemy. But at least the rain had stopped, and he felt relieved. He had worried how the Teppo could keep their powder and fuse dry, for if the guns would not fire, their positions would quickly be overrun. He thought of ways to protect the exposed firing pan of a matchlock from the rain but lacked the luxury of time to experiment. But he was thankful his men were using a weatherproofed match rope to ignite the firing pan. The barbarians had explained to Mitsunari they use match ropes made of hemp and soaked in saltpetre, but the innovative sword smiths of Tanegashima devised a match rope made from the braided strands of the cypress tree bark. When soaked in a mixture of saltpetre and rice flour, the fuse would keep alight even in a rainstorm.

Mitsunari heard shouts towards his southern flank and looked to see Tadayo's men engaged in heavy hand to hand, fighting outside the palisade lines.

So, it has begun, he thought.

Mitsunari's men readied themselves at the palisade, and Mitsunari strained to see past the ghostly mist in front of them. One of the Ashigaru yelled out that he could see shapes in the mist and all eyes now focussed on a line of dancing shapes in the distance, each becoming larger and darker by the second.

Just as the Takeda cavalry in their red lacquered armour emerged from the mist shouting their battle cries, Katsuyori belatedly signalled the official opening of battle with his war horn. The muddy rice fields slowed the momentum of the Takeda cavalry, but they ploughed ahead towards Mitsunari's lines with their infantry running behind them. As part of the plan, Sakuma waded out on foot in the mud to meet the advancing Takeda and had his men fire a volley into the advancing horde before running back towards the palisades, feigning a retreat. Due more to luck than skill, several of the Takeda cavalry fell, but the volley of fire had broken their momentum. The cavalry regrouped and charged after Sakuma's fleeing men towards the palisades. The Takeda had taken the bait.

Once the Takeda were in range, Mitsunari gave the order to fire, and Mitsunari quickly put his hands to his ears just as hundreds of matchlocks roared into life and tore into the advancing Takeda cavalry. Expecting to overrun the gunners before they could reload, the Takeda continued their charge. But three more controlled and efficient volleys of several hundred matchlocks thundered across the Shitagahara Plains, tearing men and horses to shreds. On hearing the fourth volley, Katsuie, and Hideyoshi raised their standards and swept round to attack the Takeda flanks. Still undeterred by the slaughter of his cavalry, Katsuyori gathered his remaining reserves and led another charge directly at Mitsunari's position.

Again, bullets tore into Katsuyori's ranks, decimating his cavalry. One Takeda rider who miraculously dodged the fusillade found himself trapped at Mitsunari's palisade. Unable to jump, the momentum of his charge had caused him to crash into the fence, collapsing it on top of Mitsunari. Elsewhere, those lucky enough to escape the fusillade met their end at the barriers as Ashigaru spearmen surrounded the riders and drove spears into their mounts and skewered the riders when they fell. With the tide of battle turning against the Takeda, the main Oda army under Nobunaga moved out and pushed on towards the Rengogawa, chasing the retreating Takeda and despatching the fallen. Nobunaga heard reports that Katsuyori escaped with several of his cavalry, and past mid-day at the end of the hour of the sheep, most of Shingen's revered twenty-four generals lay dead on the plain of Shitagahara alongside the bodies of 12000 Takeda soldiers.

A dazed Mitsunari crawled from underneath the pile of logs that once formed his palisade, along with several of his unit. He heard his name called, and he wiped the mud from his face and looked around him. A thick mist of musket smoke lingered with the morning mist, and he struggled to make out the direction of the call. Before long, a shape appeared before him, and he made out the outline of a Samurai in light armour.

"I am over here," Mitsunari called out, not sure if it was friend or foe. The Samurai moved closer, and Mitsunari immediately recognised him by the white hachimaki he wore.

"Yoshimasa," Mitsunari shouted. "What are you doing here?"

"Looking for you, of course," said Yoshimasa. They both stood and looked at the carnage surrounding them. Mangled bodies and dead horses lay everywhere. Many of the enemy were still alive, at least for the moment. They could still hear groans and detected movement in many of the soldiers lying on the ground. Mitsunari and Yoshimasa moved among the writhing bodies, the lucky ones left alive, with gunshot wounds and blown off limbs would gradually bleed to death. Those unlucky enough to be wounded in vital organs were consigned to die a slow death.

"Is there anything we can do to end their suffering?" asked Mitsunari.

"Their suffering will end shortly," Yoshimasa said, pointing to a group of Oda Samurai busy at work collecting enemy heads. "All the heads are to be taken and piled into mounds for tallying. Those of rank are to be brought to Nobunaga and the generals for viewing." Mitsunari noticed a couple of Ashigaru defacing one of the heads.

"What are they doing?" inquired Mitsunari.

"Blackening its teeth, I would say," replied Yoshimasa.

"Why?"

"Among men of rank, the blackening of one's teeth is a sign of status. To produce a head with such teeth would show the victim was one of worth, and glorious rewards would follow if you could prove you took it in battle."

"Isn't that dishonest?" remarked Mitsunari.

"Yes, of course, it is," said Yoshimasa.

"So those cheats are going to get rewarded?" Yoshimasa looked at Mitsunari and grimly smiled. "I think Lord Nobunaga will see through such deception, and their reward will probably be the same fate as those they choose to present before him." As Mitsunari and Yoshimasa headed back towards their lines, they stumbled across the body of a Takeda warrior clad in vermilion armour lying in the thick mud with a sodden banner draped over him. His helmeted face was concealed by his *Menpo* or armoured face mask, sculptured with demon-like looking features. Mitsunari stooped and picked up the banner and read the painted characters.

Fu rin ka zan: wind, forest, fire, mountain. Swift as the wind, silent as the forest, intrusive as fire, and immovable as a mountain. Of course, it is Shingen's motto.

"Judging by the quality of his armour, I would say he was a cavalry officer of low rank," Yoshimasa observed.

"Even with his mask on, he looks at peace," Mitsunari said.

"Come on, let's head back to camp," said Yoshimasa. As Mitsunari and Yoshimasa moved to walk away, the dead Takeda officer suddenly sprung up and thrust the Katana he was secretly clutching into Yoshimasa's unprotected back. Yoshimasa had worn only the light *Haramaki* armour designed to protect his front and fastened at the back with just cords. He regretfully saw no need to attach the 'coward's plate', which would have protected his back against such stabbings. In an instant, Mitsunari released *Jiko* and struck under the Takeda's armpit in a reverse strike. The officer's arm, still gripping his sword, dropped into the mud, and he fell to his knees, howling as blood sprayed from the wound. Mitsunari pivoted and brought *Jiko* down at the officer's neckline, but the cheap *Shikoro* neckguard buckled and *Jiko* easily severed the Takeda's head from its body. The Torso crumpled and fell into the mud whilst the head fell on a small patch of dry ground, face-up, eyes open as if staring in disbelief. Mitsunari rushed to Yoshimasa's side and pulled his face out of the mud, whilst calling out for help, and did his best to stem the bleeding.

Chapter Fifteen

Oni no Hanzō.
Summer: Third year of Tensho (1575)

While the Takeda Lord Katsuyori managed his escape from the battlefield, Mitsunari knelt in the deep mud of Shitagahara and cradled the gravely wounded Yoshimasa. With the help of Oyamada Nobushige and Obata Masamori, the last survivors of Shingen's revered twenty-four generals, Katsuyori escaped to his camp on nearby Mt Horaj-Ji and set about regrouping the remnants of his army for a hurried retreat to Kai. The battle lost, Katsuyori abandoned his Mikawa campaign against the Tokugawa and of the fifteen thousand army he had set out with, less than three thousand remained to begin the long march home.

Mitsunari carefully cut the cords of Yoshimasa's *Haramaki* armour and removed the front breastplate, exposing the sword's exit point. Using strips cut from his robes, Mitsunari plugged both wounds to stem the flow of blood and looked around for something to bind the blood-soaked strips. He noticed two figures approaching and called out for help. One dragged the banner that had covered the Takeda officer Mitsunari had just killed. As they drew near, he noticed they wore plain grey smocks and Hakama pants. They were certainly not soldiers.

"Who are you?" Mitsunari shouted. "I need help here." One of the two men appeared much older than the other, probably because of his grey beard, but neither replied. The older of the two approached Mitsunari, dragging the banner, and knelt over Yoshimasa. He inspected Yoshimasa's wound and withdrew a small star-shaped object from his obi and began cutting up the banner into long strips whilst the other tightly bound Yoshimasa's torso.

"Who are you?" Mitsunari again asked. Without replying, the two figures silently lifted Yoshimasa and walked away.

"Hold on, I am coming with you. Where are you taking him?" shouted Mitsunari. The older looking of the two men turned to Mitsunari, saying, "There is no need to worry. Our instructions are to deliver him to safety."

"I will accompany him then," Mitsunari insisted.

"No, his welfare is entrusted into our hands."

"But you have not told me who you are," shouted Mitsunari.

The older man replied gruffly, without turning. "This man's life depends on getting him to safety quickly. We have no time to explain. You will be notified shortly of his condition."

Mitsunari watched helplessly as the two figures disappeared into the mist, carrying Yoshimasa. At first, he was convinced Nobunaga had sent help, but he quickly realised Nobunaga could not have known of this situation and became suspicious. Mitsunari trudged his way back towards the Oda lines, determined to report to Lord Nobunaga what had happened. The hooves of thousands of horses and men had churned the battlefield into a muddy quagmire, and Mitsunari struggled with each step as the soft mud sucked at his woven sandals.

As he approached the Oda lines, he found the ground grew firmer, and it became easier to walk. He looked down at his mud-splattered pants, which now resembled rags, and barely held together. He was a mess.

How can I report to the lord like this?

The smoke of battle and the lingering mist had finally lifted, revealing the carnage of battle, and Mitsunari now noticed the body of an Oda Ashigaru laying in the mud before him. The corpse's eyes were still open, fixed upwards towards the heavens, and Mitsunari considered taking his clothes. He opened the stiff fingers of the corpse and placed six copper coins in his hand and began removing his armour and clothes. The Ashigaru's front chest armour, with its lacquered iron plates and cloth backstrap, although streaked with blood, was still usable. The short, badly slashed kosode he wore was also soaked in blood, and unusable, but his leggings appeared less ravaged and presentable. Mitsunari had stripped the Ashigaru and replaced his shredded pants with the Ashigaru's leggings when two Ashigaru assigned to cleaning up the battlefield noticed him.

"Hey, you." One of them shouted. "What are you doing? Robbing the dead? We should report you to the lord." Mitsunari continued fitting himself with the Ashigaru's leggings whilst explaining to the Ashigaru who he was and why he needed an urgent change of clothes. Pointing to the coins in the dead man's hands, he protested he was not stealing and had made reparation for the dead man's clothes. The Ashigaru, still dissatisfied, continued their grumblings, and Mitsunari gave six more copper coins to each of them. The grateful Ashigaru bowed and continued their way.

Outside Nobunaga's command tent, Mitsunari cleaned himself as best he could in the horse's water buckets and, still looking dishevelled with blood-stained Ashigaru armour, he was admitted and took his seat on the dirt floor alongside Hideyoshi and other generals. Nobunaga sat in front on his camp stool, still dressed in his armour, along with Lord Ieyasu and his son Nobutada. As the purpose of the gathering was to reward meritorious deeds and acts of valour on the battlefield, Nobunaga stood up and called for nominations. Hideyoshi was the first to stand and cited Mitsunari and Yoshimasa for their innovative efforts with the Teppo units in helping to deliver this victory against the Takeda. Nobunaga frowned, narrowing his eyes as he addressed Hideyoshi.

"So, you say I should reward them for doing what they were expected to do, then?" Hideyoshi, feeling foolish, apologised and quickly sat down.

"That reminds me. Where is my retainer, Yoshimasa?" Nobunaga inquired. "I do not see him here." Mitsunari stood up and asked permission to speak, then outlined the events of the Takeda officer's cowardly attack on Yoshimasa and the help that arrived.

"Where is he now?" Nobunaga asked of Mitsunari.

"I do not know, Lord. I had thought at first it was you who sent the help." Nobunaga spoke to Hideyoshi.

"Take as many men as you need and search the area. They could not have gone too far. 'Songbird', you go with him." Hideyoshi and Mitsunari immediately left to arrange men for the search and passed a group of attendants busy placing severed heads onto wooden boards. Mitsunari noticed the heads were clean from blood, and the hair of each head meticulously combed and tied, and each had a nameplate attached.

"What is all this?" Mitsunari asked Hideyoshi.

"It is for the viewing of heads," said Hideyoshi. "Once the lord has finished with the issuing of rewards, they will deliver these heads to him for inspection. Depending on whose head it is, they will judge and maybe reward those who took the head." Intrigued, Mitsunari stooped down and examined the nameplate of the head closest to him.

Yamagata Masakage, Takeda, killed with a spear, head taken by Hashiba Hideyoshi.

"It says here you took his head?"

"Yes, but there was nothing meritorious about it. Your gunners did the work for me and wounded him. I merely finished him and took his head to give to the lord. He was a prize, though. The noted Yamagata Masakage was one of the fiercest of Shingen's generals who led Katsuyori's 'Red Fire' cavalry regiment."

"The lord did not think the efforts of the Teppo were especially meritorious then?" said Mitsunari.

"Make no mistake, Songbird, the outcome of this battle would have been much different had it not been for your efforts. We had overwhelming superiority in numbers, but for the Teppo, our casualties would have been considerably higher." Still confused, Mitsunari queried Hideyoshi.

"Why then does the lord downplay the contribution of the Teppo?" Hideyoshi just looked at Mitsunari and grinned. "We do not have time for this if we are to find Yoshimasa."

With limited daylight left, Hideyoshi believed the village of Ariake Mura was the most obvious place to search for Yoshimasa, being the only one around for many kilometres. The search party led by Hideyoshi and accompanied by Mitsunari, together with thirty of Nobunaga's Samurai, set out for the village of Ariake Mura, arriving late in the hour of the rooster, just as the sun began its final descent below the horizon. Hideyoshi sat on his horse and looked around at the slowly darkening outlines of the village and the lights of lanterns erupting around him. There were around thirty or forty thatched farmhouses, some tightly packed together, others spread out at the edge of the rice fields. A few were at the edges of the forested slopes of Mount Tobigasu.

This will take some time, Hideyoshi thought, before calling out to his search party.

"Split up and search house to house. Mitsunari and I will take those farmhouses in the hills."

#

Yoshimasa lay on a bed of loose straw within the farmhouse of the village headman, nestled on the slopes of Tobigasu at the edge of the rice fields. A raised

179

platform over an earth floor formed Yoshimasa's sleeping quarters, and the open windows of the house allowed the cool mountain air of the evening to circulate and provide some relief from the lingering humidity. In the centre was a fire pit tended by an older woman, busy preparing a meagre gruel of boiled rice, while Yoshino tended to Yoshimasa's wounds.

"Consider yourself lucky," Yoshino said to Yoshimasa as she squatted to pee into a bowl. "The blade missed your vital organs, and if we can stem this blood, you should live, but first we have to clean this wound." Yoshimasa had heard the barbarians often cauterised their wounds with gunpowder that was set alight, searing the flesh. This time, he was thankful for the healing arts of the Ninja. Yoshino irrigated Yoshimasa's wounds with her urine and then, with a small fishbone threaded with silk thread, closed the open wounds. When finished, she unfolded a paper envelope she kept in her obi and sprinkled a powdered resin onto his wounds.

"How did you find me? And why are you helping me?" Yoshimasa asked.

"I followed you after the battle. I was hoping you would help me find Chiyo," Yoshino answered as she applied a bandage to the wounds. "Do not worry, for I mean her no harm. It's just that she is the key to something important I need to resolve."

"What makes you think I know where she is?" Yoshino grinned. "I know you two were, shall we say, past lovers, and I am sure you are still in contact?"

How could she know about Chiyo? Yoshimasa thought but remained silent. Yoshino explained that Katsuyori's wife, Masako, had advised her to seek Katsuyori as Chiyo will be nearby. She further explained that having discovered Katsuyori was at Nagashino, she set out to follow the same route the Takeda army had taken and arrived at Mount Takamatsuyama only two days ago only to find the Oda army assembling below. From her position on Takamatsuyama, close to Hideyoshi's camp, she overlooked the Arumihara Valley. She knew the camp was Hideyoshi's as she recognised the golden gourd standard planted outside the command tent and thought,

If Hideyoshi was here, then Mitsunari must be as well.

"Did you find Katsuyori?" Yoshimasa asked.

"No. Tokugawa scouts captured me and took me to Ieyasu."

"Well, you are here now, so you must have escaped."

"Let's put it this way, Ieyasu released me again."

"Again?" queried Yoshimasa. Yoshino sighed and was about to explain when the farmhouse door swung open and a Tokugawa Samurai in full armour, sporting a large bushy beard but wearing no helmet, made his way inside. Unperturbed, the old woman at the hearth glanced up and bowed in recognition and continued with tending to her boiling pot. Yoshino also casually bowed and continued attending to Yoshimasa's dressings.

"This is Hattori Masanari, a senior retainer of the Lord Ieyasu," Yoshino said to a confused Yoshimasa. "You may have heard of him by another name, Oni no Hanzo?"

"Hanzo? The demon Hanzo. Yes, of course," Yoshimasa said with a dry, rasping voice. "I have heard of you. I was at Anegawa and saw you surrounded by no less than a dozen Azai warriors and watched you despatch every one of them, appearing to savour each kill as a demon would."

"How is it you know the Hanzo?" Yoshimasa asked Yoshino.

"Hanzo is also Shinobi and is head of the Iga-Ryu. I have him to thank for my life." Yoshimasa was about to ask another question when Yoshino silenced him by putting her finger over his mouth and quietly muttered.

"These are stories for another time."

Hanzo was taller than average and wore a similar style of light armour to the one Yoshimasa had worn. As an undefeated *Kensei* sword saint, he could afford to use more vulnerable armour.

"We need to hurry," Hanzo said to Yoshino, "Nobunaga's men have arrived and are searching the village for your wounded comrade, and it is the wish of my lord that they do not find you with him." Yoshino was about to ask why, when Hanzo insisted, she immediately gather her belongings.

"Do not worry about your friend here," said Hanzo, "Nobunaga's men will find him and take safe care of him." Hanzo looked down at Yoshimasa and spoke.

"It would be best for the time being if you mention nothing about your Kunoichi friend being here. Lord Nobunaga detests Ninja, let alone spies, and should your relationship with her be discovered, it is likely you will be viewed with suspicion." Yoshimasa understood and grimaced in pain as he tried to nod his head before laying back on the soft straw and allowed pleasant thoughts of Chiyo to return.

He recalled the few times Chiyo would return to Izuma's hut. She would only say her visits were to inquire of Yoshimasa's recovery, yet with each visit, they both grew closer. Chiyo asked of Yoshimasa his plans for when he recovered, respectfully pointing out his dim prospects. As a masterless Samurai, he would spend his days scrounging for a living. He remembered her moving catlike across the floor to put a comforting hand on his shoulder and felt the warmth of her breath in his ear as she whispered her master would like to employ him. She told him her master was the Takeda Lord Shingen and begged him to consider his request.

It was late in the next month when Chiyo next returned and conveniently Izuma had been called away to attend a sick relative for a few days. The unseasonably sultry night air had kept him awake and in the eerie silence of the night, he was alert to the slightest of sounds. Sensing another in the room, his hand moved to rest on the hilt of his sword that lay alongside him before opening his eyes to see the outline of a naked woman standing over him. His eyes followed the contours of her body, from her slender thighs to her firm stomach and full breasts, finally settling on her face. It was Chiyo. Her fingers lingered over his mouth as if to silence him while she rested a heavy pouch of coins on his naked chest.

"Lord Shingen has accepted you, and we have a task for you. You are to deliver a message for a geisha in the capital and return."

"When do I leave?" Yoshimasa struggled to say.

"When we have finished what I came to do," Chiyo whispered as she sat astride Yoshimasa and coaxed his increasing erection.

#

With clear skies and a bright moon to guide them, Hanzo and Yoshino rode away from Ariake Mura and headed south towards Tokugawa Ieyasu's headquarters at Hikuma Castle. With the Takeda now in retreat, Nobunaga had decamped and began moving his army for the long journey back to Gifu and Ieyasu departed soon after to return to Hikuma. While his army marched back, Ieyasu rode throughout the night, and he was not expecting to reach the Hikuma until late in the hour of the hare, just in time to watch the dawn rise.

Hanzo and Yoshino made timely progress crossing the mountains, rivers, valleys and reached the edge of the Mikatagahara Plateau just before daybreak. Another hour of riding would see them arrive at their destination, but Hanzo rested the horses and took shelter within a nearby wooded copse at the edge of the plateau. The night air was not cold, but chilly enough for Hanzo to light a small fire, and Yoshino warmed her hands only to be slowly mesmerised by the flickering flames. Fire wraiths danced amidst the flames and Yoshino was taken back to the events of three days earlier.

The last thing she remembered of that day was the sight of Hideyoshi's golden gourd standard on Mount Takamatsuyama. Her next recollection was waking up groggy and sore, her hands bound above her head. Her feet were spread apart and anchored to nearby tree branches, and in front of her stood a grinning, gap-toothed Samurai leering at her. He was not alone as several more of his kind gathered around her, ogling and prodding her with sticks as one would bait a captive prey. She noticed these were no ordinary Samurai, for they dressed in peasant garb, coarse grey smocks and wore no Hakama pants, yet all carried the two swords of the Samurai class. The gap-toothed Samurai raised his smock, exposing his erect penis, and moved towards her. The next moment, she felt the weight and stench of his body on top of her and a warm liquid running down her face. Opening her eyes, Yoshino faced the headless torso laying on her stomach, spraying blood over her.

She watched a tall man with a large bushy beard clad in light armour approach methodically dispatching into the void with his sword all those who took him on while the sensible ones ran away. She felt the sudden release of her bonds as they were cut loose and sat up. Her saviour was a young Ashigaru bearing the Tokugawa crest on his chest armour, who stood over her armed with the knife that had cut her free. They both watched as the tall, bearded warrior waist-cut one of the bandits, who now begged for mercy. Wiping his blade on the dead man's smock, he approached Yoshino and politely introduced himself as Hattori Hanzo before ordering her young saviour to bind her hands again, but lightly this time and bring the spy back to Lord Ieyasu's camp.

Hanzo's sudden dousing of the fire snapped Yoshino back into reality.

"Come, let us complete this journey," Hanzo urged as the first streaks of daylight pierced the horizon.

Ieyasu had travelled all night and had only recently arrived back at Hikuma, so it would be several hours later before Yoshino and Hanzo would meet with Ieyasu. It was past mid-day, and well into the hour of the sheep that a refreshed Ieyasu took his refreshments in the main living room of Hikuma Castle and received the news of Hanzo's early return.

"Send him in at once," Ieyasu said to the servants as he wiped away some sake that had dribbled from his mouth. Hanzo later entered with Yoshino, having changed into a black Hitatare with black Hakama pants while Yoshino wore a black silk kimono bearing the Tokugawa Mon given to her on her arrival.

"You two look like a pair of black ravens," Lord Ieyasu said. His eyes flashed with recognition as they fell upon Yoshino.

"So, we meet again. You make a habit of getting captured. I should have had you beheaded before and be done with it, but Hanzo here was persuasive in convincing me you could be of some use." Looking at Ieyasu's grim smile made Yoshino feel nauseous. It was only two days earlier that Hanzo had rescued her from the Ronin Samurai on Mount Takamatsuyama and dragged her before Ieyasu as a Takeda spy.

She had resigned herself to lengthy interrogation and torture, but Ieyasu's command to Hanzo to execute her immediately had taken her by surprise. Hanzo protested, but she still noticed the grim smile on his face as they led her away to someplace outside. Yoshino found herself still bound and on her knees in the dry sand of a courtyard. She felt comforted by the warmth of the bright sunshine and squinted, expecting to see her executioner, but saw no one. She was alone. The sweat from her forehead ran down her face in rivulets, stinging her eyes, but she still noticed the outline of a tall man with a sword approach. His approach blocked the sun from her eyes, and she saw it was Hanzo. At that moment, Yoshino realised Hanzo was to be her executioner and readied herself just as Hanzo laughed and cut her bonds loose.

Yoshino returned to reality and looked up to see Hanzo pouring his master a bowl of sake, while Ieyasu again grinned at her before picking up a sliver of bonito fish in his chopsticks and devouring it.

"If you are still awake, I am talking to you," Ieyasu shouted at Yoshino. "You have yet to explain your purpose for being on Takamatsuyama. Did Katsuyori somehow get wind of our advance and send you to spy?"

"No, my Lord. I indeed sought Katsuyori, but it was not to serve him. I needed to find someone." Careful to leave out details, Yoshino reminded Ieyasu that she had admitted to her earlier role as a Takeda assassin in the service of Shingen, but pointed out that with his death she was no longer bound in his service as she had not sworn fealty to his heir, Katsuyori. She explained her purpose was to find her employer, Lady Mochizuki Chiyo. Wherever Katsuyori was, Chiyo would be nearby. Ieyasu held his bowl out again for Hanzo to refill and whispered.

"Are you sure she can be useful?" Ieyasu asked Hanzo before addressing Yoshino.

"Shinobi are sought for hire. Are you for hire?" Ieyasu asked. Yoshino knew her life depended on the correct answer. Her time as a Kunoichi for hire was over, her only focus was to find Chiyo. To answer no would end her life and any hope of finding Chiyo, but a 'yes' answer meant being bound to some form of contract but with a chance of achieving her goal.

"Yes, Lord, I am for hire," Yoshino said decisively. Ieyasu looked at Yoshino, weighing up her response.

"The question centres on if I can trust you, does it not?" Yoshino knew there was nothing to stop her agreeing and once free to disregard the contract, but the way he said the question bothered her.

"What would it take for you to trust me, Lord?" Yoshino asked.

"Aha!" Ieyasu exclaimed. "I would need a guarantee of your good faith. Say, perhaps a hostage."

A hostage. What is he talking about? Who could I offer?

"My Lord, I have no relations. Did you have anyone in mind?" Ieyasu downed another bowl of sake, wiped his lips, and replied.

"Yes. Your son, Mitsunari," Yoshino froze.

How could he know? I have told no one. Ieyasu picked up his chopsticks and again sampled the slivers of fish from his plate before speaking.

"Your eyes tell me you are surprised, my Kunoichi friend. Hanzo here will explain, for I have more important matters to attend to. You have a choice. Either I take your head now or you work for me. If you betray me, I will have your son's head. What say you?" Without waiting for Yoshino's answer, the Tokugawa Lord rose to leave the room and nodded to Hanzo, who now faced Yoshino.

"I was there those five years ago at your failed assassination attempt on my lord's life. You appreciate that Lord Ieyasu is naturally suspicious about your arrival here. Tell me, to what *Ryu,* do you belong?" Yoshino studied Hanzo before answering, at only thirty-four years of age, the grey flecks in his hair and beard made him look older than he was, and she searched his eyes for any sign

185

that would betray his true intent. To her, his eyes revealed a man of empathy and compassion,

He is someone I can trust.

"The Mochizuki Ryu of Nagano, and you?" Hanzo smiled and nodded. "So, you want to know a bit more about me, eh? You are perfectly aware I am the leader of the Iga Ryu. I am the son of Hattori Nazo Yasunaga, who, like me, was also a Tokugawa vassal, and I have served Lord Ieyasu since I was sixteen. So, tell me Kunoichi, what is your answer to my lord's proposal?"

"Do I have a choice?"

"Indeed, you do. Your head, or your son's head, that is a choice. I suspect; however, you have already decided to serve my lord." Yoshino frowned and nodded.

"Good, but first tell me all you know about this Mitsunari person," Hanzo said, adding,

"And let us not play games, Kunoichi. I will explain my lord's thinking about this. Five years ago, I watched you defiantly face death. I would have been among the first to recommend to the lord that the manner of your death be quick and not the lingering fate designed for those traitors. The lord was curious as to who would risk sending a lone assassin. He suspected his former ally Shingen's hand in this but wanted proof and so he released you to see where you would go to roost."

"And did he get his proof?" Yoshino asked.

"As I was saying." Hanzo continued, ignoring her question. "I had my Shinobi follow you, and it puzzled us to find you tutoring a young boy at the residence of Hashiba Hideyoshi. Other reports added to our interest with claims you were an envoy of the Shogun. Naturally, my lord was keen to know what was so special about this boy that attracts the attention of the Shogun, Lord Nobunaga, and you. Your visit to the boy's parents at Ishida further added to the intrigue, especially the report given by one of the castle servant girls we had primed to spy. Your conversation with Ishida Masatsugu was overheard." Yoshino became agitated, thinking.

What did she hear? As if reading her mind, Hanzo answered.

"Interestingly, the boy, it seems, was not the natural son of Masatsugu but adopted."

186

"And how does that make the boy my son?" Yoshino said.

"It does not," Hanzo conceded. "But the case builds. We had you followed to Tsutsujigasaki Yakata, the Kofu residence of Takeda Shingen and word was leaked of your conversation with Mochizuki, as was your departure in the dead of night from Tsutsujigasaki Yakata to visit the Daizenji Temple." A stunned Yoshino felt the knot in her stomach tighten, and the question she raised was barely audible.

"How could you possibly know that?"

"Very simple," Hanzo said, "wheels within wheels. Mochizuki told us." Before Yoshino could speak again, Hanzo continued. "Let me answer your next question. Mochizuki's spies noticed our efforts to follow you and sent word of your intentions to revenge yourself on the priest Hajikano Masatsugu, the man who defiled you all those years ago."

"Why would she want you to know that?"

"Mochizuki had hired the Shinobi of my clan to eliminate you, and having accepted the contract, they headed to the Daizenji Temple only to find you gone and the priest already dead."

"So, he went through with his seppuku, after all? I had my doubts, but strangely, I could not bring myself to kill him," said Yoshino.

"The manner of his death was not seppuku," Hanzo said. "His knife still lay wrapped on the table beside him and his head lay on the floor." Yoshino felt a wave of despair.

"Are you thinking I did it?" asked Yoshino.

"No," said Hanzo, "that much we agree on. The blood was fresh, and your arrival back at Tsutsujigasaki Yakata was observed much earlier. What we found intriguing is that your former employer now wants you dead." Yoshino's mind now raced, seeking answers.

There is a bigger purpose here, but what to make of it? Why silence the one person who can confirm Mitsunari is my child after he has already told me? And why would Chiyo want to betray me?

"We still have a problem," said Hanzo. "As I have said, my clan accepted a contract to kill you, and somehow, we must deliver on it, but if you are dead, you are of no use to us. For you to serve us, we must somehow find another way to honour our contract." Yoshino looked around the room, her mind racing to plan some answer to Hanzo's dilemma.

If I do not produce something, then Hanzo will have no choice but to have me killed. Yoshino's eyes finally settled on Hanzo's downcast expression, together with an idea.

"I may have an answer," Yoshino said. "Mochizuki knew I was intent on seeking revenge. She also knew I would kill him once I got the answers I came for, but the information Masatsugu revealed was not worth the expense of hiring Shinobi to kill me. All the priest did was to confirm what Mochizuki had already said. So, even if I ended up not killing him, why would she go to the trouble of ensuring his death, unless Mochizuki was fearful of another reason being discovered." Hanzo raised his eyes, shaking his head.

"All this is intriguing, but how does this solve our problem?"

"The way out of this is to get Mochizuki to withdraw the contract, and your clan to repay the money paid."

"Repaying the money is the simple part, but why would she withdraw the contract?" Hanzo said.

"If she believes I have discovered from the priest the real reason, whatever it might be."

"I cannot understand how this will help," said Hanzo.

"Don't you see? If what I suspect to be true, there is much more to this than Mitsunari being my son. Mochizuki cannot afford to have me killed without first knowing what I know and if I have told anyone else," said Yoshino.

"I see. So, how do we move on with this?"

"It is necessary to have her believe the priest told me the real reason, whatever it might be."

"And how might we achieve that?" Hanzo confusingly replied.

"By testing her reaction. Have your Shinobi report back to her that I have left for Tsutsujigasaki Yakata, and they intend to strike before I reach Kofu. They are to explain any attempt to kill me here in Mikawa will embarrass their clan leader, Hattori Hanzo, under whose protection I live. Also, inform them, I was overheard to say to an unknown visitor in my room that I finally know the truth of all this."

Hanzo looked at Yoshino and grinned, whilst stroking his thick bushy beard as if in thought. "Agreed, but first I must arrange for some insurance and have your son brought here."

188

Chapter Sixteen

Hitojichi—The Hostage
Spring/Summer: Fourth Year of Tensho (1576)

The *Hanami* or Cherry Blossom season had arrived early at Hikuma Castle. The Tokugawa Lord Ieyasu sat with his generals in the large audience room on the second floor of the castle's new three-storey *Dojon*. Outside, in the newly enlarged inner courtyard, the Sakura blossom carried by the spring breezes fell like snow carpeting the ground. The result was an expanse of white and pink hues that sparkled in the mid-day sunshine.

Since his defeat at Mikatgahara, Ieyasu enlarged many of Hikuma's fortifications and had recently renamed it to Hamamatsu Castle. The council of generals that Ieyasu now addressed talked about victory, not defeat, and Nagashino was a glorious victory.

"Without doubt, our forces were overwhelmingly superior," said Ieyasu. "Yet Katsuyori foolishly engaged us head-on, only to be beaten. Had he taken a position behind the Takigawa River instead of the Rengogawa, he could have held us up for days and we would have had to retire. Then, he could have attacked at will. It is a pity he was such a fool." Sakai Tadatsugu, hero of the night attack on the Takeda positions on Mount Tobigasu, spoke up.

"Lord, a new age of warfare is upon us. We have seen the futility of mass cavalry attacks in the face of these barbarian weapons. Were it not for the *Teppo* matchlock units, the battle as it played out could have gone the other way, despite our numbers?" Torii Mototada, who helped Yoshimasa erect the palisades at Shitagahara, interjected.

"The chief drawback of the matchlock is the slow reloading time, and they are useless in rain, but for the palisades and Nobunaga's new strategy of volley fire, the Takeda cavalry would have easily overrun our positions." Hiraiwa Chikayoshi, another trusted retainer of Ieyasu, also added his opinion.

189

"Sire, As Lord Nobunaga has shown us, we need to learn more about these modern methods and clever tactics, and as it is, we have very few *Teppo* units of our own." Ieyasu nodded, saying, "You are all correct in your observations. We need to learn more about these barbarian tactics and yes, we need more matchlocks. Lord Nobunaga has agreed to give us a young man who knows such things."

Ieyasu's cousin, Matsudaira Ietada, commented he was more concerned with the Takeda's intentions. Although weakened, they remain a serious threat.

"We shall continue to nip at Katsuyori's heels, Ietada," Ieyasu replied. "Nobunaga has already retaken Iwamura Castle in Shinano from Katsuyori, further weakening him and improving both our strategic positions. Nobunaga need only worry about Uesugi Kenshin in the north and Mori Terumoto in the west. The Takeda threat to Mikawa is diminished, but we must continue to bleed Katsuyori."

Around mid-day in the hour of the horse, Ieyasu retired to his quarters to take refreshments and deal with his new 'hostage'. He dressed in a vivid blue Hitatare with white peony flowers and black Hakama pants, in celebration of spring. Mitsunari, in contrast, stepped inside the Tokugawa Lord's room accompanied by Hanzo more sombrely dressed in all black and bowed. Instructed by Hanzo, Mitsunari removed the two swords from his obi and placed them to his side as he took his seat alongside Hanzo in front of Lord Ieyasu. Hanzo kept his swords in his obi, ready to use for his lord's protection.

"I recognise the Katana," Ieyasu commented, pointing to Mitsunari's sword. "The hilt is a little different, but the inlay on the *Tsuba* handguard is unmistakable, for I had it fashioned by the renowned artist Umetada Myoju. This is the Muramasa blade I gifted to Hashiba Hideyoshi. How is it you have it?"

"Lord Hideyoshi gave it to me on my Genpuku, Lord," Mitsunari replied. A grinning Ieyasu continued, "Legend has it that Sengo Muramasa once prayed to the Kami to make his swords 'the great destroyers', and demons overheard his prayer, granting his wish. From that moment on, all Muramasa's blades became associated with death and misfortune."

"Is that why you gave it to Hideyoshi?" Mitsunari replied.

"It is true. This blade has wrought some bad luck on the Tokugawa clan." Ieyasu said, taken aback by Mitsunari's question. "But the blade was rare and valuable, certainly worthy of Hideyoshi's standing. In gifting the blade, I had hoped it would also lift its curse."

"Yes, sometimes I feel they have a life of their own," said Mitsunari, pointing to *Jiro* and *Jiko* at his side. Clearing his throat, Ieyasu changed the subject.

"I intend to expand my Teppo units and at my request, Lord Nobunaga has permitted you to remain and instruct my Teppo, but I am curious how you have such knowledge of these barbarian tactics?" Inquired Ieyasu.

"My Lord, I have dealt extensively with the pottery merchants of Sakamoto and Sakai in seeking to learn from them about the Karamono porcelain they import from China. Among their kind are quite a few merchants that also trade in Chinese silks for Japanese silver, and others who trade in our lacquerware and silver for Portuguese matchlocks. It would seem our warring states are highly profitable for the Portuguese, who have even set up a permanent trading post on the island of Kyushu, at the fishing village of Nagasaki.

Whilst in Sakai, it surprised me to find many of the swordsmiths are now using their skills to make copies of the Portuguese matchlocks. With help from a Portuguese-speaking trader, I enquired of one barbarian trader about their use in European armies. He described one of the first major battles won, using matchlocks. It was at a place too difficult to pronounce, but it was in a country they call Italy, between the forces of neighbouring Spain and France. This happened long ago in the third year of Bunki (1503).

The French were like the Takeda and focussed too much on their cavalry, and whilst they outnumbered the Spanish two to one, they suffered a devastating loss. The Spanish drilled their Teppo units mercilessly and could even fire from horseback. I learnt of their Teppo units, which comprised three lines of five soldiers, each separated from one another by fifteen paces. When the first line finished shooting, they made space for the next line to advance and fire while they reloaded, and so on." Ieyasu stared at Mitsunari and remained silent for a considerable time before he spoke again.

"You are to drill my Teppo in such ways and assist Hanzo in arranging with these Saki merchants you spoke of and purchase more of these matchlocks."

"When can I visit my parents at Ishida?" Mitsunari asked before adding, "and check on Yoshimasa's recovery."

"Hanzo has arranged for your friend's care. When he is well enough to travel, he will no doubt resume his duties with his lord. As for you, your work is here and if it is satisfactory, then Nobunaga and I will decide your future."

"Am I to be Hitojichi (hostage), then?" said an angry Mitsunari. Ieyasu avoided answering Mitsunari's question directly. "Your Lord, Nobunaga has placed you under my authority to assist me in the matter of the Teppo, so I suggest you obey." Mitsunari bowed in obedience, but Ieyasu noticed the defiance in his eyes and felt some empathy for the young man.

I, too know, Mitsunari, what it is to be Hitojichi. Ieyasu closed his eyes and lapsed into thought. *I spent half of my thirty-four years as a hostage. As a five-year-old, my father, Matsudaira Hidetada sent me as a hostage to Imagawa Yoshimoto of Suruga, as a condition for Imagawa support in my father's fight against the Oda. But I never reached Suruga. Nobunaga's father, Oda Nobuhide, learned of this arrangement and had me abducted whilst I was on my way to Suruga. And so, I became Nobuhide's hostage. When my father refused his demands to sever all ties with the Imagawa clan, he threatened to have me executed but stayed his hand.*

Eventually, Nobuhide died during an epidemic, and I fell into Nobuhide's eldest son and heir, Nobuhiro's hands. Yoshimoto took advantage to attack and trap Nobuhiro. I again expected death but found myself saved by the intervention of his brother, Lord Nobunaga. To avoid a bloody battle, Nobunaga arranged for Yoshimoto to withdraw in exchange for handing me back as his hostage. It was only when Nobunaga won a devastating victory over Yoshimoto at Okehazama that I could escape and plan my revenge on the Imagawa.

Hanzo spoke, breaking the Tokugawa Lord's concentration.

"My Lord, we still have another matter to deal with." Ieyasu opened his eyes, replying, "send her in," Hanzo called out, and the guards outside the Lord's room slid back the screens doors permitting a woman in a plain grey *Kosode*-a smaller and looser fitting kimono tied with a vermillion obi to enter. She moved soundlessly across the room towards the Tokugawa Lord, her head down before bowing and taking a kneeling position opposite the lord, but alongside Mitsunari. The moment she entered, Mitsunari detected something familiar about the way she moved, and intrigued, he turned sideways to look more closely at her, but her loose, long, flowing black hair obscured her face.

"Hmm." Ieyasu hummed. "I believe you two have met?"

The woman returned Mitsunari's stare. Her sparkling brown eyes widened and raised a brow as she recognised Mitsunari. She then turned her attention towards Hanzo, and her eyes bored into him.

"Yoshino!" Mitsunari cried out, "It is you."

192

"Enough," Ieyasu shouted, "leave us." As he dismissed Mitsunari, adding, "You will have time to reacquaint yourself later before our guest here has to leave."

A brief time later, in his living quarters, Mitsunari found himself attracted to the castle housemaids attending to his evening meal. For the first time, he felt a strange twinge of desire surfacing within him, and he willed himself to think of other things. As the maid prepared Matcha from a steaming kettle she had carried, the other arranged his dinner of bean paste dumplings, broiled carp, and vegetable broth. He could not understand it, but the more he tried to suppress his desires, the more he thought of Yoshimasa.

It was only a few days ago that he heard Hideyoshi's shouts and responded to find Yoshimasa at a large farmhouse in the village of Ariake Mura. He recalled rushing in through the open door to find Hideyoshi standing over Yoshimasa and an older woman who appeared to be nursing him. He also remembered the joy he felt at seeing Yoshimasa again and was about to lose control and embrace him when two Samurai burst inside, declaring they had written orders for Hideyoshi from Lord Nobunaga.

It was whilst Hideyoshi read his orders that Yoshimasa beckoned for Mitsunari to approach and pulled him down by the sleeve to speak. He was finding it difficult to talk, but Yoshimasa whispered to Mitsunari that Yoshino had been here and had tended to his wounds. Before Mitsunari could reply, Yoshimasa extended his hand to cover Mitsunari's mouth and whispered, "Tell no one," he said, "not even Hideyoshi."

Hideyoshi announced his orders were to leave as soon as he had located Yoshimasa and catch up with the Nobunaga. The army had long left Nagashino for Gifu, and Hideyoshi knew to catch up to it would mean travelling most of the night. With Yoshimasa not well enough to travel, Hideyoshi handed over some coins to the old women to care for him till he can travel. Mitsunari had expected to leave with Hideyoshi but obeyed his order to remain behind in Ieyasu's service, for the time being, to help him in training his Teppo units. His last words to him were, "Nobunaga needs a powerful ally for what lies ahead."

Why did Yoshimasa want it kept secret that Yoshino was there tending to his wounds, and not to say anything to Hideyoshi? Mitsunari thought as he consoled himself with sake from the table.

While Mitsunari drank and dwelt on Yoshimasa's insistence on secrecy over Yoshino; Ieyasu and Hanzo were continuing their interrogation of her in the

Tokugawa Lord's living quarters. Hanzo informed Ieyasu that his clan elders of the Iga Ryu had unknown to him, accepted a contract by the Kunoichi leader Mochizuki to kill Yoshino. What interested Ieyasu most was what was so important about Yoshino that warranted the hire of Ninja assassins?

"Hanzo," Ieyasu said, "dead, she serves no useful purpose for us. Is that not so?"

"Yes, Lord, but all is not yet lost," Hanzo replied. "The Kunoichi has a plan, and we have sent word to test Mochizuki's response."

"What are you talking about, Hanzo?" Ieyasu said, growing impatient. Hanzo explained Yoshino believes Mochizuki is hiding a larger secret. She has falsely let it be known that she is aware of this great secret and has discussed it with others. Should Mochizuki call off the assassination, then it is reasonable to believe that the Kunoichi is correct; after all, Mochizuki would need to keep her alive to find out to whom she has talked.

"And you have agreed to this plan, Hanzo?" said Ieyasu.

"Yes, my Lord, and already it is bearing fruit. I have received news that the contract on the Kunoichi is withdrawn. Mochizuki has something to fear from the Kunoichi's death, which means she can continue to play her part." Yoshino stared coldly at Hanzo, and he felt uncomfortable but continued.

"My Lord," said Hanzo, "right now, there is nothing to change our view of her usefulness. It has increased, and I suggest we go ahead as planned. It is a three-day ride on a stout horse to Kofu, so I also suggest she leaves at first light, and we await developments."

"Agreed," nodded Ieyasu, who rose and left the room. Hanzo escorted Yoshino through Hamamatsu's maze of corridors towards her quarters for the night. The polished nightingale floors she had once tried so hard to avoid now sang out with each step Hanzo took, yet not a sound came from her feet. At the end of a long corridor, Hanzo slid back a screen door and stepped inside, followed by Yoshino.

"These are your quarters for the night," Hanzo said. "I will arrange for refreshments to be sent. Mitsunari is in the room next door." Yoshino looked around and said nothing, and Hanzo was about to leave when several grey-clad masked men silently descended from the ceiling space and surrounded them. Hanzo reacted and drew his sword, disembowelling one attacker. A rope dropped around him from above and pulled tight to restrain him, halted his next lunge at his attackers. Yoshino picked up the dead man's sword and in the space of two

194

moves severed the sword hand of one and removed the head of another. As Hanzo struggled against the rope binding him, his attacker delivered a forceful punch to his abdomen, knocking the wind out of him while telling him,

"Stay out of this." The remaining four intruders now moved to confront Yoshino. One of them swung a *kusarigama*-weighted chain with sickle above his head and whipped it forward, the chain entangling Yoshino's sword. He tightened the chain but made no move to rush Yoshino with the sickle. The delay was deliberate, for it gave his accomplices time enough to ensnare Yoshino with a net and bring her to the floor. The mesh of the net meant she could still see but found herself momentarily blinded by a spray of warm sticky liquid and then saw the severed head of one attacker lying next to her. Looking up, she saw Mitsunari, with *Jiko* in hand, methodically engaging the remaining attackers, and to her side lay the *kusarigama* with the hand that once wielded it, still attached. The severed shoulder of another attacker lay alongside it.

Mitsunari faced the last remaining attacker, who backed away only to cut his own throat with his sword and fall to the floor, making a hollow, bubbling sound as he fell. Satisfied no others remained, Mitsunari cut the net, constricting Yoshino who, once free, lunged after one of the fallen attackers' swords and advanced menacingly towards Hanzo, still restrained by the surrounding rope. When Yoshino was close enough to smell Hanzo's breath, she stared deep into his eyes and raised her sword to strike, only to find her blade instantly blocked by *Jiko* in Mitsunari's firm hand.

Hanzo, now transfixed on the arms poised above him, one to kill and one to save, noticed that arms had the same small, elongated patch of darkly pigmented skin on the underneath of their sword arms. *It is true then.* Hanzo thought. *They are related.*

When news of the attack reached the Tokugawa Lord, he could barely contain his anger and now berated those generals and officials he had summoned to appear before him.

"Honda Masanobu, how could this happen? You handle palace security." Before giving Masanobu the chance to reply, Ieyasu pointed his fan and directed his anger towards Masanobu's eldest son, Honda Masazumi.

"Masazumi, your impenetrable walls, moats and fortifications amounted to nothing. How much were you paid?" Ieyasu demanded. Masazumi had been responsible for overseeing the castle's expansion and improving the fortifications but had earned a reputation as an inveterate schemer for his shady dealings with the town artisans.

Fearful, Masazumi prostrated himself before Ieyasu, insistent he had not betrayed the lord and begged for permission to cut his belly open without delay to atone for this negligence. Masanobu also seized the moment and pleaded with Ieyasu to join his son in the void. Worried that Lord Ieyasu might vent his anger and allow the suicides, Hanzo pleaded to speak.

"My Lord, I consider your castle to be impregnable to any enemy force. This infiltration was the work of Shinobi, in fact, my Shinobi." An astounded Ieyasu rounded on Hanzo. "Explain yourself, Hanzo."

"I was curious why the attackers made no direct attempt to kill anyone and only restrained me. In removing the masks of the slain attackers, I identified one as belonging to my Iga clan. I sent word to the clan elders demanding an explanation, and I have received news that the contract was not rescinded but changed. They came to kidnap, not to kill."

"Hanzo, what is the point of an impregnable fortress if they can easily penetrate it? Tell me that?"

"Sire, did not the target of this attack penetrate this very fortress on her own some years ago?" Despite the coolness of the night, Ieyasu waved his fan back and forth in an agitated manner before answering, "Careful, Hanzo, careful."

Ieyasu closed his fan and studied the prostrated Masazumi and Masanobu before him, his anger gradually subsiding. He called for them to raise their heads and said, "I deny your request for seppuku." To Hanzo, he asked, "Where does this leave us then, with the Kunoichi?"

"Sire. We still have everything to gain and nothing to lose. Let us continue to wait out developments."

In the wrecked room that was Yoshino's living quarters, Yoshino, and Mitsunari sat together, each silent as they strived to understand the attack that had taken place earlier. Yoshino knew she would not be needing these quarters tonight, as arrangements were in place to leave the castle after sunset. She could not afford to delay, as she needed to cross the Oigawa River and be in Suruga by daybreak. Adding to her concern was the recent rains on the highlands would soon flow down and raise the water level of the Oigawa, making it impassable. Once across, she would travel to the village of Nambu on the Fujigawa River where Hanzo had arranged lodgings and a change of horse. From there, she would follow the Fujigawa River Valley upstream and arrive in Kofu in around two more days.

Mitsunari wiped the blood from *Jiko* with some paper he carried, and once satisfied *Jiko* was clean, he returned the sword to its scabbard and thought about the damage in front of him. The screen doors were easily repairable, but the blood-stained tatami flooring mats would all need replacing. And then a thought occurred to him. *For an assassination attempt, they did not try to kill anyone. Even after Hanzo killed one of them, they did not retaliate. Why?*

"By their weapons and technique, it is clear the attackers were Shinobi," said Yoshino, "and given their number, we should both be dead now."

"What do you think they wanted?" asked Mitsunari.

"They wanted one of us alive, and I suspect I was the target."

Mitsunari looked at Yoshino. She had a youthful appearance. Her unblemished skin lacked any signs of ageing, but he knew she was older than him. He again felt the strange bond that seems to exist between them.

"Who are you?" Mitsunari asked. Yoshino looked at Mitsunari and thought she detected a sense of hurt in him.

"I have many faces, and fate has set me on a path to an unknown destiny. Once I served the Takeda Lord, Shingen, once I served the Shogun Yoshiaki, and became your tutor. Now, I serve the Tokugawa Lord Ieyasu. Right now, I have a mission I need to complete and if I am successful, I will tell you more. When you finish your time here, seek Hideyoshi, for that is where your true destiny lies." Mitsunari thought he saw the glint of moistness in her eyes and felt an urge to comfort her, but replied,

"There is much more you will not tell me, but…" Mitsunari's words trailed off as the damaged screen door suddenly slid open, interrupting him. Hanzo, accompanied by two Samurai, stood in the doorway and spoke.

"It is time." Yoshino rose, lightly caressing Mitsunari's cheek, and left with Hanzo, leaving Mitsunari alone.

Chapter Seventeen

Yoshino

Autumn/Winter: Fourth Year of Tensho (1576)

The sun had just dipped below the horizon when Yoshino rode out of Hamamatsu castle towards her first river crossing at the Tenryu gawa. The warm breeze blowing across the flat plains of Hamamatsu from the southern Mikatgahara Plateau carried with it the sounds of cicadas, and a full moon lit up the road ahead.

Yoshino crossed the swollen waters of Tenryu and galloped across the flat river plain towards an inner bend of the meandering Oigawa river that served as the border between Mikawa and Suruga provinces. She had made good time and arrived at her crossing point around the hour of the ox, three hours before daybreak. The river level here was also rising and would soon breach its banks. She looked downstream and could tell by the moonlight reflecting off the water that the current was running strong. Yoshino coaxed her horse into the water, and whilst the bend in the river had slowed the current, she knew the danger lay mid-stream.

The mare seemed unsure of its footing and tried to back up, but Yoshino persisted in coaxing the horse onward. The water now lapped over Yoshino's saddle, but the mare ploughed on bravely, just keeping its head above water. Gradually, they pulled past the middle of the river and the water level receded as the ground rose. But the mare, weakened by the effort, struggled to gain her footing as she climbed up onto the bank. Yoshino dismounted into the water, keeping a firm grip on the reins as her feet searching for a firmer footing.

Eventually, she led the mare towards a section of the riverbank that had broken away and coaxed the mare up onto dry land. After a brief rest, Yoshino led the mare on foot for a few hours before remounting and then rode at a much slower pace. Although Shimada was only a two-hour ride away, it would take much longer with a weakened horse.

At Shimada, Yoshino rested in the stable, belonging to a local farmer to escape the worst of the day's heat and humidity and would set out again with a freshly rested horse at nightfall. Cloudless skies led into nightfall, bringing another night of welcome moonlight to guide her way.

At the Abegawa bridge, she found it guarded by a solitary Tokugawa Samurai, and after showing the travel pass that Hanzo had supplied, Yoshino crossed without event, heading north towards the village of Nambu in the Fuji River Valley. Dawn had just broken by the time she reached Nambu, and another day of clear skies meant more sultry weather ahead. In the east, Yoshino marvelled at the snow caps of Fujiyama gleaming in the emerging sun and noticed the quickly rising mists around her. Her stay at Nambu was brief, just enough to water her horse and refill her water pipe before continuing north, where she would follow the valley floor of the Fuji River towards her destination. With much of the Fuji in flood, she took to the densely forested slopes of the valley, where the rider and the horse trampled through a treacherous undergrowth of ferns and hidden moss-covered rocks.

Yoshino was grateful that the tall beech and hinoki cedar trees towering above provided a shaded canopy and welcome relief from the heat of the sun.

A little while later, Yoshino stopped to rest and tied the mare to an overhanging branch while she sat and ate a meal of rice balls she had purchased from the farmer at Shimada. Movement in the nearby undergrowth had caught her attention and her mare became visibly agitated whinnying. Yoshino quickly drew her short sword and crept silently in the direction of the movement but found nothing. She heard the mare again whinnying and returned to find her horse gone.

It was then that a masked stranger calmly stepped out of the undergrowth and stood looking at her. He appeared unarmed, but she nervously watched him slowly reach into his rough cotton *Kosode*. Yoshino prepared herself to deflect what she suspected the stranger would withdraw, but it was the sting at her throat from another direction that she now felt. She knew at once it was a *Fukibari*—a blowgun dart, fired by a hidden accomplice. The stranger in front of her had disappeared, and her vision was rapidly becoming blurred. As a wave of light-headedness overcame her, Yoshino collapsed to her knees and, using her short sword, she stabbed at the ground to stay upright. Then, the darkness came.

199

Yoshino woke up on the floor of the main Daizenji Temple outside Kofu. She recognised the temple from the three distinctive rough-hewn Hinoki doors that hung between its four columns from her last visit. The room was dark, lit only by two *Andon* lanterns on the wall, whose light failed to penetrate the far reaches of the room. She sat up, rubbing her neck, surprised she was not bound and smelt the lingering scent of burnt sandalwood incense. Sensing someone else lurking in the shadows, Yoshino called out and the figure of a woman edged out of the shadows into the weak lantern light. The vermillion cotton *Kosode* she wore was a little shorter than a normal kimono and only just covered her pink undergarment, but it was the *Aikuchi* (dagger) nestled in her thin white obi that Yoshino immediately recognised.

"Mochizuki Chiyo," Yoshino called out. "Why did you find the need to pay Shinobi to kill me?" Chiyo stepped closer towards Yoshino.

"Nothing personal, you understand, but you have now become a threat." Even in the weak light of the lantern, Yoshino noticed the change in her. She still wore her hair tied up at the back and fastened with her elaborate tortoise-shell comb and hairpins. Her long black strands of hair, now streaked with grey, hung loosely on either side of her face, and her dull eyes seemed cold and distant.

"The years have not to have been kind to you, Chiyo," Yoshino said before further adding, "you have yet to answer my question." Chiyo ignored the barb in her comment, and her lips trembled as she spoke.

"So, you believe you have discovered the truth. I should like to know that truth, for I suspect you are mistaken, and I may need to put the record straight."

She is probing. She wants me to divulge what I know. If I tell her, I lose any advantage and my life.

"Did you think I would not find out from Masatsugu?" Yoshino said, being intentionally vague, and without waiting for a reply, she continued to press her.

"You knew I had revenge on my mind, yet you offered not only the name of my defiler but also where he was. You wanted me to find him and kill him." Chiyo knelt on the polished floor before Yoshino and calmly placed both hands on her lap before she answered.

"My dear, I needed you, and you needed to learn the truth and end your lust for vengeance."

200

She continues to deny that there is anything more. I need to unsettle her.

"Or was it to remove the one person who knew too much?" Yoshino asked, carefully studying her reaction.

"What more could he know, other than being your child's father?" Chiyo confidently replied. Yoshino knew she needed to change tactics and recalled Masatsugu's confession that night here at the Daizenji Temple. She remembered thinking at times there was something odd about his tale but dismissed it, but now it sprung to life in her mind.

Why did the Takeda Lord have a child delivered into the priest's care? How is it that the lord himself found foster parents for Mitsunari and paid for his upkeep? Why would such a lord involve himself in such trivial matters? So many questions, but they all connect to Shingen. Let her answer why.

"Could it be, he perhaps knew about Lord Shingen," Yoshino said, gambling that the name that might spark a reaction, and she was right. Chiyo's demeanour suddenly changed. She became notably agitated and stared at Yoshino with a coldness she had not seen before.

"He was a fool. But only your word now stands in the way," Chiyo snapped.

She denied nothing. She assumes I know about Shingen. But what? Yoshino again changed tactics and turned the conversation to Masatsugu's murder.

"Why did you kill him?" Yoshino said. Another probe, another gamble.

"I did not, she did," Chiyo said, her head turning towards a corner of the room. Yoshino followed Chiyo's eyes and saw the outline of another woman emerging into the faint light. Even in the poor light, Yoshino could tell her clothing was much more elaborate than Chiyo's. She wore a *kosode* of expensive silk patterned in crimson, but over her heart, she wore the embroidered Takeda mon. Clutching her *Hiogi* (fan), the figure glided over towards them. Her loose raven black hair swayed, partially obscuring her face, but Yoshino instantly recognised her.

"Masako," Yoshino gasped. Masako knelt alongside Chiyo, flicking her head back to allow her loose hair to settle away from her face. She opened her fan and fanned herself as she studied Yoshino. Feeling betrayed by two of the women who mattered most in her life, Yoshino snapped back at Masako.

"Why would you, of all people, murder the priest?"

201

"Why, it is as you just said. The fool knew too much. When you crept out of Tsutsujigasaki Yakata Palace that night, I followed you here and waited for you to leave. I had expected to find Masatsugu dead, but he was very much alive. He was startled to see me and babbled on about having said nothing to you, which I knew to be a lie. Either way, it mattered not what he told you: he would always be a liability, and you would have eventually killed him, anyway. I noticed the fool kept the sword Lord Shingen once gave him. It took pride of place in his *Tokonomo* (alcove). With the fool's permission, I removed the sword to admire its elaborate decoration. You should be familiar with the *Nukitsuke* technique, the draw and cut with one motion, for that is how Masatsugu came to lose his head."

"Who else have you told?" Chiyo spoke, addressing Yoshino.

If she finds out that was merely a ruse, then my life is forfeited.

"Surely, you do not expect me to tell you," Yoshino said, acting surprised.

"It does not matter," Chiyo said. "Would you like some water? The air in here is becoming quite warm." Without waiting for Yoshino's response, Chiyo rose and went over to a small bucket by one of the closed doors and returned to offer Yoshino a ladle of cool water, who greedily accepted and slaked her thirst.

"Now, where were we? Ah yes, you declined to tell me who else you have spoken to about this matter; but no matter, you should have known from your training in medicines and poisons that some substances can tell me everything I need to know."

Yoshino's mind raced. She looked at the ladle and then back to Chiyo's face, whose trembling lips suddenly curled into a smile. She had to act fast before the delirium set in. From experience, she knew the drug was both hallucinatory and unpredictable, and she felt its effects. Rivulets of perspiration dripped from her forehead, panicking her. She hyperventilated to increase her shallow breathing rate as she had been, taught in training to speed up her heart rate and deliberately increase her level of anxiety to a level where she would feel nauseous and hopefully vomit the poison out.

"Well done," Chiyo said as she clapped her hands in approval. "It is good to see that you still remember your training, but sadly, your performance was in vain. The water was pure as it should be in a temple." Still shaken by her self-induced anxiety attack, Yoshino took slow, deep breaths and relaxed her muscles. She knew that somehow Shingen was the key to this, and they were still unsure what she knows.

Should Chiyo and Masako discover, all I know is that Masatsugu is Mitsunari's father, then my value to them is at an end. I am dead? They need to believe I know everything, whatever it is. Her confidence returning, Yoshino played another gamble.

"Why did Shingen do it?" Yoshino bluntly asked. Chiyo and Masako exchanged nervous glances, and it fell to Masako to answer first, without first thinking.

"Look, everyone knew the lord had an eye for young women, especially ones as young as you were. But because of your age and low birth, he could not have you as a concubine, but he had to have you." Yoshino fell silent as she struggled with her emotions. She wanted to cry out, but it was essential to hide her surprise from Chiyo and Masako.

This explains some of Lord Shingen's involvement, but this? Surely not. Then why did both Masatsugu and Chiyo lie?

"Are you unwell?" Masako asked in a curious tone. Yoshino ignored the comment. She had to remain calm, but Masako's revelation meant she struggled to stay focused, her mind racing, always looking for answers. Finally, she turned her attention to Chiyo.

"Why did you lie to me about my parents selling me into prostitution with Masatsugu?"

"Oh, that. It was not a lie of sorts. Everything I told you was true. I just failed to mention that Masatsugu also accompanied the Takeda Lord on his frequent visitations to you. As his retainer, it was Masatsugu's duty to be there and protect his lord." Masako added.

"As Lord Shingen could not have you as a concubine, he had you secretly adopted. So, my dear, you are also Takeda, but having a child threatened the Takeda succession."

Adopted. What is she saying?

"I sense your confusion, Yoshino," Chiyo inquired with some empathy. "This is something you did not know but would later find out, anyway. Ten years ago, Yoshinobu, who was Lord Shingen's son and heir by his principal wife, Lady Sanjo no kata was forced to commit seppuku for rebellion. His second son Nobuchika also, by Lady Sanjo no kata, was born blind and thus could not be the Takeda heir. He had a third son, Nobukiyo, who died at childbirth many years ago. So, his remaining eldest son, Katsuyori, by his concubine, Suwa Goryonin naturally became the heir. Katsuyori also had two other brothers, Morinobu and Nobusada, who were Shingen's sons by other concubines, but both ended up being adopted into the Nishiwa and Imagawa clans, respectively, to cement alliances. This also meant they could not be heirs."

"So, Masako's husband, Katsuyori, is then the true heir. Why then is my child a threat to this?" Yoshino asked.

"Lord Shingen's concubine, Suwa Goryonin, was also the daughter of Suwa Yorishige, Lord of Suwa, who Shingen killed, and on her death, Katsuyori succeeded his mother as head of the Suwa clan. Yoshinobu was the Takeda heir, but with his death, Katsuyori became head of both the Suwa and Takeda clans except, like Morinobu and Nobusada, Katsuyori could not legitimately be head of both. Many considered Katsuyori's rule illegitimate and, had another of Shingen's sons appeared, the Takeda would have been at war with themselves. This would have destroyed the Takeda clan, of which you are one." Chiyo studied Yoshino and continued.

"Does Mitsunari know who his actual father is?" Chiyo asked.

I sense a trap. If I say no, the Takeda succession is safe for the time being, but I remain a threat. If I say yes, then Mitsunari also becomes a threat, and his life will be in danger. Too many loose ends here, and Chiyo will get rid of us both once she finds out no one else knows. I need to play for time.

"No. Mitsunari is unaware of his adoption and knows nothing about Masatsugu or Shingen," Yoshino said.

"Then who else have you told? Surely, as a Takeda, you do not wish to see our clan destroyed?"

Another trap. I cannot now say no one as I would not leave here alive. She knows I am a spy for Hanzo and the Tokugawa, and they would be keen to use this information to sow dissent. If I had told Hanzo, she would find it impossible to get Iga Shinobi to accept a contract to kill him. She would have to rely on the Koga Shinobi and risk war between the two clans. Yes, there is a solution.

"Chiyo. I am not a fool. If I reply I have told no one, you would have no reason to keep me alive, and if I reveal the name of who I might have told, you will move the heavens to have this person killed, and then me. Therefore, I have no incentive to tell you, do I? You say I am Takeda, but I have sworn no fealty to the clan, so I have a proposition for you which should be enough to buy my silence and keep the Takeda line secure. You know I spy for the Tokugawa, so I propose I swear fealty to Lord Katsuyori and become a double agent for the Takeda."

"What guarantees do we have you will not betray us?" Masako asked. Yoshino tried a bluff. "I give you my word but, understand this I have arranged that upon my death, I will make your secret common knowledge."

"My dear, you will appreciate we need to confer," said Masako, who rose with Chiyo and sat in another part of the hall nearest to one lantern.

"Masako," said Chiyo, "it is as she says. She is a Tokugawa agent, but the Iga Shinobi inform me that the Tokugawa do not trust her. Her son, Mitsunari, is being held by the Tokugawa as an unsuspecting hostage to ensure her cooperation. They could not coerce Yoshino into spying for them unless she believes Mitsunari's life is at risk. I see an advantage in accepting her offer. This way, we can arrange a betrayal. Katsuyori will then kill her, and Ieyasu will finish Mitsunari. A most satisfactory solution to this problem, I think."

#

Spring: Fifth Year of Tensho (1577). Echizen Province.

With the passing of winter, the first signs of the spring thaw appeared, and the Myoko Mountain Pass linking Echigo and Shinano provinces once again became passable. The forest canopy of giant pines, beeches and cedars had given up their white blankets, but the snow still lay deep on the forest floor. Yoshino, riding a sturdy bay Kiso mare, descended the mountain towards the village of Ariaka at the foot of Mount Myoko. At the hour of the snake, the mid-morning sun was high overhead, gradually warming the chilly mountain air and melting more of the snow as she descended. Once in the foothills, Yoshino stopped to remove her uncomfortably thick *Mino* straw cape. She wore over her four-layered *Kosode* as protection from the cold sleet and snow that had followed her since she left Nagano.

Four days earlier, Masako had Yoshino set out for the castle town of Kasugayama in Echizen to watch and report on Uesugi Kenshin, the Lord of Echizen's movements. As a long-standing enemy of the Takeda, Kenshin was seeking a peace treaty, and Katsuyori suspected the pious Kenshin only wanted a pause in their battles to focus on Nobunaga, who was encroaching into his territories of neighbouring Kaga and Echigo.

The long journey from Kofu gave Yoshino time to reflect on her arrangement with Chiyo and Masako. She was under no illusion that she and Mitsunari would always remain a threat to the Takeda, and the only solution would be to first kill Chiyo and then dispose of Masako. Yoshino agonised over telling Mitsunari the truth of his parentage, but she knew the truth would torment him and, without doubt, place his life in greater danger. The politics of state would ensure he would know no peace. Daimyos, like Ieyasu, would exploit his Takeda connections to their advantage and plunge the country into war. It would be best if Mitsunari knew nothing about his actual parents, as no good could ever come of it.

She rested at the Kashiwabara ryokan at the foot of Mount Kurohime before attempting the climb up towards the Myoko Mountain Pass into Echizen, which would take a full-day's ride. It was at Kashiwabara that Yoshino laid the bait. She sent word to Masako that a drunk ronin here said he knew Hajikano Masatsugu well, for they were long-term friends and he had recently visited him, boasting he knew a secret that would make him rich and powerful. Yoshino indicated to Masako that she intended to stay at the Seki springs close to the Myoko Mountain Pass border until she heard word from her. She knew either Chiyo or Masako would dare not take the risk, however implausible, and would come to investigate, but they would also suspect a trap.

Yoshino followed the rocky trail and continued her slow descent down the mountainside towards the Seki springs. Her stocky mare felt its way down the steep, treacherous path, carefully navigating the moss-covered stones and streams of melting snow crisscrossing the trail. In the valley below, Yoshino took comfort at the sight of rising plumes of steam appearing from the many hot springs around. It indicated she was close to her destination, but it was much later in the afternoon, around the hour of the sheep before she arrived at the springs. Despite the bright sunshine and cloudless sky, the air remained chilly and reeked of the sulphurous steam rising over the various hot pools. At this lower altitude, most of the surrounding snow had disappeared, exposing a carpet of damp grasslands and blooming wildflowers.

Yoshino sat on a large rock, overlooking one of the many hot springs surrounding her and watched the bubbles of sulphurous air rhythmically rising and bursting open on the reddish-coloured waters. Three days had passed, and Yoshino had worried her plan was unravelling when late in the day the inn attendant informed her a lady of status was enquiring after her. Yoshino had the attendant invite the lady for a sunset viewing in the main Onsen pool by the large overhanging maple tree. She suspected this arrangement would allay any suspicions Chiyo might have, as being naked would remove the risk of any concealed weapons.

Yoshino walked along the narrow path separating the main Onsen pool from the *Kamado* or the cooking pot pool and glanced at the smallish statue of *Oni;* a red demon who sat grinning atop an iron cooking pot, warning those foolish enough to enter its scalding waters. At the large maple tree, she sat down near a set of steps leading into the bubbling pool and removed the *Aikuchi* dagger she had concealed within the sleeve of her *Kosode* sleeve and placed it on a submerged ledge, deep in the pool, and returned to the ryokan.

As the sun sank beneath the horizon, well into the hour of the rooster, Yoshino watched the sky transition from a palette of vivid hues of orange and red to purple and despite the erratic cloud cover, the moon cast an eerie light over the bubbling pools. Yoshino had finished washing with the bucket supplied and had slipped into the steaming waters. Leaning back, she relaxed and watched the sun disappear, while the hot spring waters lapped at the underside of her breasts. She looked back towards the ryokan and saw a woman she suspected to be Chiyo approach. Yoshino studied the figure as she removed her heavy cotton Yukata (robe) and washed her pale, milky skin in a bucket before entering the pool.

"My dear Yoshino," Chiyo said. "Your news is of great concern. How did you come to know of this Ronin you mentioned?"

Now she will test me. Yoshino had positioned herself at the submerged ledge, concealing the *Aikuchi* dagger, but she was still not close enough to strike.

"We must be careful and not overheard," Yoshino quietly replied as she edged closer. Chiyo settled her petite frame into the water, her arms outstretched to support her while she floated while the bubbling waters lapped provocatively against her pert pear-shaped breasts.

Her body is tense, she is cautious. She is waiting for something to happen. I need a distraction.

"You know perfectly well I was lying about the Ronin, but it is true there is another who knows our secret," said Yoshino. She saw the moon's reflection in Chiyo's eyes as they widened in anticipation and continued.

"Long ago, I was tending the wounds of someone you know well and thinking him to be at the point of death, I told him." Feeling teased, Chiyo asked, "Why are you telling me this now?" as she edged along out of Yoshino's reach.

"It was your lover, Yoshimasa," said Yoshino, "and he asked me to give you a message." Chiyo froze. It was a name she had not heard spoken for years, and it suddenly rekindled a forgotten passion. Unconsciously, Chiyo gravitated back towards Yoshino to hear more. Yoshino acted as if to ensure no one was listening and looked around before drawing closer.

"What was the message?" Chiyo asked with a sense of desperation.

"This," Yoshino said as the *Aikuchi* dagger she had been holding under the water broke the surface, rising in an arc, slicing open Chiyo's throat on the downstroke. Her blood mingled with the now darkening reddish waters of the hot springs and Chiyo's lifeless body floated face down in the bubbling waters.

Part Three

Chapter Eighteen

Mitsunari

Autumn/Winter: Fifth Year of Tensho (1577)

Around mid-day in the hour of the horse, heavy rain fell over Hamamatsu Castle and on the grassy fields beyond the castle walls, Mitsunari drilled his Teppo units in the tactics he had refined at Shitagahara. As the Tokugawa possessed only three hundred guns, it did not take long for Mitsunari to train them into a respectable level of competency. By now, he was reaching the end of his usefulness as a drill instructor and had spent most of his time experimenting with other tactics and techniques he had learnt from the Portuguese in Sakai.

As the downpour became more intense, Hanzo, despite wearing a straw hat and cape for protection, ran for shelter under a nearby cedar tree and shouted towards Mitsunari.

"Mitsunari," he shouted, "why must you practice in this weather?" A sodden looking Mitsunari looked up and carried the musket he was holding; leaving the three swordsmiths he had brought in from Sakai to run towards Hanzo.

"Do you think we will only go to battle when the sun shines?" Mitsunari shouted out to Hanzo as he tried to wipe away the water running down his face. Standing alongside Hanzo, he demonstrated with the musket the purpose of his experiment with the swordsmiths.

"The two biggest drawbacks to the Tanegashima matchlock in battle are wet weather and the time to reload." Mitsunari withdrew a small, lacquered box from his sodden robes and placed it over the musket's flash pan cover.

"The barbarians use a metal pan cover on their Tanegashima guns to protect the priming powder against wet weather. When you pull the trigger, the cover retracts, allowing the serpentine igniter to fire the pan, and when released, the pan cover returns to its position to protect the pan. The swordsmiths are here to see if they can engineer something like this that we can use."

"I need to talk to you about some things which cannot wait," said Hanzo. "Return to the castle and dry out, then we can talk."

It was much later in the afternoon, around the hour of the sheep when Mitsunari joined Hanzo in his quarters and shared a light meal and warm sake.

"What was so urgent?" Mitsunari asked Hanzo, putting down his sake bowl and wiping his mouth.

"Let us deal with the urgent matter first. Lord Ieyasu commands you leave for Sakai, to purchase more of these Tanegashima guns. We need to know how many we can buy now and when more will be available."

"How many guns is the lord looking to buy, then?" asked Mitsunari. "Even with the many swordsmiths they have in Sakai, it takes one swordsmith one month to produce one gun. So, you can see supply will be at a premium, as will the cost."

"As many as are available," said Hanzo. "Do not concern yourself about cost. The attendants who will accompany you will cater to your needs and arrange the funds." Hanzo leant over and refilled Mitsunari's bowl with more warm sake.

"The second matter we need to discuss concerns our Kunoichi friend, Yoshino. It has now been several months, and we have heard no news from her. My Iga Shinobi have heard news of the death of a hi-born woman traveller in the Myoko-Echizen area and have spoken to the local magistrate there. The woman's description fits that of Yoshino." Mitsunari said nothing for a moment and sat quietly, thinking.

Strangely, this news does not bother me. I feel certain she is still alive somewhere.

"Why are you telling me this, Hanzo?" Mitsunari asked.

"I was wondering if you have had news from her that would allay our fears."

"No, I have heard nothing. Now, when do I leave for Sakai?"

"The horses are ready, and arrangements made. You are to leave at first light and travel west, following the shoreline towards the furthest point of the Atsumi Peninsula where a vessel to take you to Ise awaits. At Ise, you will travel overland through Oda territory to Sakai." Hanzo picked up a folded parchment and handed it to Mitsunari. "You will need these travel papers. Nobunaga has signed them, allowing you and your attendants unfettered travel."

Having endured four days of uncomfortable travel, Mitsunari's arrival in Sakai with his four attendants was not without event. Officials had delayed their entry into the east gate of the city for several hours, while they scrupulously checked the credentials of a long queue of merchants and labourers seeking entry. With the city walled off on three sides and surrounded by moats, the east, and west gates were the only access to the city. When the gate officials finally attended to Mitsunari and his party, they were directed to the west side of the city where inns catering to middle-class retainers such as he were located. The officials pointed out that accommodations on the east and north sides of the city were reserved for government officials of rank and, of course, Daimyo. Commoners and foreigners were relegated to the south port area, near the waterfront storehouses.

Mitsunari later left his lodgings and walked alone down a narrow street that led towards the waterfront. Ceramic merchants, sake brewers, and stores filled with Chinese and Korean imports were prominent on both sides of the street. The many ox-drawn carts carrying baskets of pottery and sake barrels made passage through the narrow street difficult, but eventually, he could see the waterfront and the strange vessels laying at anchor just offshore. At the waterfront, he spoke with wharf workers, busy unloading cargo from longboats sent by the strange ships, and learnt they were Portuguese. The two Galleons and a four-masted Carrack had arrived on last night's tide.

Opposite the dock, Mitsunari located a wide street of tall narrow two-storey storehouses, painted white with earthen walls, and stone pillar bases to protect against fire. Annoyingly for Mitsunari, all the storehouses lacked any signage that might show either its contents or its owner. Feeling a bit lost, Mitsunari inquired of a passing worker where he might find the merchant Imai Sokyu and was pleasantly surprised to discover that the storehouse in front of him belonged to Imai Sokyu. The only visible entrance to the storehouse was a small wicket gate built into a much larger door, which Mitsunari opened and stepped inside. An enormous room filled with cedar boxes of assorted sizes and hemp bales greeted him.

Mitsunari walked over to the other side of the room, where several workers at one of the open rear doors were busy loading cedar boxes onto a cart. He ran his hand over one box, delighting in the smooth grain of the timber, and wondered what lay inside. All the boxes bore the painted characters for Omi and Sakamoto, which Mitsunari presumed to be their destination. A worker, noticing Mitsunari's presence, stopped his work and bowed towards Mitsunari, who calmly inquired if the merchant Imai Sokyu was around.

"If you are seeking Imai Sokyu, I am here," a quiet voice behind Mitsunari called out. The overweight looking gentleman who stood before him was not the Imai Sokyu he once remembered, but despite the shaven head, fine robes and fuller figure, he still recognised him and bowed in acknowledgement.

"Sokyu," Mitsunari exclaimed. "You seemed to have gained a bit of weight since I last saw you." The merchant looked at Mitsunari, and a wide grin formed across his face, revealing the few remaining teeth he had left, and returned Mitsunari's bow.

"It is young Sakichi, is it not?" The merchant replied.

"Yes, but I have taken an adult name now," explained Mitsunari. "Lord Nobunaga has given me the name Mitsunari and acknowledged my family name. I am known as Ishida Mitsunari." As was customary, Mitsunari was about to state his vassalage but confessed to being confused. He explained, "At my Genpuku, I swore fealty to Nobunaga, but Hideyoshi is my lord and now I seem to serve the Tokugawa." Sokyu smiled at Mitsunari and moved towards a nearby staircase, beckoning Mitsunari to follow.

"Come upstairs and let us take tea. You still remember the ceremony?" The second level, as Mitsunari noticed, included two conjoined rooms, each featuring a large shoji window looking out over Osaka Bay. One room served as a cluttered office, made untidy by the considerable number of paper scrolls, and writing implements that lay scattered on its polished wooden floors and tables. The other room, in contrast, showcased a theme of order and serenity. Sokyu had transformed this room into a *Chashitsu* (tea room), complete with tatami mat floors, a tokonoma alcove and walls decorated in simple subdued colours.

Mitsunari sat before Imai Sokyu in the tea room, quietly watching him prepare the green matcha. Besides being a merchant, Sokyu was also a renowned tea master, and fond memories of secretly watching his mother perform the ceremony for her guests flooded back. When he was ready, Sokyu placed a bowl of hot tea in front of Mitsunari and invited him to drink. Mitsunari responded with the customary appraisal and compliments of Sokyu's choice of tea utensils.

Impressed with Mitsunari's cultured perspective on the *Chanoyu,* Sokyu reminisced about earlier times when visiting the Enryaku-ji.

"When I lasted visited the abbot, I remember his praise for your growing knowledge of Karamono tea utensils, but tell me, what brings you to Sakai?"

"Master Sokyu. As you will recall, it has been some years since I was last here in Sakai looking for suitable pieces for the abbot's collection. On that visit, I came across one of the Portuguese barbarians in one of the ceramic trading stores, and by good fortune, a Jesuit priest who spoke his language accompanied him. I took great interest in the small teppo the barbarian carried in his waistband that he called a 'Pistola'. He was also kind enough to explain its function and went into detail about how the matchlocks we call Tanegashima were used in his native Europe. I had thought this interest in firearms to be a passing phase, but it would seem fate had delivered me to those who wanted to make use of this knowledge. For the moment, it would seem I serve the Tokugawa Lord, Ieyasu who has commanded me to purchase as many rifles, ammunition, and powder as I can lay my hands on."

"You have explained what brings you to Sakai, but how is it you sought me out?" Sokyu said as he carefully cleaned and put away his tea serving utensils.

"I knew of your good relations with Lord Nobunaga, as he, too, is a keen follower of the *Chanoyu* and an avid collector of valuable tea utensils. I was privileged to view his Meibutsu tea collection at Inabayama." Having finished putting away the utensils, Sokyu now gave Mitsunari his full attention.

"So, did Lord Nobunaga send you then?"

"No, master Sokyu. It is common knowledge that Sakai is one of the major centres of trade in firearms and ammunition and that you supply Lord Nobunaga with such items."

"I fear you confuse me with someone else," Sokyu said.

"Master Sokyu," Mitsunari said, becoming a little annoyed. "I was at Gifu when you visited Lord Nobunaga. Nobunaga himself has said that aside from being a wealthy merchant, you are also a descendant of the Sasaki Samurai family of Omi. Your warrior ancestry has elevated you above the lowly merchant class, and I know you provisioned and lent capital to finance some of Nobunaga's military campaigns. You also own the ammunition factory at Abiko, just outside Sakai, and Lord Nobunaga has made you a magistrate of the five districts formerly ruled by the Miyoshi clan with the added benefit of a sizeable stipend." Sokyu's eyes widened in surprise and, feeling uncomfortable, he shifted position.

"How is it you know so much about my dealings with Lord Nobunaga?"

"Lord Hideyoshi told me."

215

"Ah!" exclaimed Sokyu. "One purpose of the tea ceremony such as we have just had is to communicate beyond words and learn fundamental truths about each other. I know little of your background, but you have expert knowledge of mine. As for your interest in arms, this age of war has shown not only is the nature of war is changing but society as well. Merchants continue to be despised for their trade, but we have become invaluable suppliers of arms, provisions and capital for the warring Daimyo. For the merchant class, war has become a very profitable business." Sokyu breathed deeply as if absorbing the peace and serenity of his surroundings and continued, "The problem with war is that demand has overtaken supply. If I supply one lord, his enemy demands the same or more, leaving my neck exposed. Can you tell me why I must help you?"

"Master Sokyu, I have been honest with you. I come as an agent from the Tokugawa seeking to purchase arms. As you are no doubt aware, the Tokugawa are allies of Lord Nobunaga, so I doubt this transaction will cause trouble for you with Nobunaga."

"I think you miss the point," said Sokyu. "As I have said, demand has outstripped supply. I cannot supply all of Lord Nobunaga's' requirements now and even though the Tokugawa are allies, I suspect the quantity Lord Nobunaga receives from me will not please him. No doubt, he would be annoyed to discover that his ally has deprived him of the rest." Mitsunari knew Sokyu had a valid argument, but he also knew Sokyu was not the only merchant in Sakai with firearms for sale. Pressing Sokyu, he asked.

"What of the other merchants here in Sakai? Do they have any firearms available I might buy?"

"I cannot speak for the other merchants, but I suspect, like me, they are also struggling to meet demand. However, give me a day or two, and I will make enquiries with the other merchants and see what I can do on your behalf."

"Do you wish to know where we are staying?" asked Mitsunari.

"That will not be necessary, Mitsunari." Sokyu laughed, adding, "we know where all the customers are in Sakai." Mitsunari bowed in gratitude at the offer of help but felt despondent at the thought of returning to Hamamatsu empty-handed. As he rose to leave, Mitsunari noticed the ink landscape painting hanging in the Tokonoma alcove which reminded him of something. Pointing to the painting, he asked, "Is that Mount Hie with Sakamoto at the base?" Sokyu looked towards the Tokonoma before replying to Mitsunari. "Yes, it is. It is an old painting I picked up in Sakamoto some years ago. I remember liking the brush strokes. Does it interest you?"

"It's just that it reminded me of the markings on the boxes I saw in your storehouse below being loaded onto a cart. Are they destined for Sakamoto?" Mitsunari asked.

"Yes, an intermediary for an anonymous Daimyo has paid for his shipment and we are arranging delivery." Mitsunari nodded at Sokyu's answer and bid him farewell. On his way out, he glanced again at the few cedar boxes that remained and thought,

Anonymous Daimyo? Sakamoto is Akechi Mitsuhide's Fife. I wonder if Lord Nobunaga knows of this. And where is he getting the gold for this?

On the second day of his stay in Sakai, Mitsunari watched the dark clouds rolling in over Osaka Bay and felt the light rain that had fallen. He was helping to saddle the horses outside the inn they were staying at for an early departure before the heavier rains arrived with the approaching storm. Distracted by a commotion in the street, he watched as a cart pushed by several men came hurtling directly towards him. He instantly recognised the portly man sitting atop the cart, dressed in fine robes and clutching a colourful *Wagasa* (umbrella) for protection against the rain.

"Sokyu!" he shouted. The cart came to a stop alongside Mitsunari, and Sokyu stepped down onto the muddy street.

"It would seem I have only just caught you then?" Sokyu said. Mitsunari bowed and wiped away the water, settling on his face.

"I wanted to prevent you the embarrassment of a failed mission and return empty-handed, so I have come with Ten Tanegashima rifles for you to take back with you," Sokyu called out as the first crack of thunder roared. "As regards to payment, on receipt of gold coin to cover this shipment from your master, another twenty will be available together with ammunition and powder." Mitsunari felt elated. Ten muskets were not much, but it should be enough to appease Ieyasu.

"Will this make trouble for you with Lord Nobunaga?" Mitsunari asked.

"Your visit was auspicious, Mitsunari," Sokyu said, smiling. "I could locate more rifles to complete Lord Nobunaga's order and had thirty left over to supply you," Sokyu called out to his workers to unload the cedar box from the cart and

217

remove the Tanegashima rifles. Mitsunari quickly asked Sokyu to leave them in the box and had the attendants go to the waterfront and purchase oiled canvas to have the rifles tied to the horses. The characters for Omi Sakamoto, painted on the cedar box, did not escape Mitsunari's attention.

"Sokyu," Mitsunari called. "Are these not part of the shipment you are sending to Sakamoto?"

"Indeed, they are, Mitsunari," Sokyu grinned.

"Will you not be in trouble with the anonymous Daimyo, though?"

"I have indicated to him I have supply issues and I suspect he will be angry, but he can hardly do anything about it for fear of it coming to the attention of his Lord." Sokyu still clutching his umbrella held his other hand out to test if the rain was becoming heavier, and said to Mitsunari, "Always prepare for rain, Mitsunari. We must always expect the unexpected." Mitsunari was unsure what Sokyu was trying to say, but it sounded profound enough, and he nodded in acknowledgement as Sokyu shouted to his men to move on.

Chapter Nineteen

Yoshimasa
Autumn/Winter: Sixth Year of Tensho (1578)

The westerly winds sweeping in from Lake Biwako brought a chill to the night air, but did little to cool the raging fever and delirium besetting Yoshimasa. He lay on the matted floor of his living quarters, his brow dripping in sweat, his haunted mind immersed in a time long gone.

Eight years ago, on the battlefield of Anegawa, he steadied his agitated horse, fearful of the ghostly shapes emerging from the dense mists. Before him was an armoured mounted warrior with raised sword racing towards him. He wanted to flee and turned his horse but felt the heavy blow across his face armour and the long fall into darkness. He could see his body lying on the battlefield amongst the gore of many other fallen warriors. His breathing became laboured, and he felt smothered by the warm breath on his face. He saw eyes in front of him glowing yellow with black vertical slits as the Kitsune stood over him.

Suddenly awake, Yoshimasa's eyes flickered and opened. He sat up and felt the wetness of his sweat on his shaven head. The dim light provided by the lantern in his room suggested it was still night, and he rose from his bed to open one of the Shoji screens opening out into the garden. Staring out into the darkness, Yoshimasa watched a band of light appearing on the horizon and knew daybreak was not far off. Still wet from his night sweats, Yoshimasa felt the full chill of the night air and shivered.

Wearing the fresh white Kariginu robes of a Shinto priest, Yoshimasa stepped out of his modest lodgings, intending to walk the short distance into the township of Kunitomo towards the blacksmith's forges and workshops that dotted the banks of the Anegawa River. Kunitomo was a post town conveniently placed astride a major trading route connecting it with the castle town of Nagahama, Lord Hideyoshi's new home.

The sun had yet to rise, but even at this hour, the village he walked through was bustling with activity. Workers loaded carts with charcoal and iron ore destined for the foundries, and the women set out to till the drained rice paddies to prepare for the spring planting. As he walked, Yoshimasa also gathered a following of curious children as he made his way towards the river. He paused momentarily to adjust his robes and caught sight just ahead of him, a red fox standing its ground in the middle of the road, fearlessly looking directly at him. It was not until Yoshimasa moved towards the fox that it turned and loped away.

Ah... Kitsune! he thought. *How many times must I die?*

It was a question he had asked himself many times, for most of his restless nights involved the recurring dream of being visited by a fox.

His injuries at Shitagahara had taken a long time to heal, and he was lucky to be alive, but the months passed quickly enough, and he soon felt well enough to travel and resume his place in the land of the living. News had reached him of his lord's plans to build a new castle on the flatland plains of Mount Azuchi overlooking Lake Biwako, and he set out before the first snows of winter on a horse provided by Hattori Hanzo to re-join his master. He would first head for Gifu and rest there awhile before continuing to Azuchi.

It was at Gifu, Nobunaga's old capital that Yoshimasa heard first-hand from the common folk the cruelty of his lord, in his zeal to unite the country. He served Nobunaga in the belief that he alone could finally bring peace to the divided country. Although death and hardship were constant companions in this period of the warring states, Yoshimasa learnt that the common folk found their suffering increased, for this was no longer a war just between ruling elites.

Daimyos enthusiastically embraced the use of barbarian matchlocks, for it meant the common folk could effectively fight and die instead of the Samurai. Farmers found themselves conscripted, and not only was their tax burden increased, but they also faced new and inventive tax levies to fund the wars waged by the elites. It was with a heavy heart that Yoshimasa learnt the people's suffering had only grown under his master's excesses. Nobunaga had entire towns, temples, and shrines raised to the ground, and their inhabitants butchered by the thousands, and Yoshimasa questioned if his lord was indeed mad.

By the time Yoshimasa had reached the workshop compound, daylight had broken. Wind flurries now scattered the fallen maple leaves covering the ground and Yoshimasa looked skyward to see a line of dark clouds rolling in from the west and felt the air become even colder.

The snows will soon appear, he thought.

Yoshimasa rang the bell of the compound and sniffed the sulphurous odours permeating the air, and a tallish but emaciated looking elderly man opened the gate. Whilst it had been many years, Yoshimasa instantly recognised the old man as Kunitomo Zenbee, the renowned swordsmith. Zenbee also had not forgotten his visitor and enthusiastically welcomed Yoshimasa. Together, they crossed the courtyard towards the sounds of ringing hammers and met with the swordsmith, Tokyusaemon, who was busy pounding a glowing red block of metal, his smock barely concealing his sinewy arms.

On seeing Yoshimasa, Tokyusaemon laid down his hammer and bowed. Like Zenbee, he too was thin and elderly, but much shorter. Zenbee and Tokyusaemon, along with the ironmaster Sukedayu, had set up the foundry some twenty-five years earlier under the edict of the then Shogun Yoshiharu. They were commanded to produce copies of the matchlock muskets the young Lord Tanegashima Tokitaka had bought off the barbarian Portuguese. It was several years later that Lord Nobunaga assumed full control of Omi province, and Kunitomo fell under his domain.

"It has been a long time, Yoshimasa. I see you have become a priest. How may we be of help?" said Tokyusaemon, smiling. Yoshimasa suspected Tokyusaemon's relaxed manner hid an inner intensity and couched his words carefully.

"I have come with coin and instructions from Lord Nobunaga," Yoshimasa said.

"More instructions?" Tokyusaemon grumbled. "We can barely keep up with his demands now. We already have another visitor here today from Nagahama castle, also with instructions from Lord Nobunaga." Tokyusaemon left and went inside with Zenbee to return with their visitor, Mitsunari.

"Yoshimasa. Is that you?" exclaimed Mitsunari with a wide grin. "I see you are still a priest."

"Ah, young Mitsunari. I never expected to find you here, but to answer your question, I am not a priest, even though, as you can see, I carry no swords. Lord Nobunaga sees an advantage in having me dress like one in his dealings with the barbarians and Portuguese missionaries."

"But at my Genpuku, you dressed as a priest?" Mitsunari noted with a puzzled expression. Yoshimasa briefly explained he had sought the help of the local priest who presided over Mitsunari's Genpuku for guidance as to the meaning of his recurring dreams where a Kitsune talked to him in a tongue he could not understand.

"The priest believed the Kitsune was a *kami no tsukai,* one of the messengers of Inari, a patron deity of blacksmiths and the warriors. He suggested I stay a while with him and pray, for he was convinced the *Kitsune* was reaching out to me."

"And did you find those answers?" Mitsunari said.

"No, not yet, but I felt it was time for me to return to Lord Nobunaga."

"Are you here at Lord Nobunaga's bidding?" asked Mitsunari.

"Yes. As you know, the lord has built a new castle in Azuchi. He intends it to be the grandest of any castle in Japan. Azuchi sits at the crossroads that links his army to the north and the Uesugi, the Takeda in the east and the Mori in the west, and importantly, it controls the route to the capital in the south. A whole new castle town is under construction, and Nobunaga has decreed all residents are to be exempt from all taxes. He has even decreed that all travellers who pass through Azuchi must spend the night there. Lord Nobunaga has ordered me to have cannon for Azuchi Castle's defences cannon cast here at Kunitomo. May I ask what your purpose here is?"

"If you recall at Shitagahara, we were lucky the rain held off, otherwise our muskets could have proved useless. I learnt that the Portuguese barbarians use a cover of sorts to protect the flash pan from the wet and with Lord Nobunaga's permission, I am experimenting with several designs which require the services of the skilled gunsmiths of Kunitomo."

"The last I heard, you were serving Lord Ieyasu," Yoshimasa said.

"Yes. Lord Nobunaga sent me to Lord Ieyasu to drill his Teppo units into the tactics we developed at Shitagahara. Lord Ieyasu, realising he was embarrassingly short of Teppo himself, sent me to Sakai to buy guns. Which reminds me, at one merchant I noticed boxes of firearms consigned to Sakamoto Castle. Is that not Mitsuhide's fife?"

"Yes, it is," Yoshimasa said as it now occurred to him the oddity of one of Nobunaga's generals receiving such scarce firearms at his home castle.

"Have you told anyone about this?" he asked Mitsunari.

"No, but I was thinking about informing the lord."

"Just as well," Yoshimasa replied. "Remember, Akechi is cunning and plans forty moves ahead. He will have a ready-made excuse ready to counter your accusation. My advice is to say nothing and wait. He will reveal his hand soon enough." As an afterthought, Yoshimasa asked Mitsunari, "Your time with Lord Ieyasu was not long. How is it you have returned to Nobunaga?"

"All I know is that Lord Ieyasu had a visit from the Sakai merchant, Imai Sokyu, and soon after, Nobunaga sent word for me to return."

"By the way, what news of your old tutor, Yoshino?" asked Yoshimasa. The mention of Yoshino's name resurrected forgotten feelings, with Mitsunari delaying his response.

"Hanzo believes she is dead. The local magistrate reported finding the body of a lady traveller fitting her description at the Seki springs in Myoko. Somehow, he is wrong."

"What then of the Lady Mochiko?" asked Yoshimasa.

"According to Hanzo, she too appears to have vanished from the face of the earth. Why is this of interest to you?" Yoshimasa paused.

"It is just that our paths have crossed many times, but right now we need to sort out our expectations of these swordsmiths," pointing to Tokyusaemon and Zenbee. Yoshimasa faced the two swordsmiths and spoke.

"I have noticed that your entire village has become an estate of artisans, each devoted to performing their craft in the production of the Teppo rifles. From the *Taishi* carpenters who craft the stocks to the *Karakuri* who make the intricate mechanical parts and components, any disruption to one of these trades would be ruinous to meeting your obligations to Lord Nobunaga. My friend's request for help in developing a protective cover for the flash pan does not interfere with your production. So, I encourage you to supply whatever help you can. My Lord Nobunaga's directive is simple and affects only your iron casting." Yoshimasa reached into his robes and showed the two swordsmiths a large silver coin embossed with Nobunaga's seal of flowering quinces. Tokyusaemon and Zenbee immediately recognised the importance of the seal, for the bearer spoke with the authority of Nobunaga himself.

"What does the lord require?" inquired Zenbee as he bowed.

"The light cannon pieces you have cast for the lord have proved their effectiveness on the battlefield but are not suitable for besieging and defending castles and strongholds. The lord requires you to produce cannon of much heavier calibre suitable for defence of his new fortress at Azuchi. How long before you will have a sample ready for testing?" Tokyusaemon and Zenbee looked at one another with worried frowns on their faces, and Tokyusaemon was the first to speak, "Come back in the spring." Yoshimasa thanked the swordsmiths, indicating he would return to Azuchi straight away and report the lord.

"Why not join me, young Mitsunari? We both have much to tell?"

#

Winter/Spring: Seventh Year of Tensho (1579)

Nobunaga had just returned from Settsu province, having paused his siege of Arioka castle for the *Shogatsu* New Year's celebrations at Azuchi. The rebellious Settsu Daimyo, Araki Murashige, who had faithfully served Nobunaga in several campaigns against the Ikko-Ikki warrior monks had now betrayed him and sought alliances with the Ikko-Ikki bonzes of the Ishiyama Hongan-Ji and the Mori clan who continued to supply them.

Yoshimasa and Mitsunari had also returned to Azuchi Castle to report to Nobunaga on the Kunitomo swordsmith's response to his directive to provide heavy cannon. While Yoshimasa briefed Nobunaga, Mitsunari wandered the grounds of Azuchi Castle, fascinated by the amount of construction still in progress, and watched as hundreds of workers toiled away under cold, gloomy skies. He stood in awe at the structure before him. Although still incomplete, the Donjon that towered above him was already six storeys high, with a seventh still under construction. He had never seen a castle so huge. The cold misty rain that had fallen partially obscured the vivid hues of the red and gold mural of tigers and dragons that decorated the Donjon's facade above and below its unusual octagonal fifth storey.

With the construction of the retainer's quarters at Azuchi incomplete, Yoshimasa and Mitsunari stayed in one of the several estates allocated for visiting Daimyos and their families in the castle's new town of Azuchi. The first snow of the season had just fallen, and the townsfolk enthusiastically began their preparations for the coming *Shogatsu.* The customary bonfires were made ready as townsfolk gathered the old decorations of the previous year to burn in a symbolic breaking of the past. Nobunaga had announced that Azuchi's New Year's celebrations would be an extravaganza to be talked about for generations to come. He summoned all his generals who were not away on front-line duty to Azuchi to take part in the celebrations and, of course, view the grandeur of his castle. Azuchi was to be a visual symbol of his might and rule.

In the hour of the dragon, just after daybreak, Yoshimasa and Mitsunari responded to their summons and set out for Azuchi Castle. Fierce icy winds blew that day, and Mitsunari chose the warmest overcoat he could find, supplementing it with a straw cape and hat as protection against the sleet and snow. Yoshimasa, meanwhile, made do with just his priestly robes and straw cape and hat. They took the forested east-west path along the southern face of Mount Azuchi; the journey led to a junction at the nearby Azuchiyama Jesuit Seminary where Yoshimasa pointed to the long steep path ahead of them that they needed to climb to reach the castle.

The castle sat on a flat mountain plain atop Mount Azuchi that jutted out into Lake Biwako to form the Azuchi Peninsula. Cold westerly winds blew in from the lake, bringing with it flurries of snow that quickly settled on the straw cape and hats Yoshimasa and Mitsunari wore. By the time they reached the end of their steep climb, the needle leaves of the mountain umbrella pines were already sagging heavily under the weight of snow.

At the castle, they were escorted to the audience hall on the second floor of Azuchi's towering Dojon, where Yoshimasa and Mitsunari sat and gaped at its lavish decorations. Walls were decorated with paintings of Sakura blossoms, geese, monks and pheasants by the famed artist Kano Eitoku, and in front of them sat Lord Nobunaga on a raised dais alongside his eldest son Nobutada and the Tokugawa Lord Ieyasu. In keeping with the grandeur of his Azuchi Castle, Nobunaga was suitably attired in an elaborate and expensive silk red and gold embroidered *Hitatare*.

"Gentlemen," Nobunaga called out to his assembled generals and notable retainers, "the first full moon of the year will soon be upon us, and I intend to celebrate the *Shogatsu,* here at Azuchi, before returning to Arioka and dealing with the traitor Araki Murashige. Lord Akechi Mitsuhide, who is away campaigning in Tango and Tamba provinces, has sent messengers on my behalf to Arioka Castle, petitioning Murashige to surrender peacefully, although his son and wife and his mother are our hostages. As for the *Shogatsu,* the traditional *Dondoyaki* bonfires are to be lit in the town, and the castle will host a riding exhibition the likes of which the country has never seen. Consider it a rehearsal for next year's *Shogatsu* when the Dojon will be complete and the emperor himself will grace us with his heavenly presence." Murmurs of approval rumbled throughout the gathering as several boasted of the contribution they would make to the proposed exhibition.

"Then it is settled." Boomed Nobunaga, allowing the conversation to develop into light-hearted revelry. "I will require you to be dressed in your finest livery and armour for the celebrations." Nobunaga rose and strode towards the staircase, beckoning to his gathering to follow him upstairs. On the third floor, Nobunaga showed off his private living quarters, sumptuously adorned with more paintings by Eitoku. The gathering quickly passed the fourth floor as it was the inner quarters of Lady No, Nobunaga's legal wife, and climbed the stairs to the octagonal-shaped fifth floor which Nobunaga explained represented the heavens, and again suitably decorated with more of Eitoku's paintings, this time depicting vast landscapes of the capital and Sagano. Nobunaga opened one of the screen doors to access the vermillion painted balcony and his entourage stepped out in turns to watch the falling snow and the panoramic views of Lake Biwako, which was unfortunately shrouded in a grey mist.

"Imagine the view on a cloudless day," Nobunaga said proudly. The sixth and seventh floors above were incomplete and Nobunaga explained he intended to house his famous *meibutsu* collection of tea utensils on the floor above and that the final seventh floor was to be covered entirely in gold leaf and would serve as a tea room. The challenge of having a seventh floor was unique in castle design, and Nobunaga knew achieving such a feat would cement his greatness. With the grand tour over, Nobunaga guided his guests back to the audience hall, where he had arranged refreshments. Individual trays of sake and dried sea bream with pickles were placed at the guests' seated positions to which Nobunaga invited them all to enjoy. He would attend personally to each guest and pour their sake.

On reaching Niwa Nagahide's table, Nobunaga poured his sake and praised Nagahide for his efforts in building Azuchi. As a reward, he announced to all that Nagahide would receive the Obama fife in Wakasa province together with a stipend of one hundred thousand Koku. Nagahide poured Nobunaga's sake, and Nobunaga drank it up in one gulp and a chorus of approval roared from the assembled guests. By the time Nobunaga reached Yoshimasa's table, he had become decidedly more jovial.

"Tell me, will the Kunitomo smiths have cannon ready by the first full moon?" Nobunaga asked.

"They have promised one for trial by then, my Lord," Yoshimasa replied. A pleased Nobunaga eagerly poured Yoshimasa his sake and gleefully accepted the offer of sake in return.

"One more thing," Nobunaga said, "get rid of those priests' robes. I have decided I want my old retainer back looking as he should be." Moving to Mitsunari's table, Nobunaga poured the young man his sake and whispered.

"Have you had the pleasure of Azuchi's pillow world yet?" A startled, Mitsunari felt a flush of embarrassment creep over him, and he stuttered.

"No, my Lord. I have been too busy to think of such things." Nobunaga grinned before rebuking him. "Have you forgotten your manners? Are you not going to pour your lord a drink?" Feeling foolish, Mitsunari apologised for his rudeness and poured his lord a bowl of sake, which Nobunaga again gulped down in its entirety. With a flushed face, Nobunaga rose and clapped to gain everyone's attention. He reached into the sleeve of his *Hitatare* and withdrew a folded letter, which he then flourished over his head, signifying its importance.

"This is a letter of introduction and a guarantee of expenses to be paid to the owner of the *Ageya* (entertainment house) in the town for which I now give to young Mitsunari here." The room erupted into applause and laughter, for they all knew the 'entertainment house' as Azuchi's pleasure quarters, staffed by some of Kyoto's finest courtesans. Hideyoshi, who had sat nearby alongside Mitsunari, playfully interjected, and called for Mitsunari to provide all in attendance a detailed report on his experiences.

"Lord Hideyoshi is correct," said Nobunaga, addressing the room, "we expect young Mitsunari to report back to this assembly by the first full moon with a detailed account." The thunderous applause and laughter that followed left Mitsunari further embarrassed. Unable to refuse, Mitsunari bowed to Lord Nobunaga in gratitude and accepted the letter presented.

At Hideyoshi's table, Nobunaga again exchanged drinks, but his mood became more serious. "Monkey, return to Harima province at once, for we have another traitor. It appears Bessho Nagaharu, emboldened by Murashige's rebellion, has announced he is severing his ties with me. I want you to punish him accordingly. I am counting on you." An unsteady Nobunaga finally returned to his seat alongside Nobutada and Ieyasu and continued to drink with them, but it was not long before Nobutada stood up and addressed the room, first to thank them for coming and to continue to enjoy their time together, as he would now leave to assist his father to his quarters prompting a roar of laughter.

Several days had passed since the New Year's gathering at Azuchi, and Mitsunari, eager to put behind him his obligation to Nobunaga for his gift, entertained Yoshimasa in his quarters to seek his advice. He knew that to refuse

Lord Nobunaga's gift would be an unforgivable insult, but the thought of such intimacy terrified him. Mitsunari asked Yoshimasa if he had any experience of the pleasure quarters, who immediately broke out laughing but quickly changed to protesting that he had no experience in such things. Yoshimasa continued to persuade Mitsunari that he must accept the inevitable and face his fears and offered to take care of the arrangements and accompany him for support.

True to his word, Yoshimasa surprised Mitsunari the very next day with news that a meeting with the head courtesan of Azuchi's pleasure quarters would take place this evening. He explained to a confused Mitsunari these were not common whores. The courtesans of the pleasure quarters had a reputation to uphold and were experts in all the classical refinements expected of Samurai women, with additional skills in dance, music and conversation. Yoshimasa pointed out to Mitsunari it was not uncommon for several meetings to take place before they even accept you.

As dusk fell, within the hour of the rooster, Yoshimasa dragged a reluctant Mitsunari outside into the fading light and braved the chilly evening air. Luckily, it had stopped snowing, and the moon made its appearance from behind the clouds to help guide their way. Yoshimasa had Mitsunari dress in his finest winter outfit and presented him with a fresh pair of straw sandals, and Mitsunari reluctantly followed him towards the town's main street that led to the district's pleasure house.

Townhouses, together with sake and merchant shops, lined the length of the narrow main street, at the end of which lay the *Ageya*-geisha entertainment house. Mitsunari paused outside one of the crowded sake shops, savouring the prospect of a drink and an excuse to abandon his appointment, but Yoshimasa tugged at his sleeves and coaxed him along.

"Come on, it is not far to go now," he urged.

By now, most of the lanterns in the street were alight, and the air had become noticeably colder, for when Yoshimasa and Mitsunari spoke, their warm breath mingled with the frosty night air like two cloud breathing dragons. At their destination, Yoshimasa pulled on the bell-rope outside the establishment's heavy wooden doors. It was not long before a young girl in a brightly coloured kimono appeared and ushered them into one of the elaborately decorated rooms used to entertain clients. The girl asked if the room was satisfactory and, noticing their confused looks, explained that all the rooms varied in size and catered to a variety of tastes. She added that each of the rooms on the ground floor overlooked the garden, but each room had a different view. The smaller rooms upstairs allowed for more intimate interactions with the geisha or courtesans. Mitsunari blushed and gravitated to the welcoming warmth of a charcoal brazier in the centre of the room. To his delight, the young girl offered to provide warm sake while they waited for the head courtesan. Mitsunari and Yoshimasa sat in front of the brazier, warming their hands.

"What are you going to say to her?" Mitsunari asked nervously.

"The lady will first ask for a letter of recommendation, which I will provide. Then, she will address her questions to you."

"Me!" exclaimed Mitsunari.

"Yes, you. She will first ask about your pedigree, your knowledge of the classics and your experience in lovemaking, that is. In the end, it is all about money and Nobunaga's guarantees will smooth any ruffled feathers she might have about your ability to pay."

"You led me to believe you have no experience in these matters. How is it you know so much?" queried Mitsunari.

"I said, I have no experience in these matters, but I have heard from many that do."

"What if I do not want to pillow with her?" asked Mitsunari.

"Oh. You misunderstand. She is not for you. She will assign a suitable courtesan for your pleasure once she has accepted you."

Before Mitsunari could ask Yoshimasa another question, the screen door slid open, and the young girl entered with other servants carrying trays of refreshments and sake. As the young girl poured their sake, the screen door again slid open, and the Tayu dressed in a long plum-red kimono decorated with white peony flowers floated into the room and took her seat alongside Yoshimasa and Mitsunari. The young girl now poured sake for the Tayu, and when Mitsunari and Yoshimasa had drunk their sake, she raised the bowl to her chalky-white face and sipped. Mitsunari noticed the oddity of her lower lip covered in a blood-red make-up while the upper was natural.

There is something familiar about her, but I cannot yet place it.

Yoshimasa reached into his sleeve and presented Nobunaga's letter to the Tayu who carefully unfolded it, read it, and refolded it to place it at her side. Yoshimasa had expected the Tayu's line of questioning to go in the manner he outlined to Mitsunari, but the Tayu asked only one question of Mitsunari, "Will you come again?" And without waiting for a reply, she rose and asked Yoshimasa to arrange another meeting, and left the room with the young girl.

A surprised Yoshimasa, and an equally surprised Mitsunari, looked at each other and prepared to leave when the young girl returned and pleaded with them to stay and finish their sake. Not relishing the cold walk back to their quarters and having to leave the warmth of the charcoal fire, Yoshimasa, and Mitsunari eagerly obliged. With the sake finished, Yoshimasa and Mitsunari finally rose to leave and followed the young girl through another room connecting with a small courtyard at the rear of the *Ageya*. The young girl pointed to the heavy door a short distance away underneath a lit lantern and explained that the establishment valued discreetness and while clients entered by the front, they always left at the rear. She bowed and pressed a folded letter into Yoshimasa's hand and withdrew inside, leaving Yoshimasa and Mitsunari to make their way out.

The courtyard door opened out onto a dark narrow lane behind a row of townhouses, and with just enough moonlight to tread safely, Yoshimasa and Mitsunari braced themselves against the chilly night air and headed for their quarters. Meanwhile, Mitsunari counted out the distant sound of nine bells, *midnight*, he thought. The hour of the rat had arrived.

"That was short," Mitsunari remarked to Yoshimasa, back at their quarters.

"I thought she was not interested, which does not bother me in the slightest."

"I had explained to you it might take more than just one meeting," said Yoshimasa.

"By the way, what was the message she passed to you?" Mitsunari asked.

"Probably instructions for your next meeting," Yoshimasa said, withdrawing the letter and reading.

I would ask of you to meet me here again tomorrow at the same time to discuss matters of grave importance. Have your friend remain and come alone. Tell no one.

"As I thought, just instructions for your next meeting," Yoshimasa said, quickly sliding the letter back into his sleeve. Mitsunari was about to ask what the instructions were, but the need for warm sake was more pressing.

"Come, let us have some sake before retiring," he said.

230

The next night at the *Ageya,* Yoshimasa found himself ushered into the same room as before, but, this time, the Tayu was already present and seated by the brazier. Yoshimasa took his seat and the young girl provided trays of refreshments and poured his sake.

"You may leave us, Ona," said the Tayu as she reached to fill a *tokkuri* (flask) with sake and placed it in the water pot above the brazier.

"Just like old times, I seem to remember you prefer your sake warm," the Tayu quipped, taking Yoshimasa by surprise.

"Who are you?" Yoshimasa asked, sensing something familiar about her. The Tayu smiled and gently bowed before pouring Yoshimasa's sake and waited till he had drunk his fill.

"Tell me, have your wounds healed?" the Tayu asked. It was as if a lock had opened, Yoshimasa now remembered.

"So, what do we call you this time? Yumiko, Yoshino, or do you now have another name?"

"You may call me Kasumi."

Chapter Twenty

Kasumi

Two Years Earlier: Spring: Fifth Year of Tensho (1577)

Yoshino continued to relax in the hot healing waters of the Seki springs, while those same bubbling waters carried Mochizuki Chiyo's lifeless body over to the far side of the pool. In the night sky, wisps of clouds moved to obscure the face of the full moon, and a surreal atmosphere of darkness and utter silence descended. Not an insect stirred, and the sound of bubbles breaking the water's surface echoed loudly.

The cloud cover soon passed, and the moonlight reappeared, but the eerie silence remained. A naked Yoshino emerged from the water and walked over to Chiyo's lifeless body, which was now wedged in the rocks at the edge of the pool. Only a narrow path separated the main Onsen from the steaming cauldron of an adjacent pool where the grinning statue of the demon Oni looked on to warn wary bathers of its dangers. Yoshino dragged Chiyo's body by her hair, up onto the bank and launched her into the adjacent steaming waters of Oni's pool. She watched the dense steam envelop the body and disappear into the mists. Moments later, the grotesquely bloated shape of Chiyo's remains bobbed around in its churning waters.

Quickly retrieving her discarded clothes, Yoshino dressed and walked back towards her quarters, intent on catching the attention of the waiting pool attendant to inform her that her friend had stayed longer to enjoy the waters of the Onsen pool. On hearing the news, the attendant bowed in acknowledgement but inwardly seethed at the prospect of another sleepless night waiting for a guest to finish.

The inn's guest rooms were all on the ground floor and each occupied room had a welcoming lantern and prepared bedding. As she approached her room,

Yoshino noticed the faint glow of lanterns through the paper screens in only two of the rooms.

So only two of the rooms have lit lanterns. One is mine, the other must be Chiyo's. Sliding open the door to her room, Yoshino recognised her belongings placed at the foot of the prepared futon and then opened the second door to what she surmised to be Chiyos' room. She carefully examined the pile of folded clothes at the foot of the futon for anything that might identify her. Yoshino grabbed the unique Aikuchi styled dagger she always wore that lay in her travelling bag and patted down her riding Kosode. Finding something concealed within the Kosode, Yoshino carefully removed from the lining a small pouch of gold coins.

She is not likely to need these anymore; besides, I have better use for them.

It was well past midnight into the hour of the ox when the sounds of wailing and loud shouts roused Yoshino from her sleep. She slid open her sliding door and stepped into the corridor to find a hysterical pool attendant at her feet. The attendant stopped crying long enough to tell Yoshino that her friend had somehow foolishly entered Oni's pool and died from its scalding waters, and behind her, the elderly proprietor of the inn suddenly appeared and in an agitated voice cried out.

"Who is going to pay her bill?" Yoshino gave the old man an icy stare.

Someone has died and all this wretch worries about is losing rent. She reached into her sleeve and removed a solitary gold coin before tossing it at the proprietor's feet.

"That will more than cover what the lady owes. Have her horse and mine saddled and ready to depart at first light. Do not forget her belongings. I will deliver them to her family." Snatching up the coin, the old man cowered before Yoshino and remained silent.

"One more thing," Yoshino said, "I suggest you report this to the local magistrate without delay or you might lose your head." The proprietor, who had toyed with the idea of keeping this quiet out of concern as it would be bad for business, was now reminded of the consequences of covering it up.

"Concerning your friend," the old man asked, "by what name do I give the magistrate?"

"I believe she called herself Yoshino."

Yoshino rode out of Seki springs, with Chiyo's mare trailing behind her as a band of ominous dark clouds appeared from the west; she had hoped to cross the Myoko pass into Shinano province before the rains came. Having dealt with one threat, she considered dealing with Masako but decided it would be too risky to return to Kofu and would instead head back to Hamamatsu and smooth things over with Hanzo.

By the time she crossed the Myoko pass to reach the foot of mount Kurohime, the heavens opened, and the rain fell, forcing her to take shelter at a ryokan in the nearby village of Kashiwabara. For two days and nights, it rained relentlessly, dislodging huge rocks onto the steep mountain road that led to the Ueda Plains below, making it impassable. Once the rains cleared, she would have to cross the dense forest slopes of Mount Kurohime on foot, to reach the Ueda plains.

The journey on foot, hampered by leading her horses through dense undergrowth, took much longer than Yoshino had expected, but the dark canopy of trees overhead finally opened to clear blue skies and bright sunshine. Ahead, she could see the flat plains of Ueda, and by late afternoon in the hour of the monkey, she reached the Hokkoku Kaido Road, post town of Ueda that connected the Kanto with the Sea of Japan.

Yoshino found the town buzzing with a large influx of travellers, merchants, and salt traders and lodgings were scarce. Flush with Chiyo's gold, Yoshino had little difficulty in securing lodgings. One guest, a salt trader, found himself unceremoniously evicted to accommodate Yoshinos' payment of a higher rate.

In search of new clothes, Yoshino wandered the narrow streets of the town, seeking the clothing guilds. As she crisscrossed the many small water canals used for washing clothes and draining the winter snow, she came across a busy street housing silk and cloth producers, cloth dyers, and clothing makers. Inside the silk and cloth producer's store, Yoshino browsed the range of cloths on display. Bolts of expensive Chinese silk and patterned cotton lay piled on tables, over which two merchants were haggling with the proprietor.

"These are beyond Kyoto prices," argued one merchant, but Yoshino, tired of waiting, interrupted them, shouting,

"Then go to Kyoto and buy them." Ignoring them, Yoshino caught the attention of the proprietor and pointed to two bolts of patterned cotton on the table.

"I will take those," and handed him a gold coin, adding, "have them delivered to the cloth maker's shop, and tell them I will be along shortly." The two merchants facing a grinning proprietor finally accepted the asking price and left.

Yoshino was leaving the cloth maker's shop, which was across the road from the cloth producer's store when she saw the two merchants, she had met earlier in the store struggling to secure their cartload of clay jars. As she walked past, one jar fell and broke open on the road, spilling its contents of white crystals. Thinking it was salt, Yoshino approached the merchants to inquire if their destination was Kofu, for despite being enemies, the Echigo Lord, Uesugi Kenshin, still supplied salt to the Takeda. The righteous Kenshin held the view that common folk should not suffer for politics and if they were heading for Kai, it could be an opportunity to travel with them and enter Kofu undetected, and deal with Masako.

"Are you bound for Kai?" asked Yoshino.

"No, we are bound for Omi," said one merchant.

"Oh, Omi? I did not know Echigo traded salt with Omi as well."

"Salt?" Looking down at the white crystals glistening in the fading sun, the merchant laughed.

"No, these are saltpetre crystals obtained from Korean traders in Joetsu. We are arranging delivery to Tokyusaemon in Kunitomo."

"Tokyusaemon, the swordsmith?" Yoshino queried.

"Yes. Sir Yoshimasa, a senior retainer of the Oda Lord, Nobunaga, has paid for this cargo. He is making a special powder for the cannon Tokyusaemon is casting for Nobunaga's grand project at Azuchi."

So, Yoshimasa is at Azuchi. I wonder if Mitsunari is still at Hamamatsu.

"Have you heard of Lord Hideyoshi's whereabouts?" Yoshino again asked.

"You ask a lot of questions. You're not a spy, are you?" Yoshino laughed.

"No, it is just that I am looking for someone."

"Well, the last we heard was that Lord Hideyoshi is at Nagahama overseeing gun powder production."

So, Hideyoshi and Yoshimasa are both nearby. They will surely know where Mitsunari is.

After a two-day delay to await delivery of her clothes, Yoshino once again set out at daybreak, this time for Nagahama. The journey over the Kiso Mountains would take several days and having to trail Chiyo's horse behind her would add to the time. She had thought about selling the horse here at Ueda but reasoned a spare fresh horse could be useful. Once over the mountains, the cool mountain air gave way to the warm humidity of the lowlands as she approached Lake Biwako.

The thriving castle town of Azuchi lay at the foot of Mount Azuchi, and many of the streets and houses were still under construction. The area was teeming with workers and artisans. Lord Nobunaga had conscripted labourers, masons, carpenters, tile moulders, artists, blacksmiths and lacquerers from the surrounding provinces to build his castle, and these workers also built their own homes here, as did the merchants and traders. As she trotted into Azuchi, in search of an inn, she noticed gangs of workers toiling to widen the road she travelled on. They were also planting cypress trees on either side of the road to provide shade for the travellers Azuchi sought to attract. As she rode past the workers, she looked behind and smiled as they raked the freshly laid clean sand and pebbles to remove the imprint of her horse's feet.

In the days following, she discovered Mitsunari had returned from Hamamatsu and now lived at Lord Hideyoshi's Nagahama castle. Using Chiyo's gold, Yoshino bought herself a new life and a new identity. She bought a patch of land at the end of one of the streets under construction and later had a villa built that would eventually service the pleasure needs of Azuchi's town folk.

#

Spring: Seventh Year of Tensho (1579). Present.

Yoshimasa stared intently at Kasumi as she poured him another bowl of sake. He tried to imagine what lay beneath her porcelain white face, while Kasumi returned his stare, curling the single red line of her painted lip and raising a smile.

"Is the boy a virgin?" Kasumi asked. "It would help to know, to smooth out any embarrassment." A flustered Yoshimasa looked surprised. He neither expected the question nor had he an answer for it, instead, he deflected it.

"Why are you here?" he asked.

"To put things right," Kasumi replied.

"Why all this pretence, then?"

"I believe Mitsunari's life is in danger."

"Why would anyone want to harm him?"

"He is in danger because of me," said Kasumi. "There is much about his life I have kept secret from him. If it were to become common knowledge, a bloodbath between certain clans would erupt. Only two people know his secret. I am one of them, and the other will kill him to preserve the secret."

"Why is he important to you?" a confused Yoshimasa asked.

"He is my son."

Your son! The thought reverberated in Yoshimasa's mind.

"How do you know he is in danger?"

"My private quarters are above the rooms the courtesans use to entertain their clients. By design, when removing a particular mat, I can hear even the most private of conversations." Yoshimasa felt the urge to complain but held his tongue, and Kasumi continued.

"Recently, I overheard a courtesan conversing with a presumed client of ways to lure Mitsunari to this establishment. I later thought that the briefness of the conversation meant it was unlikely to have been a client, so I carefully monitored her. Discovering she had left to go out in the dead of night, I followed her and saw her secretly met with someone at a copse of trees just outside the town."

"I know it is an obvious question, but did you see who she met?" Yoshimasa asked, quickly gulping down the warm sake.

"The person she met wore simple, dark, loose clothing, and a mask, not just any mask, but a *Fukumen* complete with a *Zukin*-hood as used by ninja. I could judge by the person's gait he was a man," Kasumi firmly replied. "I have long suspected this courtesan to be Kunoichi. Only last year, she complained to the other courtesans that she was assaulted by a client who is known to us. The very next day, his body was found floating in the sewer canal without a mark on him. It was assumed he was drunk and fell into the canal and drowned. Being suspicious, I walked alongside the same canal and came across a single pronged long Kanzashi hairpin of brass lying in the dirt nearby. Such hairpins are speciality instruments used by Kunoichi to insert into the ear canal to puncture the brain, leaving little if any trace of blood." Yoshimasa's eyes narrowed as he also remembered Kasumi's trade as a Takeda Kunoichi.

She would know, he thought.

"I know a Kunoichi does not act independently. She must be under contract, but to who?" Yoshimasa asked.

"Precisely," Kasumi said. "I have a plan, but I need your help." She poured Yoshimasa another bowl of sake, and added, "How is your aim with a *Yumi-bow?*"

"Let us hear your plan," Yoshimasa said, ignoring her comment.

"I will arrange with the Kunoichi to receive Mitsunari after the *Hatsumode* (the first shrine visit of the year), which is in two days. Arrange for Mitsunari to pay his customary respects at the Soken-Ji Temple and then accompany him here. By then, it should be nightfall. He will be escorted here, into the same room as on his last visit. It will also be a night of the full moon, and I will arrange for the room here to be open to the garden for the viewing, but even with the screen doors shut, the room will be well lit, and you can easily make out their silhouetted positions. Everything you need will be ready for you here. As soon as you see the courtesan reach for her hair, aim true with the *Yumi,* and strike quickly for Mitsunari's sake. I will take care of the rest."

"Why do you need me? Surely, with you being a Kunoichi, can you not take care of this yourself?"

"She suspects me and will be on guard." Yoshimasa's jaw tightened as he glared at her.

"You presume much. What makes you think I will agree to this?"

"Because you care for him, and that, my friend, is the only reason you are still alive." Yoshimasa glared at her, his anger rising, but memories of her nursing his wounds at Shitagahara resurfaced and his anger subdued.

If his life is truly in danger, I cannot let him be killed. But do I believe her? Can I even trust her?

At the hour of the hare, just after dawn, the bells of the Soken-Ji Temple at nearby Azuchi Castle rang out, signalling the start of the *Hatsumode.* Lord Nobunaga had the three-storey pagoda Soken-Ji Temple moved from its humble position in far off Chugoku province and reassembled here in the castle precincts to provide a spiritual focus for the good people of Azuchi in his grand endeavour. So, it was that the good people of Azuchi, undeterred by grey skies and falling snow, began their pilgrimage to the temple to make the traditional wishes and prayers for the coming year.

It was late afternoon, around the hour of the monkey, when Mitsunari and Yoshimasa, after finishing their prayers, departed for the town. The light snow that had fallen for most of the day now became heavier, and despite the heavy robes they wore, they felt the cold biting intensity of the onshore westerly winds from Lake Biwako.

At the *Ageya,* Ona once more received them and escorted Mitsunari to the empty room where he had first met the Tayu, whilst Yoshimasa waited in the foyer for Ona to return. Mitsunari sat alongside the warm brazier and helped himself to the various plates of refreshments and warm sake prepared for him.

Escorted to one of the other entertainment rooms, an agitated Yoshimasa waited for Kasumi to arrive. He opened a screen door overlooking a small courtyard of snow-covered gravel and stepped outside. Cloud cover had masked the brilliance of tonight's full moon, but at least the biting wind and snow had ceased. Kasumi had earlier indicated that this courtyard overlooked the garden room where Mitsunari would be, and from his position, he could see the silhouetted outlines of Mitsunari and his courtesan lover.

Kasumi arrived carrying a *Yumi* war bow in the shorter, *hankyu* style, which was ideal for restricted positions and a quiver of arrows. Yoshimasa cautiously took the bow from Kasumi and made for the cover of a line of black pines directly in front of Mitsunari's room. Meanwhile, Kasumi returned to her room and removed the outer blue silk kimono she wore, replacing it with another, one of vivid crimson red patterned with white peony flowers. She placed a two-piece *Kanzashi* hairpin in her hair and entered the garden room, where Ona was entertaining Mitsunari with refreshments. At Kasumi's silent signal, Ona poured Mitsunari another bowl of sake and left. A relaxed Mitsunari studied the beautiful courtesan before him and his heart fluttered, but something about the courtesan was familiar.

"I have a feeling we have met before, but that would be impossible," asked Mitsunari as he gulped down the sake. Ignoring his question, Kasumi knelt alongside Mitsunari and poured him yet another bowl of sake.

"I am told you have yet to pillow with a woman," Kasumi bluntly stated. Mitsunari's agitation was palpable, and he was lost for words. He knew she spoke truthfully, but the subject was not open for discussion. Kasumi, sensing his embarrassment, changed the subject and asked about his family.

"Tell me, are your parents well?"

"It has been many years since I last saw them, let alone heard from them. I live in hope that one day I might be allowed to visit them." Kasumi sensed the despair in Mitsunari's voice and replied comfortingly.

"I am sure you will, and soon," Kasumi said as she reached into the sleeve of her kimono and withdrew a folded letter, which she handed to Mitsunari.

"Please give this to your friend, Yoshimasa, when next you see him." Mitsunari found the request strange.

"Why not give it to him yourself? He is surely still here?"

"Your friend has returned to his lodgings and hopes you will enjoy what is on offer," Kasumi said, emptying the last of the Sake into Mitsunari's bowl.

"Now drink up. It is nearly time for the moon viewing, although I doubt *Tsukuyomi-no-Mikoto* (the moon god) will be as radiant tonight." Kasumi and Mitsunari rose, and Kasumi moved to open the screen doors overlooking the garden. They both felt the chill of the night air but fortunately, the cloud cover obscuring the new year face of *Tsukuyomi-no-Mikoto* had dissipated, and in the eerie glow of the moonlight they looked out over a garden of dark shapes and shadows. Kasumi looked towards the line of pines at the edge of the garden concealing Yoshimasa and silently prayed.

A concealed Yoshimasa stood ready with the bow in hand, three arrows standing upright in the snow beside him. He had watched the screen doors of Mitsunari's room opening and prepared himself. Slipping his left arm out of his *Hitatare*, Yoshimasa exposed his bare shoulder to the chilly night air and shivered. He gripped the *Yumi* Kasumi had given him and looked again at the figures in the room. Judging his range was correct, he silently nocked an arrow against the string and aimed.

Within the room, Kasumi beckoned Mitsunari to step onto the veranda.

"Come and see, Mitsunari, *Tsukuyomi-no-Mikoto* has come to life." Mitsunari joined Kasumi and looked up at the bright silver orb floating in the night sky.

"Sit for a moment and I will bring over more warm sake, so we might enjoy this view," Kasumi said. Yoshimasa had Mitsunari in his sights. Behind him, his target, the courtesan who wore a patterned red kimono, approached Mitsunari carrying a small table. His grip on the *Hankyu* tightened, and he gently pulled back the bowstring with his right hand to a point behind his ear. Kasumi had refilled Mitsunari's bowl with warm sake and she smiled as he drank. Glancing upwards to *Tsukuyomi-no-Mikoto*, Kasumi momentarily closed her eyes as if in

240

prayer before allowing her left hand to reach for her hairpin. Alert to the move, Yoshimasa releases the arrow and as the string returns to its position, the bow grip spins in his hand. He remains still, trancelike in a state of *zanshin*. His mind follows the arrow to its target.

The arrow passed close enough for Mitsunari to detect a brief disturbance in the air and then heard a gentle thud. He looked up to see Kasumi, an arrowhead protruding from her neck, and her blood mingling with the white *oshiroi* make-up she had painstakingly applied, turning her throat pink. Her eyes bulged as if in shock, but strangely, she is smiling as she falls forward into Mitsunari's arms.

Seeing his target fall, Yoshimasa breaks cover and runs towards the veranda in time to see Mitsunari awkwardly dragging the courtesan inside. Hearing someone on the veranda, Mitsunari gently lays Kasumi down and reaches for his swords. Fearing another assassination attempt, Mitsunari stands over Kasumi's body with sword drawn ready to strike, but Yoshimasa's sudden appearance in the doorway bewildered him.

"What are you doing here? Where are they?" Mitsunari shouted.

"There is no one else. The arrow is mine."

"Why?" a bewildered Mitsunari cried out. Yoshimasa looked down at his kill and froze. He knew he had killed Kasumi. The costume and hair ornaments might be different, but the smile on her face gave away her identity.

"I do not understand," Yoshimasa stammered, and he frantically tried to explain to Mitsunari his arrangement with Kasumi to eliminate the courtesan.

"What have I done?" Yoshimasa shouted. "Why did she deceive me?" Mitsunari knelt and snapped the arrow shaft at the back of Kasumi's neck and pulled out the protruding arrowhead.

"I do not understand any of this," Mitsunari said, as he unknowingly shed a tear. Remembering Kasumi's earlier request, Mitsunari reached into his Hitatare and gave Yoshimasa the letter she had given him.

If you are reading this, then I have succeeded, and you have killed me. With my death, the reason to kill Mitsunari dies with me. For now, he is safe. I wish there were another way, but whilst I am alive, Mitsunari will always be in danger. You should know that I killed our benefactor and employer, Lady Mochiko Chiyo. As you slept recovering from your wounds at Shitagahara, you often called out for Chiyo. I suspect she was your one genuine love and hope my death provides some satisfaction for you, knowing you have avenged her. Chiyo had kept a secret from me, which I have since discovered and set out to kill me. I simply took her life before she took mine.

The courtesan I spoke of who wanted to kill Mitsunari does not exist. That part of my plan was a lie, but there is more to this tale that I have time for today. If you seek Hanzo, he will explain.

Look after Mitsunari and care for him, as he will care for you. That is the reason you are still alive today.

"What does it say?" Mitsunari asked. Yoshimasa handed him the letter, and Mitsunari read it several times before handing it back.

"I still do not understand," Mitsunari said. "She died for me, but why? I must seek Hanzo for an answer." Yoshimasa looked down upon Kasumi's lifeless form and closed his eyes. He clapped his hands in prayer and silently vowed to protect Mitsunari until death and keep from Mitsunari that he had just killed his mother.

Late next morning, Mitsunari and Yoshimasa gathered at the Soken-Ji Temple to watch Kasumi's departure from this world into the next. The sun had just broken through the rolling grey clouds, adding some warmth to the icy still air, and Mitsunari and Yoshimasa both watched the smoke carrying her spirit rise and dissipate just beyond the roof of the temple pagoda. Both knew she had earned no redemption for the road she travelled in this life. The flames suddenly crackled and hissed loudly, prompting Mitsunari to ask Yoshimasa.

"What did you place on the body just before?"

"Just some possessions of hers to accompany her into the afterlife."

"What possessions?" a curious Mitsunari asked.

"Her collection of special tea bowls. The strange-shaped ones she had specially lacquered and gilded." Mitsunari looked at Yoshimasa and he asked no more.

Chapter Twenty-One

Akechi

Autumn/Winter: Seventh Year of Tensho (1579)

In the second month, the first hint of spring arrived at Azuchi with a modest thawing of snow. With the inaugural Shogatsu celebrations finally over, Nobunaga had returned to his army besieging Arioka Castle in Settsu province. Araki Murashige's continuing defiance had continued to stroke Nobunaga's anger, but he was also pragmatic and shrewd. Nobunaga summoned his adjutant, Kazukage, to have a message sent to Akechi Mitsuhide in nearby Tamba province.

"Mitsuhide is still languishing in his siege of Yakami Castle," Nobunaga said to Kazukage. "Remind him that we still hold Murashige's daughter-in-law, wife and mother as hostages, and he is ordered to contact Murashige and mediate a surrender on good terms." A confused Kazukage asked permission to speak.

"Forgive me, Lord, why not just send a delegation up to Arioka Castle and deliver the terms to Murashige instead?"

"Murashige has spurned all other attempts to mediate, and if anyone can convince him, Mitsuhide can," Nobunaga replied. "Murashige's daughter-in-law is Lady Shizen, Mitsuhide's daughter from one of his other informal wives."

Two days after he received Nobunaga's message, Mitsuhide and twenty of his men rode into Nobunaga's camp outside the besieged castle of Arioka with the news that Murashige had fled the castle months ago.

"What!" Nobunaga screamed as he stomped his foot. "What do you mean, he is not here?" Mitsuhide bowed and did his best to conceal the smirk on his face as he replied.

"My Lord, I learnt from one of his captains that Murashige was holding out on the promise of reinforcements from his Mori allies, but none arrived. Having decided it would be impossible to hold out much longer, Murashige under the cover of darkness left the castle last autumn with five or six of his close retainers and travelled by boat down the Ina River towards Amagasaki, another Araki Castle held by his son Muratsugu." Nobunaga clenched his fist, his anger again simmering.

"You mean my army has sat here all these months for nothing?"

"My Lord, as you commanded, I then went to Amagasaki and pleaded with him to save his family and surrender."

"What did he say?" Nobunaga asked.

"He refused." A stony-faced Nobunaga remained silent for some time before quietly ordering Mitsuhide to return to his siege of Yakami Castle. Faced with having to siege both Arioka and Amagasaki, Nobunaga summoned his son Nobutada to relieve him. Before the end of the month, Nobunaga left Arioka and returned to Azuchi to finish his Dojon, but not before sating his anger by burning Arioka's castle town of Itami to the ground and slaughtering its inhabitants.

After five long months, Yakami Castle finally fell to Mitsuhide, and he returned to Azuchi with the Lord of Yakami, Hatano Hideharu as a hostage along with his younger brother, Hatano Hidehisa and their mother. Hideharu, like Murashige, had also rebelled against Nobunaga but had now agreed to come to Azuchi and seek Nobunaga's forgiveness. It was around mid-day in the hour of the horse when Mitsuhide rode into the grounds of Azuchi Castle. He was in good spirits, for the journey to Azuchi was a pleasant one. He had developed a rapport with his prisoner, Hatano Hideharu, over their shared passion for hawking. Hideharu had earlier presented Mitsuhide with a gift of a pair of falcons he had specially bred to cement their friendship. At Azuchi, Hidehisa, together with his mother, rested at the guest estate and awaited the fate of Lord Hideharu.

Nobunaga had just begun his council with his generals and other lords in the castle's audience hall when Mitsuhide and Hideharu arrived. At Nobunaga's direction, the pair took their seats in the vacant spaces three rows back from Nobunaga's dais and sat alongside Yoshimasa and Mitsunari. Lord Hideyoshi, as one of the first to arrive, sat in the front row opposite Lord Nobunaga, who sat nestling a war fan on his lap, which he occasionally tapped on his thigh when agitated.

Mitsuhide smiled at Mitsunari as he took his seat. It was a look that made Mitsunari think of a fox toying with its prey.

"Excellent work in taking Tamba!" Nobunaga called out to Mitsuhide. "I will reward as soon you as Lord Hideyoshi here finally finishes with subduing Harima." Nobunaga watched Hideyoshi squirm, as was his intention.

"Now, where is this traitor, Hideharu?" Nobunaga said to Mitsuhide. All eyes fell upon Hideharu, prompting Mitsuhide to explain that Lord Hideharu regretted his actions and begged forgiveness for his crimes. He added that safe conduct to Azuchi to plead his case was a condition of Hideharu's surrender, thus saving many lives on both sides. Nobunaga studied Hideharu. He sat erect and proud, and he returned Nobunaga's stare with a steely glare of defiance.

"I do not see any signs of contrition here, Mitsuhide," said Nobunaga, goading Hideharu into speaking.

"My Lord, my crime is that I have resisted your invasion of my lands for these past three years, but now I accept defeat and respectfully ask that I may live in peace with my family." Nobunaga waved his war fan to signal the guards to have Hidehisa and their mother brought in. They stood before Nobunaga with their hands bound and feet tied together.

"My Lord," Mitsuhide protested, "I have given my word to undertake safe-conduct for Lord Hideharu and his family."

"My patience is at an end with traitors." Nobunaga nodded to his adjutant and several more guards entered to arrest and restrain Hideharu before leading them all away.

"My Lord," pleaded Mitsuhide, "what is happening?"

"What is happening, Lord Mitsuhide is that the traitor and his family are on their way to the execution grounds on Mount Kinsho for immediate crucifixion."

Outside in the castle courtyard, as Mitsunari and Yoshimasa walked towards their quarters, light rain fell and Mitsunari commented on Nobunaga's decision to execute Hideharu and his family.

"I never thought I would say this, but I felt sorry for Mitsuhide. He gave his word and is now dishonoured. Do you think he will commit seppuku?"

"No. He has to ask permission first and the lord will forbid it," Yoshimasa said. "It is not for us to question the Lord's decisions. Consider how many enemies he has forgiven, only to have them betray him again. He pardoned his brother, Nobuyuki, for conspiring against him only for him to try again, as did another brother Nobuhiro. Now it would seem Nobunaga has added Murashige and Hideharu to the list."

"Maybe so but, I thought it unnecessary to kill Hideharu's family, though," Mitsunari replied.

"The family are, but an extension of the head of the household, his crimes are their crimes."

#

In the tenth month under grey autumn skies, an angry Nobunaga returned to Arioka to deal with Araki Murashige. This time he took with him Akechi Mitsuhide, Hashiba Hideyoshi, and Takigawa Kazumasu. Yoshimasa also accompanied Nobunaga.

Nobunaga's latest anger stemmed from the humiliating news circulating in the capital of Murashige's audacious attack on Nobutada's Kamo Fortress. With only five hundred men, Murashige overran the fortress, which was garrisoned with three thousand seasoned Mino and Oda soldiers. Nobutada was lucky to escape without injury. It was just before dawn in the hour of the tiger when Nobunaga arrived at Arioka and set up a camp at Murashige's abandoned Ikeda Castle, which lay across the Ina River opposite Arioka Castle. Yoshimasa was sent to scout Arioka's defences and report back.

With Nobutada's forces reassigned to Amagasaki castle to put a stop to the frequent forays out of the castle by the Amagasaki defenders, Nobunaga depleted siege force waited patiently for Yoshimasa's return.

"The castle is well defended and provisioned with water from the Ina River," Yoshimasa reported on his return. "Moats and fortresses surround its inner and outer citadels."

"Yes, we know all that," an annoyed Nobunaga replied. "What do you suggest?"

"My Lord, the castle is impregnable to frontal assault, but they are vulnerable to attack from within." Nobunaga slapped his war fan on his hip in annoyance at the suggestion.

"I assume you have more to tell than this, Yoshimasa," Nobunaga said dryly.

"My Lord, the lord of Arioka, having abandoned the defenders to their fate, presents us with an opportunity. Morale is low and with the right inducements, Arioka's commanders might be ripe for defection."

Nobunaga snarled, "The only inducement they have to consider is sparing their lives, but I take your point."

246

Following the failure of negotiations with Arioka's defenders, a determined and visibly angry Nobunaga launched a full-scale night-time assault on the castle led by his general Takigawa Kazumasu. The first attack was against the Jorozuka Fortress protecting Arioka's gates. Teppo units fired volley after volley into the fortress and archers let loose with fire arrows, setting fire to the residences behind the wall.

Kazumasu's advance met with little resistance, and they easily breached the castle gates. Once inside, Kazumasu's men faced the defector Araki commanders, Nakanishi Shinhachiro, and Miyawaki Heishiro. The commanders had earlier sent word to Kazumasu that the garrison would surrender, but Nobunaga refused to accept it and overruled him. Kazumasu pressed his attack, reinforced by Hideyoshi, who, along with Mitsunari, chased the Araki commanders into the inner citadel. Surrounded by water-filled moats on three sides and a dry moat on its southern flank, the inner citadel was only accessible by its drawbridge spanning the dry moat. Kazumasu moved his forces in front of the drawbridge and called out to the defenders. He warned he would have his men fill in the moat and storm the citadel and they would spare no one, whereupon the citadel commander Araki Kyuzaemon lowered the bridge and opened the gates, ending the siege of Arioka Castle.

Nobunaga had Araki Kyuzaemon brought to him, and he was not inclined to spare the castle inhabitants unless Kyuzaemon persuaded Murashige to leave Amagasaki castle. Taking fifty of his soldiers, Kyuzaemon went to Amagasaki to deliver Nobunaga's demands, and given the perilous situation Murashige was in, Kyuzaemon was confident his lord would see reason. Despite his pleadings, Kyuzaemon failed to persuade Murashige and not wanting to face Nobunaga's wrath, he fled with his soldiers and melted away into the Rokko Mountains. Nobunaga patiently waited well into the twelfth month, but having not heard anything from Murashige or Kyuzaemon, he closed the chapter on the Araki clan. Kazumasu, Hideyoshi, and Mitsuhide, out of concern for the fate of Arioka's inhabitants, petitioned Nobunaga for leniency.

"Murashige has abandoned his family, his clan and his people to their fate," Nobunaga said. "He is not fit to be a Daimyo, and Kyuzaemon has broken his promise and not returned despite knowing the consequences for his people." Nobunaga slapped his war fan against his thigh to ease the anger within him and decreed the following.

"Murashige's wife, mother, and all of Murashige's family, along with their retainers, are to be taken to Kyoto for execution. The rest are to be sent to Nobutada at Amagasaki Castle." Hideyoshi suspected he knew the answer but asked, anyway.

"What will become of the garrison at Amagasaki Castle?" Hideyoshi asked.

"Nobutada has his instructions."

"My Lord," Mitsuhide shouted. "As you well know, my daughter is Murashige's daughter-in-law."

"I am aware you once had a daughter, Mitsuhide. She is no longer Akechi but an Araki and is expected to share their fate." Mitsuhide begrudgingly bowed his head to the inevitable. He wanted to beg for her life, but he knew it would be useless. Nobunaga was right, his daughter married an Araki, and her fealty is to the Araki clan, but he felt powerless and grew angry at the thought Nobunaga allowed his sister, Lady Oichi, who married his enemy Azai Nagamasa, to live. A brooding Mitsuhide excused himself and returned to his quarters, determined to get drunk and obliterate the pain he felt.

On the next day, in front of the defenders of Amagasaki Castle, Nobutada following his father's instructions and his penchant for cruelty had ninety-seven crosses erected to crucify a portion of the hostages, for ninety-seven was the quantity he was restricted to in materials and time. One hundred and twenty women with children were lined up and shot by Nobutada's Teppo units, and the remaining castle survivors in their hundreds were herded into four nearby farmhouses which were set on fire. Nobutada's example in front of Amagasaki Castle did little to elicit a reaction from the castle defenders, and spies reported to Nobutada that once again Murashige had slipped away and escaped to the last Araki Fortress of Hanakuma Castle.

It took Nobunaga until spring the following year to mount an effective siege against Hanakuma, and a further five months to breach Hanakuma's defences, only to discover that Murashige had again abandoned the castle and fled to the safety of the Mori clan.

#

Winter/Twelfth Month: Seventh Year of Tensho (1579)

248

Following the fall of Amagasaki Castle, Mitsuhide petitioned Lord Nobunaga to be allowed to return to his fife at Sakamoto. To reach Sakamoto meant passing through his intended destination, Kyoto and his daughters' execution.

Mitsuhide left Amagasaki and rode alone, while his six retainers followed behind. His need for solitude grew strong, and he had a lot on his mind. Upon reaching the outskirts of Kyoto, Mitsuhide broke into a trot, and enormous wisps of warm vapour rose from the labouring nostrils of his horse as it mingled with the frosty morning air. Overhead, the clouds rolled away and blue skies with radiant sunshine appeared. The snow glistened on the ground and were it not for such a heavy heart, the magnificent view of the capital would have lifted his spirits.

The notice pinned to the veranda post of the inn he stopped at reminded Mitsuhide of why he was here. It announced the schedule for thirty-six executions to take place at dusk today at the Rokujo-gawara. His home at Sakamoto castle was but a half-day's ride away and Mitsuhide had three of his retainers continue towards Sakamoto and prepare for his late arrival. Meanwhile, he would rest at the inn for the rest of the day.

Six bells rang out to signal the hour of the rooster had arrived, marking the beginning of the dusk period. Accompanied by his three retainers, Mitsuhide set off for the Sanjo Ohashi bridge spanning the Kamogawa River. The execution grounds of the Rokujo-gawara lay a short distance ahead in one of the dry riverbeds that once fed off the Kamogawa.

They found the bridge congested with hundreds of spectators making their way to the execution grounds for their evening entertainment. Mitsuhide's retainers, with their hands menacingly resting on the hilt of their swords, cleared a passage through the throng and over the bridge. A steep path led down an embankment to the Rokujo-gawara and as they descended, the tops of crosses used for crucifixion came into view. At the bottom of the path, a large crowd had already gathered, and shouts of laughter permeated the air, creating an almost obscene, carnival-like atmosphere. Mitsuhide's retainers again cleared a path and pushed through towards the Samurai guards in charge, passing the crucified bodies of long-dead souls with birds feasting on their eyes and open wounds.

One of the guards, recognising Mitsuhide, bowed and cleared a space for him among the crowd while another guard rushed to provide a camp stool. The crowd, upon seeing Mitsuhide as someone of significant importance, kept a respectful distance, and while he sat, he dwelt on the fate of his daughter Shizen. A nearby peasant girl playing with her brother immediately caught the attention of Mitsuhide and memories of Shizen as a little girl flooded his mind. He remembered a time when she wore her favourite bright blue silk kimono and played at skimming flat stones across the surface of the garden pond with her older sister, Tama. As children, the pair were inseparable, but having been raised by different mothers, they also grew up with distinct personalities. Tama, his daughter from his formal wife, Tsumaki Hiroko, was headstrong and loved learning about history and the arts, and when the time came, she was married off to Nagaoka Tadaoki of the Hosokawa clan. Shizen's mother was Mitsuhide's concubine, Hachijo-in, and became Mitsuhide's favourite, and she too was eventually married off to Murashige's son, Araki Muratsugu.

As his eyes glazed over, Mitsuhide woke from his memories to the sounds of shouting and opened his eyes to see guards leading the Arioka hostages onto the old dried out riverbed. They all had their hands bound and were tied together in a line with rope. Mitsuhide's heart sank when he recognised the lead prisoner as Shizen. They had dressed her in white clothes, the colour of mourning, and her eyes looked downward, oblivious to her father's presence. The Samurai leading them stopped and readout for the benefit of those assembled the charges for which they were to be executed and a thought flashed in Mitsuhide's mind.

I could stop all this. I outrank them all.

Without thinking, his body tensed, and he attempted to rise, but his intentions were transparent enough for his retainer to place a restraining hand on his shoulder.

"If you do, my Lord," the retainer said, "Lord Nobunaga will order your seppuku and she will still die." The moment to act had passed, and he resigned himself to the inevitable. Not wanting to witness her death, Mitsuhide rose and walked away with his retainers. He had taken only half a dozen steps when he heard a dull thud and the roar of the crowd behind him, and he stopped. Anger again welled up inside him, and he inwardly cursed Nobunaga.

He could have spared her for me like he spared his sister.

250

The snow had become heavier, and Mitsuhide had lost no time in leaving Kyoto. At the inn, he had the horses re-saddled, and his retainers sent to purchase fresh straw capes. It was late into the hour of the rat, well after midnight, by the time Mitsuhide arrived home to Sakamoto Castle. With the household roused, servants scurried off to prepare refreshments for their lord. Mitsuhide was in no mood to eat, but he had planned on drinking. Yukishige, one of Mitsuhide's trusted castle retainers, informed him that a priest from the Daito-Ku-Ji Temple had arrived earlier in the day with important news and was resting in the drawing-room.

"Send him in later. First, I need a drink," Mitsuhide said as he handed the reins of his horse to Yukishige. Mitsuhide took his refreshments in the garden room. In summer, the room would be wide open to view the garden's beauty and receive the cooling breeze coming off Lake Biwako, but tonight the wintry winds and heavy snow decided that the doors would remain shut. Servants brought in a warming charcoal brazier, and Mitsuhide warmed both his hands and his sake. Tonight, he would pour his own sake and he ignored the plates of fresh Bonito, Miso soup, and pickles laid out before him. He downed two bowls of warm sake in quick succession and then summoned the priest.

The Zen priest Sakugen Shuryo, expecting another cold room, stepped into the garden room, clutching his patchwork *Kesa* (priestly outer robe) tightly against his chest. He welcomed the warmth of the brazier and, at Mitsuhide's invitation, sat down and warmed his hands.

"Greetings, Shuryo," Mitsuhide said. "How is Mother? And What brings you here at this time of night?"

"I bear grave news, my lord. Your mother, Omaki-no-kata, has died." Mitsuhide fell silent and eventually stammered his reply.

"How is this possible?" Mitsuhide exclaimed. "Before I left for Tamba I had visited her at your temple, and she was in fine spirits enjoying seeing out her days as a nun?" Shuryo, who had momentarily bowed his shaven head in prayer, looked at Mitsuhide. His sunken eyes were full of pity, but it was his duty, to be honest with him.

"Lord. The noble Omaki-no-kata has been killed."

"How?" Mitsuhide demanded. Shuryo hesitated before replying.

"It is gruesome, Lord."

"Tell me," Mitsuhide again demanded.

"We found her body nailed to doors of the Daito-Ku-Ji. All her fingers were missing." First anger, then a wave of depression swept over Mitsuhide as he choked on his words.

"Who is responsible?" Shuryo reached under into his robe and withdrew a folded note and handed it to Mitsuhide.

"My Lord, they nailed this notice alongside your mother's body." Mitsuhide snatched the note and read the simple wording.

In revenge for Hideharu's mother. The note fell from his hands, and he reached for his sake bowl, hurling it across the room. He cursed as he watched it bounce off the mat, tearing a hole in one of the papered screen walls.

"Damn Nobunaga to the lowest levels of the Avichi hell."

Chapter Twenty-Two

The End of the Takeda
Spring: Tenth Year of Tensho (1582)

Two more winters had passed, and Nobunaga looked forward to consolidating his conquests. Hideyoshi had finally subdued Harima and Inaba provinces and brought the Mori clan to its knees, closing the supply route to the rebel monks of Ishiyama Hongan-Ji and ending their decades-old rebellion. General Shibata Katsuie, accompanied by Yoshimasa and his Teppo rifle brigade, added more misfortune to the rebel monks of Kaga Province and brought it under Nobunaga's umbrella.

In the third month, as Mitsunari languished at Nagahama castle, he worried that he might one day die in battle without ever finding out the truth of Kasumi's secret. He had just explained to Hideyoshi the events surrounding her death and the letter she wrote. The key was Hattori Hanzo, and Mitsunari sought leave from Hideyoshi to seek him out.

"Where would you find Hanzo?" asked Hideyoshi.

"Perhaps at Hamamatsu, where Lord Ieyasu is."

"Ieyasu is not at Hamamatsu. In case you have not heard, Katsuyori's retainer, Kiso Yoshinaka of Shinano, has rebelled and sworn allegiance to Nobunaga. Katsuyori has responded by sending a large force into the Kiso Mountains to deal with Yoshinaka, and that is where Ieyasu is heading."

"Then with your permission, which is where I must go," said Mitsunari.

"You cannot just wander into an attacking army and have a chat. I will write a letter outlining your mission and a request for safe passage to Ieyasu. One more thing, Ieyasu is joining up with Nobutada's army, so do nothing silly." As Mitsunari rode out for Shinano, a journey that would take the best part of five days, he looked back and noticed the dark clouds rolling in over Nagahama.

The spring rains are early this year, he thought.

As he neared the pass at Mount Ibuki, which would take him into the Sekigahara Plains, he heard the shouts of a rider coming up from behind, calling for him to halt. The rider, a messenger sent by Hideyoshi, had news of a change in Ieyasu's location. The messenger explained to Mitsunari that Yoshinaka had repulsed Katsuyori's army, forcing Katsuyori to flee back to his new capital of Shinpu in Kai. This defeat had spurred a mass of defections, and even Katsuyori's cousins and uncles had forsaken him. Of the fifteen thousand Katsuyori fielded against Yoshinaka, he returned to Shinpu with less than five hundred. Nobutada was now attacking Shinpu from the west and Lord Nobunaga from the south. Ieyasu and the Hojo had joined up to attack from the north and east to complete Shinpu's encirclement. The messenger added that Ieyasu's last sighting was two days ago at Monjudo in Kai as he headed towards Shinpu.

"How far is Shinpu from Monjudo?" Mitsunari asked the messenger.

"A single rider would make it in under two days, but an army would take three, maybe more."

"I can make Kai and follow Ieyasu's route to Shinpu in under three days. Tell Lord Hideyoshi of my gratitude for his news." With that, the messenger turned, saluted, and galloped back the way he came.

Mitsunari crossed the Kiso Mountains and reached the village of Ina in Shinano just before dusk where he would rest before daybreak. From Ina, he would head east towards the Kamanshi River Valley and his destination, Shinpu. Wearing a new straw cape and hat, Mitsunari left Ina at daybreak under the same dark skies and drizzling rain that had persisted since yesterday, and it was several hours later that he reached the Kamanshi River, and the weather had eased. Despite the spring thaw, the snow line of Mount Nyuskasa extended to the river's edge, covering the road to Shinpu in a thin layer of snow and ice, now turned to slush by the feet of many men and horses. All along the river valley melting snow cascaded off the mountains into the Kamanshi, swelling its waters and forming raging torrents of white water along its shallows.

Mitsunari rode carefully along the road in fear of his horse stumbling and breaking a leg. When he reached the next bend in the road, he noticed that the snow line here had receded away from the road into the lightly forested slopes of the valley. The road ahead was blocked by a fallen pine tree, and he dismounted. By now, Mitsunari was eager to rest and eat and judging by the warmth of the horse dung he just stepped in, whoever came past this way was not long gone. He sat on the fallen tree chewing one of the rice balls he had purchased at Ina and watched as plumes of rising black smoke blended with the dark clouds in the distance. The unusual silence and absence of birds had just struck him when he felt the damp mesh of a net unexpectedly envelop him. The more he struggled, the tighter the net became. Then he felt the dull blow on the back of his neck and then blackness.

When Mitsunari next opened his eyes, he saw the dim light of a single lantern and noticed the walls rippling in tune to the sounds of the wind he could hear from outside.

I must be in a tent, he thought. The cold wet cloth covering his forehead startled him, and he quickly sat up. Seated in front of him was a middle-aged man with loose, long, flowing black hair that matched his robes.

"Who are you? Where am I?" Mitsunari called out.

"My name is of no importance to you, young man. I am a physician to Lord Ieyasu. I believe the gentleman over there is an acquaintance of yours?" Led by the physician's eyes, Mitsunari turned his head and gasped.

"Hanzo!"

"So, we meet again," Hanzo said. "To answer the rest of your question, you are at Shinpu Castle, or rather, what they left of it. All that remains is a pile of smouldering charcoal and rubble. We learnt that Lord Katsuyori, having realised his four hundred defenders were no match for the 180,000 arraigned against him, set fire to the castle and fled in the night."

"What happened? And why am I here?" snapped Mitsunari.

"You are here because you wanted to see me. My men were searching the woods for Katsuyori's men when they came across you. Unsure of your clan and in Takeda territory, they naturally assumed you to be a Takeda spy. Your head would have been taken, but for a letter addressed to Lord Ieyasu that was found on your person." Hanzo handed Mitsunari back the letter and continued.

"As your mission was to see me and we are here. My question to you is why?" Feeling better, Mitsunari got up from the coarse straw matted floor and rubbed his neck.

"Do you remember the Kunoichi, Yoshino? Your spy." Mitsunari said. Hanzo's eyes narrowed, and he looked directly at Mitsunari.

"Ah, the Takeda spy. Yes, I remember her. We have heard no news from her since she left us. We heard reports of the death of a lady traveller in Seki springs and believed it was her."

"That was Mochiko Chiyo. She wrote as much." Mitsunari explained to Hanzo about Yoshino's alias of Kasumi and the scheme she concocted to get Yoshimasa to kill her. He told Hanzo of the letter Kasumi had written to Yoshimasa, which mentioned her killing of Mochiko Chiyo.

"The letter also mentioned how you could answer, why Yoshino orchestrated her death to protect me," said Mitsunari.

"When the Shogun became focused on an insignificant Samurai child, we became interested. Our intelligence also led to some suspicions about the Kunoichi's relationship with you. We confronted her with our suspicions when she was at Hamamatsu."

"What suspicions?" Mitsunari asked.

"Only that our evidence points to you being her child," said Hanzo.

"Impossible," Mitsunari protested. "My parents are at Ishida."

"That is true. The parents who raised you are at Ishida, but they adopted you. Your parents admitted as much."

Adopted, how can this be? Mitsunari thought.

"If Yoshino or Kasumi is my mother, then who is my father?"

"If your mother is to be believed, the priest Hajikano Masatsugu of the Daizenji Temple in Kofu."

"A priest!" Mitsunari shouted incredulously.

"Yes, but not just any priest, but one of Takeda Shingen's twenty-four generals. That would give you an impressive pedigree."

"Where is this Masatsugu now?"

"Oh, he is dead. Slain by unknown assailants. For what purpose, I do not know. One thing still puzzles me, though. I have yet to see the connection how the Kunoichi's death protects you."

"Anyway, we have only your word for all of this?" said Mitsunari.

"Yes, that is true, but Mochiko Chiyo knew, and you say she is dead. There was also one other that knew, Takeda Katsuyori's wife, Masako."

"Where can I find her?" pleaded Mitsunari.

"Oh, she is here. At least her head is." Hanzo explained that Katsuyori, having finally accepted all is lost, set fire to Shinpu, before fleeing into the nearby Katsunuma Mountains with his immediate family to seek refuge at the Takeda Kogakko Iwadono Fortress.

"It turns out that Katsuyori's castellan of Iwadono, Oyamada Nobushige, denied him refuge, leaving him trapped with his thirty retainers to face an Oda and Tokugawa army of fifteen thousand closing in on him. Katsuyori made his last stand at the foot of Mount Tenmokuzan, and, by the reports, Masako was a brave warrior in her own right for one so young. Skilled with the Naginata and Yumi, she fought with skill and desperation at Katsuyori's side. When her Naginata broke in two, she resorted to her Yumi and made every arrow find its mark until mortally wounded. Three of Katsuyori's retainers then closed ranks around their lord to give him time to do what needed to be done. Acting as Masako's second, Katsuyori swiftly decapitated her. He was less fortunate and completed his battlefield seppuku unassisted. His son, Nobukatsu, kept fighting to the very end, losing his head to an opponent." Hanzo moved closer to Mitsunari and whispered.

"Take note, Mitsunari, the Takeda clan ended here at Tenmokuzan. Lord Nobunaga's forces currently scour the mountains with orders to execute summarily any Takeda, found."

"Why are you telling me this.?" inquired Mitsunari. Hanzo eyed Mitsunari and stroked his bushy beard before replying.

Because your mother told me who you are, and you will never know. Hanzo secretly thought.

"Just be careful in these woods, Mitsunari, and wear something identifiable as being one of us. Now, I have been rude and kept an important visitor of yours waiting."

"A visitor?" Hanzo opened the flap of the tent and called out, and Hideyoshi stepped inside.

"Have you finished chasing your ghosts?" Hideyoshi called out. A surprised Mitsunari bowed before his lord.

"Yes, my Lord," Mitsunari answered in a resigned tone.

"Good. We need to leave immediately, as we have a long journey ahead to Takamatsu in Bitchu province. We must arrive before the rainy season and prepare to crush the last line of defence of the Mori." Mitsunari turned towards Hanzo and bowed.

"I still have this feeling you are keeping something from me. Another time perhaps."

"Perhaps young Mitsunari, perhaps," said Hanzo.

Hideyoshi and Mitsunari rode out of Kai ahead of an army of five thousand in the drizzling rain that had again returned, just as a grim-faced Hanzo walked across the muddy ground towards Ieyasu's command tent where Lord Nobunaga and his son Nobutada were seated. He had a particular had a task to perform. To find Katsuyori's head from amongst the pile of unwashed heads that lay piled on the muddy ground outside the command tent.

On seeing Hanzo with Katsuyori's head, Nobunaga rose from his seat, grinning and called out to all in attendance.

"Here is the Takeda leader, who now finds himself at the feet of those he sought to conquer." Lord Ieyasu, however, stood and saluted his fallen enemy with his war fan and commanded Hanzo to have Katsuyori's head along with his wife and son buried with respect at the Kogan-in Temple in his homeland of Kai. With the head viewing finished, the matter of the captured Takeda prisoners was addressed. Ieyasu, having conferred with Nobunaga, agreed they were to be given the option of seppuku or crucifixion. Once given their choice, the prisoners bowed before Nobunaga and Ieyasu except Oyamada Nobushige, who had denied Katsuyori refuge at Iwadono, stood upright and protested loudly that his betrayal of Katsuyori proved his loyalty to the Oda cause. Nobunaga, surprised by Nobushige's response, rose and addressed Nobushige directly.

"You claim loyalty to our cause, yet you betray your master. What is worse, is that you even denied him sanctuary in one of his castles, condemning him to death? Is this the action of loyal vassal?" Nobushige dropped to his knees and begged the Oda lord for forgiveness. Nobunaga's eyes radiated pure anger.

"For you, Nobushige, the option of seppuku is withdrawn. We will return after refreshments within the hour and take our seats to witness your crucifixion."

Chapter Twenty-Three

Honno-ji

Summer: Tenth Year of Tensho (1582)

In the sixth month, the rains came early to Bitchu province, just as Hideyoshi had predicted. Braving the relentless summer rains in sodden straw capes and hats, Hideyoshi, and Mitsunari sat on their horses watching the progress of the labourers conscripted to build a series of dykes along the raging Ashimori River. Just ahead lay the Mori stronghold of Takamatsu Castle on a small hill, a few feet above sea level in a natural valley of marshy ground. The Ashimori River, now swollen with rains, ran alongside the castle and the dykes Hideyoshi had built would soon divert its waters and flood the castle. Pointing to the swamp forming around the castle, Mitsunari shouted at Hideyoshi through the noise of the rain.

"You cannot possibly take this castle. There is no access."

"I do not intend to assail it," Hideyoshi shouted back. "The rains will do the job for us. Come, we must tell them to build the dykes higher." Hideyoshi stirred his mount into action and headed for the dyke builders, closely followed by Mitsunari. The work on building the dykes had begun at first light yesterday and continued throughout the night. By late afternoon around the hour of the monkey, they raised the dyke walls a further three feet, causing the swollen Ashimori River to raise the water level of the flooded area right up to the castle gates.

"Higher. We must go higher," shouted Hideyoshi to the dyke builders. "There is plenty of rice, sake, and gold for you if we take this castle." Hideyoshi knew his plan depended on the rain continuing to feed the Ashimori River. He estimated if he could increase the dyke level by a further two feet, the castle should be well and truly flooded by daybreak, guaranteeing its surrender and with it, total control of the Chugoku region. Hideyoshi and Mitsunari turned their horse to ride back to camp when they heard shouts behind them. Two of Hideyoshi's scouts on horseback were struggling on the muddy ground.

"Stay here," Hideyoshi shouted above the noise of the rain to Mitsunari and made his way over to the scouts. As Hideyoshi neared, the first scout called out.

"My Lord, there is a large Mori army heading this way. The rain is slowing them down, but they will arrive here by daybreak."

"How many?" Shouted Hideyoshi.

"At least thirty thousand."

"So, Terumoto is aiming to break the siege. Though, we are no match for his army, he cannot engage us with the floods. He will have to halt his army once he reaches our new lake," considered Hideyoshi.

If the rains stop now, the water level will drop, and we lose everything.

Hideyoshi shouted to the riders,

"Lord Nobunaga is at Azuchi. Hurry there and let him know of the Mori army and our need for reinforcements, else Takamatsu is lost." The two riders saluted and turned their horses away, carefully crossing the muddy terrain heading East for Azuchi.

#

Azuchi Castle. Omi province.

From the fifth floor of the Dojon at Azuchi Castle, Nobunaga looked out over the distant grey expanse of Lake Biwako and watched the line of dark clouds creep closer to Azuchi. He had not long returned from Kai and was looking forward to the tea ceremony he was to host in Kyoto for the imperial regent and his court nobles when Hideyoshi's scouts arrived, imploring him to send reinforcements to Takamatsu. A troubled Nobunaga walked over to a table and unfurled his campaign map of the Chugoku region and studied it for some time. Having summoned Yoshimasa, Nobunaga informed him of the latest developments.

"Ah! Yoshimasa, word has come from Hideyoshi that a large Mori army has unexpectedly appeared at Takamatsu."

"I assume Lord Hideyoshi seeks reinforcements," Yoshimasa observed.

"Yes. Hideyoshi is on the cusp of taking Takamatsu, and now the Mori appears. Shibata Katsuie's army is too far away in Echizen to help, and I find myself here in a bind."

"How so, Lord?" asked Yoshimasa.

"I am to meet the imperial regent and members of the court, at the Honno-ji Temple in the capital for a tea ceremony I am hosting in the next few days. I am also taking some of my meibutsu collection for the occasion. As the emperor continues to flatter me with titles, I dare not offend. Did you know that the imperial regent has offered to adopt me and give me the office of Shogun? Do you think I should accept?"

"Congratulations, my Lord," said Yoshimasa. Turning his attention to the view over Biwako, Nobunaga further explained.

"As you know, Yoshimasa, I have never needed, nor sought, imperial titles. Only might will possess this realm under heaven, and not by any fancy titles. However, I am leaning to think that being Shogun will make my control easier." Nobunaga glanced at the map on the table and quickly abandoned his fanciful thoughts to return to the matter of Takamatsu.

"Yoshimasa, I have a mission for you. Akechi Mitsuhide's has an army of thirteen thousand in Tanba garrisoned at Kameyama Castle, which is much closer to Hideyoshi. Mitsuhide has left Sakamoto for Kameyama to pay his respects to his recently departed mother Omaki-no-kata at the Daito-Ku-Ji temple, where she gave service as a nun. Go to Kameyama and convey my orders for him to leave for Takamatsu and relieve Hideyoshi immediately. The bulk of my army will leave for Bitchu by daybreak tomorrow, and I will follow with the rest when the tea ceremony is over." Yoshimasa bowed and prepared to leave the room when Nobunaga called out.

"One more thing, Yoshimasa, Hideyoshi's messengers are still here resting, ensure they return straight away and inform Hideyoshi that reinforcements are on the way and to hold on at all costs."

#

Kameyama Castle, Tanba: Twentieth day of the sixth month

Having ridden throughout the night, Yoshimasa was pleased with his progress. The expected rains had not yet come, and the roads were still dry. By

261

daybreak, he had crossed into Tanba province and reached Kameyama Castle around mid-morning in time to hear the five bells of the hour of the dragon ring out.

Kameyama was an imposing but bleak-looking wood and stone fortress that lay exposed on flat land with no natural barriers to protect it. Mitsuhide had Kameyama built as a forward base for his campaign to subjugate Tanba province and had no intentions of permanently garrisoning the fortress. Yoshimasa found getting access to Mitsuhide was proving to be difficult, as he was busy holding a Renga poetry session to a select audience of noted scholars and poets. The servants had instructions; he was not to be disturbed, and they made Yoshimasa wait in the anteroom until he had finished.

As Lord Mitsuhide recited the first stanza of his poem for the scribe to note, he became visibly annoyed at the commotion taking place outside the room. Yoshimasa had disregarded the instructions to wait and barged into the room. As it was a scholarly session, Mitsuhide took no precautions to post guards outside the room.

"Forgive me, Lord Mitsuhide, but I am commanded by Lord Nobunaga to convey urgently his orders to you."

"What is so urgent that you disregard my instruction?" Mitsuhide asked as he prepared to return to his poetry.

"I suggest you clear the room first," Yoshimasa said, for he had little respect for Mitsuhide. Seething with anger, Mitsuhide knew he had to hear Nobunaga's message and had little recourse but to apologise and excuse his guests. Once he had the room cleared, Mitsuhide took to admonish Yoshimasa for his rudeness, when Yoshimasa again interrupted.

"Lord Mitsuhide. We have no time for this. Lord Nobunaga commands you leave for Takamatsu castle immediately and relieve Hideyoshi." Yoshimasa explained Hideyoshi's predicament with the sudden arrival of a large Mori army.

"How many are in this army?" Mitsuhide demanded.

"Hideyoshi reports around thirty thousand," Yoshimasa replied.

"Even with my army and Hideyoshi's, they still outnumbered us. Is Lord Nobunaga committing troops?" Mitsuhide said.

"Yes, the main army at Azuchi will have already left by now and Lord Nobunaga will follow in several days."

"Why is Lord Nobunaga delaying?" queried Mitsuhide.

"He has commitments with the court and is hosting a tea ceremony at the Honno-ji for the imperial regent."

"I see. So, you are telling me that Lord Nobunaga's army has departed for Bitchu, leaving their lord alone then?"

"Not quite. He has his usual retinue of attendants and retainers to comfort and protect him," replied Yoshimasa. Intrigued, Mitsuhide pressed home his questions, seeking more intelligence.

"What about the heir, Nobutada? Can he not be of help?"

"No. Nobutada is still lodging at the Myokakku-ji Temple at the Nijo whilst he oversees the rebuilding work at the palace."

"What about our Tokugawa allies?"

"Lord Ieyasu has been touring the sights around Lake Biwako as Nobunaga's guest and has since departed for further sightseeing in Sakai. The main Tokugawa army has already departed Kai and returned to Mikawa," Yoshimasa said, becoming curious about Mitsuhide's line of questioning.

I have misjudged him. He seems concerned for our lord's safety. In an unusual show of politeness, Yoshimasa excused himself to return to Kyoto and report back to Nobunaga. Mitsuhide quickly summoned his generals, Akechi Sama, Akechi Jiemon, Fujita Dengo and Saito Kura to discuss Nobunaga's command to relieve Hideyoshi.

"How soon can the army be ready to move out?" Mitsuhide asked.

"We can leave by the afternoon, Lord," Akechi Sama said with the others concurring.

"The rain is light, and the roads are still dry enough. If we travel through the night, we can make Takamatsu before sunset tomorrow," Akechi Sama continued.

Just before dusk, Mitsuhide, and his army of thirteen thousand set out in the drizzling rain for Bitchu province and Takamatsu Castle. Akechi Sama and Fujita Dengo led the vanguard while Mitsuhide languished on his horse towards the back of the column with his trusted retainer, Saito Kura. The army snaked its way up the Kitayama Mountains towards the Oinosaka pass, and with the moon obscured by cloud cover, torches, and lanterns were lit to help guide their way. As they neared the pass, Akechi Sama sent a rider down the column to inform Lord Mitsuhide.

"Kura," Mitsuhide shouted to get Kura's attention.

"Consider this. If we take the left fork at the pass, we have another day's march to reach Takamatsu, where we will risk our lives for Hideyoshi's glory. If we turn right, we will reach Kyoto by daybreak and catch Nobunaga without his army and unprotected at the Honno-ji. What would you do?" A stunned Kura looked at Mitsuhide, who returned the stare.

"Lord. Are you intending to betray Nobunaga?" Kura asked.

"Come now, Kura, you are a strategist, are you not? Again, consider this, Hideyoshi is preoccupied at Takamatsu, and Nobunaga currently lodges unprotected in Kyoto. His son Nobutada has only a token bodyguard at the Nijo, and Nobunaga's main army has left Azuchi for Takamatsu. Also, Lord Ieyasu is on his way to Sakai with what I presume to be a small escort, having left his army behind in Mikawa." Kura rubbed the stubble on his chin, deep in thought.

"I would say it is an opportune moment. Swift action on our part could end Nobunaga's rule."

"Exactly my thoughts, Kura. This opportunity may never present itself again."

"Then, it is a turn to the right, Lord?" Kura said with a wide grin. Mitsuhide and Saito Kura spurred their horses forward and trotted towards the head of the column to seek Akechi, Sama and Fujita Dengo.

"Gentlemen," Mitsuhide quietly addressed his generals, "we will take the right fork towards Kyoto. I will explain later, but first I have a task for you." Mitsuhide instructed Sama and Dengo to send fast riders ahead towards Saki and locate Ieyasu's whereabouts.

"You will take the left fork," Mitsuhide said to Saito Kura. "Head towards Takamatsu and seek Mori Terumoto to offer an alliance against Hideyoshi." He handed Saito a folded letter.

"This is my word, and I trust your judgement on the terms. Either way, if we bottle Hideyoshi up in Takamatsu, he cannot intervene in Kyoto."

As the first rays of a rising sun crept over the horizon, the Akechi army crossed the Togetsukyo Bridge spanning the shallow, slow-flowing Katsura River, where Mitsuhide halted to admire the blossoming Sakura trees lining the riverbanks. For Kyoto, the blossom season had come late and Mitsuhide, seeing this as an auspicious omen, rode out to the front of his army and led them eastwards for the quick march to the Honno-ji.

#

Mitsuhide's army approached the Honno-ji just before daybreak, while Nobunaga, who had risen earlier to wash at the stone water basin outside the main temple hall, listened as the bush warblers in the nearby trees came to life with the approaching dawn. Nobunaga had the Honno-ji Temple expanded at his own expense to use as a base for his visits to Kyoto and to accommodate his ever-expanding retinue; he had thirty residences constructed within the temple grounds. On this occasion, he brought only a small entourage comprising Yoshimasa, a retainer, his formal wife Lady No, and several ladies-in-waiting together with a few servants.

Having finished his ablutions, Nobunaga stepped aside for Lady No and her attendants to take their turn at the washbasin while he focussed on the sounds of a commotion emanating from beyond the compound. As the noise grew louder, Yoshimasa and Fuwa Mitsuharu, Lord Nobunaga's elderly retainer, emerged from one of the temple residences that circled the main hall and ran towards Nobunaga.

"Yoshimasa, find out what is happening?" Nobunaga commanded, but before Yoshimasa could respond, Mitsuharu shouted out.

"They are battle cries. Someone is attacking the temple." A confused Nobunaga was about to ask who would dare? When he saw about fifty Ashigaru carrying matchlocks, taking up firing positions in front of his quarters. He recognised the bellflower emblem on their armour.

"Akechi. They are Akechi. What is the fool playing at?" Nobunaga shouted. Yoshimasa, suspecting Mitsuhide's intent, called out.

"Lord, we must go. The compound is breached," Nobunaga reached for his swords, but he then realised his swords still rested on their stand within his quarters, which were now surrounded by the Akechi riflemen.

"Hurry, Lord," Yoshimasa pleaded with Nobunaga. "Into the temple." Nobunaga and Yoshimasa sprinted towards the temple doors, but Nobunaga stopped at the sound of muskets firing and glanced back to see his wife's attendants being shot down by the Akechi riflemen as they fled. The delay was costly. A group of Akechi Ashigaru armed with Naginata's and Yari spears swarmed around Yoshimasa and Mitsuharu, but it gave Nobunaga's precious seconds in which to enter the temple. Yoshimasa and Mitsuharu, with swords drawn, kept Lady No, who had only her *Kaiken* close behind them.

Yoshimasa easily parried the first thrust, made by an ill-trained Ashigaru wielding a Naginata as a spear. He deflected the Naginata upwards enough to follow through with a reverse cut, nearly slicing the Ashigaru in two. Mitsuharu was not as lucky and felt the point of a Yari spear penetrate deep into his abdomen. He gripped the shaft tightly with one hand and pulled it towards him, drawing the spear deeper inside him and with it his opponent, while his sword hand arced in the air, decapitating the Ashigaru. Lady No quickly dropped to her knees and grabbed the fallen Naginata and attacked, slicing through bone and sinew. Fearfully, the Ashigaru momentarily backed off enough for Yoshimasa and Lady No to flee into the temple hall and bolt the heavy door behind them.

Inside the temple, Nobunaga, Yoshimasa and Lady No cowered on the floor as bullets ripped through the wooden walls of the temple. Nobunaga, realising his position to be hopeless, bellowed to Yoshimasa,

"Set it on fire. Buy me some time and allow me to die an honourable death and promise me you will not let them have my head." While the Ashigaru reloaded, Yoshimasa removed one of the lighted candles from the altar and emptied lantern oil onto the temple floor in front of the thick, heavy doors, setting it alight. The fire quickly took and roared into life. Fearing the smoke would soon overcome him, Nobunaga asked for Yoshimasa's short sword and sat in front of the roaring flames enveloping the doors and prepared himself for seppuku.

"Will you be my *kaishakunin*?" asked Nobunaga. Yoshimasa nodded. He also realised the situation was hopeless, and now thought about his death. Lady No knelt before her husband, weeping as she said goodbye to her husband. Rifles again cracked and bullets again pierced the thin wooden walls but not the burning doors which became their blazing shield. Yoshimasa positioned himself on Nobunaga's left side and with his right hand, he raised his sword in preparation.

"We are almost out of time," Nobunaga panted as the smoke became denser.

"We have no time for the full ceremony," Nobunaga rasped. "Sadly, there will be no death poem for me. When I stretch out my hand thus, it is the signal to strike. Goodbye, old friend." Without any hesitation, Nobunaga tightly gripped Yoshimasa's short sword midway along the blade with both hands, badly cutting himself. As blood continued to drip from his hand, he thrust the blade into his abdomen, making a slow left-to-right cut. His eyes bulged with pain, but he continued the cut. When he could bear the pain no longer, he held out his left hand and Yoshimasa's blade flashed downward, severing Nobunaga's head. Without bothering to wipe his blade, Yoshimasa knelt and withdrew the short sword from Nobunaga's abdomen. The time had come to consider his seppuku and that of Lady No. As he retrieved the sword, he heard a loud crack and the huge beam above him collapsed in flames, breaking through the floor where it landed. Yoshimasa drew Lady No closer to him, as roof embers continued to rain down.

"Are you ready, my lady? It is time we must do it now." Lady No readied her *Kaiken* against her throat and Yoshimasa also readied his sword when suddenly, another beam collapsed. It had just missed them but had them trapped against the altar. Even with the dense smoke and fires raging around them, the gap in the collapsed roof now acted as a chimney, drawing some of the smoke upwards. The smoke cleared a little, and Yoshimasa noticed the two Kitsune statues atop the altar. He knew the Inari gods of Shinto were always welcome in the same space at Buddhist temples, but to find the Kitsune here confused him, as did seeing the statue's yellow eyes glow brighter.

Outside, Mitsuhide stood watching along with Akechi, Sama and Fujita Dengo, the temple hall being consumed by fire. With grim satisfaction, Mitsuhide ordered the rest of the buildings in the compound to be set alight. A smirk of satisfaction crossed his face as he thought about the first part of Nobunaga's legacy being erased.

"Dengo," Mitsuhide called out. "The scouts have just reported that Ieyasu has arrived in Sakai with about fifty men. Take two hundred and kill him. He is too dangerous to leave alone." Mitsuhide worried he had little time left in which to consolidate his position. With Hideyoshi preoccupied with Bitchu and Ieyasu out of the way, he needed to pacify the Kyoto citizenry and gain the emperor's favour. Addressing Akechi Sama, Mitsuhide issued new instructions.

"We leave for Azuchi at once. Leave a contingent here to watch over the fire. Nothing can survive that, but I want those ashes thoroughly raked. I want Nobunaga's head."

Chapter Twenty-Four

Tokugawa Ieyasu

Azuchi Palace: Summer: Twenty-second Day of the Sixth
Month

Tenth Year of Tensho (1582)

The news of Nobunaga's death had travelled fast, and the castle town of Azuchi was in panic. Not knowing what to expect from the slayer of Nobunaga, many of the townspeople fled to nearby Kyoto while others took advantage of the chaos and joined in the looting and burning begun by the recently arrived Akechi soldiers.

Having raided Nobunaga's treasury at Azuchi, Mitsuhide sent parcels of silver coins to many of the court nobles in Kyoto as donations. A written proclamation declaring himself as *Sei-i Taishogun* accompanied this investment, he argued that, unlike Nobunaga, he, as a true descendent of the Minamoto clan, had the pedigree to claim the title. With Nobunaga dead, he believed the emperor would have no excuse to deny him. So confident was he in this claim that Mitsuhide gathered his men at Azuchi and announced his premature Shogunal appointment. Content that such an announcement would cement his legitimacy for usurping Nobunaga and dispel any grievances. As a reward to his army, he stripped Azuchi of its treasures and gave them to his men.

While he waited for news on Mori Terumoto and Ieyasu, Mitsuhide returned to the Honno-ji to claim what was left of Nobunaga.

"What do you mean, there is nothing?" Mitsuhide barked at Nagano, the captain assigned to find Nobunaga's remains.

"My Lord. We have inspected every smouldering ember and raked all the ashes. There is no body to be found."

"This cannot be. We all saw it. Nothing could survive that inferno, let alone escape. How is it possible?" Mitsuhide asked, pacing nervously.

"Maybe the fire was so intense that it left no trace?" Said, Nagano.

"Yes, that must be it, Mitsuhide replied." Inwardly he knew it could not be, for even funeral pyres leave bones. Nagano produced the two stone statues of the Inari Kitsune unscathed by the ravages of the fire and some badly discoloured pieces of pottery.

"These, my Lord, are the only items that survived the temple blaze."

#

Myokoku-ji Temple, Sakai: Twenty-second day of the sixth month

Ieyasu was enjoying a light breakfast of grilled fish, pickles and rice in one of the Myokoku-ji Temple rooms reserved for visitors when Hasegawa Togoro, an Oda retainer assigned by Nobunaga to assist the Tokugawa Lord as a guide during his tour of the provinces, interrupted his meal.

"Sire. There is a merchant outside who claims to be an old friend of your Lordship," Togoro said, performing a perfunctory bow.

"What is his name?" asked Ieyasu.

"He says it is Chaya Shirojiro."

"Shirojiro. Send him in right away," Ieyasu snapped.

"That will not be possible, my Lord. He says he has ridden all night to bring you grave news, and he fears if he dismounts at his age, he cannot get back on for the return journey." Ieyasu laughed.

"Then let us attend to him ourselves, Togoro."

It was around early morning, into the hour of the dragon, and the heat of the sun was becoming intense. Beads of sweat quickly formed on Ieyasu's forehead as he approached the tired-looking elderly merchant who leant forward astride his horse as if he was about to fall off. His hands tightly gripping the reins of his horse and that of the packhorse behind him. Upon seeing Ieyasu, Shirojiro straightened up and bowed as best he could.

"Forgive me for not greeting you as I should, Lord Ieyasu, but I fear these old bones will not make it to the ground."

"What brings you here, old friend?" Ieyasu asked. Straining his hoarse voice, the merchant asked,

269

"Could I trouble you first, for a drink of water?" Ieyasu walked over to the temple water basin and filled a dipper with clear cool water and presented it to Shirojiro. With his thirst slaked, he continued.

"Lord Nobunaga is dead," Shirojiro casually announced. "I have in my packhorse exquisite pieces of Karamono that Lord Nobunaga purchased off me in Azuchi as gifts for you. He informed me you were sightseeing in Sakai. With the capital engulfed in flames, many are panicking and fleeing to the countryside. It is from them I learnt about the attack on Lord Nobunaga at the Honno-ji where he was staying and his slaying."

"Who killed him?" an impatient Ieyasu asked.

"The Akechi. Akechi Mitsuhide and he has proclaimed himself Shogun." A stunned Ieyasu remained transfixed, his mind racing to comprehend the import of this news. The merchant looked at his friend and continued.

"Akechi riders stopped me earlier on the road seeking news about you. They seem determined to find you and kill you. You must flee from here."

"But how did you find me?"

"I met your retainer, Honda Tadakatsu, on the road earlier. He told me where you are."

"Oh, yes, I sent Tadakatsu earlier with a message for Nobunaga, which appears will not now be delivered. Where is he now?"

"He continued on to find out more news and will return. Farewell, old friend, I must get back to Kyoto before the mob loots my store." Dropping the rein of the packhorse, Shirojiro turned his horse and trotted out of the temple compound back towards Kyoto.

Ieyasu summoned his generals, Anayama Nobutada, Hanzo Hattori and Sakai Tadatsugu, the hero of Nagashino, for an impromptu council in the courtyard.

"Togoro, have the servants and our men ready to leave at once," Ieyasu said. Despite the heat of the sun, Ieyasu stood firm and announced the grave news Shirojiro had brought. Tadatsugu was the first to respond.

"We must return to Mikawa straight away. Maybe a ship at Sakai can take us?"

"No, it will be the first place the Akechi will look," Hanzo chipped in, as he picked up a stick and drew a crude map on the dusty ground to explain.

"If I were Mitsuhide, I would expect Lord Ieyasu to take the quickest route back to Mikawa. Which means heading for Ise and seeking passage on some vessel. He will not be expecting the lord to cross the Suzuka Mountains to reach Mikawa. That reasoning is simple. The terrain is steep and too difficult for horses and must be made on foot. Also, the area is rife with bandits, but if we can reach Iga alive, my ninja clan stand ready to help us."

Accepting Hanzo's reasoning, Ieyasu gave orders to leave immediately. Hanzo added they will head eastwards first, then turn north towards the Kizugawa River. Once across, they will strip their horses, abandon them, and climb the Suzuka Mountains on foot.

#

Juraku-no-tsu, Ise province: Twenty-seventh day of the sixth month.

As dusk fell, Ieyasu and his small band emerged from the wooded lowlands on the outskirts of Juraku-no-tsu, a major seaport on the east coast of Ise. After five days of rough travel, in their torn and dirty garments, they looked like Ronin. Hanzo suggested they make camp in the surrounding woods and light no fires. Of the fifty men accompanying Ieyasu from Myokoku-ji, only Hanzo, Honda Tadakatsu, Sakai Tadatsugu, and Anayama Nobutada survived. Several times in the Suzuka Mountains, bandits attacked them.

On the first day of their travel, Hasegawa Torgoro sat down to rest and succumbed to an arrow in the neck. Ieyasu lamented at having to leave his body behind, which would by now be missing a head, but haste was essential. The servants were the first to run away, and after each attack, the bandits dwindled their numbers to the point none remained, save Ieyasu and his generals. Even in Iga with Hanzo's clan for protection, bands of Ronin scoured the land looking for Ieyasu, tempted by the offers of large rewards for each Tokugawa head taken.

The group made camp in a small clearing within the forested lowlands they had just emerged from, which lay just outside the port of Juraku-no-tsu. Ieyasu rested on the ground and removed a pouch of silver coins from the torn rag tied around his waist that not only served as his Obi but held the remnants of his kimono together. Keeping a few coins, Ieyasu handed the pouch to Honda Tadakatsu and instructed him to sneak into the port after dark and find a boat that will take them across the bay to the Mikawa Port of Atsuta and safety. The remaining coins he gave to Sakai Tadatsugu and tasked him with finding Lord Hideyoshi at Takamatsu.

"Tell Lord Hideyoshi what has happened," Ieyasu said. "And tell him I intend to march soon and avenge Lord Nobunaga, and it would please me for him to accompany me on that mission." Tadatsugu bowed and quietly left the camp on foot, heading west for the perilous journey to Takamatsu. Meanwhile, as Tadakatsu prepared to leave for Juraku-no-tsu, Hanzo called out.

"Leave your swords behind. You look like a bandit." Tadakatsu laughed and handed Hanzo his swords for safekeeping and left the camp. A little while later, Anayama went to relieve himself and standing in front of a low bush, he heard the distinct crunching sound of feet on dried leaves and turned to see several attackers he took to be bandits lunge at him with swords. He drew his sword and shouted for help just as he dodged the blade of the leading attacker but felt the cut of another blade on his upper right arm. Blood quickly leaked through the sleeve of his *Hitatare*, but he still had use of his sword arm. Any deeper, he thought, and he would have lost his arm.

Anayama retreated a few steps and readied himself. The attackers paused as he thought they would, giving him time to assess the situation. He faced four attackers with swords, the quality of their clothes, and the swords showed these were not opportunistic bandits, but neither were they Akechi Samurai. With the element of surprise gone, the attackers were cautious in testing Anayama's response. One attacker lunged at Anayama but became momentarily distracted by the head of one of his comrades landing in front of him. It was enough of a distraction for Anayama to follow through with a downward stroke and cleave the attacker's head in half. Hanzo had emerged from the bushes and slashed at the back of one of the remaining attackers, instantly felling him, leaving the sole remaining attacker to flee into the forest. Ieyasu also appeared and stood over the bodies.

"Are they Akechi?" He asked.

"No, Lord," said Hanzo as he examined the bodies for signs of identification.

"If they were," he continued, "they would not be ignoring us. Their target appears to be Anayama."

"They are Takeda," said Anayama as he inspected the wound on his arm.

"How do you know this?" asked Hanzo.

"By the head, you chopped off," Anayama said, pointing to the head at Hanzo's feet. "I recognise him. The head belongs to Masatada Masayuki, the younger brother of Oyamada Masayuki, one of Shingen's senior retainers who perished at Nagashino."

"Is this revenge for your betrayal of Katsuyori?" asked Ieyasu. Anayama was once one of Shingen's generals and Shingen's nephew. His mother, Nanshou-in was Shingen's older sister and his wife Kensho-in, was Shingen's daughter from Lady Sanjo.

"You served your clan faithfully before defecting to me after Nagashino. Is your clan still holding a grudge?" said Ieyasu.

"Possibly," said Anayama. "Katsuyori was an impetuous fool who would lead the Takeda into destruction. That is why I serve you."

"Enough of this," Ieyasu said angrily. "There may be more of your disgruntled clan about." Ieyasu, Hanzo, and Anayama returned to the clearing to await the return of Tadakatsu, and while Ieyasu rested, Hanzo dressed Anayama's wound.

"The wound is deep, but you will recover," Hanzo reassured Anayama.

"Hanzo, I cannot stay here. I must leave," Anayama whispered.

"Where will you go? You will be safer in Mikawa and need, I remind you; you are Ieyasu's vassal now and require his permission." Anayama glanced towards the resting Ieyasu and, satisfied he was still asleep, again whispered to Hanzo.

"Yes, I am grateful to Lord Ieyasu for accepting me, but I must find my mother if she is still alive."

"Why is this so urgent?" Hanzo replied. Anayama drew closer to Hanzo and whispered.

"As you know, I have sworn fealty to Lord Ieyasu, but I still long for the day when the Takeda will have an heir worthy to wear Shingen's mantle. My wife, Kensho-in still lives in Hamamatsu. In the event of my death, I ask that you take care of her."

"Look, the Takeda are finished, Anayama," Hanzo said. "Nobunaga went to great lengths to eliminate the Takeda line at Tenmokuzan. Shingen's remaining sons, Nishiwa Morinobu, and Katsuayama Nobusada are all adopted into other clans through marriage and cannot inherit. Katsuyori was the last of Shingen's line and his sons were all dead. Who is their left? And you have not explained the urgency of visiting your mother, who may well have died in Nobunaga's purge." Anayama again glanced at Ieyasu to satisfy himself he was still asleep and continued.

"Some years ago, while visiting my mother at the Tsutsujigasaki Palace, Kensho-in and I were enjoying the garden when we overheard Mother and my uncle arguing in a room opening onto the garden. My mother was admonishing my uncle for his philandering ways and demanding to know his intentions for the bastard child he had sired."

"What did he say?" Hanzo eagerly asked.

"I do not know, as other guests in the garden interrupted our eavesdropping. I need to confront my mother and find out."

"As you say, all this happened a long time ago. Why does it matter what became of the child?" Hanzo said, knowing the answer. If found, the child would be a rallying point for a Takeda resurgence, and if the boy were anything like his father, he would pose a grave threat to the Tokugawa. Hanzo promised Anayama that he would concoct some story to explain his absence. Both knew that should Ieyasu believe Anayama has betrayed him, Kensho-in's life and that of his child would be forfeited. Anayama quietly slipped away into the forest and before long the warning cry of an owl disturbed the peace, waking the Tokugawa Lord.

"Where is Anayama, Hanzo?" Ieyasu said, looking around.

"I have sent him to Kai, Lord."

"What?" Ieyasu exclaimed incredulously.

"I must explain later, my Lord." Ieyasu was plainly angry, but he also knew Hanzo did nothing without a purpose, and he was about to insist Hanzo tell him now when Tadakatsu returned.

"Ah, Tadakatsu. What news? And what do you have there?" Tadakatsu unwrapped the cloth bag he carried, revealing six large rice cakes.

"Forgive me, Lord, I spent a coin on getting us food."

"What news of a boat, then?" Ieyasu said, ignoring the food.

"The only boat in port is a vessel carrying salt to Edo, but for a price, he will divert to Atsuta and then continue to Edo. The vessel casts off on the next outgoing tide, which is just after daybreak around the start of the hour of the dragon."

Hanzo's eyes quickly looked skyward. A thin patch of light appeared over the horizon.

"Dawn is not far off. We must leave for the boat now."

"Are there any Akechi soldiers at the port?" Ieyasu asked Tadakatsu.

"Yes, Lord, a small group of six guards at the dock."

"So, with Anayama gone, it is just the three of us against six. Should not be much of a problem," Hanzo said with a smile, "but first I need to make sure we are not attacked by bandits from behind." Hanzo left to scout the vicinity and a short while later returned just as the sun began its climb over the horizon.

"We must hurry," said Hanzo, looking at the sky. As they moved to leave, Ieyasu noticed the acrid smell of burning, and a nearby column of rising smoke caught his attention.

"Hanzo, it seems we have company," said Ieyasu. Tadakatsu hastened towards the smoke, and Ieyasu and Hanzo followed. Ieyasu noticed the smell was unusual, not the smell you would associate with a campfire. They circled warily around the source of the smoke and realised it was a tree on fire but attached to the tree was a burning black shape that crackled and hissed loudly. Ieyasu knew he was looking at the body of a man and the distinctive hilt of the sword laying on the ground told him it was Anayama.

"We cannot delay any longer, Lord. We must catch the tide," Hanzo urged.

Taking cover behind a sake warehouse, Ieyasu, Hanzo and Honda Tadakatsu watched the coastal trading vessel that would take them to Atsuta being loaded with its cargo of salt. They could see only three of the six Akechi soldiers that Tadakatsu earlier confirmed were guarding the loading pier.

"We can only see three. Where are the others?" Hanzo whispered to Tadakatsu.

"They cannot all guard night and day. There were six, however, that was much earlier on. I am inclined to think they are resting to relieve these on duty."

"Or there is possibly another six, ready to relieve them," Ieyasu said.

"I hope not," Hanzo whispered.

"If we do not board soon, the vessel will leave without us and our coin," Tadakatsu added.

"How well do you trust this boat's master, Tadakatsu?" Hanzo asked.

"As much as I would trust you to guard my daughter," Tadakatsu shot back. Hanzo stifled a laugh.

"If we take on these three Akechi guards, the boat's master is likely to take fright and leave straight away. We need to get one of us on board to prevent him from leaving, but that would leave just two of us to deal with these three and possibly more." Glancing back at Lord Ieyasu, an idea struck Hanzo. Whispering to Tadakatsu, he explained.

"Look, notice the workers with sacks of salt on their backs are bent so far forward that their faces are obscured, and the guards are ignoring them."

"So?" said Tadakatsu, unsure of Hanzo's point.

"Look at us. With our torn clothes, we already look like peasants, and we stink. If we take the place of some of these workers, we can board the vessel without a fight."

"What. You want me to humiliate myself and break my back carrying a sack," Ieyasu said upon hearing Hanzo's plan.

"Yes, my Lord, either that or we fight our way to ship and risk the ship leaving before we can get aboard." Ieyasu reluctantly agreed for he could see the logic behind Hanzo's plan, and he felt he had not misplaced his trust in him.

The three sneaked into the nearby salt warehouse housing the vessel's cargo and hid amongst stored bales of cotton. Hanzo noticed there were only a few sacks of salt left, and they would have to move fast. Hanzo slit the throat of the first unfortunate worker who came in to pick up a sack and hid his body among the bales. Tadakatsu tied Ieyasu's swords around his lord's back and loaded Ieyasu with one of the salt sacks. Meanwhile, Hanzo despatched another surprised worker and loaded Tadakatsu with a sack. Together, Tadakatsu and Ieyasu headed for the vessel.

As Hanzo had hoped, Tadakatsu and Ieyasu easily passed by the Akechi guards who took no notice of them, and once onboard dropped their sacks into the hold. Tadakatsu saw the boat's master standing on the bow of the vessel, watching the tide, and hurried towards him. The master caught sight of Tadakatsu and nervously glanced towards the Akechi guards at the gangplank. Fearing a betrayal, Tadakatsu lunged at the boat's master, pressing his dagger on his abdomen.

"If you want to live, do not make a sound," Tadakatsu whispered. "When is the vessel ready to leave?"

"Now. The tide is running. I am just waiting on the last sacks."

"Good, have your men ready to cast off in a moment." The boat's master shouted a command to the crew, who began preparations to drop the vessel's single sail. The crew urged the few workers approaching the gangway to hurry as they were about to cast off. Hanzo bore the last sack on his back and tried to run ahead, only to trip over, attracting the attention of the Akechi guards. A worried Tadakatsu thought about creating a diversion, but Hanzo had already taken care of that. The guards instead turned their attention to the rising plume of black smoke coming from the warehouse, and a moment later, flames appeared on the warehouse roof. Soon, the entire building was alight. As Hanzo expected, workers and guards alike rushed towards the fire, like moths to a flame.

He picked himself up, leaving the last salt bag on the ground, and casually walked aboard the vessel.

Once underway, Icyasu sat down amid deck and retrieved from inside his ragged kimono, the rice cakes Tadakatsu had left behind.

"Eat," he commanded.

"Hanzo, when we get back, take care of Anayama's wife, will you? They murdered him so horribly, all because he served me." Hanzo bowed in acknowledgement and with a painful smile thought of Anayama.

I promised you I would think of something to explain your absence and save your family, just as I promised Lord Ieyasu that I would eliminate all threats to the Tokugawa. My regret, old friend, was the manner of your death, but it had to be convincing. Forgive me.

The vessel under full sail pushed along by strong south-westerly winds ploughed through the swell and soon entered Ise bay and tacked northeast to the port of Atsuta and safety.

Chapter Twenty-Five

The Thirteen Day Shogun
Summer: Takamatsu Castle: Bishu Province
Twenty-second Day of the Sixth Month
Tenth Year of Tensho (1582)

The lengthy period of rain Hideyoshi had hoped for had ended, and as the clouds dispersed, patches of blue sky were left in its wake. At the edge of the lake surrounding the flooded castle of Takamatsu, Hideyoshi, and Mitsunari steadied their mounts and looked at the fluttering banners of the Mori army encamped opposite.

"Is there any news yet from Nobunaga?" Mitsunari asked Hideyoshi.

"No, but Muneharu Shimizu, the castellan of Takamatsu, is now completely cut off from his supply lines and with the lake separating them, there will be no rescue from Mori Terumoto's army."

"It also means you cannot take Takamatsu unless you breach the dykes and let the water level drop," Mitsunari observed.

"Yes, but we need time. The runoff from the mountains should keep the water level high for a while longer yet. The quicker Lord Nobunaga can get here, the better." Hideyoshi and Mitsunari turned their horses to head for camp when one of Hideyoshi's men approached with news.

"Lord, we have captured someone trying to skirt our lines and head for the Mori camp. He was carrying this." Hideyoshi received a folded parchment from the soldier bearing Mitsuhide's name and read its contents.

"Where is this man?" Hideyoshi asked the soldier.

"Back at camp, my Lord. Unfortunately, we wounded him."

"What does it say?" Mitsunari asked.

278

"It is a letter from Mitsuhide to Mori Terumoto suggesting an alliance against me," said Hideyoshi.

Why would Mitsuhide seek an alliance with the Mori? Hideyoshi thought *unless he plans on betraying Lord Nobunaga.*

"Take me to him," Hideyoshi barked at the soldier.

At Hideyoshi's camp, a messenger had arrived from Kyoto with urgent news. Expecting word from Nobunaga, Hideyoshi forgot about the prisoner and received the grave news that Mitsuhide had killed Lord Nobunaga, his son Nobutada, and had proclaimed himself Shogun.

"What of lady No?" Hideyoshi asked of the messenger.

"It is said she died alongside her Lord, as did his retainer Yoshimasa." Hideyoshi grimaced.

"Who else have you told of this?"

"No one save you, my lord."

"Then on your life, say not a word to anyone," said Hideyoshi. A troubled Mitsunari spoke up in anger.

"Mitsuhide's motive in that letter is now clear. He meant to betray Nobunaga; we must avenge them. I swear I will take Mitsuhide's head for this."

"Everyone stay here," Hideyoshi commanded as he stormed out of the tent towards the screened area where the prisoner was held.

"I have read the letter you were carrying to Terumoto," Hideyoshi said calmly, addressing the prisoner who lay on the wet ground before him. "Who do I have the honour of addressing?"

Surprised by the civility, the wounded prisoner replied, "I am Saito Kura, retainer to Lord Mitsuhide. You must be Lord Hideyoshi."

"Yes, but I have sad news about your master. I am sorry to tell you Lord Nobunaga survived the attack on him and his army is scouring the lands for your master, who has fled." Saito Kura tried to rise but fell back, remaining silent.

"I will give you two choices for a simple explanation of your master's betrayal," Hideyoshi said as he knelt alongside Kura.

"The first choice is I will permit you, seppuku. The second is I will roast you alive and have all your family put to death. I shall leave you for a moment to meditate on this." Hideyoshi returned to the command tent only to deal with yet another messenger. This time, the Mori envoy Ankoku Ekei, sent to parley with Hideyoshi.

279

"We meet again, Ekei," Hideyoshi said, greeting him warmly. He had known him as the abbot of the Ankoku-ji Temple at Fukuyama and became good friends.

"You had scant luck in negotiating a settlement with the traitorous Shogun Yoshiaki, so I hope you fare better this time," said Hideyoshi. Bowing his shaven head, Ekei gathered up his brown kayasa robes and took a seat alongside Hideyoshi, a straw mat hurriedly laid down for the occasion.

"It is good to see you again, Lord Hideyoshi, but I will come to the point. We are aware of your appeal to Nobunaga for reinforcements and given the declining situation here in Takamatsu, Lord Terumoto would like to enter a reconciliation with Lord Nobunaga." A surprised Hideyoshi knew this to be an opportunity he cannot pass up. *Terumoto does not know of Nobunaga's death,* he thought. To strike at Mitsuhide he had to move now, and a negotiated peace with the Mori would enable him to leave Takamatsu.

"Ekei, as we already hold Bitchu, Mimasaka and Hoki provinces, I recommend you surrender Takamatsu. In exchange, we will divide the land between the Kawabe-gawa River and the Yahata-gawa River. The Mori will control the west and the Oda, the east. And one last thing, your castellan Shimizu is to commit public seppuku for wasting my time."

Ankoku Ekei returned to Terumoto to deliver Hideyoshi's terms, which under the circumstances he found most acceptable. So, it was that Muneharu Shimizu and three retainers boarded the boat sent by Hideyoshi, and on the banks of the lake overlooking Takamatsu, Shimizu ended his life for all to see. On the twenty-fourth of the sixth month, Hideyoshi formally took control of Takamatsu and immediately departed with his army for nearby Himeji Castle in Harima province to regroup. Two days later, ahead of an army of twenty thousand, Hideyoshi marched towards Kyoto and Mitsuhide.

#

Sakamoto Castle: Twenty-Ninth Day of the sixth month

The new Shogun sat in his audience room at Sakamoto Castle, attended by generals Akechi Sama, Fujita Dengo and Mimaki Kaneaki. Dressed in the trappings of his self-appointed office, a worried Mitsuhide wore an expensive silk black kimono and black eboshi hat. He had struggled to consolidate his gains since the slaying of Nobunaga and the sacking of Azuchi Castle and he had yet to bring any of Nobunaga's enemies into his coalition. The court as he expected had accepted the fait accompli of his self-appointment as Shogun and formally petitioned him to restore order in the nation, but the absence of any news from Saito Kura and his offer of an alliance with Mori Terumoto weighed heavily on him.

"Do we know of Hideyoshi's whereabouts?" Mitsuhide asked out aloud. Akechi Sama reported,

"Our spies inform us he is approaching Amagasaki with an army of at least twenty thousand." To state the obvious, Mimaki Kaneaki reminded all in attendance that the Akechi army of thirteen thousand was therefore outnumbered. Mitsuhide moved quickly to quell any fading morale brought about by Kaneaki's observations.

"We still have the advantage," said Mitsuhide. "Remember, he is coming after me. Where I go, he goes. Therefore, we dictate the battlefield." As the generals gathered around, the battle maps Mitsuhide had been working on all day were brought in. On one such map, Mitsuhide pointed to the Yamazaki Plain that lay in the shadow of mount Tennozan and outlined his strategy.

"If we position our forces on the east bank of the Enmyoji river, the adjacent Yoda River will protect our right flank and the terrain of Mount Tennozan to the west protects our left. Hideyoshi's only viable approach, therefore, is from the south. This also means he must force a crossing over the Enmyoji River onto the Yamazaki Plain where the terrain is to our advantage. The hills there provide natural choke points against any army. A small force can easily withstand one much larger. Also, we have the nearby castles of Yoda and Shoryuji to fall back on if needed." An Akechi messenger interrupted Mitsuhide's presentation with further news of Hideyoshi.

"Reporting," said the Messenger. "Hideyoshi has joined with Niwa Nagahide and Oda Nobukatsu outside Osaka. Their army has swelled to at least forty thousand." Akechi Sama was the first to react among the chorus of sighs and whistling through teeth.

"My Lord, your plan is good, but if we are to draw Hideyoshi to Yamazaki, we need to make haste. If Hideyoshi is in Osaka, he will reach the Yamazaki Plain by first light about the same time as us if we leave now." Mitsuhide continued to study the maps before finally commenting.

"I agree. We must reach those hills first. We leave now." Unknown to the generals, Mitsuhide also had another plan in play. It failed the previous Shogun

Yoshiaki, but it might just work now with Nobunaga removed. As Shogun, Mitsuhide had decrees posted and messages sent to all potential allies and enemies of Nobunaga that he alone acted in the emperor's name. As the legitimate military ruler of Japan, Hideyoshi was defying lawful authority, and as such, he was a rebel. All men and Daimyo therefore must rise and support the Shogun in the emperor's name.

#

Yamazaki Plain: Second day of the seventh month.

As the sun rose, Hideyoshi and Mitsunari looked out from their vantage point atop Mount Tennozan.

On the Yamazaki Plains below, they could see no sign of the enemy, just vast clouds of a dense mist still lingering over the plains. Hideyoshi gave the command and cautiously, the army moved to descend the mountain and prepare for the battle to come.

With his army marshalled on the Yamazaki Plains, Hideyoshi looked across the Enmyoji River and within the mist watched the moving, indistinct shapes of the Akechi army getting into position. He rode up and down the banks of the river, surveying the area before returning to where he had left Mitsunari.

"The river is running fast, but upstream there is a fording point," Hideyoshi said to Mitsunari. "It is there that Mitsuhide will attack first and where we have the best chance to cross and attack. Come with me." Hideyoshi took Mitsunari to the fording point, where he instructed him to set up his Teppo squads. Generals Kato Mitsuyasu and Ikeda Tsuneoki planned to set up behind Mitsunari's guns while they prepared to cross the Enmyoji. Hideyoshi, meanwhile, would lead the rest of the army downstream to cross and attack their left flank.

It was well past daybreak and late in the hour of the dragon. By the time the sun finally penetrated the clouds, the mist lifted. Mitsunari had arranged his musket units into three lines of one hundred and fifty Ashigaru. Just as Hideyoshi had predicted, the first Akechi assault began with a probing attack on Mitsunari's position. Several hundred Akechi Ashigaru stormed across the fording point towards Mitsunari's Teppo units, which opened fire on the forward Akechi infantry. Mitsunari's second line opened fire, and the third line, which was ready, waited for the assault that never came. The Akechi had pulled back, leaving the bodies of hundreds lying where they fell. Behind Mitsunari, the war horns of Mitsuyasu and Tsuneoki roared into life and hundreds of mounted warriors entered the river at the fording point to cross the Enmyoji, followed close behind by thousands of Ashigaru.

Further east, Hideyoshi had crossed the Enmyoji in deeper water with fifteen thousand to attack the Akechi from behind. Mitsuhide had correctly assumed that the defensive nature of the Yamazaki Hills would act as natural choke points against an attacking army, but they were of little use if the enemy was behind you, blocking your retreat. Realising they were being attacked from the front and rear, the Akechi troops quickly broke ranks and by noon, the battle was over.

Across the Enmyoji river, Mitsunari saw the carnage wreaked by Mitsuyasu and Tsuneoki's assault, bodies of Akechi soldiers littered the ground, and in the near distance, he noticed two riders galloping away from the battlefield towards the forest slopes of Mount Tennozan. He was close enough to recognise the distinctive helmet, crowned with a big bold *Mitsu-kuwagata* (three hoe shaped crest) worn by one rider.

It is Mitsuhide. I would recognise that helmet anywhere. Mitsunari immediately rushed towards the fording point and waded across, grabbing one of the riderless horses milling around the battlefield. And took after the two riders. At the edge of the forest, he dismounted and drew Jiko from its scabbard, and quietly led his horse through the thick undergrowth. Cautious of the broken branches and loose rocks concealed beneath him, he knew Mitsuhide would also be forced to dismount.

The forest floor was a world of shadows existing in the dappled light as the sun shone through the tall canopies of black pines. A cautious Mitsunari led his horse through the treacherous undergrowth, only to stumble over a fallen branch and fall heavily to the ground. As he picked himself up, he noticed the face of a man hidden amongst a dense thicket of ferns.

"Who are you?" Mitsunari called out as he waved Jiko at the face.

"Please don't kill me," the face pleaded. "My name is Hidemitsu."

"Come out now," Mitsunari demanded as he readied his sword. He felt anxious as if other eyes were watching him. Mitsuhide, who had been hiding close by, rushed Mitsunari from behind, but, sensing another Mitsunari, swung around in time to dodge Mitsuhide's sword strike. He was unprepared, his feet unsteady on the hidden loose stones and moved backwards to avoid the follow-up strike that was to come when he again tripped over a hidden snag in the undergrowth and fell facedown, his sword falling from his hand.

Mitsunari quickly rolled over, but Mitsuhide was faster and took a position astride him, his sword raised above his head to deliver the inevitable death blow. He looked helplessly at the dark figure towering above him. Mitsuhide was still in his black lacquered battle armour, which had enabled him to melt into the dark shadows of the forest floor. He closed his eyes for the strike that never came, and as he felt the touch of Mitsuhide's blade resting against his throat he opened his eyes. Above him, fierce eyes radiated through a grotesque facial armour, a crimson *Menpo* resembling the face of the demon *Tengu*.

"I should have killed you when I had you in my grasp at Enryaku-ji," he heard Mitsuhide say just as he felt the pressure of his blade increase against his throat. Mitsunari resigned himself to the death that will surely follow.

"As much as I would like to, I now find myself asking what good it would do to kill you?" Mitsuhide said in a calm voice as he relieved the pressure on Mitsunari's throat.

"If you are going to kill me, then do it now," Mitsunari said defiantly in a hoarse voice. He again shut his eyes, tensing his body for the blow that would end his life, but all he felt was the relaxing of the blade against his throat. Mitsunari opened his eyes to see Mitsuhide remove his helmet and *Menpo* and discard them at his feet. With his sword still poised above Mitsunari's throat, Mitsuhide spoke in a calm but resigned voice.

"It never had to be this way; Nobunaga was a butcher who deserved his end."

"Just as you who led your army to slaughter the thousands at Enryaku-ji. You are a traitor, Akechi, and there is nowhere left for you to run," said Mitsunari.

"Am I to be hunted down and killed like a dog then, and for what? Avenging my mother, my daughter, and the thousands of others that have met their deaths at Nobunaga's cruel hands?" Mitsuhide said, his voice wavering. In the scattered light filtering through the forest canopy, a glint of a tear became visible in his eyes as he continued to talk.

"I had no choice at Enryaku-ji. Nobunaga commanded that all be put to the sword. As much as I regret my actions, it is our sworn duty to obey the commands of our lord even though we might disagree. Yes, Nobunaga was a cruel man. I even came to wonder if he was mad. That is why I allied with the Shogun Yoshiaki in the hope he would end Nobunaga's reign of terror." Mitsunari knew what Mitsuhide had said was true, but he was also Nobunagas vassal, and he had sworn to avenge his death.

"If it is your sworn duty to serve and obey your lord's commands, why then did you betray and kill him? Your oath requires you to protect your lord with your life."

"What you say is true," said Mitsuhide, lowering the point of his blade to rest it on Mitsunari's chest. He suddenly slapped his head with his free hand as if to banish the painful memories that now flooded his mind. Imagery of his daughter Shizen's head on public display at the foot of the Sanjo Ohashi Bridge refuelled his anger, and he quickly returned the blade to Mitsunari's throat.

"She didn't have to die," Mitsuhide spat. "Yes, she married the enemy of our lord and as is the custom shared his fate, but Nobunaga's sister Oichi was also the wife of his enemy, the Azai Lord, Nagamasa, and she was spared. Even when this was pointed out as I pleaded for her life, he still insisted on her death. I have nothing more to live for." Mitsunari looked up into Mitsuhide's eyes. The fire and anger had gone, replaced by reflections of sadness and pain. He felt sorry for him, but he swore to revenge his lord and that is what he must do.

It was as if Mitsuhide had read his mind. If he were to die at the hand of his enemy, he could wish for no better death. He immediately removed the point of his blade away from Mitsunari's chest and moved to walk away. Mitsunari, seizing his chance, rolled over and lunged for his sword that lay nearby. With Jiko now in hand, he sprung up and launched himself at Mitsuhide, attacking him from behind. As a seasoned warrior, Mitsuhide had easily seen the strike coming and instinctively moved to block Mitsunari's strike. The two swords clashed at close quarters, momentarily locking both fighters in a *tsubazeriai* where each of the swords become locked with the opponents' *tsuba* handguard.

With the advantage of weight, Mitsuhide easily broke the *tsubazeriai,* and pushed Mitsunari away, giving him time to position himself in a basic *chudan* stance. Mitsuhide stood, feet apart, with the tip of his sword pointing horizontally at his attacker. It was a simple move that balanced the advantages of both attack and defence, but importantly, it bought Mitsuhide more time to arrange what he must. The heavy body armour he wore came with a single thick breastplate, both front, and back, which meant Mitsunari had limited choices to wound his opponent, but the major advantage he had was mobility. Mitsunari made a lunge at the one weak spot Mitsuhide had under his armpit. It was a move he expected

Mitsuhide to block, for he hoped the feint would allow him to get closer and then knock Mitsuhide to the ground.

Anticipating Mitsunari's move, Mitsuhide unexpectedly dropped his sword to the ground and raised both his arms towards the filtered sun, as if offering praise to the kami of the forest and, in doing so allowed Mitsunari's thrust to penetrate deep into his rib cage. Mitsuhide collapsed to the ground on his knees and smiled.

"Why?" Mitsunari shouted. "You let me kill you." Mitsuhide was barely alive and rapidly losing blood, but he spoke.

"My life here is done. You will find on my horse something I salvaged from the ashes of the Honno-ji. Guard it well, for others will come to claim it." Mitsuhide's voice grew fainter. He beckoned Mitsunari to come closer, who knelt to hear his last words.

"Now, Shogun slayer, take my head and make a name for yourself."

Mitsunari found Mitsuhide's horse tethered to a nearby fallen tree branch and removed the padded straw satchel that hung from its saddle. Inside was a discoloured Karamono tea caddy still covered in ashes and grime, but he instantly recognised it as the famous *Tsukumo Nasu*, the same one he had seen in Nobunaga's meibutsu collection at Inabayama Castle in Gifu. Mitsunari quickly mounted the horse, but he hesitated and looked back into the forest. He had left Mitsuhide laying in the forest where he fell, his head still attached. He had killed him, but he had let himself be killed and he had not earned the right to claim his head.

Mitsunari sat in the saddle while Mitsuhide's words reverberated in his mind. He had finally come to understand the man who had once spared him and unknowingly shaped his destiny. Was it destiny that brought him to discover his genuine mother and a father of whom he had never heard? It was a question Mitsunari grappled with. Yet he felt something was missing and doubts again tugged at him.

Why did she die? What was she hiding?

He thought about his friend Yoshimasa, Mochiko Chiyo, and Masako, wife of Katsuyori, his mother Yoshino, or Kasumi, or whatever her real name was. Everyone connected to her life is now dead. Save one, Hanzo Hattori.

286

Does Hanzo know more than he is letting on? Thought Mitsunari as he sighed.

Whatever she died for, died with her.

Spurring his horse forward, Mitsunari shielded his eyes from the bright sunshine as he emerged from the shade of the forest and broke into a gallop, racing out towards his lines with the *Tsukumo Nasu* hanging securely from the pommel of his saddle. Ahead of him on the plains of Yamazaki, soldiers were busy collecting heads for Hideyoshi's viewing pleasure.

The End

Epilogue

The death of Nobunaga and his son and heir, Nobutada, ended Nobunaga's ambition to unite Japan under his rule. Hideyoshi, along with Mitsunari, continued Nobunaga's legacy and united the warring states of Japan to become the second 'Great Unifier'. An exciting new era was to dawn on Japan. It was an era where old friends and allies became foes and a time of dramatic change in Japan's society and culture. Thus, the 'Age of War and Tea' had entered a new phase, a golden age.

As for Yoshimasa, it was rumoured he escaped the burning of the Honno-ji temple, taking Nobunaga's body and head with him to bury it secretly away from Nobunaga's enemies and honour the promise he had made. A warrior fitting Yoshimasa's description was seen serving as a priest at the Tamatsukuri Inari Shrine that Hideyoshi had built near Osaka. The fate of Nobunaga's wife, Lady No, is uncertain, but along with Yoshimasa she appeared to have escaped the flames of the Honno-ji and disappeared into obscurity.

Mitsunari, meanwhile, rose in Hideyoshi's service to be known as the great *Kanrisha* or administrator. He became governor of Sakai and Daimyo of Sawayama Castle in Omi province. He remained a thorn in Tokugawa Ieyasu's side and the intrigue concerning the 'great secret' of his parentage continued to shape events. The rival Fuma ninja clan of Takeda, Masako's mother eventually killed Hanzo Hattori, and Anayama Nobutada's wife, Kensho-in, who was also one of Shingen's daughters, remained under the protection of Ieyasu and secretly continued to pursue the identity of her father's bastard child.

Glossary

ANEGAWA: The Battle of Anegawa refers to the battle which took place in the region around Anegawa (Omi Province) in 1570 between the allied forces of Oda Nobunaga and Tokugawa Ieyasu, against the combined forces of the Azai and Asakura clans.

ASHIGARU: Foot-soldiers who were employed by the samurai class.

ASHIKAGA: The Ashikaga shogunate, also known as the Muromachi shogunate, was the feudal military government of Japan during the Muromachi period from 1336 to 1573.

CHADO: Chado (The way of Tea) Chado and Chanoyu are often translated as the 'Tea Ceremony'.

CHAKAI: A chakai is the main informal Japanese tea ceremony. The event does not last long and includes a serving of traditional Japanese sweets and thin matcha tea known as usucha. And although the event is informal, there is still a rigid set of rules that are followed.

CHANOYU: Translated as 'hot water for tea', refers to the tradition of preparing and serving powdered green tea in a highly stylized manner. The art of Chanoyu, also called 'tea gathering' by practitioners, combines elements encompassing fine and applied arts, architecture, landscape design and etiquette. Through Chanoyu, sharing a bowl of tea becomes an act of evoking self-awareness, generosity towards others, and a reverence for nature.

CHAWAN: A bowl used for preparing and drinking tea.

CHUDAN: A middle-level stance in Japanese martial arts.

DAISHO: A daisho is typically a matched pair of Samurai swords such as a katana (long sword) and wakizashi (short sword) and/or a tanto (knife). Daisho eventually came to mean two swords having a matched set of fittings. A daisho could also have matching blades made by the same swordsmith.

ENRYAKU-JI: Enryaku-ji is a Tendai monastery located on Mount Hiei in Otsu, overlooking Kyoto.

FUKIYA: The fukiya is a blowgun. It comprises a 1.2-metre-long tube, with darts approximately twenty centimetres long.

FUKUMEN: The zukin and the fukumen were coverings for the ninja's head. Two pieces of triangular cloth, with the zukin the hood covering the head, and the fukumen covering the ninja's face.

FUNDOSHIN: An unshakable mind and an immovable spirit is the state of fudoshin. It is a demonstration of courage and determination to face difficulty, danger, pain, and even death without fear.

FURINKAZAN: Translates as Wind, Forest, Fire, Mountain. A battle standard motto used by Takeda Shingen. The banner quoted four phrases from Sun Tzu's The Art of War: 'as swift as wind, as gentle as forest, as fierce as fire, as unshakable as mountain'.

GENPUKU: Genpuku was a coming-of-age celebration for boys, a rite of passage held among court nobles and Samurai families. The coming-of-age celebration for noble girls was called 'Mogi'. Genpuku was held to declare that a boy who became 15-years-old had transitioned from child to adult status with the full assumption of adult responsibilities.

HAKAMA: Traditional trousers or pants tied at the waist and fall to the ankles. They are worn over a kimono specially adapted for wearing hakama, known as a hakamashita.

HITATARE: The formal robe of Samurai. A crested linen robe designed for everyday wear characterised by V-shaped necklines accentuated by inner-robe neckbands of white.

IGA/KOKA NINJA: Ninja clans originating in the province of Iga (modern Mie Prefecture) and the adjacent region of Koka (later written as Koga).

ISHIYAMA HONGAN-JI: The Ishiyama Hongan-ji was the primary fortress of the Ikkō-ikki, leagues of warrior monks and commoners who opposed Samurai rule during the Sengoku period.

KAISHAKUNIN: A person appointed to behead an individual who has performed seppuku, Japanese ritual suicide, at the moment of agony. The role played by the kaishakunin is called kaishaku.

KARAMONO: Broadly refers to artworks and other cultural objects from China.

KITSUNE: The Japanese word for fox. In folklore, Kitsune possesses paranormal abilities that increase as they get older and wiser and can shapeshift into human form.

KOKU: A dry measure. One koku was considered a sufficient quantity of rice to feed one person for one year.

KOMOREBI: A Japanese word used to describe sunlight filtering through trees.

KOSODE: A short-sleeved garment, and the direct predecessor of the kimono. Though its parts directly parallel those of the kimono, its proportions differed, typically having a wider body, a longer collar, and narrower sleeves.

KUNOICHI: A kunoichi is a female ninja or practitioner of ninjutsu. During the feudal period of Japan, ninjas were used as killers, spies and messengers.

MAEDATE: Maedate is a crest or decorative fitting mounted on the front of a kabuto (samurai helmet).

MEIBUTSU: Translates as 'famous things', such as famous tea utensils, or Japanese swords.

MON: Emblems used to decorate and identify an individual or clan.

OKASAN: The mother of a geisha house is called an Okasan.

RONIN: Samurai without a lord or master during the feudal period of Japan. A Samurai became masterless upon the death of his master or after losing his master's favour or privilege.

SAYA: A scabbard or sheath for a sword.

SHINOBI: A Ninja.

SHOGATSU: The celebration of the New Year based on the Chinese lunar calendar.

SUTEGO: Abandoned child.

TANEGASHIMA: A type of matchlock or arquebus (firearm) introduced to Japan by the Portuguese in 1543. The name Tanegashima came from the Japanese island (Tanegashima) where a Chinese junk with Portuguese adventurers on board was driven to anchor by a storm in 1543. The lord of the Japanese island, Tanegashima Tokitaka (1528–1579), purchased two matchlock muskets from the Portuguese and put a swordsmith to work, copying the matchlock barrel and firing mechanism.

TAYU: A specific category of high-ranking courtesan who does not engage in sex work at all.

TEPPO: A snap matchlock gun, also referred to as teppo, hi nawa ju, or tanegashima.

TSUBA: A round (or occasionally squarish) guard at the end of the grip of bladed Japanese weapons such as the Katan.

TSUBAZERIAI: The locking of sword to sword (in a duel) and pushing.

UGUISUBARI: Translating as 'bush warbler guard watch'. Uguisubari are specially constructed floors, more commonly referred to in English-language texts as nightingale floors. Planks of wood are placed atop a framework of supporting beams, securely enough that they won't dislodge, but still loosely enough that there's a little play when they're stepped on. As the boards are pressed down by the feet of someone walking on them, their clamps rub against nails attached to the beams, creating a shrill chirping noise.

YUKATA: An unlined cotton summer kimono, worn as a bathrobe.

Author's Note

The historical characters represented in this work follow traditional Japanese customs and are referred to by their family surname followed by their personal name. Unlike in Western convention, 'John Thomas' would be referred here to as 'Thomas, John'. In the example, 'Tokugawa Ieyasu', you will note the family or clan name of Tokugawa precedes his personal name of Ieyasu.

Concerning dates and times, readers will observe that, in some reference works, the dates of events cited differ with our Gregorian calendar. For example, the Battle of Mitagahara is sometimes referenced as occurring in October 1572 but is widely accepted as occurring in Genki 3/12/22 which refers to 25th January 1573. It should be noted that during the Sengoku period, European notations were based on the Julian calendar, and it was not until the late 1800s that it was superseded by the Gregorian calendar we use today.

At this time, the Japanese lunar calendar was numbered according to a system of era names. Each new Japanese era was usually started soon after the beginning of the reign of a new emperor and was also changed because of other events. As the Japanese lunar year ends twenty to forty days later than our solar year, problems arise with dates occurring late in the lunar calendar. For example, the Japanese twelfth month fell in February of the next year of the European calendar, and it was not until Meiji 6 (1873) that their calendars aligned with years beginning January 1. Throughout this book, for consistency, all dates align with the European year of the Gregorian calendar.

In Japanese timekeeping, the typical clock had six numbered hours, from nine to four, which counted backwards from noon until midnight; the hour numbers one, two and three were not used in Japan for religious reasons, because these numbers of bell strokes were used by Buddhists as calls to prayer. The count ran backwards because the earliest Japanese artificial timekeepers used the burning of incense to count down the time. Dawn and dusk were therefore both marked as the sixth hour in the Japanese-timekeeping system. Besides the numbered temporal hours, each hour was assigned a sign from the Japanese zodiac. Starting at dawn, the six daytime hours were:

Rabbit: Six bells: Sunrise
Dragon: Five bells: Morning
Snake: Four bells
Horse: Nine bells: Noon
Sheep: Eight bells: Afternoon
Monkey: Seven bells
From dusk, the six night-time hours were:
Rooster: Six bells: Sunset
Dog: Five bells: Evening
Boar: Four bells
Rat: Nine bells: Midnight
Ox: Eight bells before dawn
Tiger: Seven bells

Measures are a greater problem than dates and times. For simplicity, those measures referenced in this text should be considered as a rough modern equivalent.

Whilst '*War and Tea*' chronicles the life of the warlord Ishida Mitsunari and is woven around genuine characters and events of the period, I have had to apply a certain amount of artistic license. It should be noted that many of the chroniclers of this era were inconsistent in their recordings of events. The premise that Takeda Shingen fathered Mitsunari is, of course, fiction. His real father, Ishida Masatsugu, was a low-ranking Samurai farmer from Omi province, but nothing is known of his mother. As noted in the character listing Mitsunari's mother, Yoshino is also fictitious. But according to 'Koyo Gunkan' (a record of the military exploits of the Takeda family), Shingen had fathered at least six sons and five daughters from various concubines besides his principal wife, and rumours of other illegitimate children were rife. Importantly, the rise and fall of the Takeda clan played a vital role in shaping Oda Nobunaga's outlook and that of the real Mitsunari.

Selected Biography

Adolphson, Mikael S. (2007). *The Teeth and Claws of the Buddha: Monastic Warriors and Sōhei in Japanese History,* United States: University of Hawaii Press.

Berry, Mary Elizabeth. (1989). *Hideyoshi,* United Kingdom: Harvard University Press.

Chaplin, Danny. (2018). *Sengoku Jidai. Nobunaga, Hideyoshi and Ieyasu: Three Unifiers of Japan*, United States: CreateSpace Independent Publishing Platform. Cummins, Antony, Minami, Yoshie. (2018). *Samurai Arms, Armour & the Tactics of Warfare: The Collected Scrolls of Natori-Ryu.* United Kingdom: Watkins Media.

Deal, William E. (2007). *Handbook to Life in Medieval and Early Modern Japan*, United Kingdom: Oxford University Press.

Denning, Walter. (1955). *The Life of Toyotomi Hideyoshi*, Japan: Hokuseido Press.

Ehara, Tadashi. (2011). *Shogun & Daimyo*, United States: Different World Publications.

Fróis, Luís. (2014). *The First European Description of Japan, 1585: A Critical English-language Edition of Striking Contrasts in the Customs of Europe and Japan by Luis Frois, S.J.*, United Kingdom: Routledge.

Lamers, Jeroen. (2000). *Japonius Tyrannus: The Japanese Warlord Oda Nobunaga Reconsidered*, Netherlands: Brill.

McCullough, Helen Craig. (1976). *The Taiheiki: A Chronicle of Medieval Japan*, United States: Greenwood Press.

Ōta, Gyūichi. (2011). *The Chronicle of Lord Nobunaga,* Netherlands: Brill.
Pitelka, Morgan. (2015). *Spectacular Accumulation: Material Culture, Tokugawa Ieyasu and Samurai Sociability,* Germany: University of Hawaii Press.

Sadler, A.L. (2009). *Shogun: The Life of Tokugawa Ieyasu*, Japan: Tuttle Publishing.

Sadler, A.L., Satoko, Iwasaki, McCabe, Shaun. (2011). *Japanese Tea Ceremony: Cha-No-Yu*, Japan: Tuttle Publishing.

Sakai, Atsuharu. (1940). *The Memoirs of Takeda-Shingen and the Kai-no-gunritsu*, Japan: Nippon bunka chuo renmei (Central Federation of Nippon Culture).

Sansom, George Bailey. (1961) *A History of Japan: 1334–1615,* United Kingdom: Stanford University Press.

Toyo, Yoshida. (2005). *Koyo Gunken: Military Exploits of the Takeda,* Tokyo: Kodansha Press.

Turnbull, Stephen. (2013). *The Samurai: A Military History,* United Kingdom: Taylor & Francis.